ALL THE
GOLD

WORLD OF TERRAGARD™
BOOK TWO

BY
D.S. TIERNEY

Cover Illustration by Raymond Minnaar
www.raymondminnaar.com

Terragard & Salaz Maps by Daniel Hasenbos
www.danielsmaps.com

Editing by Drew Tierney

All the Gold by D.S. Tierney
www.dstierney.com
© 2020 D.S. Tierney
ISBN: 978-1-7347614-2-9

For Orvis, The Getaway:
Can't think of a better story to dedicate to your
memory than a heist. You left the world too soon.

Special Thanks to the Mechanics:
Jay, Elisabeth, Michael, Genevieve, Wayne and Chris

Also from Author D.S. Tierney

Dark Ages (2019)

Are you a thief for hire? Or all that stands between Terragard and a new dark age?

Grint, adopted son of the God of Thieves has been running cons across the countryside. When Eleanor, an envoy of the evil necromancer, Count Danghier, hires Grint to steal a rare artifact before the convergence of Terragard's two moons, his first instinct is to run. When she tells him it's in the Terrastags, a legendary city that's never been robbed, the challenge and prestige are too good to pass up.

What he finds is more than he bargained for. A sinister plan to unleash a new dark age using the blood of an innocent child in the artifact. Against his normally selfish mindset, Grint rescues the girl and flees into the mountains. In their desperate race against the moons, he'll have to outwit necromancers, assassins and rival thieves, never knowing what's worse... The monsters at his back or the mysterious girl at his side.

So what are you Grint? A thief, an opportunist, or a hero?

Terragard Tales - The Lunar Sundering (2020)

The Hit Audiodrama Podcast, now in Print! The Lunar Sundering follows three adventures during the cataclysm that created the world of Terragard. *Birth of the Bhanyu, The Grummahrand, The Last City in the Sky.*

Available at: **www.dstierney.com**

Note From the Author

How to Read The World of Terragard

Each novel in the World of Terragard series is written as a standalone story that you can pick up and read in any order. While there are crumbs and connective tissues sprinkled through each narrative, it is my goal that your enjoyment of this book only be deepened by, without relying on, events in other stories.

My suggested reading order is the order in which they were published, as denoted by the book numbering. Feel free to ignore this, as it is, after all, just a suggestion.

Thank you for joining me on this adventure, and the many more to come!

Cheers!
D.S. Tierney

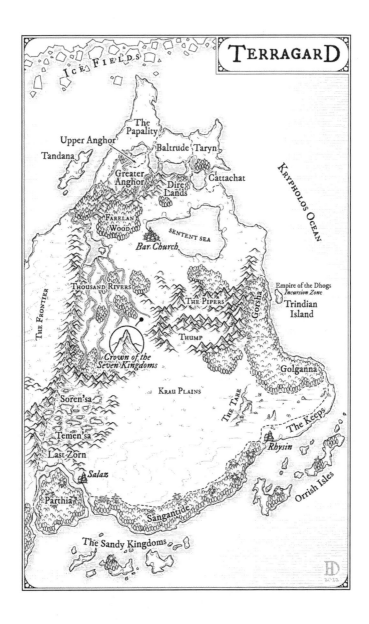

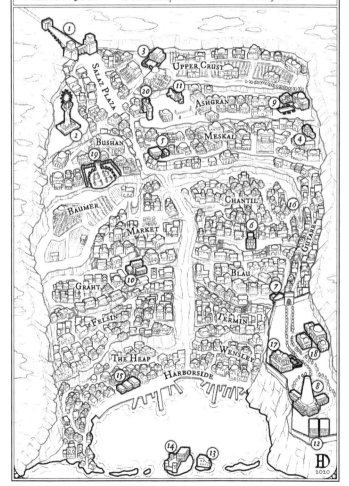

The CITY of SALAZ

1. Tiber's Bridge
2. Statue of Ashgra
3. Borismere's Manor
4. Orsava's Manor
5. Café of the Runway
6. Nazara's Apartment
7. Chain of Weebles Tavern
8. Seastone Tower & Palace
9. Gallery of the Sun & Ashgra's Temple
10. Courtyard and Tenement Buildings
11. Abandoned Church of Krypholos
12. Palace Guest Apartments
13. Allast Island Prison
14. Fort E'lo"Prakk
15. Old Warehouse
16. Winding Road
17. High Priest Home
18. Military Command Building
19. Overlook
20. Arch of the Sun

Thief in the street, Thief in the gutter,
One coin, two coin, poor as butter.
Thief on the roof, Thief in the night,
Three gold, four gold, all is right.
Thieves getting drunk, Thieves like to skim,
All gold everywhere, the drinks are on him!

- Sons of Hobbe

1

*"And with that, the trap is disarmed
and the danger passed."*

*- The last words of Hamilton C. Fields
Annum 1212*

Salaz, Annum 1369

There is nothing like gold. The luster, a gentle sheen of reflective bliss. Its weight, solid and balanced, the heft proportional to its value. The draw, nothing else calls the way gold does. Not jewels or antiquities or objects of power. They all paled in comparison to the natural elegance of a golden coin. Countless thieves fell ill to the fever brought on by gold. More than any plague ravaging the landscape, but never Grint. He learned well to avoid that sickness.

Keep your eye on what you're there to steal. Blue Fingered Hobbe, the God of Thieves, cautioned his many wards of the danger the golden fever carried.

Grint ran his finger along the curved arm of a golden candelabra and flicked it at its lowest point. The answering thud made him smile. A solid piece, neither gilded nor hollow, and when melted down would keep him floating in drink for a few turnings of the moon. Tempting, perhaps a bit too tempting considering the piece fit in his bag. To-night's foray into larceny had a specific goal in mind, but why not something extra?

A deep, pleasing silence filled the ancient manor. The palpable, deafening absence of sound forced him to be at his best or invite disaster. One errant mistake, false step or indulgence of fancy would bring about a flood of trou-ble. Upon slippered feet wrapped in cloth, the ends tied off in strips of leather, Grint moved with impunity as the last hours of night dwindled away. The occupying lord slept, un-aware of the intruder stalking his halls.

Grint had watched the manor for a week leading up to tonight. The original house, a squat, square structure of yel-lowed sandstone, remained half-visible beneath additions of lacquered wood frames, clay walls, and scalloped tile across the roof. The perfect depiction for the city of Salaz. A place caught between progression and protecting heritage. The lord in residence, Borismere caused quite an upheaval all on his own, courting the queen and elevating his status beyond what Grint's benefactor found to be suitable.

Through careful study, Grint watched, moving closer every day. First, from the window of a fine tavern where he could see the comings and goings. Then at night, from the branches of a tree he shared with three old mungles chatter-ing incoherent grunts to each other over a single piece of fruit. Each time, Grint familiarized himself with the guards' faces, routines, and patrols. The kry-damned fools, embold-ened by a lack of anything meaningful to do, passed most nights throwing dice in the small confines of the guard-house. Grint laid upon their roof the last night, listening to war stories - most outright lies - and complaints about the despotic rule of the wizard in Borismere's employ.

Unlike most jobs, Grint had the luxury of time. The man who hired him, Lord Sem Orsava, was not the typical benefactor doling out opportunities while contriving ways to cheat you. Instead, as a minor Salazian noble, Orsava wanted to set certain balances right and see family heirlooms returned to his care. Such as his lost painting of a boat in a storm. The painting, which Orsava described as older than the Sangantide Treaty, was last seen with his estranged brother. Through the lucrative market of trading favors, Orsava learned the queen's collectors seized it. Brother Orsava's reputation as a poor gambler was legendary, piling up a substantial amount of debt.

A pity I never met him, Grint thought. Rich fools at the table often put more coin in the pocket than theft. It just wasn't as fun. Grint never asked the fate of the brother, but with a debtor's mark, he was likely imprisoned on Allast Island. The jail sat on the center island in Salaz's harbor, just a deadly swim through siren eel infested waters.

Proper handling of debts meant the painting should have been auctioned toward the brother's account. The queen chose instead to gift it to Lord Borismere. Orsava described the rival lord as the worst kind of Salazian - one who wasn't from there. Grint held to the suspicion that if the painting ended up with anyone else, he would have left it there. Seeing it with Borismere was not an option Orsava would entertain. Given Borismere's standing and his connection to the queen, it was of paramount importance that Grint make no mistakes, or leave even the barest of footprints behind. A fate worse than Allast Island waited for anyone who crossed the vindictive monarch of Salaz.

"Not to worry," Grint told his benefactor just that morning. The details of entering the manor and leaving with the painting were all worked out.

Be careful you don't become too emboldened yourself! Hobbe laughed. He wanted to scream at Hobbe, but it would do no good. The annoying bits of knowledge doled out by the smirking god in Grint's mind were just that - voices in his head. Spectral communication wasn't among Hobbe's many talents. Debating with the voice, as he often did, was just arguing with himself. And foolish. When his conscience chimed in, he found it best to listen.

Fine, Grint gave in, putting the candelabra back on the hall table, adjusting the angle to match the position he'd found it.

Trouble enough existed on any job without tempting the hand of Lady Lorelai, Goddess of Chance. If tonight, Borismere remained late in his study, or the wizard woke from a harsh dream - all the spirit glue ever mixed wouldn't put the broken pieces of the plan back together. Grint knew how to adapt to changing landscapes with the tools on hand, and with those tools he was the best there was. It wasn't hubris - *maybe* - but he never doubted the fact that there wasn't a thing in the world he couldn't steal.

Fine rugs ran the length of the manor hallway, squishing beneath his feet. A pair of hard-soled boots sat in his bag, just in case he needed them for a getaway. Most of the roads in Salaz were cobblestone or cracked brick in need of repair. Either would be murder on slippered feet. Skirting the wall, he stepped light, trying not to think about the prospect of escaping. Lord Borismere lived here when he was not at the palace, but also housed his staff within the manor. Four maids, a secretary, and the wizard lived in rooms scattered around the house. None should have any need to be awake at this hour, but it helped to keep him sharp if he imagined they were right beside him.

Pausing beside the study door, he sucked in a deep breath, listening for sounds on the other side. No light spilled beneath and nothing moved, so he turned the knob. It was an old, copper thing that screamed in protest at such an untimely hour. Grint's jaw ached with tension, but he kept at it, squeezing his eyes until a loud click echoed the release of the latch. Shimmying through the opening, he closed the door within a hair's width. Not open enough to notice unless someone tried to come in and not shut far enough that he'd have to mess with the knob on the way out.

Effulg's blue moonlight spilled through the window behind Borismere's desk. The study was a disappointment for Grint. An unassuming room, sparse in its decor. Just a plain, oak desk centered beneath the window and an old reading chair in the far corner. Three golden busts of Borismere's ancestry sat on the shelves, interspersed between books that appeared purchased for their aesthetic value and not the words they held. Looking at the first bust's gaunt features pinched in expressions of dismay reminded Grint of willen bonecasters who beheaded intruders as a warning. Grint flicked the nose and heard a hollow sound. Tin with a gilding of gold.

All that remained in the study were two paintings hanging on either side of the window. To the left, an old chapel of Ashgra and its believers during a meteor shower. Somber tidings to look upon every day. Not that the painting on the right offered any better. Orsava's family heirloom depicted an old boat on rough waters. Torrential rains drenched two fishermen fighting to stay afloat. Fishermen was Grint's initial thought, but looking closer at the rough scratch the artist used on their faces, the deep-set eyes and gaunt, frail arms. *They look like escaping prisoners.*

Growing up on the streets of Dirty Gull, he knew the type well. Salt fishers, condemned prisoners used as bait, walked under guard when their boats were in port. Or maybe it was just his occupational bias. When you're a thief, everyone looks like a criminal.

Orsava mused at substantial length on the painting, about how the waters drew you in as they moved. Grint didn't see it. Just a boat lost at sea.

Not a musing, Hobbe whispered in warning.

"You're right," Grint said, his fingers hovering over the intricate detailing of the frame. Orsava made it clear this painting moved. An enchantment of the oils and brush. Animated paintings were a fad that spread through aristocracies, ebbing and following over the last century. Grint never cared for them. The unnatural motion made him feel green when he looked too long. Things meant to be still should stay that way.

The revelation that this one sat still inspired him to proceed with caution. Grint pulled an agot stone from his bag and scraped the edge onto his blade. The dust it left behind had the uncanny ability of revealing hidden enchantments. It saved Grint's backside more than once, warning him about traps that otherwise would kill or ensnare.

Grint blew the dust into the picture. If nothing happened, there were no enchantments. Otherwise, the color of the dust would reveal the magic used. Borismere may have enchanted the painting to stop moving. Or his wizard... Grint watched the result as his mouth hung open. In all the many years of thievery, this was one he'd not seen before.

Wherever the dust landed, the painting vanished, revealing a rough texture beneath and the scribblings of what appeared to be a complex map. The image lasted two breaths before the painting reappeared.

Wanting a better look, Grint pulled the thing off the wall and set it face down atop the clean surface of the desk. A handful of brackets held the canvas to the frame, each pried loose with the tip of his dagger. Setting the frame aside, he flipped the painting face-up and smoothed it out. His mind expected the rigid contour of scraped paint, but that was a lie. This wasn't a painting at all, just a map pretending to be. Grint produced a long leather tube, removing the spool of paper within. A thin layer of wax protected the mimicrum - magic cloth that took the image of what it touched - wax being the exception. Using it took skill. Even the slightest brush of a finger could trigger transformation, rendering it useless.

With delicate precision, he laid the painting onto the mimicrum. In a few ticks it would create a perfect copy of what lie beneath. Mimicrum cared nothing for enchantments, taking its shape from the original. Once done, Grint could put the original back in the frame, giving himself ample time to study the duplicate. Borismere would never know someone else had a copy of his secret map. Grint paced while he waited for the mimicrum, imagining what the map might lead to. Something important. Who hid a map to their larder or grandmother's old day dresses?

While his mind dreamed of bejeweled crowns and magic swords, the mimicrum sizzled, the audible cue that its magic was at work. At the very least, Grint hoped it might lead to the real painting. A tad disappointing if that was all, but it would mean a job completed and a pouch of coin paid. *Take what is...*

"Not now," he told the voice, wanting to indulge in a few more flights of fancy. "The lost sword of Zorn," he whispered. "Or the Flute of Gray Renown. A hundred coins from the haul of ancient pirates. An elixir to raise the dead." Grint knew far too many people to bring back with such a thing.

When enough time passed, he trotted back to the desk, unable to contain the excitement. His foot tapped as he peeled back the painting. The mimicrum had done its job. Perhaps too thoroughly, he thought. The map, in all of its glory, was a complex thing of lines, notes, warnings and directions - most overlapping one another in confusing layers.

"What in the charffing name of Maguire am I supposed to do with this?"

Grint flattened the painting inside its frame, using the butt of his knife to tap in the brackets. All the while studying the new map, trying to make sense of what it led to. Turning away to hang the painting, it struck like a bolt from the heavens. The map showed the floor plan of a manor. This manor in particular. And the line was a path leading to a series of tunnels. At the end? A sizable room marked only with a golden circle.

Now came the time for truth. Did he follow the map to its end or retreat and come back another night? Dawn was fast approaching and would make skulking nigh impossible. Leaving led to the possibility that Grint's interdiction would be discovered, rendering the map useless.

"What's life without a minor risk," he asked one of the golden busts, lightly slapping its cheek.

The hunt began in the study, continuing past a sitting room and kitchen before ending in a hall with no outlet. A staircase existed on the map, but no doorway through. A bridge to cross when he got to it. Light spilled through the kitchen threshold. Followed by the whisper of voices. A man and woman. Grint tucked himself beside the sitting-room door and waited. One guard and a maid? Their conversation centered on her making him a sandwich and her attempting to shoo him off. Stealing food and fraternizing was an excellent way to get sacked, but that wasn't leverage enough to convince them to ignore Grint if they happened upon him.

A black and brown shepherd dog padded through the door and sniffed the air. Grint froze. *When did they get a bloody dog?* He never once saw it during his reconnaissance.

"What is it, Cur?" The guard said as his bulky frame blocked the light. The dog whimpered and looked up, but found no affection from the man. With a disgruntled sound, he walked back into the kitchen.

"Who was it?" The maid whispered.

"No one, Cur is just a jumpy thing."

"She's an obedient girl," she laughed. "Better close the door just in case. Lord Borismere's all-powerful wizard has been on a rampage."

Grint let his breath out as the kitchen door closed, bringing blessed darkness back to the hall. The dog sat, licking her chops while the eyes reflected what little ambient light existed. As soon as Grint shifted, she turned his way. A low growl sounded as her hackles raised. Head low, Cur stepped slowly toward him.

"Easy there, Cur," Grint whispered, reaching into his bag.

The dog stopped a few feet away, baring its teeth. One wrong move and Grint could picture his insides splattered across the expensive rug. Careful not to make sudden moves, he held out his hand, showing the dog a meaty bone. It was something his own dog, Newman, liked to chew on. The effect was immediate. Cur stopped growling, settling onto her haunches and pawing the air. Grint tossed the bone, and she caught it, retreating to the kitchen door with her prize.

Grint tip-toed past. The dog watched, then returned to her important work. Ahead was where the hallway ended. An odd thing to build a hall without windows or doorways. Not even a closet. Grint shook a glow orb, the liquid lit, brightening so he could look at the map. If the guard came out, he'd have to stow it in the bag or fight his way out.

The map showed a series of symbols in three columns. *What language is this?* If it was an ancient tongue, this was a dead end in more ways than one. Grint couldn't recognize the glyphs, or even approximate them with something he'd seen before. Running his hands along the wall, he looked for panels or gaps and even slammed a shoulder into each of the walls to see if they moved. Nothing. As a last-ditch effort, Grint pulled out the agot stone and blew dust at the wall. Waving it around, he hoped to show hidden enchantments. Again, there was nothing.

Grint fumbled with the glow orb as the guard reappeared. He cradled the thing against his belly and fell on it before the guard spotted the light. Stuffing a sandwich in his mouth, the guard looked down at the dog and asked, "You making that noise, Cur?"

Grint watched from the dark-end of the hall, crouched low with the orb held tight. Light threatened to escape from the gaps between his clothing, so he tightened his grip, hoping the sudden shift of shadows didn't draw attention. Unable to see now, Grint could only listen as the guard cursed.

"Stop trying to trip me," he snapped at the dog. "Spilling my food." Grint heard the bone drop as the dog lapped at the fallen bits of sandwich.

"Careful," the maid whispered, her voice giddy. "If they find a mess, it's my hide."

"Cur will clean it up," he answered. Grint risked a peek, seeing the guard pushing the bone with his foot. "Where did you find this?"

"Make sure she does," the maid replied as she planted a smooch on the guard's cheek. The door closed, stealing away the light.

"It's dark in here," the man whined. Grint heard the maid's laugh fading away. There were more inaudible grumbles to which Cur growled back. "Ungrateful," the guard muttered, walking toward the front door. Left alone, the dog picked up the bone and trotted over to Grint, laying it by his feet to keep chewing.

"I wish all guards were as easy to bribe as you," Grint said as he scratched her ears. Alone, he released the orb, hoping to find the answer.

"You know what these glyphs are, girl?" He asked, unrolling the map. If he lingered much longer, daylight would force him to flee. The dog drew Grint's attention to the floor beneath the carpet. She pawed at the edge, trying to lift it. Looking closer, Grint saw the third rune from the map under the frayed strands. Pulling the carpet away, he found an unbroken line of runes scratched in the floorboards. Smiling, he fed the dog a treat and scratched her face. A gesture returned with a wet tongue across his cheek.

Lining the map on the floor, he matched four of the runes. Grint touched them in order, pressing down on the wood until each glowed. Fulfilling the list, a latch in the wall clicked. The panel shimmered, turning from solid wood to clear liquid. It hummed when he touched the surface, but allowed his hand to pass through with no effort. The dog lifted its head, licking its lips, and whining at the portal.

"Dangerous?" He asked. She cocked her head. "Only one way to find out." Grint leapt through and turned to call for the dog, but the wall turned solid as soon as his feet touched down.

Holding out the glow orb, its magical light illuminated a long stone stairwell leading deep below the manor. Grint took account of what tricks he had left in his bag. Bits of magic for concealment, poisons, blades, a rusty compass, and three lock picks. The jumble of things made him wish he'd spent an extra hour this morning organizing the mess. With the old bag, it knew what he needed and just made it available. This bag needed training. Neither contained magic, other than the warding on the clasp, but even a good inanimate object required a bit of cajoling here and there.

"Could be there's a magic bag at the end of this hunt," he smiled. He'd always wanted one of those. They were charffing expensive to get the right way and rarer to find the less legitimate route. He traced his hand across the stairwell on the map, wondering for the first time whether Borismere posted guards in here.

Thank you for thinking of that now.

According to the map, after the stairs he'd find three rooms and another staircase. Notes scrawled atop the rooms revealed a myriad of directions for someone who could read them. Grint learned a few written words in Basic. Enough to get him by. Traps, chest, treasure, death, wanted. The rest of it was all a bunch of jumbled letters in a secret alphabet. Except, this time, some of it was a secret alphabet. Lord Borismere used cyphers in the notes. Boxes and circles around numbers and letters. Traps and puzzles annoyed Grint, even if his greatest skill was working out how to circumvent and escape their deadly clutches.

That's what you think your greatest skill is? Hobbe asked.

The stairs led to an ancient set of halls with arched twenty-foot ceilings. Ancient stonework with no seams were smooth to the touch, as if someone had carved them from a single block. The craftsmanship was exquisite, forming intricate patterns and mosaics from a culture markedly different from most he'd seen. As the glow orb faded, he stuffed it in his bag to recharge. Pulling a torch from a bracket, the black iron ring clanked against the stone, dropping a shower of dust. Grint felt around the base of the bracket. They were recent additions, pounded into the wall and cracking centuries old pictograms. Lord Borismere held little sentimentality for Salaz's past, it seemed. Grint passed his hand through the torch fire. It didn't burn.

"Evertorches," he whispered. An expensive enchantment to make a torch that never died and didn't burn. A single one would fetch double what Orsava was paying him to steal the painting. Tempting to be sure, but they would miss such an expensive item. Or not. Grint gawked at a hallway lined with at least twenty of the torches.

"Find the room first, steal the torches later."

Reaching the first puzzle, Grint burst out in laughter. The sound echoed through the dusty chamber. For all the cryptic words scrawled on the map, he'd expected a harrowing journey. What he found instead were ropes tied along the path one needed to take. Borismere held this secret so long he'd lulled himself into thinking he didn't need to hide it. Smart if you were the only one coming down and you didn't want to take an accidental step. But secrets never kept. Someone always found them. It made Grint's mouth water, anticipating what he might find. Something that Borismere visited often enough to rope off a path.

Grint stood a foot to the side and tested the rope with his blade, plucking it like a lute string. When nothing rumbled or collapsed, he gripped it and traced the path through the dust. He tested each step before committing. In the first room, a hundred tiny statues depicting Dohlar, God of Plagues, stared inward. The many yawning mouths waited to release poison darts or gases to choke the life out of anyone foolish enough to disturb their slumber.

Allowed a moment to breathe, Grint shimmied through a cramped tunnel leading to the next chamber. Within the sunken room loomed two glimmering glass statues of Asper, Goddess of Oceans. Each bent along the curve of the ceiling, reaching out to clasp the other's hands at the apex. Golden light danced through the liquid churning inside the glass. Would she drown Grint if he stepped wrong? Three materials covered the floor. Sturdy stone slabs, solid and sure. Cobbled brick, uneven, yet unmoving. Loose gravel, giving way underfoot. *The most like water.* The rope led through the gravel and back again to center as the chamber fed into the last room.

Here, Grint stared at an angry red statue of Ashgra standing with a bloody sword raised. Underfoot of the statue was a crude depiction of Krypholos. Salaz accepted Asper and Dohlar as deities. Krypholos did not enjoy the same courtesy. The bloody sword dripped fire, hissing where it struck the floor. Fire fit with the motif of Ashgra as a Sun God. The rope ended at a wall to Ashgra's right with no clue why. Grint looked over the map, seeing nothing but a scribbled hand. One yellowed stone out of all the others looked worn.

Sweat beaded on his temple as he let his fingers dance before the stone. Pushing it seemed obvious. Stop the fire and open the door. Or would it dump an ocean of lava on him? Grint shook his head. "I'm overthinking it. Borismere won't get tricky at the end."

Closing his eyes, he pressed his hand against the stone, hearing it scrape as it moved. The door beneath Ashgra swung open, but the drips of fire did not stop. Grint counted the time between and jumped through without getting singed. Still, he patted himself down and checked to make sure. Satisfied, Grint passed into the second stairway. At the bottom, he discovered a large cave-like chamber filled with statues of galloping horses ten-times too large for any person to ride. The map depicted this room with a crudely drawn horse and a doorway leading to the larger chamber where the golden circle waited. What he saw when he lowered the map were a dozen tunnels branching off in many directions. The map didn't show this. It was something Borismere came up with.

Borismere won't get tricky at the end? Hobbe laughed.

Grint crouched, picking up loose pebbles from the floor and scattering them. They bounced into each cave. The tunnels weren't illusions. Each pebble disappeared into a wall of darkness a dozen feet in. There was no breeze or hint of light offering clues to the correct path. Even the dust from the agot stone was useless. Each tunnel glowed red as the dust crossed the threshold. *They're all enchanted somehow.* The spying glass, a small monocle supposed to show secrets when held to the eye, revealed nothing. *Charffing useless,*

Grint thought as he tightened the bag over his shoulder. *I knew Zephen cheated me with this thing.*

He stepped into the first tunnel, groaning, "I'd better get started."

The best plan left to him was walking into each. If the tunnel branched off or ended, he'd go back and try another. It would take time, but in this darkened underworld, he had plenty. Dawn could come and go as he'd have to remain here until dark settled on the city once more. Unless Borismere made a habit of coming down to gawk, the odds of being disturbed were slim.

One step into the tunnel and the air collapsed inward, trapping the breath in his lungs. Grint tried to jump backwards, but the tunnel's entrance vanished and his shoulder struck a solid wall. The pressure increased the longer he stood still, and relieved a bit as he moved, so he kept forward, struggling to breathe without blacking out. The tunnel curved in a tight circle. *How can that be?* It should have intersected with another tunnel or come back around to where he started.

Maybe it has no beginning, Hobbe warned, voicing the fear Grint knew too well. Irrationality set in and he started running, the surrounding pressure pushing harder every moment. A rumble of rocks showered the uneven floor as the tunnel collapsed, cascading in his direction. Grint ran until it was right on top of him and jumped with his eyes closed. When the rumble stopped and his breath returned, he opened his eyes. Back in the entry room, he thought, looking at the twelve tunnels.

"Charffing bender puzzle," he coughed, wiping the very real debris off his coat. A nasty bit of magic popularized in the pre-Zorn days when Bar Church was the center of cultural significance. Each path would present its own horror to tax the mind and body, getting worse each time he chose the wrong way. From what Grint knew of the magic, he'd have two more tries before it killed him. And there were eleven tunnels left. Grint paced back and forth, looking for clues. Something. Anything to give him the answer. Footprints? Markings? Stumbling like a blind beggar into another tunnel was foolhardy, but there wasn't a way in all the known hells of Astapoor he'd give up the hunt.

Rummaging through his bag, Grint sought anything that might help. The collection wasn't as impressive as the one he used to have, but he'd still pulled together more than a few tricks. Unfortunately, none offered any help in this situation. *Make the right choice. Resign yourself to momentary failure. Find a mage in the city who knows ways of revealing bender puzzles.* The voice was right. If anyone like that existed in Salaz, they could unwind the bender with a snap. The last time Grint encountered such a mage was years ago, planning a crypt-job in the Thousand Rivers. It would take months to find him again, and there was no certainty they still lived.

"I could always try one more passage. Lorelai willing, might get lucky," Grint said, pointing his finger at one passage and then another.

No, leave.

"Yeah, I'm trying," Grint shut out the voice, breathing in deep and exhaling. Bouncing on his heels, he repeated the breathing, trying to will himself forward. It all felt like the moment before you dove in a body of water you knew would be freezing.

A dog's bark and muffled a voice alerted him to someone's approach. Two sets of boots walked down the stairs to his right. Grint clambered on top of the closest stone horse, pressing himself low in its saddle. In his bag he had a vial of shade leaf, but it was too late to go rooting around for it.

Lord Borismere walked in with the dog, who sniffed around the room, growling. *Turncoat*, Grint thought. Another figure stepped in after them. Dressed in blood-red robes, they hid their face beneath a silver mask with horns protruding from the edges. The house wizard.

"When she paws at the glyphs it wakes me," Borismere yawned. "Can we not change that?"

"I can, or we could punish the mutt," the wizard replied. Cur whimpered and darted into the tunnel Grint first tried.

"No," Borismere shouted. "Foolish dog."

He pulled out and flicked a medallion. The tunnels wavered, allowing the dog to return with a rat in her mouth. "Was that what the fuss was about? You'll be spending your nights in the yard with the rest of the louts." The dog glanced at Grint with the rodent in its mouth - did it wink at him? *Not so foolish.* Smart enough to know Grint woke the house by touching the glyphs.

"I can do a sweep," the wizard said.

"No, I'm tired." Borismere clicked his tongue as he left the room and the dog ran to follow. The Lord never looked up to see the smiling face of Grint. And why was he so happy? The medallion revealed the tunnel he needed to enter.

Grint waited well beyond the fading sounds of their footsteps, wanting to be sure no one doubled back. When he was satisfied, he hopped off his petrified mount and stepped into the third tunnel from the right. The illusion wavered and fell apart. Before him stood a giant wall with two golden doors. Pounding the surface with his fist, he felt the giddy realization that these doors alone were worth more than what Hobbe claimed to have in his secret vaults. Handles made of carved golden ropes felt right in his hands.

Grint pulled on them and they swung open easily. Golden light poured over his face as his heart skipped a beat. The evertorch fell from his hand and he didn't care. An ocean of gold, jewels, and treasure filled the room beyond. And more. So much more.

"Hobbe, I've done it. I've become richer than you," he said, falling to his knees.

Grint picked up two heaping handfuls of gold, letting the coins, knuckles, squares, triangles fall through his fingers. A bejeweled crown fit snug on his head. To the side, leaning against a rack of golden spears, sat Orsava's painting. True to his word, the waves rolled as the men in the boat fought to stay alive. Grint fell onto his back, waving his arms and legs in a childish game of snow angels.

And just like that, the thief succumbed to the one thing he swore he never would. Gold Fever.

2

"Dragons are often believed to be myth due to their infrequent appearances in many provinces, but they are quite real. As are their hoards of gold!"

- Wizen Freid, The Temptation of Dragons

Grint leaned against a stone wall, letting the sun kiss his face. In Salaz, it rose first over the Upper Crust district, proof in their eyes that Ashgra rewarded the nobles. The city was waking up as hawkers and laborers started their days. A mixture of smells filled the air. Baking bread and frying fish, smoke from forges and tanning leathers. Present too was the pungent spice they used in great abundance, bassal. Sunlight reflected off the tile rooftop of Borismere's manor, which remained the sole focus of Grint's attention. He clutched the single golden coin in his pocket. The only piece of treasure he dared leave with. Taking more risked showing his hand, and he didn't want a single handful. He wanted it all.

A man walked by, adjusting the smoky, semi-translucent veil across his face. Grint couldn't make out his full expression, but enough of the man's disapproval showed through. In Salaz, they wore veils, scarves, and even masks as more than mere fashion statements. To most, it was a religious necessity. Ashgra, the sun god looked down on the world. If the proud god saw someone looking back, she would bewitch them, making them insane. People wore the coverings, believing they protected them from Ashgra's gaze. On sunny days, cloudy days or during storms - As long as the light of the sun shines, so too does Ashgra.

All a bunch of rubbish to Grint. There was a god of light, and it wasn't Ashgra. Krypholos and Ashgra. Were they the same? Hobbe said the gods used other names as they adjusted to the world and their place in it. Perhaps ten thousand years ago, Krypholos wandered through Salaz under the name Ashgra and cursed someone. Whatever the origin, the sun didn't dole out curses and the god of light was too busy drinking to care who looked up. For the past few hundred years, old Krypsie had been hiding away in a Kryphatic monastery sampling their wines. Another nugget of wisdom, courtesy of the real Hobbe.

Trying to explain any of that to a devout Salazian would get you whipped, sent to Allast Island, or drowned in the harbor. Asking a Salazian for proof of Ashgra's presence was equally annoying. All they would do was point at the crimson statue of the god, looming over the Bushan district, her arms supporting a great sun overhead. They revered the monument and claimed it as an immutable testimony of the god's existence.

The golden lining was that not everyone wore masks. After the slow conquest of Zorn through Terragard, many cities like Salaz learned of Krypholos and the Papality. It set many of their ideas about religion and deities on a dangerous path. Where once everyone in Salaz hid their faces, there now existed a mix of those who did not. The controlling majority held to the beliefs, looking down on their rivals as sun-facers. They offered visitors a modicum of leeway in the matter, but not much.

Grint ignored the scornful glares and comments on all but one occasion. After a costly tavern brawl, Orsava told him to wear a veil blend in. Grint refused, giving in to it would be a declaration that Ashgra was real. Aligning with ideas like that could have dangerous consequences. Orsava shook his head, unable to wrap his mind around the notion. Not when Grint mocked worship and belief.

"Oh, I believe in gods," he told his friend and benefactor. "I just don't like them. All one hundred of the krydamn bastards." And most didn't like him, so calling their attention to his actions was something he tried to avoid.

Sweat ran in streams around his ear, then down the side of his neck. The sun had barely risen, and it was already shaping up to be hot. Air, thick with moisture, made it feel like a person could swim from one place to another. That was Salaz. At least the winds weren't blowing in from the swamps today, bringing the smell of rot with them. Though it wouldn't be so bad if they did. A strong southern wind would carry out the muggy air even if it left a stink behind. On rare occasions, the wind shifted in from the Gellanore River, beyond the harbor, carrying the sweet scent of flowers. Those days were few, and Grint had yet to experience one.

A pack of mungles sat along the edge of the roof overhead. The gray things looked like hairless monkeys with useless bat wings. The entire city was lousy with foy. Mungles, siren eels in the harbor, bloodsucking foy flies - even rumors of halflings living in the glades around the city.

Why was Salaz such a hotbed? Grint couldn't say any more than he could articulate his disdain for them. They were just nasty pests. A wizen in Edelgrah once told him there were fifty distinct ways a foy fly's bite would kill you and spent the evening listing them.

"Two rollies for a plick," a veiled woman said with a basket under her arm. Rollies were fish treats rolled in batter, then baked. Not bad if you had a sauce to go with it, but the locals preferred to eat them without. Grint didn't have any of the local currency on him. Plicks were much like a copper bit but stamped with the queen's seal. Aside from the gold in his pocket, he never carried money on a job. Bringing coin was an excellent way to lose it unless you needed it for some part of what you were up to. And even then, you'd somehow lose it.

"No plicks on me," Grint said.

The old woman lifted her veil enough to spit and stomped off, muttering something about sun-facers.

"Salaz hospitality," he smiled as he looked back at Borismere's manor. Getting out before the dawn had been a close thing. Grint slipped out the front door as the wizard walked downstairs for a morning bite.

With sweet freedom and knowledge of the treasure, came other problems. He needed to contrive a way to get the coin and transport it before he approached Orsava. The lord might despise Borismere, but would that be enough to convince him to join in on a heist of this magnitude? The answer was likely no. Lord Orsava feared retaliation from the queen, and that would give him cause to pass on the opportunity.

Yes, that's why you don't want to go to him, Hobbe said, picking apart Grint's excuses.

To tell the truth, Grint rankled at the idea of sharing the gold. Going to Orsava meant dividing it by half or more. Why take only part of the hoard when he could have it all? The answer became one of feasibility. Grint had few connections in Salaz outside of Orsava's circle. *Few?* He knew one other person, and bringing her in would open a new chest of horrors.

Grint walked to the corner, looking down at the Grand Runway. The longest, widest street in Salaz, it ran from the base of the Meskal district down to Harborside. They had built Salaz on a staggered downhill slope nestled between thick, inhospitable swamps with only one roadway out. The city gates and Tiber's Bridge were close to Borismere's manor, but he'd need a hundred carts moving single file while the guards looked another way. *Bribe them?*

Better to keep the coin you have, Hobbe said. *By the time you pay off the guards, that's what they'll leave you with.*

It might work if he brought the gold out a little at a time, but that would require finding a safe place to stash it while hoping nobody stole it. Or he could take it in wagons down the Runway and load it onto a ship. Set sail before anyone knew what he'd done. A massive if, but at least it was something. Hobbe didn't have to speak, he'd given Grint the answer every day of his young life, but the god never wasted an opportunity to hear his own voice. *The best plans - all my plans - involved the mark giving me their wealth without a care in the world.*

How do I get Borismere to give it to me?

A steady commotion rose from Salaz Plaza, quieting the voice Grint never could. Urchin children shouted as they ran past, shoving anyone in their way. As word spread, windows and balconies filled with people. The shops emptied as citizens tied veils or strapped masks on their faces. Grint lingered, letting the crowd grow around him, as curious about the fervor as anyone else. The reigning queen might cause such a clamor, even being as spiteful as Orsava claimed. The lord's opinion on the matter aside, even unpopular monarchs were a sight to behold. *A visiting monarch?* No. If that were true guards would line the streets to keep crowds back.

Grint didn't have long to wait and was glad he stayed. The sight was the second most surprising thing he'd seen today. Atop a broad-backed tan horse sat a Parthian of considerable size. A foolish distinction, Grint realized. The smallest Parthian he'd ever seen was still two heads taller than himself. Like all Parthians, shaggy hair covered the rider, this one blond with a smattering of gray, save for the black snout and jowls hanging beside his mouth. And it was a 'him' - female Parthians bore six breasts and no shyness in showing them. Bright red eyes sat in the deep recesses of his face, focused on nothing beside the road ahead. With a long sword strapped to his back, he wore a leather harness, briefs, and boots. Barbarian gear. A Parthian barbarian crossing the Gellanore wasn't a thing to celebrate. Meant he was atoning for something. Wouldn't be hard to stay clear of him. The crowds he'd attract would be enough to give Grint warning of his presence.

"Not something we see here often," a woman said in a confident voice. Grint glanced to the side, finding a woman of height with him, but he could say little else about her appearance. A large, floppy hat covered her hair while a shiny silver mask hid her features. Even the thick burgundy robe concealed all but the nape of her neck. What concerned Grint more than how she wore such thick robes in this heat, was how she got co close without his noticing.

I'm tired, he told himself, knowing it was time to leave. *Too many eyes on the street.* Too many chances for someone to notice and remember him later. Grint offered the woman a smile and walked away, heading in the opposite direction of the Parthian. If she was a pick-pocket, she was wasting her time. There was nothing interesting she'd find on his person. The bag he carried would shock her, and the golden coin remained clutched in his hand.

The Ashgran sat below the Upper Crust. There a Salazian could find the holy shrines to Ashgra and smaller temples to approved deities. Below that was the Meskal, where Orsava lived. Wealthy, but not enough to live on top. *Not yet.* Grint kept his stride casual, sensing someone a dozen steps back. *Sloppy,* he thought. The cadence of their footsteps was off by a click, and they cast a long shadow. *A long shadow with a floppy hat.* Could be coincidence, but he'd avoid Orsava's manor until he knew, continuing into the Market district.

The Market District was a maze of streets filled with covered carts attended by barkers. Banners waved from ropes as advertisements and crown edicts, criss-crossing the space between shops. The wares offered here varied as much as the carts themselves. Fish and seafood dominated the selections, but you could always find swamp fruits and roasting critters. The quality meats and fruits brought in by ships were more expensive and sold only inside the stores catering to Salazians. Finding such a treat on the street was a good deal or the perfect way to end up sick. Veils and decorative masks hung from pegs beside cloaks, clothing, and beaded jewelry.

The last piece to the puzzle of Salaz were the colored armbands the citizenry wore. Each color marked a guild or social class. They had issued Grint a white band with two red slashes forming a V when he arrived. Orsava wore a divided red and blue armband with this house emblem in the center. Nothing stopped someone from wearing the armband of another guild, except for the guilds themselves. A first offense carried with it a punishment decided by the guild itself. A second offence earned you a visit to the city tribunal.

As Grint browsed the carts, he caught sight of several red band city guards milling about. Another coincidence? Idling at a stall selling leather bracelets, he noted the blue and white checkered armband - a merchant willing to deal with sun-facers. Those with yellow armbands and the red insignia of Ashgra would not deal with him at all. Floppy Hat was still with him, hiding behind a squid seller's booth. But her shadow was distinct. Why was she following him? Had she seen him leaving Borismere's or was this a sun-facer thing? Grint kicked himself for not noticing her armband in the Plaza, and the booth hid it now.

"Ten plicks for that," the barker said.

"Ten? Sounds steep," Grint said without looking at what he'd picked up.

"From the finest beasts in all Terragard," the Salazian said. "Ten plicks is a bargain."

"I guess," he answered. The woman hadn't moved, content to look at scarves while Grint browsed leather bracelets. Were there others watching him?

The barker, a tenacious fellow, stepped out from behind his booth, pressing the bracelet into Grint's hand. "You drive a hard bargain for a sun-fa... visitor. I like that. Nine plicks."

"I'd give you three if I had it on me. Maybe later."

More guards appeared at either end of the street, none of them in formation. Grint looked for the woman and her shadow. Both vanished. Maybe she wasn't following at all.

"I insist," the man said, giving the bracelet back again.

"No," Grint said with more force. The barker backed off, his disdain for Grint's tone clear. But then why was he smiling? When Grint stopped at this cart, the man had displayed a blue and white armband. He was sure of that. But now the merchant wore yellow.

"Thief! Thief! Sun-facer thief!"

"I'm not stealing, I'm just not interested." Though he may not have been, the guards were. Six on each end of the street, they turned in unison. The coordinated effort triggered a warning that all may not be what it seemed.

"Thief! Help me, guards!"

Guards in blue chain armor adjusted red armbands and drew blades, walking toward the commotion. The crowd parted to let them pass. *Charffing mungle-dipped...* Grint pulled a red mallet from the cart and threw it at the barker. The man fell in a flutter of robes. A woman wearing a mask painted to look like an Orrish sailor screamed and pushed her way through the gawkers.

"Sun-faced miscreant," she cried to the guards, pointing at Grint. *That's enough of that,* he thought, ducking into the crowd. Markets worked well for disappearing. Among enough people you could vanish, and that had gotten him out of a lot of tight scrapes. In cities, there were always those who despised authority enough to offer a bit of help and point a guard the wrong way. Unless they hated you more than the guards. Masked citizens spat insults as they locked arms, blocking his way through. The guards shouted as they cracked their swords against bucklers, expecting a fight. Behind the group of guards to Grint's left, he saw the floppy hat bouncing.

"Charffing luck," he growled, wanting to curse Lorelai in the same breath, but wisely choosing not to. The Goddess of Chance was vindictive. Instead, Grint climbed through a cart without a canopy and stepped onto the head of a man who'd chosen to do his civic duty and block his path. Screams of protest and swatting hands followed him as he jumped from one head to the next. Until the last person moved aside, sending Grint crashing onto the stone street. He groaned, feeling the twinge of something angry in his ribs.

Grint ignored the pain, rolling onto his feet and racing into an alley. The guards reached where he'd been, shouting in rage for people to move. The very trap they set now turned against them. Clutching an arm around his side, he checked for breaks. Perhaps Lorelai was smiling on him after all as nothing moved or dropped him to the ground in agonizing pain.

The space between buildings in the Market was slim and littered with mungle droppings and slop from Krypsie knew what. Strange piles squished beneath his thick boots. At least I have these, he thought. Having to traipse through the muck in slippers was an image he didn't relish. Warning shouts and alarm bells rang out, but those on the street he came out on didn't know why. Lowering his head, Grint wished he'd listened to Orsava and gotten a mask. Anything to pull attention away.

Eyes fell upon him as he moved from one side of the street to the other. Ringing bells and the sudden appearance of a sun-facer from the alley were more than enough to draw attention, but Grint's pale skin stood out in a city of darker complexions. Add the mop of red hair on top of it all, something as rare as a Parthian riding into town, and he might as well have come out screaming they're after me.

The whispers grew into open shouting as a lock of soldiers turned onto the street, spreading out to cut off escape. Grint started walking back the way he came when a powerful hand gripped his arm, easily wrapping around his bicep. Callouses covered the knuckles from years of fighting. Scars stood out against the tiger-stripe tattoos running up the length of the muscled arm. The man, much taller than Grint, wore his long, black hair in a ponytail and covered his face with a veil dyed to look like a tiger's face.

"Sun-facer," he roared as he dragged Grint toward an outlet. "Is this madness your doing?"

"There's no madness here," Grint said with a smile, knowing that getting away from the man would require a fight, drawing more attention to himself. "Just a misunderstanding involving leather."

The tiger-man looked back at the guards as he pulled Grint onto a stairway leading down to the next district. "Shut your fool mouth," he bellowed.

A *bit too loud*, Grint thought, still trying to figure a way out of the man's grip. A knife in the ribs would work, but stabbing someone and then getting caught would earn him a spot on the next transport to Allast.

"Run," the man whispered without looking down at Grint.

Grint blinked at him like an idiot. Giving the man a second, appraising look. The tiger motif aside, nothing familiar stood out. This wasn't someone introduced through Orsava or even Nazarra. Grint looked for the man's armband, but he wasn't wearing one. An unaffiliated man opened another mystery. While Grint ran through all of this, the guards converged on their spot, shouting for the tiger-man to hold on to Grint.

"Run," he said in an exasperated voice.

"Who are you?"

Without answer, the tiger-man tossed him down the steps. Four sets of stairs led from the lower edge of the market to the Graht district below. Grint felt every jarring step as he rolled. Salazians walking up the steps stood aside to let him fall, shaking fists in the air at what they deemed foolishness. Somewhere around the third landing he slowed and came to a stop. Grint allowed himself a moment to breathe before the terror set in. Patting his pockets, he found he'd lost most of his belongings. The bag lay a few feet to the side, but the gold coin spun on edge, threatening to tumble over the next step and make its way down without him. Grint dove for it, clutching it tight in his fist.

As Grint grabbed the coin, an urchin boy jumped from the wall beside the stairs, looping the bag's strap over his head. A second boy waited atop, holding out a hand to lift him back up. Grint reached for his dagger, not to hurt them, just threaten, but that had gone missing too. A step away from losing his bag; the greed of the urchin saved the day. The boy tried to undo the bag's clasp and received a nasty shock from the ward. He fell to the ground, yelping as he shook his hand.

The second boy abandoned him as Grint limped over. An obnoxious pain stiffened his right leg. That would take a few days to loosen with a hot bath and a jug of spiced rum. He pulled the boy to his feet and reclaimed his bag. The kid looked scared until Grint smiled and ruffled his hair.

"It was a good try, but next time, make your getaway first. Count all the loot later. Got it?" The kid squinted and nodded with a smile. Grint lifted him onto the wall as soldiers started down the stairs. "Get out of here."

The kid didn't need to be told twice, disappearing over the wall. It was time for Grint to follow his own advice and keep running.

The Graht district was a packed cluster of tenement buildings rising into the air, housing dozens of families in each. Rope lines ran from building to building with wash hung out to dry. The high roofs gave a good vantage of the other districts and were a favorite of the thieves' guild. Dressed in light leathers or cloth, the thieves leapt from one roof to the next. A smart way to escape soldiers weighed down by heavy plate or chain.

Every instinct told Grint to go high, get on the rooftops, but there was no kry-damn way he that would happen. He'd rather a lengthy sentence on Allast Island than deal with the rooftops. Hobbe never understood his fear of heights. As if a god could relate to a mortal's fear of dying. Friends and rivals took great delight in mocking him for it. Grint just grimaced and told them, *It's not so much the being up high. It's the falling down.* Grint may be a talented thief and escape artist, but his getaways often left him banged, bruised, and worse for wear. Getting into one of those situations on top of a tower would lead to an untimely death.

"No thanks," he whispered with an upward glance.

Climbing a crack in a stone wall, Grint jumped into a courtyard between two buildings. The sun hadn't reached this far yet, so the chill of night lingered, keeping the residents indoors. Alone, he jogged to the opposite side, hearing the shouts of guards and additional tolling of bells. He just needed a spot to hide, somewhere they wouldn't think to look. Once night fell, he'd make his way back to Orsava's. A haven that grew further away with each step.

Between the squat tenements sat a third, taller building blocking the alleyways and trapping Grint within. Was Lorelai toying with him? She gave him luck before, but now seemed bent on pushing him to the rooftops. Guards converged outside the courtyard, rattling the locked gate. What other choice did he have? A long balcony ran along the third floor, stretching around the side. The only way up to it without climbing gear was inside and through someone's apartment.

"Check this block," a woman shouted. Was it Floppy Hat?

Grint ran inside, climbing steps three at a time until he got to the third story. Any of the rooms would do. He just had to orientate himself on which side of the hall it was. He heard people moving around inside the first and second rooms and passed those by. Pressing his ear to the third door; he heard only silence and tried the knob. *Locked.* Grint pulled out a pick and went to work, releasing the lock as someone opened a door further down the hall. Slipping in before they spotted him, Grint put his back to the door and breathed. The guards wouldn't check every home in Salaz over a bracelet. He'd hide here until... *Until when?* Hobbe asked.

A man sat on a pallet of cushions, smoking a long pipe of tabac. He watched Grint without expression or movement.

"Hello," Grint said with a smile, wondering if the man was alive. "From the city. Here to make sure you're happy with the... um... Queen?"

The man took the pipe from his mouth and looked at the door. An old fellow with long wisps of white hair, his expression unreadable under layers of wrinkled skin. Grint held up his hand, worried the man would start shouting. Already the soldiers stomped around the hall outside. But the man didn't shout. He pointed at the door with the end of his pipe, making a twirling motion. Grint turned and locked it a moment before the guards tried the knob.

"Thank you," he whispered. The man smiled back and pointed at the balcony door. Grint wasted no time, jumping onto the balcony railing as the guards thumped against the door. How were they finding him so fast? Did they have a thief-catcher with them? Was that what the woman in the floppy hat was?

The golden coin sat plump in his palm. The face smooth with the barest of etchings. An old thing. The years had worn away the original image. Was the coin working as a tracer? Grint cocked back his arm and got ready to throw it and then stopped. Convincing himself it was clean, he put it in his pocket and looked out at the alley across from the balcony. Three stories up was enough to make him dizzy, but not enough to dissuade him from doing something stupid.

As the door broke, the old man shouted in anger at the guards. Grint jumped into the alley. He'd hoped to grab onto a clothesline to break the fall, then drop to a lower line before the ground. It snapped under his weight and he fell, hitting the next line and the next. Then the ground. Clothes fluttered down as people yelled out their windows.

It was just mid-morning, and already he was ready for the day to be over with.

Grint limped away, hoping it would take the guards time to backtrack around to this alley. Between then and now, he needed to slip the tracking spell. What were they using? Grint hadn't bought or picked anything up beside the coin. *Not the coin*, he thought, cocking an arm back to throw it away.

No, not the coin, he convinced himself. *Has to be something else.*

On the next street, he mixed in with the crowd going about their day. He found a spot to rest beside a fountain of Ashgra. Cupping a handful of water, he splashed his face, wincing at the sting of chilly water against his scrapes and bruises. Then another, and this one he drank. Graht led to Felsin, and Felsin to The Heap. In the shanty town next to Harborside, he'd find someone or something to disrupt the tracker.

The guards, still tenacious in their duty, kept pace. Grint walked without running. He just had to stay ahead of them. Another block or two and he'd reach the stairs to Felsin. As he passed by a butcher shop with its no sun-facer banner, a hand reached out from the alley and pulled him in. Before he could shout, he felt her lips press against his.

"Nazarra," he said when the kiss ended, his eyes squinting in a shaft of sunlight. The youthful woman wore a purple dress and matching veil.

"Come on, you kry-damn fool," she laughed. "That's the saying, yes? Kry-damn?"

"Yeah," he answered, letting her lead him away. A pack of mungles watched them move through the alley, screeching at the intrusion. "You need to get out of here. The guards are looking for me."

"I know," she said, stopping them.

"How?"

"Later," she answered, running her fingers through his hair and then down his chest and into a pocket. Nazarra grinned like an addle-brained Taryn woman as she pulled out a cream-colored ribbon.

"What's that?" He looked at it, wondering where it came from. *Floppy Hat*, he thought.

"How they're tracking you," she said, then bent over and tied the ribbon on a moldy piece of discarded bread. Giving the knot a flourish, she threw the bread to the mungles. One caught and juggled it, then squawked and ran from the rest.

"That'll confuse them," Nazarra laughed. "Come on, or do you want to go to prison?"

Grint nodded, the gold coin still clutched tight in his hand. To think, he'd almost tossed it away. The thought made him shiver. As for Nazarra, he'd get answers out of her yet, though somehow, he thought that might be harder to do than stealing all that gold.

3

"You are hereby banished until such time as you atone your mistakes in the world of the dreego and foy. Begone now and let your exploits be worthy of our notice."

- The Tale of Teelo Tane, Parthian Barbarian;
p.Annum 9874

Fleck whinnied and shook his giant head as the noise of the dreego echoed through the city streets. Chell had never experienced such a thing, never traveled beyond the borders of Parthia. Even warnings of the cacophonous nature of the dreego did not prepare him. Salaz was the first of their cities he'd seen, and it left him to wonder if this was how they all lived, in small boxes on top of one another. Already he missed the deep jungles and tribal homes carved into baska trees. The symbiotic relationship between Parthian and baska provided harmony - the tree directing the Parthian where to make shelters and the baska feeding on the breath of the Parthian. *Perfection.* Nothing like the stone crypts these Salazians dwelt within.

Children ran alongside the horse, trailing colorful streamers at the end of sticks. The thin tissue flapped in time with their laughter. Older dreego gathered in windows or along the street, watching him pass with little expression or fanfare. What must they be thinking? How many others of his kind ventured this way on their road to atonement? Surely, one must have, but who and when? Would there be an opportunity to discover that?

No Chell, he told himself. *Contemplation led to my banishment. Inaction in the face of treachery.*

The warmth of the sun on his fur chased away unpleasant thoughts. With sweat bathing his skin, his musk would be strong. He should remain wary that it not addle the minds of the dreego women. Such temptations would not sidetrack Chell, but if the men of Salaz grew angered, he may have to slaughter some unnecessarily. Would that count towards atonement? No seer could answer that, atonement was personal and different for each Parthian. Returning before achieving it promised the endless death for banished warriors.

Fleck bucked his head as the noise grew. Chell reached forward to pet his flank, sharing the horse's fatigue. Their journey had been long, with many days on the move. It was time for respite and refreshment. Painted planks on either side of the street, covered in dreego scrawl, offered no help. Chell could speak their tongue, but not read it. He continued until he found one with a picture of a mug and dismounted. The gathered dreego scattered, giving him a wide berth as he tied the horse to a post beside the street. A weak thing, improperly anchored, Fleck could pull it out easily should he get the mind to.

"Be at ease," Chell said, brushing the horse's mane with the claws on his hand. Fleck turned his head just enough to glare, then shook with a laughing sound.

At seven feet tall, Chell was forced to duck beneath the top of the door. Mercifully, the inside was high enough for him to stand upright, but just barely. Deer antlers adorned the ceiling, nailed into the wood with the tips pointed down. Chell's head brushed the ends, an annoyance, but would he find better elsewhere in the city? The owner kept the room dark, lit by a faint handful of candles and the meager remnants of the previous evening's fire. Weathered planks of wood creaked under his weighty steps, and bits of mortar fell from the flagstone walls. For the hour of the morning, the dreego occupied only one table. Even their legendary laziness did not extend to drinking so early, it seemed. Chell sat on a wooden stool facing the bar and worried it might collapse under his weight and thanked The Builder it did not.

Builder, he thought. *Why did you forsake me?*

The Great Builder was not a deity to commune with. The Teachings were a way for the many generations to hand down his lessons. After a young life of tragedy, Chell dove into the Teachings and built himself a tribe of hungry warriors who consumed victories like drink. A mighty warlord, the vastness of what Chell conquered rivaled any Parthian since the time Zorn crossed the Gellanore.

His should have been a mighty name worthy of song. Not a lone barbarian on a forced quest of atonement.

"You speak common?" The dreego behind the bar asked as he wiped sweat from his face with the same rag used to clean the counter. "Common?" He asked again as he pulled a mug off the rack and set it before Chell.

"I do," Chell replied, his voice gruff from disuse and desperately in need of beverage.

"You're not here for me, are you?" The barman's hand lowered out of sight. Chell imagined a cudgel hidden there for dealing with unruly visitors. What the man thought he could do with it against a Parthian offered a moment of amusement.

"I am here to slake my thirst. Be quick about it," the Parthian said, pulling a silver piece from a pocket on his harness.

The barman took the mug to a cask set in the wall. "Only have ale this early," he said as he pulled on the tap. "The boys have not returned from the market and it's their job to bring the bottles up from below. They'll get a tanning if they dally much longer."

"And food?" Chell's stomach rumbled at the thought of something warm.

"No, my cook won't be in for a few hours. Just drink." The barman set the drink down, his hand trembling. Chell threw it back in one deep gulp and slid the mug back to the barman.

"Another. And find me bread and cheese. You don't need a cook for those."

"Ales are two plicks. Bread and cheese I can do for five. You able to pay?" The barman's voice cracked like a maturing cub, and he even backed away a step.

Chell smiled, dropping the silver on the counter, "Make your plicks from this, but do not treat me poorly. Or I will come for you."

The barman nodded as he picked up the silver, poured another drink, and scurried off to the kitchen. Chell sat in silence, watching bubbles float to the top of the tan liquid. His mind wandered to a place of happiness, but found only heartbreaking sorrow. *Marra. Sweet Marra. Why did you betray me? This long march will lead only to my death, I fear. Marra.* A memory of moonlight danced atop the ale. Marra beside the flowing waters of the Belgeist River, beckoning him. When had their love turned sour?

A plate of bread and cheese appeared in front of him. The barman lingered until Chell looked up, then dropped a stack of thin brown coins with the etched likeness of a long-necked woman. *Plicks*, Chell assumed. "I took what you owe already."

Chell availed himself of the bread, picking up the half loaf and tearing off a chunk. "It's cold," he said before shoving it in his mouth.

"I told you, the cook isn't here," the barman replied, using his all-purpose cloth to wipe out mugs.

Chell shoved a handful of cheese in after the bread and washed it down with ale, wondering how hard it was to heat a piece of bread over the hearth. He almost said as much until two dreego joined him, one on either side. They lounged with casual demeanor, but Chell could smell their tension. If they harbored a desire to cause trouble, they would wish very much they'd looked for their sport elsewhere. Both removed colorfully painted masks, setting them on the counter. Depictions of jungle birds graced each. Deep olive skin with dark pockets under their eyes marked them as locals of Salaz, unlike the barman, whose lighter complexion reminded Chell of the dreego living in Last Zorn. The two waited in silence while Chell ate his food. The watery ale washed down the dry bread, and against better judgment, he slid the mug so the barman would refill it.

"That one is on us, Merv," the dreego closest to Chell said, sliding a plick.

"It's two plicks," Chell laughed.

"Two for sun-facers. One for the good folk who fear Ashgra," the buyer remarked. "I am Prince Mikil of the Opposition party. My friend is Tobor."

"What about my face reminds you of the sun?" Chell asked before he shoved more cheese in his mouth.

"Reminds me? No, it is our masks and worship of Ashgra," the prince answered.

"I don't care," Chell leaned back on the stool, staring at the man. "Why is a prince buying me a drink?"

Merv returned with another ale in a much larger mug. The fresh batch didn't taste like dying bug larvae. Proving the Ashgra fearing dreego received better treatment. The friend called Tobor reached into his thin red jacket, but before he could pull anything out, Chell grabbed his arm. The quickness of the movement shocked both dreego, and the prince fell from his stool.

"Parchment," Tobor stammered. Chell relaxed his grip and let the dreego produce the paper. Gathering himself, the prince took it and unfolded it atop the bar. A strange thing filled with dreego scrawl.

"I don't read your writing," Chell said, sliding the parchment away.

"That's fine. It's a proclamation from the queen," Mikil said, running his finger across black ink letters.

"A nasty woman," Mikil continued as Tobor righted his stool, allowing him to sit down.

"Very nasty," Tobor remarked.

"And does this proclamation say anything about sun-faced Parthians drinking ale and minding their own business?" Chell gave them both a toothy smile. He downed the ale, slamming the mug on the bar. "I'll have another, Merv. My unknown friends will pay for it."

Merv looked at Tobor, who slid a plick across the bar.

"I'm happy to keep buying if you're happy to listen?" Prince Mikil smiled, blocking the mug as Chell reached for it.

"Until I tire of the drink, I will sit here and listen to the strange noises your mouth makes," Chell waited for him to move the hand before picking up the mug.

"Right," Mikil said with a hint of uncertainty. "The words on this parchment enact a law to close businesses like this one and harass the kind people of Salaz. For nothing more than supporting my Opposition. A group willed into existence by the first king and anointed by Ashgra herself."

The dreego continued his blathering, lamenting the loss of their livelihood as if Chell would care or offer his condolences. Additional ales appeared to replace the ones he finished. A pleasant warmth filled him. Much more and he would lose his clarity and require rest. Perhaps that would be for the best.

"Where can I find a room," Chell asked as he paused between drinks.

"I have rooms downstairs," the barman answered.

"Down?"

"The stone keeps the rooms cool," he answered. "Ten plicks."

Chell slid the pile toward the barman. "Keep the rest and have the cook send food whenever they arrive." He straightened the sword across his back as he stood.

"Except there is more to discuss," the prince said, putting his hand on Chell's shoulder. The Parthian looked at it sitting there, contemplating whether to tear the limb off. It looked like such a fragile thing.

"Never lay hands on a Parthian. Especially a drunk one," Chell grinned. Mikil pulled the hand away, color draining from his face. "I have heard nothing worth discussing in anything you've said."

"Atonement. That's why any Parthian leaves their jungles. Your jungles," Tobor said.

"What do you know of Parthian atonement?" Chell asked, feeling the heat of anger rising. A dreego speaking of the Great Builder's Teaching? An affront to all the spirits in the baska trees.

"We have a problem and you have a need," Mikil added. "I think it works for us all."

"I have yet to hear what you think I can do for you," Chell said. "Speak it plain or stop speaking altogether."

"I have said," Mikil answered. "Our queen is killing us. We need you to kill her."

"I am not an assassin," Chell slammed his fist into one of the support struts, shaking the entire tavern. "If you have a problem with your queen, deal with it. My atonement comes from loftier pursuits, not your pithy vendettas. Where do I find the way to the basement?"

The barman pointed at a door on the back wall. Chell shouldered past the dreego. Annoying as they were, gratuitous violence against them would make time in this city unpleasant. After a day of rest, he would continue on. Something about remaining in Salaz felt wrong. Lingering would make that feeling worse.

"Except that's not all," Mikil called out. "I have tried to do this the civil way."

"Carrig benthun, dreego." He said in native Parthian. Calling them animal fodder and dreego publicly meant his wits had taken leave.

"I am afraid you've left us no other option but to compel you to do as we've asked." The smiling demeanor dropped from Prince Mikil's face, replaced by a weak attempt to be menacing. Chell almost laughed as Mikil placed a small blade on the bar.

"And that tiny thing does so?" To emphasize his amusement, Chell drew the two-handed broadsword.

"Not the blade," Mikil answered, less sure of himself. The other dreego backed away from Chell, equally shaken and afraid. "But the poison in the ale you drank will."

"The what?"

"Poison in your ale," Tobor repeated.

Chell did not attack the two, instead brandishing his sword at the barman, who shrieked and grabbed his hidden cudgel. Filled with rage, the bar would not deter him from striking out. A mighty swing of the sword cracked the thick, oiled wood. His rage unquenched, Chell struck a table, cutting it in half. Mikil grabbed the knife, holding it in front of him. But even he must have realized how pitiful the decision was. To believe such a small weapon offered any protection. If the Parthian turned the sword on them, they'd all die bloody.

"Give me the antidote," Chell commanded.

"When you've completed the job," Prince Mikil said with an audible swallow.

"Now," he screamed.

"No," Mikil found some backbone as he spoke. "Kill the queen and you get the cure."

"You do not understand what you are asking. Give me the cure now or I will slaughter you." Holding the blade in one hand, he slapped the dagger away from Mikil. *The fool weighs less than a cub*, Chell mused as he grabbed the prince around the throat, lifting him off the floor.

"Then you will die," Mikil choked. "Only I know where the cure is."

The low growl the Parthian uttered went on as the man turned blue, then purple. Giving in, he tossed him to the side. Mikil fell onto the smashed table and yelped as a broken splinter skewered his arm. Uncaring of the pain he'd inflicted, Chell rested the sword on the bar, turning the tip toward the barman.

"My silver and plicks, give them back to me," he said, holding out a hand. "Now."

"All of them?" Merv stammered.

"Do it," Mikil coughed and rubbed his throat, shoving Tobor away as he tended to the splinter in his arm.

"You will also pay me," Chell said to the Salazians.

"Your payment is your life," Tobor spat. "And the generosity of food and lodging."

"You will also pay me," Chell repeated as he leaned across the bar. Several nondescript jugs hung on the wall. Chell never believed the barman had only ale to drink. Only poisoned ale. Shaking a jug, he heard the contents swishing around, and he pulled the cork loose with his teeth, spitting it onto the floor. A glorious scent of aged rum greeted him. Merv watched as he returned with the silver finger. The barman smelled displeased, but remained silent. Chell took a drink, letting the spices tickle his throat.

"We will also pay you," Mikil relented. "In gold. An associate keen on seeing me take the throne will provide it."

Chell smiled. When he finished the liquor, he tossed the jug against a wall. The way it made the dreego jump as it shattered pleased him all the more. "How long do I have?"

"Five days," Mikil said.

"I need rest. Remember to send food when the cook arrives." With that, Chell excused himself. The mad dreego of Salaz would be the death of him.

4

"Their piety toward Ashgra is a well-perfected ruse. A Salazian wears many masks. Who they are is never who you think."

– Admiral Ta'rak Odeshah, Orrish Fleet,
Annum 1367

Duty, Nazarra thought, sitting in front of her vanity, brushing her long black hair. Duty strangled like a set of black chains wrapped around her neck. Drowned her in the ocean as they weighed heavily upon her shoulders. Never had she reason to question or resent her duty. From a young age, they had trained her to accept it as a part of herself, an inherent need. A suit of armor protecting her and her family. Why then imagine it as chains after all this time?

Nazarra's eyes slid across a variety of powders arranged neatly on a shelf, each categorized by the season of their effectiveness. And again, by the time of day. For the late spring month of Renduan, when humidity gripped tight, she used a moderate powder to dry the glossy sheen on her dark skin. More make-up sat below the mirror, but the lip balms and shadows for her hazel eyes were there for show. Her real stash waited in a secret compartment under the vanity's surface. Along with an extensive selection of knives, poisons, swords, and a crossbow.

With the hidden items, she could change her appearance when a mask or veil wouldn't do. A prosthetic nose and cheekbone shaded just right would fool the casual observer. All very helpful for someone in her line of work. Years of methodical training and experience elevated her to a Master of the Disguise Arts. She'd even fooled her own sister on a handful of occasions. Glancing at her red-haired thief in the mirror, she wondered if she might fool him as easily. So far, she had, or so she believed, but he kept thoughts to himself like a seasoned gambler at the Cheat Me table.

My thief. As if I own him. If she believed the palace seer, even the God of Thieves struggled to corral Grint. From the first moment she caught sight of him riding into Salaz atop a mummer's cart, he'd intrigued her. Such a casual man, laying back, letting the sun kiss his face with reckless abandon while the mummer yelled at him to get off. It seemed for sure the Opposition would ensnare him in their web. A common trick they used on newcomers was dosing their drink, forcing them to do their bidding, but Grint didn't stop at a tavern, disappearing instead into the Meskal. Accomplishing that feat deserved merit. Few wiggled out of her grasp.

For two days she searched, finding him again outside a pawnbroker's shop in Wensley. A known fence of stolen goods, who when pressed, told her what she wanted to know. A thief from the far north, Grint, came to Salaz under the contract of a lord. The broker didn't know who it was, but the items the thief sold were minor things, baubles. Bracelets and goblets, nothing too extravagant, and nothing that suggested the Opposition's involvement.

Making contact was easy enough. An evening brush, letting him feel the soft curves of her body against his. She breathed in the cool, winter scent of his northern roots, and then vanished. The next day she returned, expecting to leash him like a puppy, but he never showed. Nor did he return the next night. Nazarra prepared herself to move on when he turned the tables.

Sitting atop a barrel, popping grapes into his mouth, he smiled at her. "I don't like when people follow me," he said. The affable demeanor could be mistaken as laziness, but she recognized a coiled viper waiting to strike. How quick could he produce a weapon? Faster than her? Nazarra almost wanted to discover.

"I haven't seen one like you in many years," she smiled. "I only wished to entice you with an invitation."

"No thanks," he said, hopping off the barrel.

Nazarra reached out, grabbing his arm. The tension in his muscles multiplied and she let go. "Then a drink? I've never been outside the city and love the stories. Please?"

"A drink?" She watched as he weighed it out. "Yeah, we can have a drink, but I'm not a bard. Can't promise any magnificent stories set to song."

The emotional entanglement they developed was far less convenient for them both. Well, inconvenient for her. She could not speak to how it affected him.

Bringing him to the safe-house burned it if things turned out badly between them, but she had a handful more like it throughout Salaz. Small, one-room flats full of costumes, weapons, and money, though this one held a special place in her heart. Occupying the top floor in a three story, chestnut brown storefront along the lower arm of the Chantil, it provided her with much-needed solitude. A tough thing to come by in most places. The floor beneath sat empty. A place the baker, occupying the first floor, used as storage. On certain mornings, she would wake up to fresh-baked goods, scents of cinnamon and lavender, or melting chocolate. Her favorite times were when the wild blackberries came in from Ogriliah. The smell from that lingered for days, reminding her of a simpler time.

Was there ever a simple time growing up? Nazarra's youth was nothing more than a series of lessons. Spy-craft, diplomacy, decorum. So many more, each day of each month. Her sister had different lessons, being the older of the two, but Nazarra didn't mind. At night, Akkie laid beside her as the moons lit their bedroom in shades of blue and red. And her sister would share what she learned, acting out the part of both teacher and student. It was hard to reconcile that girl with her sister, a hard, angry woman who wore sullenness like a badge.

All those lessons and every one after slipped away when she got within ten feet of Grint. He'd beguiled her like a siren eel and not the other way around, a fact that both infuriated and impressed. She knew so little about his purpose in Salaz. Who was he working with? Grint wasn't with the Opposition, that much she gathered, but his incursion into Borismere's manor bothered her. What was he after in there? For whom? Had Prince Mikil gotten to him after all? No, she thought. *The man is too proud and independent to join someone else's war.* And the realization splashed icy water on her face, waking her from the trance he'd put her under. Grint was the stray dog you fell in love with, but shouldn't keep. Eventually, he'd bite her, because that's what the stray knows. She'd have to let him go, but didn't know if she could.

Grint hissed as he pressed a wet cloth against the scrape over his eye. Sitting shirtless in the bay window of her tiny apartment, the sun reflected off his pale skin. A map of scars covered his arms, back, and chest, with fresh bruises appearing daily. As adept a thief as he might be, he was also a magnet for trouble. The escapade of today's flight was evidential proof of that.

"I've never seen such a display," Nazarra said, rolling her eyes. Tilting his head back, she took the cloth and cleaned the cuts.

"You could be gentler," he said, squirming.

"And you shouldn't tempt Ashgra so," she replied, running the back of her hand across his cheek.

"Nonsense."

"Yes, I know," she said, dabbing the bruise on his chin harder than necessary. "Ashgra is fake and Krypholos is a drunk monk."

Grint snatched the cloth away with a grimace. "I'd rather have a salt witch tending my wounds. And Krypsie isn't a monk. He just lives with them."

"But the drunkard part is right?" She asked, smiling at the absurdity of a god neglecting their duties to consume alcohol.

"How did you find me?" The question was one she'd deflected three times since pulling him out of the guard's snare. Doing so again would raise suspicions. *How* was a simple enough question to answer, but it would lead to why, and why was the one that kept her mind racing.

"It's not a mystery," she shrugged, sitting on the edge of the bed. She wore a simple black robe of fine silk with lace slippers and bracelets. Enough to drive most men crazy. Grint glanced at her, but kept his focus outside the window. "Talk of a Parthian spread quick. I wanted to see. When the alarm bells started, I thought it was the barbarian rampaging. Turned out the guards were after a sun-facer with a head full of fire. I don't know too many of those in Salaz, do you?"

Grint shrugged his response, pressing his forehead to the window. "Can I use the Parthian as a distraction?" He whispered. A faint sound few others would have heard, but Ashgra had blessed her with keen ears. A gift maybe, but it was also a curse.

"Did you see it? The Parthian?"

"Yeah," Grint said. "Big lunker too."

"Never seen one," she lied. "How big were his muscles?"

"Hard to tell under all that hair," he laughed, stretching his shoulders and pressing a finger into bruises just starting to purple.

"Why were they after you?" She asked, wondering if he would continue his own deflections.

"I don't know," he lied. "A crazy merchant tried to sell me a leather bracelet, and when I told him no, he accused me of theft."

"Buying me a sweet gift?" She batted her eyes, for all the good it did. Grint chuckled, but kept looking out the window. What did he find so interesting?

"Who handles contracts?" He asked, sipping the same cup of wine he'd nursed the last hour. "For moving things, I mean."

"Legitimate or not?" Nazarra picked up the decanter of wine and brought it over to give him a refill, but he waved her away. Over the last couple of weeks, she'd found there wasn't a drink the thief couldn't consume in a matter of minutes. This change in behavior further puzzled her. Did the questions arise from breaking into Borismere's manor? What did he find in there?

"Or construction?" He asked. "I haven't heard of a building guild."

"Construction runs through the Palace," she answered. "They use prisoners from Allast. As for moving things, best to ask at the docks. The Harbormaster and his Fish Mongers. Why?"

"Occupational curiosity," he said, stepping away from the window for the first time in hours.

"And what occupation is that? You've never said," Nazarra sat back at the vanity, miming the act of applying make-up.

"Import-export," Grint answered, standing behind her chair. His hands, rough and strong, kneading the flesh of her shoulders. Nazarra knew it was another lie, but didn't pull the string. When she brought the wine, she saw what he'd been looking at. Two guards roughing up a merchant. The new edict from the Palace about foot traffic taxes wasn't sitting well with the marketers, and some were refusing to pay. Not that such politics entered Grint's mind. He wanted to watch the guards outside. Put his mind at ease that they weren't following him.

"I'm afraid you can't stay tonight," she said, spritzing perfume from the Sandy Kingdoms. A pleasant aroma of coconuts and scorching sand that made her wish for a trip on the sea. Other duties needed performed.

"Clients?" And the way he asked cast doubts that he still believed her job was a courtesan. Why would he? She'd never given him reason to question it. And to his credit, he never treated her any differently than he would a lady of the court. "For someone who entertains, no one ever comes or goes."

"I have the privilege of seeing who I want when I choose," she smiled. Was he watching her when they were apart? The idea never occurred to her before now. A sloppy mistake, if so. One of many she'd made today.

"Will it be safe?" He asked, walking back to the window. Nazarra breathed a sigh of relief, afraid that he would keep at the question of her job. His mind had gone back to the world outside and for whatever he needed transportation. Someone to smuggle him out if things got bad enough?

"It's dark. You can slip out and skulk back to where ever it is you go," she said, wishing she'd left the ribbon in his pocket. Maybe then the question of who in the Meskal hired him could find an answer.

"I never skulk," He laughed. "But I am a mess. Can I borrow something from you? I ruined my shirt." Grint walked over to the wardrobe, intending to open the double doors.

"Stop," she blurted out, the tone too harsh. A look of perplexed curiosity crossed his eyes in the way new ideas formed. "That's my personal attire, meant for me. I have some things in a chest by the door." Pointing him toward it with her hairbrush.

What would it have cost her to let him look inside? A dozen costumes she could pass off as outfits for her clientele. The burgundy robe and over-sized hat with the brim hanging low enough to cover her face were both tucked away beside the bathtub. When they returned this morning, she'd stepped behind the screen to change, using the moment to stash her gear.

"You get a lot of pirates?" Grint waved a brown leather tricorn hat he found within the clutter. Nazarra didn't have an inkling of what clothing was in the chest. It was a prop set by Palace security officers meant to make the apartment appear lived in.

"This is Salaz," she replied.

"What about eye-patches? Where are those?" He said, digging through the chest, spilling the across the floor.

"Just what's in there," she said.

"You've got everything from wizard robes to silken waistcoats, but no eye-patches," he said as he shoved things back in.

"Not all pirates wear them. I'm sure with the hat and a rugged cloak you could board a ship without question," Nazarra rolled her eyes, wanting to laugh.

"But more pirates wear them than people on land," he gave her a smile as he plunked the hat on his head and spun a cloak round, swishing the fabric until it fell to rest across his shoulders. Clasping it tight with the loop and bone white toggle.

"I'm not sure that's true."

"How do I look?" Grint asked, posing with fists on his hips.

"Like someone who forgot to put something on under their cloak." Nazarra grabbed a cotton shirt and threw it to him.

Grint looped his bag across his shoulders with a wry smile. "I like to breathe a bit at night." Then grabbed her in a kiss. When he finished, he darted to the window with a flourish of the cloak and stopped.

"What?"

"I always forget this is the third floor," he said, stepping away from the window and bowing his way out the door instead.

Nazarra waited until his footsteps faded to throw the powder brush at the mirror. It bounced, clanking off a glass jar before rolling onto the floor. Clenching her jaw, she swept the jars off the desk in one motion. Each shattered, the contents puffing up in swirling clouds throughout the room. All the preparations she'd made for tracking him. Every string she'd pulled and none of it amounted to a single thing. Nazarra knew nothing more than she had yesterday.

The Court would ask questions in whispered voices. In the back rooms and quiet corners where she wouldn't hear. A summons to Military Command would follow. And what would she say when two hundred sets of eyes burned into her from the Inquisition floor? Why had she called off the manhunt? Why destroy the ribbon and take the thief to safety? How long before someone asked if she'd become besotted with the mark?

"No," she said, stepping around the broken glass to look at herself in the full-length mirror by the tub. Streaks of powder formed colored patterns across her face. "I didn't let him go because of love."

I wanted to build trust... To save him so he would... What? Gush out every secret he's ever kept? She wiped away the powder with a damp cloth, knowing everything she told herself was a lie. Evidence contradicted her statements and Nazarra knew it. She would need to remedy these mistakes before it came to inquisition.

Donning the burgundy coat and floppy hat, she lifted the desktop, retrieving two daggers and a rapier. Buckling the sword belt and cinching it tight, she put the last touches on her outfit. The white mask and red armband with her sister's insignia; A wreathed shield with two alligators. Tonight, she would find where in the Meskal the thief went to roost, even if she had to kick in every door in the district.

"Or just ask Racko," she said, halfway down the stairs. The option hadn't occurred before now. The master of the thieves' guild would have an idea. Thieves from outside the city weren't forbidden, but expected to pay a fee of whatever they stole. Grint's mysterious benefactor would know that too and make the arrangements, or suffer the ire of the Blue Hands.

Breathing a sigh of relief, she reached the street. Nazarra felt like herself for the first time in weeks. Grint could hold on to his anonymity for another day. Leaving her free to investigate the more pressing problem on her plate. The barbarian. After that surprise, she sent an operative to tail the Parthian. Now was the time to reconnect and find where he landed.

People kept their faces down, giving her a wide berth. Masks came off when the sun went down, so she saw the fear in their eyes as they looked away. A fear that grew over the past months, coinciding with daily edicts from the queen. And what did any of it accomplish? It bolstered the Opposition and Prince Mikil's standing.

Nazarra struggled to understand why. The edicts began after the queen started up with Lord Borismere. Grint broke into the Lord's manor. Was it connection or coincidence?

It didn't take long to find where the Parthian had gone. Traveling into the Bushan district, she spotted the massive horse tied outside a tavern. Her operative signaled from a rooftop across the road. Nazarra cut through an alley and climbed a wall thick with vines to meet him on the roof.

"Is he in there?" She asked.

"Yes, Spymaster General," he answered. "Stopped here after we parted. I went in before sunset. The Parthian cracked a table in half while drunk and is sleeping it off in a room."

"Did they recruit him?" She watched the door, weighing out the cost of charging in. She should never have let the Parthian out of her sight. Following him was of greater consequence than Grint and his escapades in the Upper Crust. If the Opposition dosed the Parthian...

"I believe they may have. Prince Mikil and his guardian were here earlier," the operative said. "They left before I entered."

Nazarra wanted to scream. "Go," she ordered. "I'll handle it from here."

"Should we not rally the guard?"

"That would be a bloodbath," she answered, imagining a hundred soldiers torn apart by the beast. Nazarra had never seen a Parthian fight, but her father's top advisor told her stories. Dark, bloody tales that left her with nightmares. "I have ways to bring him down without risking our men."

"As you wish, Spymaster General," he said with a deep bow.

A warm breeze blew in from the harbor. It would be a pleasant night. She imagined sitting on a beach, Grint's arms wrapped around her waist...

Duty, she thought, chasing away the thief's image. The weight of the chains grew with each new link she forged.

5

"A superstitious man thinks, never roll a twenty four. I think, just keep a couple of twelves up your sleeve."

– Grint

Do you trust who she is? Hobbe asked. A question Grint had no answer for.

Standing beside the window in a small curio shop, he watched a troop of four armored guards walk up the street. Their presence in the Meskal tripled from any other day. Were they still looking for him? The stink of bassal overpowered the eviscerated gull guts and thick clouds of incense in the room. Grint crinkled his nose as he turned away from the window. The shop and its proprietor were a means to an end. Nazarra meant something more.

He'd always known she had her own agenda. Played her own game. Until this morning he thought she was running a Hasker Judy, grifting visitors as they passed through. Nothing wrong with that, as long as she knew not to pull it on him. They were kindred spirits, developing a mutual understanding that the other was off limits. So then - what was she doing in the Graht? The Parthian excuse held water, but Grint felt the frayed edges across the tapestry of her rehearsed tale.

It took her two breaths to find that ribbon in your pocket, Hobbe warned.

That didn't mean she'd been a part of it. Floppy Hat planted the ribbon as the Parthian rode in. Nazarra recognized what was happening and took it out - simple as that. What motivation did she have to betray him? Money? Did the guards have something on her? Grint spent most of his time looking out her window, waiting for footsteps on the stairs. Why hide him if she'd been in on it? The entire thing gave him a headache.

"Why did Floppy Hat plant the ribbon in the first place?" None of the targets he hit leading up to Borismere had any connection to the lord. Nor were they large enough to garner proper attention. Someone could have followed him. Grint wasn't infallible, but even an experienced tracker would have tripped one of his wards over the past week. That's what he told himself. Whatever the reason, they showed up looking to grab him today.

"Do you talk to your god?" The exotic woman in multi-colored silks said, looking up from the gold coin on her table.

"I talk to myself," Grint answered, turning a chair around to sit on it backwards. "My god doesn't care to listen."

"It might surprise you," Marielle answered, re-focusing her eyeglass on the coin. "What Hobbe hears."

The slender woman with olive skin and thinning hair wasn't a salt witch or necromancer. Just a simple spirit-monger selling antiquities and trading in minor magical artifacts. Grint found her shop useful. It was here he'd purchased the mimicrum and glow orb.

"The coin," he said, drumming his fingers on a worn tablecloth of blue and gold stars.

"There are no curses or magic on it, I can see," she said, sliding it back to him with great reluctance. "If you wish to spend it in my shop, I have many exotic items worth your interest."

"Go on," Grint smiled, making the coin disappear into a pocket.

"Firejacks encased in Calamat silver. Exquisite in both construction and destruction," Marielle said, flashing a smile full of bronze teeth.

"That's a lethal bit of demomancy," Grint said, standing. "Where did you come by it?"

"A pair of goblins passing through," she replied. "They made a nuisance of themselves and landed on Allast Island as I've heard."

"I'll let you know about the firejacks," Grint replied. Carrying live demomancy in his bag was a tricky proposition, but it never hurt to have something with punch to get out of tricksome situations.

The sky was a tapestry of reds by the time Grint left the shop. Stone dust crunched under his feet as the hard soles of his boots crushed loose paving. There was no sign of moisture from the afternoon storm, just the trickle of water from one drain to another. Heat and sunlight evaporated the rest. Salaz at night turned into an unfamiliar world, still and silent under the queen's curfews.

A block away from the curio shop, Grint faded into the shadows beside a cobbler's stand. Eight guards walked in two-by-two formations. Stepping deeper into the alley, he crushed a rotten crate underfoot, setting a swarm of foy flies loose. The racket he made incited a stray dog to bark. Three mungles hopped into the alley, their useless, leathery wings flapping. Each picked up pieces of the moldy wood, sniffing and tasting, then fighting over the rest. Grint held his breath as the guards passed by, then crossed the street, mumbling to himself about all the foy while swatting the flies away.

"You make too much noise," an old woman shouted from her fourth-story window, white hair blowing in a breeze that wouldn't reach the street. "I call the guards."

"It's okay," Grint said, tipping his tricorn cap. "I'm leaving."

Today should have been a joyous day. Grint wanted to dance through the streets, clicking his heels. He wanted to grab strangers and plant wet kisses on their face. Buy a round for every two-coin thief and criminal from here to Rhysin. Wake up in a strange gutter with no memory of how he got there. Instead, he'd gotten chased, beat up, and left to question one of the few people he liked in Salaz.

Both of them, Hobbe said.

Both, he repeated in his head. If Nazarra wasn't responsible for the guards and there wasn't a curse on the coin - that left Orsava. The only other person who knew where Grint would be and what he'd been up to. But that scenario made even less sense.

Pausing at a knee-high stone wall, Grint sheltered himself beneath a tree, watching people rush home with their carts and goods. Horses voiced their objections to the pace, preferring to take their time rolling along the uneven street. Merchants looked out shop doors before closing shutters and locking up. Four-man guard patrols stopped anyone within reach, checking their wares and collecting tolls. Throwing those who didn't pay to the ground. Grint remained still under the hanging branches of the tamarind tree, letting the guards pass without a second look. He exhaled a nervous breath. Their focus may have been on spot-checking merchants and fattening their own pockets, but it didn't matter to them who they shook down. Outsider or official guild merchants were all fair game.

The armbands worn were as varied in color as the robes. Shades of blue, yellow, gold, red, and a hundred more variations. With all the guilds, factions, and nobility in the city, Grint bet someone had to handle transportation. Whoever that was, he'd also need to keep them from nosing in on Borismere's fortune. Thinking of the gold, he slipped a hand in his pocket. The smooth surface of the coin against his thumb calmed him. A hundred fancies slipped over the surface of his mind. A coin for every fantasy he'd ever had, and a lifetime more after.

The sun became a recent memory by the time he strolled up the back streets of the Meskal. Multi-story, block style manors and elegant apartment clusters rose above alabaster walls. Gas lamps created flowing shadows as city torch-bearers made their way around, lighting them. Lord Sem Orsava, the great benefactor, lived in a three-story manor of white stone along the curved arm of the Meskal's back end. At the top were open air gardens the lord rarely perused. Orsava was a strange man, happy to admire his wealth but with little need to indulge in it. Grint asked him what the point of the money was if he didn't spend it. Orsava gave it a long thought.

"My money buys me time," he said. "Time to read and drink my wine."

"Too each their own," Grint laughed, then and now. Standing in the light of a gas lamp, he watched Orsava's white manor. Not for guards or floppy-hatted women, but Grint hadn't decided what to tell Orsava yet. He could easily deliver an excuse about how the painting was a fake, collect his dog, Newman, and leave. Or lay all the cards out, filling Sem in on all that happened. Both options had their benefits and drawbacks. *Sharing the gold with anyone is a drawback,* Grint told himself.

Be smart for once, Hobbe answered.

I'm trying, Grint thought. The smart choice was bringing Orsava in. Doing this alone would be nigh impossible. Grint didn't know enough about the city or how to maneuver its pitfalls to get a fraction of the wealth out. *If I wanted the gold for myself, I should have taken a bag's worth and run with it.* Even a sack's worth would have kept him going for a year or two.

A woman screamed back the way he'd come. Grint stepped around the gas lamp, watching the guards drag a family from their home. A red cloaked inquisitor oversaw the operation from the seat of a prison cart. The mother wept as they took away her two young children, slinging their tiny bodies over armored shoulders like sacks of flour. The father took umbrage with the treatment and tried to fight back. *Fool,* Grint thought as the guards beat him down. Blood dripped from his chin as his left eye swelled. A deep purple bruise shining in the scant light. The family's light olive skin, enriched with the warm undertone of sunset, hinted at an origin outside Salaz. *Golganna maybe? Or Bhanyu? Sun-facers, for sure.*

Was that their crime? Or was this the city graft? Grint couldn't be sure. No one could from day to day. Just two days past, Orsava shook his head sadly at news of a renowned lord hauled away by inquisitors. A devout Salazian who always supported the queen, especially in the conflict against her cousin. Orsava offered no further explanation, but Grint felt the fear radiating off him. And the unasked question, when would it be his turn?

The inquisitor looked toward Grint, freezing the beat of his heart. They wouldn't need an excuse to throw Grint in jail. Just snap him up and drop him in the deepest cell they had. He'd get out. Always did. Nobody built a prison that could hold him, but it would be a kry-damn inconvenience.

The father screamed, telling his wife to run as he swung at the guards. The inquisitor stopped looking, laughing now as the guards beat the man unconscious. Nothing Grint could do about it. He tried being a hero once and it charffing well killed him. Wll, nearly killed – not truly dead and gone, but stuck in a limbo realm. Thank Lorelai's Luck; Hobbe had a trick up his sleeve and brought him back. Hard to stay mad at a guy when he's saved your life a dozen times over.

The prison cart rolled away, taking with it Grint's indecision. Orsava's friendship exceeded being a simple broker. If he could help the lord get out of this bloody city and start a life somewhere quiet - it was the least he could do. *Half of an uncountable fortune is still uncountable.*

The way you count, it is, Hobbe laughed.

Grint slipped into the stone garden beside the manor, moments before the slow trot of a torch-bearer reached the corner. As much as he wanted to trust Orsava, a small voice, more annoying than Hobbe's, cried out for him to run. There wasn't any way in all the Hells of Astapoor he was leaving without his dog. Newman was inside, under the care of Orsava while Grint worked. If things turned sideways, he'd grab Newman and run.

"Maybe I should have picked up a firejack," Grint said as he flipped the gold coin, hoping that chance would decide how to proceed. Front door or roof. The answer made him grimace. A cruel joke from Lady Lorelai. *My fault for giving her the choice.*

Grint cracked his knuckles before finding handholds in the uneven plaster. Puling himself up the wall, he peeked in a first story window. The dining room was still and empty, shrouded in the darkness of night. Beyond, a slim arm of light ran across the carpet, courtesy of burning candles in the hall. Orsava rarely used the room, preferring to take meals in his study, but it would make a delicious spot for an ambush if one waited for him. An unwitting thief, returning from a night of larceny, wouldn't think twice about checking dark rooms.

That's why unwitting thieves die young, Hobbe laughed.

The footholds above the dining window were plentiful, letting Grint ascend quickly, telling himself over and over not to look down. By the time he reached the upper window, sweat drenched his body, something he attributed to the heat rather than nervousness. Listening at the pane of glass, the only sounds within were the soft scratch of a quill on parchment. The clink of a cup against wood as the resident lord sipped his wine, and the snore of a bulldog.

Grint used his dagger to slip the lock and open the window. Swinging his legs through, he hugged the side of the sill and looked down. "It's only two stories, you kry-damn coward," he chastised himself.

"I have a door," Orsava remarked, looking up from his work. The lord worked on penning notes, with plans to write a book one day. His faithful goblet of wine and pitcher close at hand. A small bell appeared from under the desk and when he rang it, Angis appeared with a second goblet. How the butler always knew what Orsava needed from the sound of that bell remained a grand mystery.

"I wasn't entirely sure about the reception I'd receive." Grint looked around as he stepped into the room. The dog snorted as he woke, groaning with a big stretch. Newman lumbered to his feet and wiggling his backside, approached. Grint sat cross-legged on the wine-colored carpet, letting the dog climb into his lap where they showered each other in kisses.

"Did I give you an ill impression?" Orsava stopped pouring the wine, a hint of disappointment clear in the sour tone his words imparted.

"The woman tailing me after the job gave me several impressions," the thief said as he scratched his dog.

"Woman? Who?" Orsava finished pouring and brought the goblet over, but seeing how excited the dog was, chose instead to place it on the table beside the reading chair. The carpet was another family heirloom, and Angis was fastidious in its care.

"We didn't introduce ourselves," Grint said, climbing into the chair as Newman laid back down. "Big, floppy hat. A coat to match your carpet. Commanded soldiers. Any ideas?"

"No," Orsava sighed. "I am afraid I am not versed on the inner workings of the queen's soldiery. I take it that being followed meant you were unsuccessful in last night's foray?" More disappointment, not just in voice, but in physicality. Orsava's shoulder sagged as he looked upon the empty frame meant to display the stolen painting.

Grint could still change his mind. "Yes, and no," he said, silencing the last voice of doubt. "I found the painting, but also this." And he tossed the golden coin to Orsava.

The lord caught the piece in the air, bringing it down for study. He took his time, mumbling and clucking. The bell rang and Angis appeared with a monocle. Orsava took more time to study the coin, turning it over in his hand, feeling its weight and density. "This is nice, but not at all what I am paying you for. Did you get the painting?" Orsava glanced up as he set the coin down. "Please tell me you don't have it folded up in that crazy bag of yours."

"No, I left the painting where I found it."

"Why in Terragard would you do that?" Orsava asked, his face reddening. For the first time since meeting him, the man was losing the eternal cool he displayed. "Did I hire the wrong thief? The directions seemed simple enough."

"Simple if you wanted me to steal a poor forgery of your painting. The one in Borismere's study is a fake." Grint stood, disturbing Newman's slumber. The dog gave him an irritated look and laid back down.

"How did you discern that," Orsava looked intrigued, sitting back in his chair. The anger dissipated as he scratched his chin in thought.

"The mimicrum," Grint replied, unfolding the sheet stashed in his bag. Curiosity cut through the man's stately demeanor, and he beamed while making room on the desk. Angis lurked in the doorway, displeasure alive in the crinkled recesses of his brow for not being asked to clean the desk himself. Orsava paid the needs of the manservant little mind as Grint laid the map out, and placed the monocle to his eye once more, studying the map, tracing each intricate scrawl. The notes were of particular interest, earning more than a few grunts and studious noises on the side. Reaching a passage along the left edge, Orsava picked up the bell. Delighted at being summoned, Angis strode in the room, picking a book from the shelf, leafing through the pages and setting it down before his master.

"If I ring the bell," Grint said looking up, "would you bring me one of those roast beef sandwiches with the crispy bread and cheese sauce?" Angis sniffed, straight-backed and insulted, but when Orsava cleared his throat and nodded, the manservant bowed.

"That sounded delicious," Sem said. "He'll bring two."

"Some day you must tell me how you communicate with bells and grunts," Grint laughed. "Could be useful in a heist."

"There is no trick to it," Orsava answered. "Angis and I have been together since childhood. It is just the experience of long years."

The explanation wasn't as fun as what Grint hoped. Maybe one day, when he sat at the Cheat Me tables in some distant kingdom gambling away pieces of gold like copper, he'd embellish the tale. Make their connection a thing of magic.

"This part of the structure is reminiscent of early Salaz," Orsava ran his finger over curved lines on the upper portion. "And the Upper Crust. But here, the lines of the building intersect too often. Were there multiple layers?"

"Just the one," Grint said, his attention pulled from the map to the massive sandwich Angis brought. Setting the first by his master, he gave Grint his with the barest of nodding bows, the most the manservant had done to acknowledge him since his arrival. *Maybe he's warming up to me?*

"You didn't investigate further?"

"I was in a rush," Grint said through a mouthful of food. Newman woke at the smell and waddled over, sitting down with his chin resting on Grint's knee.

"Walk me through this," Orsava said. "How did you discover the map?"

Grint washed the bite down with a cold ale before speaking. "That's not really the important part, Grint said, dropping a bit of meat for Newman.

"I beg to differ. If we want to decipher this and find the location, I need to understand it more." Orsava took a large bite, lifting his eyebrows in appreciation.

"Find the location?" Grint stopped. "Sem, I already found it. I followed the map underground. Vanquished the ancient traps and entered the vault."

"You've already been there?" Orsava's awe towards the thief returned in the form of a gleeful smile. As he picked the coin up, he held it between two fingers, seeing something in it he had not before. "How many of these does Borismere have?"

"So much more," Grint stood, his giddy excitement too great to contain. "Mountains of gold and jewels. Dozens of paintings, the moving boat among them. The genuine one. Crowns and weapons. A dozen dragon's hoards all in one beautiful chamber."

"Dozens?" Orsava asked, his disbelief growing at the sheer size Grint described. "Is that thief-speak for a chest or two?"

"No. Mountains, Sem. Literal mountains," Grint opened his arms, feeling all the gold he'd rolled around in as if he was still in the vault.

"Ashgra's fortune," Orsava exclaimed, slapping a fist into his palm.

"Is that an expression or a thing?" Grint asked.

"Well, it's both," Orsava said. "Here, I am speaking of the thing."

Before he could pick up the bell, Angis appeared, pulling down a bound book of aged blue leather. The tome creaked as Orsava opened it, and the thick parchment pages groaned with displeasure at the disturbance. "Yes, Ashgra's fortune. This is one of the few books remaining on the subject the High Priests haven't burned."

Orsava found the page and turned the book toward Grint, showing a hand-painted picture of Ashgra with her hand buried in the sun above. A shower of golden coins fell upon dancing people in veils. "In the ancestral histories, it is said, Ashgra reached into the sun, pulling out a handful of molten gold and forming it into wealth for the people of Salaz. She rewarded those who followed her, but soon they wanted more, turning on the god when she would not give it. Ashgra hid the fortune to spite the people and cursed those who looked to the sun for what they'd lost."

"Sounds about right for gods and their tempers," Grint laughed, feeling nice and warm from the ale.

"Indeed. Now, when Zorn conquered Salaz, the tale of the gold spread through his ranks. Hundreds tore the city apart looking for the wealth until Zorn himself began hanging them for treason."

Grint heard many stories of Zorn. Some painted him as a merciful uniter of the lands, seeking to learn. Others, a wrathful tyrant wanting to control the world beneath an iron boot. Hobbe never spoke of the dennel Emperor, but every story named him the child of Myrilee, Goddess of Hope. Given that, he leaned towards believing the kinder tales.

"Was this the last place he conquered before Parthia?"

"Yes," Orsava nodded. "Zorn died a year after leaving, and the High Priests used the vacuum of power to rebuild the faith of Ashgra. They re-wrote the stories, not wanting to depict Ashgra as one who needed to bribe her followers."

"No one ever found the gold," Grint said.

"Until now," Orsava laughed. "Ashgra's fortune is an expression, as you asked earlier. People use it when something lucky befalls them, but nobody says it thinking about an actual hoard of treasure."

"And you think this could be it?"

"If it's as vast as you say, how could it not?" Orsava looked again at the map, shooing away a foy fly hovering over the crumbs of his sandwich. "I'm not saying Ashgra is real, or she molded gold from the sun. It might be as you say, that Ashgra is Krypholos. Or the god was a woman who found a dragon's hoard. Even someone who stumbled across a molten river churned up during the Lunar Sundering."

Grint threw his head back, laughing, kicking his feet onto a cushioned ottoman. Angis brought a fresh glass of ale and took the time to refill Lord Orsava's wine. If there was ever a time to rejoice and smoke his pipe, now was it. Grint retrieved it from the bag and tamped down a thumb's worth of tabac, striking a match. Orsava had the same idea and followed suit, both men grinning like idiots as they puffed smoke rings into the air.

"Grint," Orsava said after a time. "I can't help but ask, why bring me in on this?"

"Why, you ungrateful, bloody, charff-riddled mungle!" Grint shouted in mock anger. The litany of profane words made Orsava laugh. He did quite enjoy the crass nature of the thief, frequently saying it provided a nice counter-balance to the stuffy aristocracy Salaz forced him to mingle with.

"Truthfully," Grint said, taking the pipe from his mouth. "I thought about going it alone. Coming here and telling you I couldn't find the painting. Bagging off with

Newman to a nice quiet room while I figured out how to steal the gold."

"And yet, here you are," the lord responded with no hint of hurt in his voice. Did the admission that he considered cutting him out bother Orsava?

"I don't know this city and never will. Not like you do," Grint admitted, listening to the phantom sound of coins falling through his fingers.

"You need my help," Orsava smiled.

"I can't do it without you, and frankly, don't want to." Grint got up and walked to the window. Salaz at night could be a beautiful sight. Sparkling firelights danced in windows across the sloping vista. The splendor could almost entrance one into forgetting the rancid layer of political corruption beneath. "I spent half the day running from city guards and watching them beat up people of all types. If the gold can get you out, maybe retire to a lakeside villa where you can read your books, then I'm happy to help."

"Generous," Orsava said without the usual sarcasm Grint heard with other thieves. Such a rare thing. Most people in Grint's life were wary of betrayal or actively trying to betray.

"How do we go about this?" Orsava set a tin cart on top of the map. "It's reasonable to think we could get six chests into a cart and back here. Divide it in half and live a life of leisure."

"Six chests?" Grint turned from the window, scowling.

"You can make your case for eight, but I think we'd be working the horse too hard. That is a lot of weight." Orsava pulled out a scale as Angis brought him fresh ink and quills to continue scrawling notes.

"No," Grint said, causing the lord to pause. "I don't want a sack, a chest, or even a cart's worth. I want it all."

"Be reasonable, Grint," Orsava pleaded, looking up from the papers. "What you're describing would take an effort beyond anything we're capable of. Even with hiring on hands, and we will have to if you want more."

Grint squeezed his fists. Splitting the gold any further sent pains through his chest. "As long as we limit the number of people."

"And their pay?" Orsava raised his eyebrows, blowing out a relieved sigh when Grint shook his head.

"When they see the gold, if they don't think they're getting a fair shake, we'll have knives at our throat and fires at our feet." Grint had worked with enough crews and lived to know how to play the game. "We pay them, but only what we need to." Was an uncountable fortune split eight ways, ten ways, still uncountable?

"You will need a plan worthy of the God you follow," Orsava sat back in his chair, staring down at the half-written formulas he'd begun.

"Hobbe would be proud," Grint laughed. "I'm not there yet, but let me assure you. By the end of this, Borismere will hand us the entire pile with a fat smile on his face."

"Won't that be a sight to see," Orsava laughed.

Grint snapped his fingers, "Speaking of, in all the excitement I almost forgot about the Parthian riding into town!"

6

"Let your hand be your own. The guiding star of another will always lead to ruin."

– The Tale of Teelo Tane, Parthian Barbarian; pAnnum 9874

Chell woke from the alcohol-induced blackout with his feet hanging off a dreego-sized bed. Stalks of straw poked through the flimsy mattress, stabbing him from every direction. Beetles, frightened as he stretched the stiffness away, scattered across the basement floor, flattening themselves as they squeezed their way through cracks in the stone. A rickety table sat beside the bed with an unlit candle atop it. Parthian eyes focused well in the dark, so Chell needed no help from it to find his gear. His thick leather boots went on first and required several tugs to fit over swollen feet.

Standing in the corner, breathing through the anvil strikes behind his eyes, he recalled the dreego cowards dosing him with poison. Chell closed his eyes, focusing on the flow of blood through his veins. Total awareness of one's body was an old practice the shamans taught. Useful for a chief who believed a rival might poison their food, but Chell never mastered the technique. Today was no different, but he'd learned enough to recognize that his muscles sagged and moved as if drowning in mud. Was that from the drink or the poison?

The sparse lodgings offered by the tavern showed Chell how little he knew of the dreego. How did one attain true rest without the calming energy of the stars? Or wake without the gentle hand of the sun? Below ground, in a windowless basement, Chell experienced a disconnection with nature, and did not care for it. Musty stones dripped with condensation. The stink made his nose itch as if a hundred ants crawled inside. How the dreego withstood these conditions eluded his understanding. Their feeble attempts to keep cool in the inhospitable heat rendered them soft. Chell battled through worse temperatures in the jungles of Parthia, the viscera of his enemies running through his fur.

"Now is not the time or place to pleasure myself with the songs of magnificent battles," Chell said, tightening his back scabbard.

A flimsy curtain acted as the door to his room. Chell accidentally tore it down as he exited, surprised that a fragile thing like it lasted so long. The low ceiling forced Chell to walk with a hunch, but still he scraped his head with every step. "Must I crawl to find relief?"

A wooden thing clattered to the floor, and he spotted an adolescent dreego at the end of the hallway sweeping dirt. The child picked up his broom and stared in wide-eyed wonder at the hulking Parthian. Chell said nothing until the boy reached out to touch his fur. The impetuous action earned a deep growl as he flashed a mouthful of sharp teeth. It made the cub scream as he fell into a tight ball at the base of the stairs.

"Check on your brother," the barman called out as Chell ascended the stairs. Another small dreego, some years older than the first, stood in the doorway as Chell reached the top. This one screamed too, falling backwards and scrambling away as Chell righted himself to full height.

"Calm down boy, that is our guest," Merv said.

"Guest? Is that what you call the hospitality of poisoning those who sit at your table?" Chell asked. The barman waved a hand as if he wanted the poisoning to remain a secret, but backstabbers deserved no favors.

"Is my other son all right?" Merv asked, looking past him to the basement stairs. Chell smelled the deep terror that sullied the dreego's sweat. Fear of dying to the barbarian's rage. Fear that Chell tore the young cub asunder.

"The little dreego is unharmed," Chell said as he walked up to the bar. "He attempted to pet me like a dog, so I growled at him like one. I would ask if you taught these little ones any manners, but clearly you do not understand the idea."

"Chaz, check on your brother," Merv repeated in a harsh whisper, picking the older boy up from the floor. The one called Chaz stayed well clear as he trotted to the cellar door, but he never took his eyes off Chell.

"I scared him. Nothing more." Then after a moment of thought Chell added, "I am not so savage as those who break the Rule of Bread."

"It was not my fault," Merv said, his voice cracking. The Rule of Bread was a universal concept and needed no explanation. When you accepted a guest, you treated them as blood. It did not include poisoning or murder, even if some ignored the rule.

"Save your piteous excuses," Chell snapped. "Unless you have an antidote to atone with, I will take a mare's milk to regain my strength and rid myself of this foul place."

The barman agreed by pouring the milk in a clay tankard. Chell's belly raged with fires even this cool liquid failed to soothe. In that moment, a vague recollection of the previous day returned. A space littered with splinters remained where he smashed a table in rage. The section of bar he shattered hid beneath a draped cloth. Chell pulled the sheet aside and ran his finger over the cut. Clean was his stroke, but the blade did not go through, and that surprised the Parthian. The wood caught his blade, stopping it short.

"What is this material?" Chell asked.

"Steel oak," Merv said, the scowl deepening. "It comes from the north and is very expensive. Very."

"A misfortune for your friends. I hope they can compensate you for the damages," Chell said, crushing the clay tankard in his fist. The shattered bits dropped as he opened his hand. Chell shook his hand, scattering dregs of milk across the bar. Merv stared at the mess, afraid to look into Chell's eyes.

A sharp pain stabbed into his stomach, blossoming throughout his chest. Perhaps the first sign of the poison taking effect. How long had they told him it would be? Five days? Four now that he'd slept one away. If the poison's effects grew worse over time, he would lose a day at the end. *Three days then*, he thought. *Three days to kill a queen.*

The task set before him was not one of leisure. Killing a monarch would incite the ire of the entire kingdom, putting a legion of killers on his back. Neither was it insurmountable. Kings and queens were not unreachable fig-

ures. A personal lesson he'd learned at great cost. His fall
from grace a testament to that reality. Though a war-leader no more, he would take back his mantle and punish the
fool who dared defy him.

Four men entered the tavern. Humid air fought the
cool comfort of the common room as they swept in, one
at a time. They chose a table by the door, each pulled back
their hoods before setting light blue masks down with
great reverence. That each hid a dagger beneath the mask
amused Chell. Merv made an annoying squeak with his
mouth and replaced the armband he wore - deep blue with
conjoining white circles - with one of similar color, but
checkered in white squares.

"Why change that?" Chell asked, reaching toward the
band. Merv pulled away, the blood draining from his face
as he shook his head. The men at the table watched, all
dressed in thin, silk robes with blood red armbands. None
intimidated Chell. Slender dreego with beady eyes buried
beneath folds of ebony skin. Could any hold a sword? Every
cub learned to brandish a weapon. Few mastered the art.
None of these dreego were masters, Chell judged, ready-
ing his own gear for the day ahead.

"Where can one find this queen of yours?" Chell asked.
The barman hissed at the question, looking again at the table.

"There are eyes and ears everywhere," Merv whispered. Although their table sat by the door, he spoke as if
they gathered round the bar.

"Are they not of your kind?" Chell asked.

"They are not," Merv said. "They're Inquisitors." A
Parthian's nose detected many things. The stink of dreego
lies being one. The fragile creatures couldn't help secret-
ing a nasty stench undetectable to their own kind. But it

was the primary thing Chell smelled throughout the city. For once, Merv did not stink of lies.

"Had I more time, I would take care. You have not given me that luxury. Now where can I find her?" Though he cared little for the man's safety, he lowered his voice to a harsh whisper. Getting the barman killed from foolish action might prompt the others to deny him an antidote from their wretched poison.

Merv leaned over and whispered, "The Seastone Tower. You can't miss it. A great blue jewel watching over the city, glittering as Ashgra's light reflects off the water."

"And what protection does she have?" No monarch left themselves exposed, not when opposition reared its head. A rarity even in times of peace.

"Well, her army," the barman shrugged.

Chell's hand surged out in the blink of an eye, yanking him close. "I am Parthian. I am neither immortal nor capable of fighting an army alone. If I were, we would have left our jungle home long ago and rid Terragard of your hairless plague."

"Please," Merv whined.

"Do better," Chell grunted. "Or bring me the fools from yesterday."

"I can't," the barman said. "Please. I'm not with them. They threatened my children if I didn't help." This time the lying stench stung Chell's nostrils with the thickness of his fabrication. The barman's eyes glanced at the table of men and Chell heard their chairs slide as each stood.

Chell released him, listening to the soft shuffle of feet moving toward the bar. "What do I owe you for the room?" He raised his voice so the men would think their business done. Best to keep them relaxed and oblivious to the rage boiling within.

"The room?" Merv stammered. "Nothing. Nothing, please just go." The inquisitors fanned out behind him. To their credit, Chell didn't detect a trace of fear among them.

"Captain Basto is looking for you," a man's oiled voice said. Chell smiled, wondering if the fool thought himself clever, hiding a blade up his sleeve. Perhaps he could have kept it hidden had he not oiled the steel with such fervor.

"I do not know anyone named Bastard," Chell said, facing the four. The fear they kept in check until now bubbled between the cracks of their emotional armor.

"Basto," the oily inquisitor said. "Captain Basto. You will need to come with us." As he looked past Chell, the man's face twisted with manic glee. "And you, barman."

"I do not recognize your authority to take me anywhere," Chell answered. A terrified sound, like that of a dying mouse, escaped Merv's throat.

"It matters not what you recognize," the inquisitor said. "When we walk the city, we are the fingers of the queen's hand. The tongue in her mouth and eyes of her spirit. We are the queen in all but form."

"Is that so?" Chell asked. Drawing a sword was a skill Parthian children learned alongside walking. The action became so natural that one performed it the way they took a breath - without thought. It took Chell a moment to draw and swing the blade. Such folly for the four to line up in Chell's reach. The oily inquisitor's mouth moved as the sword sliced through his neck. It continued moving after the head struck the floor. Odd, garbled sounds from a brain not realizing its own demise took place.

"No," Merv wept. Chell heard the man fall, striking the ground hard. The elder of his children stood in the basement door, watching.

"Attend to your father," he said, wiping his blade on the robes of an inquisitor before sheathing it.

Killing these men would have consequence. Someone would miss them. Three days was no longer enough to visit his wrath upon the queen. He may now only have one. The one called Prince Mikil would answer for this treachery, and again for setting him on this path. Until then, Chell would focus on ways to assassinate the queen.

As it was past time to leave. Chell strode through the dim tavern, pleased by the release of his anger. It had been too long. The cubs of Merv averted their eyes as he passed. Chell hoped to find more combat soon. The taste of blood sat like a tantalizing treat on his tongue.

Outside, the brightness of the day struck him in a way he'd not expected. A wave of nausea descended upon him. Chell slumped against the wall, hot clay baking through the fur on his shoulder. Soon enough the vertigo subsided, and he shook his head, spraying sweat in all directions. Chell looked to the sky. Ominous clouds rolled across the horizon. The promise of rain sat thick on the air. An unpleasant storm if he guessed, and one accompanied by Tockra Silvertongue. As if summoned by thought, lightning flashed, followed by the anger of Silvertongue's thundering voice.

"Horse?" He called out, smiling at the skies. A good rain would cool his mind, giving him the proper perspective. Chell whistled when the beast did not appear. "Fleck? Where have you gone?"

Missing was the post he'd tied Fleck to, pulled from the ground, leaving a crater in the stone. A disconcerting thing for Fleck to have run. What frightened the beast? Silvertongue's anger would not. The horse was well used to the frequent storms showering the Parthian jungles. Parthian horse-masters trained Fleck to serve him from the day each was born. He would not have wandered. Chell crouched, running his fingers over the stone. Years of wear and etching could not hide the fresh scuffs from Fleck's hooves or the chips of steel from errant sword strikes.

"You the owner of that beast?" Chell looked at a veiled man with red armband matching that of the inquisitors. A cudgel of knotted wood rested against a shoulder covered in silver-blue chain-mail. Two eye-holes cut in the opaque red fabric hid any hint of expression, but the stink of violence around this person was thick enough to make Chell gag.

"I am. Where is he?" Chell stood, towering over the man by a good two heads. The bravado faded as the guard stepped back. Seven others lurked nearby, watching from the mouths of alleys or shaded doorways. Chell didn't need his nose to know their terror. All of them, young unblooded pups who spent their days chasing pickpockets through the streets. To them, combat was a bard's song told in drunken boasts.

"It bit the arm off one of my men," the cudgel wielder said. "When another stepped in it bit him too. Both may die."

"They should have known better than to challenge a Parthian horse," Chell grinned. "Where have you taken him?"

"We killed it," the soldier said. At the proclamation, the soldiers jogged from their hiding spots, forming a line beside their superior. A pre-determined phrase calling the young ones to action. The older guard desired this fight.

"A mistake," Chell said, letting the rage re-ignite. Fleck's loss was one he could not bear. Chell would visit the inferno of his displeasure on any who stepped in his way. Losing the horse was akin to losing a part of himself. "For your sake, pray to your foolish sun god this is a joke. And a poor one."

"It's time you come with us," the guard said. "You've become addled under Ashgra's gaze. Some time on Allast Island will help get your mind right."

"Captain," a young buck whispered. "The inquisitors have not come out. Where are they?"

"Indulging in drink," the captain replied. "Who cares? They'll just get in our way."

"My horse," Chell repeated as the captain ordered the soldiers into a semi-circle around him. "Bring him to me, or this will end poorly." Judging the distance, the dreego spread out too far to dispatch them the way he had the inquisitors.

"Didn't you hear me? Or all Parthians as dumb as you?" The captain laughed, turning to his underlings for confirmation. "We killed your horse and cooked it up." That was all Chell needed. Joke or not, there would be recompense for the slight.

An old memory bubbled to the surface. Three young cubs thinking to make a name for themselves by slaying Chell. They came at him while he relaxed in the great steam baths of the Ochinee River. Even in such a disadvantaged state, he'd leapt from the water, rolled to retrieve his weapon, and stood ready before they finished taking their second step into the grotto. It did not take much to turn the tables on them. A great remembrance and hymn sprang from that battle. That day was not this one.

Unlike before, the sword stuck in his scabbard like a thing drowning in tar. The dizziness he'd felt when waking returned, clouded his mind. Foolish dreego to administer a poison that affected his reflexes. Much like the horse, his sword was a part of him, an extension. Yet, never had it rested so uncomfortably in his hands. Chell's fingers trembled as he gripped the hilt. Both biceps quaked in the attempt at holding it steady. The captain swung his cudgel, knocking the sword from Chell's skilled hands. The cursed poison would prove the death of him, but not in the way it intended.

Seeing him unarmed, the soldiers rushed in like fools. Wild, uncontrolled beasts stinking of fear and false bravado. The result of hearing stories rather than living them. Chell palmed a youthful man's face and squeezed. The fragile skull cracked. An ugly gurgle emanated from his throat as death came to collect the debt. Now a lifeless thing, Chell used the body as a weapon. Crouching below the swing of the cudgel, he used the corpse to topple four others. As they cried in horror, he leapt, bringing the body down in a crushing blow on the captain. The cudgel fell from his twitching hand.

Chell retrieved it, hefting its weight as he inspected the wood. The weapon was not his sword, but the knotted wood felt pleasant in his hand. Perhaps it was more of the steel oak they made the bar from. The Parthian swung the cudgel in controlled arcs, careful not to overextend himself. What he failed to identify were the signs of over-exertion. Fatigue claimed him in its weak grip, and the world spun. Chell stumbled, lurching into a wooden door that cracked under his weight. In his weakness, a soldier carrying a pronged claw weapon stabbed Chell's left pectoral.

The barbarian howled like a lion and pulled the assailant close, tearing out the man's throat with his teeth.

Dropping the body, he spit the gore at rushing guards, swinging the cudgel in mighty strokes, pulping any soldier within reach. Glorious rage filled him, chasing away the weakness. Bones crunched, armor collapsed, and blood showered in time with the first drops of rain. A handful of cowards ran, dropping their weapons as they went. Perhaps he over-estimated these dreego. If Parthia rose as one, could they conquer them? Was that the path set before him? Not atonement, but education in how to bring the dreego low?

A weeping sound rose and drew his attention. An injured soldier limped toward the tavern door, trying in vain to escape. Chell grasped the collar of his thin cuirass and slammed him into the wall. His wail of pain mirrored the anguish Chell felt at losing his beloved Fleck.

"Where is this queen of yours?" The rains came down in a torrent as Silvertongue cried out in forked bolts of lightning. The cool water calmed his rage, but nothing would quell it.

"What?" The soldier moaned, blood trickling from the corner of his mouth.

"If I allow you life, will you bring me before your queen?" Chell felt the drippings of viscera through his fur while the rain washed him clean. A haunting image to be sure, but not terrifying enough to loosen the man's tongue.

"You're a mad animal," the soldier choked. "We will see you hanged and then tear you apart..."

Chell punched him square in the chest, feeling the soft metal collapse inward. The blow crushed his heart. Tossing the body aside, it landed in a puddle, splashing mud onto the last surviving soldier. The dreego sat with his back against the dented pole of a gas-lamp, holding a broken arm close to his chest. Trapped in the downpour, the trembling dreego reeked of urine and blood, some of it his own. The rest of his squad lay in tatters and the guard knew it. Chell offered no pity. Grabbing him by the ankle, he tossed him on top of the piled bodies. The soldier's helmet rolled away, revealing a cub yet to grow hair on his face. Crouching over him, Chell forced the boy's gaze onto the dead.

"You saw what denying me leads to. Tell me what I want and I will allow you to see another day," Chell said, smelling the boy urinating himself again.

"So be it," the Parthian grunted, and tore the veil from his face. The boy screamed as Chell forced his face to the skies. "This god you fear looks on you now. Even through the clouds, yes? Maybe I will scare them off if you tell me what I want."

The cub screamed in anguish, "The queen is in the tower, but I can't bring you there. They won't let us in."

"Disappointing," Chell said. "I see no reason to let you live."

"Wait," the cub said, his eyes squeezed shut. "It's the Cognispyre."

"I don't know what that means," Chell forced open an eye with his sharp nails.

"Please don't make me look!"

"What is this Cognispyre?"

"The festival," he said. "The queen comes down to the city each day leading up to it. To witness the progress of the people building their effigies."

"And today is one of these days?" This could be what he needed. Finding where and when she planned to be, he could accomplish this task and win his freedom.

"Yes," the soldier said, convulsing as the salt witches did when possessed. "But it will do you no good! I will eat your flesh before the day ends!"

The sudden change of personality shocked Chell. Could this god Ashgra be real? Or had the cub used the circumstance to free himself of the notions of civility? Whatever the cause, Chell had no use for a madman. He snapped the cub's neck. Kicking aside a corpse, he found his sword and held it out before him. The shaking in his hands ceased, but the battle left him injured. Horns of reinforcement blew from many directions. Silent, terrified eyes watched from darkened windows. The stench they let off strong enough to choke a boar-ox. It was time to move.

Losing Fleck would require further atonement. His decision to enter the city of Salaz bore no fruit but the bitter, rotted kind infested with misfortune. The Parthian loped along at a jog. With no plan on how to evade the guards and find the queen, he was a rudderless ship, lost in the endless sea. But he would do what he must, even if it meant tearing down every brick in the city.

Silvertongue laughed.

7

Kanto Key was no stranger to dark magic, but the irides-cent blue fire dancing around the arm he'd taken from the corn farmer proved to be nothing but trouble.
"Well?" Kristoff said, lashing a sword to his arm so he could carry it. "Neither of us thought we'd live forever."

— *The Longest Tale, Bard Grensly*
p.Annum 5899

The first drop of rain against her face sent ripples through her dream of laying on a beach. The sunny day turned bleak as the sand eroded beneath her. Sea water flooded in churning waves as she struggled to stay above the surface. The second raindrop landed beside her nose, shattering the dream. Nazarra waved an arm, slapping her face. When the thunder boomed, she opened her eyes, breathing in morning air full with the certainty of a terrible storm. Realizing she'd fallen asleep on the roof, she sat up, trying to recall the exact moment when.

Two bells after she'd begun watching the tavern. That was when the operative returned with food.

"This is for you," he'd said from the darkness. Nazarra heard him coming, but had drawn her sword in case it was someone from the Opposition, or even one of Racko's Blue Hands.

"I'm not hungry," she said. When he didn't move, she pointed the sword at his face. "Go," she commanded. The man placed it down and nodded.

"For later," he said, leaving with a backward glance.

Nazarra wouldn't have used the sword on him. Not after the kind gesture of bringing food, but she needed to remain cautious. Anyone could become compromised, then poison her. It was best to keep others at arm's length. That was Grint's influence on her, his inherent mistrust of anyone he didn't know. There was too much confusion in her life with the thief and her attachment to him.

Thinking of Grint tugged at her. A small voice crying from the drowning pool of her subconscious. Nazarra closed her eyes to meditate the way Master Barriss taught her. The sword-master was long dead, but his lessons still comforted her. Barriss was the closest figure she had to a father, as her own had no time for her. Within the stillness of her meditations, she slept.

Until now. The storms rolled in early today, covering the morning sky with clouds racing west to east. Nazarra dusted off the floppy hat as she watched a wall of rain marching up the street. A drenching rain, cold and hard. The wind whipped drops around the wide brim of the hat to slap her cheeks. Nazarra recollected the distant dream of a girl who ran in the rain, a bright smile on her face as she splashed through puddles. Only now, it seemed nothing more than the story of someone else's life. Emotional emptiness was the goal of her meditations, and she became adept at achieving the state.

Nazarra stepped to the edge of the roof. A dozen men lay dead on the street as the Parthian kicked aside a body to retrieve his sword. The beast slaughtered a full squad, and she'd slept through it. Horns blew from the Upper Crust, Meskal, and Bushan. Then another from the Blau. Reinforcements called too late to save this lot. Nazarra watched the barbarian jog away with the graceful ease of someone enjoying a day of leisure. There was no panic in how he moved. No second guessing his direction. A dangerous thing to behold after he'd killed so many. The Parthian cared little for Salazians. If the Opposition got hold of him as she believed they had, a very dangerous game was now being played.

Nazarra grabbed a pastry from the plate, stuffing it in her mouth as she ran along rooftops. Buildings crammed together made it easy to jump the narrow spaces between. The rain concealed any noises - if she made any at all. Streams of rain water poured across slanted clay tiles and around her soft boots. Thunder cracked as the storm raged. An unusual thing for this time of day. Morning storms in Salaz were quiet affairs, over before the sun knew to climb above the horizon. What angered Ashgra to make her displeasure known so early? The Parthian? Or her dereliction of duty?

The woman laughed at herself, leaping across a ten-foot span. Such hubris and self-importance to think she caused the storm. The High Priest would whip her in the Sun Chamber for such an admission. Or call her down as sun-addled. The priest was a rigidly orthodox follower of the Sun Book, keeping his chambers shuttered from daylight and avoiding the sun. Not even her sister, Akosha, was that devout.

Water ran beneath her silver mask, mixing with droplets of sweat that stung her eyes. Nazarra removed the covering to wipe her face. *Ashgra forbids sunlight, even on a stormy day. Another whipping from the priest.* Did she believe in the Sun Book still? Grint's stories sounded like romantic notions at first, but he never spoke of them as ideals to live by. The man hated and feared the gods he mentioned. Gods of Chance, Murder, War, Bargains, and so many more. Even his patron, the Thief God, Hobbe, was not immune to his criticisms.

The Parthian stopped, lifting its black snout into the air. A few paces away was a stairwell leading to the Blau, but he did not move toward it. Did he sense her? Hear her? No, it was not her that caught the barbarian's senses, but a squad of guards running through the downpour. Nazarra pondered jumping down to assist them, but the Parthian squeezed into the space between buildings, hiding himself behind the spout of an old gutter. The guards ran past, oblivious that the one they sought slipped through their fingers. Perhaps that was best, Nazarra didn't believe these six would fare any better than the twelve who'd already fallen.

Clear of the guards, the Parthian stepped out, shaking his long fur in great sprays of water. Taking a few tentative steps, he studied the buildings and roof line. His gaze passed over her perch to another across the street. When it did, Nazarra caught the slightest hint of movement. Surely, it was not mungles. The nasty beasts hated rain and hid during storms. Satisfied that he was alone, the barbarian started down the stairs. Nazarra saw the movement again. Not a mungle, but two people in a low crouch.

As always, her first thoughts gravitated towards Grint. The thief had followed her before, watching her when she tried to ensnare him. Had he done it again when she left the safe house? A silly notion. Thieves in Salaz were plentiful, including more than just her northerner. Racko's Blue Hands treated the rooftops as their domain. The guild operated under the rule that they not rob the churches of Ashgra or interfere with the queen. The Council created the law to limit them in their activities. If caught in the act, the penalties were severe. But that was not the result. The law gave them legitimacy as a guild, allowing the fools to wear armbands identifying themselves as Blue Hands. Inquisitors and guards turned a blind eye, accepting pay offs or hiring them to smear a competitor. Unless forced to act against the thieves, no one touched them. Nazarra didn't play by their rules. When the two curious fools spotted her, they scattered, leaving her alone in the pursuit.

The Parthian's path down the stairs forced Nazarra to descend to the streets if she wanted to follow. Remembering her tutoring as a child, and what she learned of Parthia, she kept herself downwind, pausing anytime her quarry did. Her lessons taught that Parthians were little better than feral animals, incapable of complex thought, but their senses were acute.

The rainstorm quieted as the thunder faded to a soft rumble in the eastern sky. A drizzle fell, more mist than rain, prompting the shops to re-open. People in the streets would help her blend in, but could also complicate things. One person screaming in terror might send the barbarian into a blood-rage she couldn't contend with. The Parthian had felled twelve armed guards in a matter of moments, how many citizens could he tear apart in the same span?

Nazarra watched his movement and found it odd that he looked north each time he stopped. They'd just come that way. Nazarra tried to puzzle out what compelled the barbarian's gaze. Guards? Worry of them chasing him? Or was the Parthian sporting for a fight? An old woman pushed a cart through the door of her shop. Nazarra bashed into it, spilling a pile of crawberries into drainage grates.

"Cullie bash, nah guhd," the woman said in the thick voice of someone raised deep in the Glades.

Nazarra nodded, wanting to keep the woman quiet. Through the tears in her veil, the woman spat insults, lamenting the loss of the fruit. Nazarra attempted to help her, but when she looked up, the Parthian had vanished. "Ballishoi!" The Glades-woman shouted the expletive as Nazarra knocked the cart over once more.

The Glades-woman yelled after Nazarra, her voice trailing off as she reached the spot the barbarian had been. A three-way junction with a moneylender on each corner. South would lead to a staircase and the Termin district. The eastern path was little more than an alley with small shops. To the north, a small inclining road of uneven cobbles, wet with draining water. There Nazarra spotted the Parthian rounding a crook in the road. Sprinting, she weighed the fear that he might see her against losing him, but his focus never left the road. Even when shutters flew open and the veiled residents screeched, he never broke stride.

The cobble street ended at a second stairway leading back to the Chantil district. Blowing out an exasperated breath, Nazarra watched the barbarian take the stairs three at a time. A supposition began forming from the evidence. *The Parthian hid from the patrol* - he wasn't circling back to fight them. If she believed the Opposition turned him, his attention would be on the task they gave him. *Prince Mikil wouldn't poison a barbarian to blackmail a sympathetic noble.*

He'd poison one to kill. Nazarra ran through a list of names in her mind as her gaze lifted.

Along the eastern edge of the city, high above the other districts, was the Gutarr. A long approach flanked by barracks and officer's homes, and the one road to the palace. *Mikil is sending the beast after the queen herself.* The idea terrified her. Would the palace guards be capable of repelling him? A day ago she would have laughed at the thought, but seeing what damage he'd wrought, Nazarra now doubted the outcome.

Running at a full sprint, her desire for subterfuge fell away. The brewing conflict would have to go through her. As she thought it, a strange sensation snaked up her spine, pulling the feeling out of anything above her waist. A shaking fear, imagining the head-to-head duel with the barbarian. Stray dogs, emboldened by the lack of rain, barked at her from the alleys. *No, I'm not afraid.* And she wasn't. A slow draining sensation drained the blood from her arms, dumping everything into her legs. Nazarra struggled against the weight as she reached the stairs, finding it impossible to lift her foot. A wave of intense nausea embraced her. Breath would not come. When her vision fogged over, she dropped to the ground, slumping against the stair she failed to climb.

Nazarra pulled the mask from her face, gasping for air. It fell from her hand, clacking and rolling as it hit the ground. Ashgra's wrath was the least of her worries. The suddenness of the strange illness terrified her. A clangor of voices and shouts grew closer. Nazarra blinked through the blurred spots clouding her vision. Somewhere beyond, shapes of dull color flitted about.

"Give her room, you flap-mouthed maggots!" The voice came from deep within a cave, echoing off cold, wet stones. The thought disoriented her, making her question reality. There were no caves like that within thirty miles of the city.

Shadow wraiths dominated the edge of her vision, blotting out the rays of sunshine breaking through the storm. Nazarra waved a feeble arm, but it flopped uselessly back and forth. Someone's hand took hers, warm against the clammy sweat of her palm. They gripped her wrist, gently directing it to her side.

"Easy there, Commander," the voice said in a thick Glades accent. A cool shadow passed over as they placed the mask back on her face.

Something cold touched her wrist, shocking her back to a state of lucidity. Colors returned in a flood so vivid she screamed at the stabbing pain it lit between her eyes. The helpful voice whispered something encouraging, patting her on the shoulder. And when she regained enough of herself to focus, she saw a private kneeling beside her, his veil lifted and a terrified smile on his face.

"What?" Confusion ruled her thoughts, as she spoke through a hoarse voice. "Where is the barbarian?"

"I didn't see it," the private said. His hand gripped hers uncomfortably, squeezing tighter as he tensed. When she pulled it free, he shifted it to the hilt of the sword hanging off his hip.

"Help me up." With reluctance, he pulled her to her feet. The strength she'd lost was slow to return, and her muscles shook with the effort of staying upright.

"This looks like papasil poisoning," he said, checking her over. "You should lie down."

"There's no time," she said, shaking the fog from her brain. Papasil was the plant they made the bassal spice from. The pulp of the stalk could be toxic in large enough quantities, but what would she have eaten? "The pastry," she said, placing a hand on her stomach.

"That could do it," the private said. "Cullie bash bakers are too dumb to keep the pulp out."

Had someone poisoned the pastry on purpose? *I warned you not to trust anyone,* Grint laughed. And she imagined the thief shuffling a deck of cards as he visited her bedside.

The private continued talking as her mind wandered, shutting up when she held a hand to his mouth. "I need to find the Parthian," Nazarra stopped him.

"There's a Parthian in the city?" The private shrieked.

"Yes. It doesn't matter. Help me up the stairs. I need to get to the Gutarr." As he shouldered her weight, she saw a small glass bottle, missing its cork, peeking out from a pouch on his belt. The concoction that revived her to be sure, but for now she'd keep hope that it wasn't from a salt witch.

They kept a steady pace, but nowhere close to the barbarian's speed. It wouldn't be enough. They'd be far too late to intercede. Instead of circling around, perhaps she could reach a tower and sound the alarm. Alert the palace guards to close the gates.

"Leave me," she said. They were only halfway up the stairs and already her breathing struggled. "Run to the guard towers and sound the alarms."

"I shouldn't leave you," he said.

"Go," Nazarra snapped. "That's an order."

The private grunted as he ran, shouting ahead for the alarm bells. Urchin children sat along the walls, watching her. Where they all came from or went was another Salazian mystery. Not one pressing enough to warrant investigation. But a curiosity. More clouds rolled overhead, blocking out the taste of sunlight Ashgra had given them. Another storm was brewing. Nazarra's drenched robes trailed a watery snake as she gripped a railing to help her along. The urchins followed, making chattering sounds to one another. Their dirt-smeared faces alight with mischief. Not a one of them wore masks or veils.

Reaching the top felt like an accomplishment. She limped along, feeling a tingle of sensation returning to her extremities. She'd visit a healer later. Until then, her focus remained on the barbarian. If they could tie it to Prince Mikil, they could finally hang the treacherous bastard.

There was no trace of the Parthian in the street or on the winding cliff road leading to the Gutarr. A few centuries ago, city engineers built the road into the cliff. The king wanted something they could collapse during an invasion, or used to move troops through the city. Horse carts moved up and down, weaving through people on foot. No one panicked, screaming in terror at the sight of the beast. Was she mistaken in his intention to attack the palace? Nazarra shut her eyes, focusing through the pain. The answer was in front of her. If she could just think through the kry-damn swill in her head... An image of the thief laughing invaded her thoughts. That was not what she wanted to focus on.

Nazarra listened to the city. Two elderly women argued, shaking rug-beaters at one another. Competing carpet makers by the signs dangling above their respective doors. They spoke fast, in shrill accents more at home in Harborside slums than the Chantil, but Nazarra knew the half-speak enough to discern the argument. Each blamed the other for missing rugs left out to dry. Their creations were too large for urchins to take - but a Parthian could use them to cover itself. Nazarra scanned the cobbles. Water drained from the storm, and a trail of oils swirled in the puddles, creating a trail that led onto the cliff road.

"You there," she shouted at a man leading his horse. The loose green shirt, unbuttoned to the navel, had become spotted with moisture. In a gesture of greeting, he smoothed out the veil. But his stance changed abruptly at seeing her red armband with the Queen's insignia. His own blue armband displayed concentric white circles. Being aligned with the Opposition was not a crime, but a duty of Salazian citizens to maintain a benevolent monarchy. Prince Mikil tarnished the idea, fomenting rebellion over discourse.

"Yes?"

"I need that horse," she said, yanking the reins from his hand.

"By Ashgra's grace, no," he protested. "This is all I have after the queen's last edict."

"And you will see it returned," she said, struggling to get in the saddle. "Or compensation of twice its value."

The man took a moment to ponder the offer before helping her into the saddle and slapping the horse's hind quarter. A thick, dappled mare unaccustomed to moving at speed trotted along - it's pace faster than anything Nazarra could reasonably expect from herself. Pedestrians grumbled whenever Nazarra forced them to step aside. No one behaved as if they'd seen a hulking beast lumbering through the crowd. Would they pay attention to one covered in carpets?

Alarm bells sounded from a tower in the Chantil. Bile rose in her throat, making Nazarra want to scream. The private alerted a tower in the wrong direction. The call to arms wouldn't spread quickly enough to reach the palace. *It doesn't matter,* she tried convincing herself. *The private sounded an alarm. More will follow.* She made a silent prayer to Ashgra that the guards would hear and close the palace gates.

As she reached the top of the cliff road, the second storm spat out fat drops of rain. Those still traversing the road rushed along, shaking fists at the skies. The Gutarr wasn't an active district. Finding a crowd blocking the road struck her as peculiar. A hundred people filled the street, and Nazarra's heart skipped a beat, fearful that a full insurrection had begun. Another lesson from her youth, tactics and strategy, taught by General Argus, came back to her. During the invasion of Grel Somas in Annum eight-hundred and fifty-seven. When the Lyzan slithered through the Glades to attack the city, they barricaded the Gutarr every five hundred feet. Arrows rained down from windows as the attackers struggled over the endless blockades. By the time Grel assaulted the palace gates, his numbers had dwindled to thirty. Easy enough for the Salazian infantry to sweep up.

There were no barricades today, or archers firing from windows. The people stood, cheering and waving little flags with the royal emblem. Some hoisted wooden effigies into the sky or pointed at the stick figures hanging off balconies. *I'd forgotten the Cognispyre tradition.* The holiday was a week away, and the people were displaying their creations for each to admire. Some came just to look at the creations, but many gathered to see the queen as she began her tour to see the city's progress in preparing for the day. Akosha wasn't in the palace, but out on the street. An easy target for the barbarian.

Nazarra shouted as she rode the horse into the crowd. She knocked aside people who refused to move. They screamed at the mistreatment, but Nazarra did not care. Her focus sat on the terrified herd of citizens running from the palace. She kicked the horse hard. When it didn't move any faster, she kicked it again. In the distance, the hulking Parthian shed its stolen rugs, freeing his arms to swing a massive sword. Three guards tumbled like dolls on the first arc. Behind them, atop an open-air litter, sat the queen on a golden chair. Akosha lounged, eating a piece of fruit as she watched the carnage unfold. The High Priest's chair sat empty, as the old fool hid himself behind it. Servants rushed to unfurl a covering over the queen, concerned more about keeping her dry than safe from the beast. Their efforts ignored the man atop his black steed. The wind fluttered his cream and gold coat. *Lord Borismere.*

People now leapt aside as she galloped through. The rain stung her bare face, and she couldn't say when she'd lost the mask. The storm turned torrential, then stopped. Nazarra looked over her shoulder at thick sheets of rain just an arm's length away. An invisible wall separated her from the deluge and extended over the Queen's procession. The anomaly perplexed her. No mages rode in the retinue. Who then conjured the barrier? And why did they deem the rain more pressing than the barbarian? If the hidden mage didn't act, the Parthian would surely kill the queen.

To fear is a human trait, and worthwhile. Fear allows for courage, the strength needed to conquer the cowardly emotion. Another lesson. Nazarra's fear came to life. Courage would not will the distance between her and the barbarian to

shrink any faster. The Parthian drew his sword back and
crouched, preparing to leap. Two guards swung chain
hooks in vertical circles as they cross-stepped onto his
flanks. Too far from the fight, she could only watch as the
Parthian re-sheathed his sword and held his arms wide - in-
viting the guards to take advantage.

Don't fall for it, you fools, she thought, but they could no
more read her thoughts than help themselves from such
an opening. Slinging their chains around his arms, the
Parthian laughed. The strength it took to pull the chains
taut looked like such a simple thing for him. The guards
screamed as he yanked both off their feet, stealing their
weapons. Now armed with two steel whips, he struck out,
driving the remaining guards back in stumbling droves.
Akosha never moved.

The queen would be dead in moments. *Why doesn't
she run?* Nazarra kicked the horse again, but this time its
strength gave out. Together they tumbled forward, spilling
onto the street. Nazarra rolled as she hit the ground, and
sprung to her feet, head down in a mad sprint. The Parthian screamed in pain, not rage. Impenetrable black smoke
spilled outward like a pool of blood. It whipped in furious
streaks at the barbarian and his chains, melting the steel
coils wherever they struck. More strands split off, ensnar-
ing the barbarian in great fists. He writhed in their grip,
struggling to break free. Nazarra skid to a stop, her mouth
dropping open in shock. The magic came from Akosha.
*Who taught her to conjure? Why did she learn? The laws of
Ashgra forbid the ruling monarch from using magic.*

Akosha smiled from her seat and opened her fist. The
smoke evaporated, freeing her attacker. Moving in fluid
motion, the Parthian pulled his blade and lunged. A wave

of red energy flared from the Akosha's eyes, wrenching the sword loose while tossing the massive barbarian aside. But the Parthian was of sterner stock. Recovering with a growl and resorting to fists, he charged again. The result of his second attack was the same. The red energy flared, pinning him to the ground. The queen looked bored as he made a third attempt and waved a hand in dismissal.

More soldiers flooded the street, each carrying thick chains used to bind the attacker tight. When they got close, the barbarian made one last attempt. Struggling to his feet, he slammed two men together. The gray masks they wore shattered in sprays of blood. The rest screamed, diving away from the barbarian's reach. Still Akosha did not move.

A deep tickle in her throat grew to a fit of coughing that took Nazarra's feet from under her. Unable to run any further, she watched Akosha step off the pallet and approach the Parthian. The only weapon she'd ever seen her sister wield was a staff, and even that she could barely manage. Armed now with sorceries of unknown origin, Akosha held an open palm before the beast's face and blew. A fine powder swirled through the air, enveloping his head, then disappearing into his wide nostrils. Eyes wide with shock, he scratched at his face. A moment later he fell onto his back.

"Better late than never," Akosha said with a wide grin as she walked beyond the barbarian to where Nazarra had doubled over, coughing blood onto the stone.

"Isn't your duty to warn the queen about these things?" Borismere laughed as he joined her.

"Now dear," the queen replied. "Don't tease my sister, or I'll let her peel the skin from your bones."

Borismere laughed again but slowly stopped, unable to decipher her statement as joke or truth. "Apologies, my love."

"You've looked better, sister," the queen said. Placing the back of her hand against Nazarra's forehead, she pulled it away with alarm. "You're burning up."

Uttering a whispered sound, red light flashed from Akosha's fingertips. The energy wormed its way into Nazarra's pores, digging beneath her skin until it located the itch. A searing pain racked her, and she groaned until the fever fled, pulling with it a sickly green liquid. It levitated in the air until the energy faded, and then it splashed to the cobbles, mixing in with rain water.

"Poison," Borismere said. "Like the Opposition uses. Perhaps that was why your sister was lax in her duty of stopping this creature."

Anger flashed behind Akosha's hazel eyes. A twisted thing of irrational intent. A warning sign that her sister was no longer a sibling sharing secrets in bed - she was a queen. And everyone in a queen's life was capable of betrayal.

"No," Nazarra croaked, trying to find the words to convince her sister she had not been a part of this. No words would come.

"You are trying to kill me? Me?" Akosha screamed. "I am the queen! Not you! I am the anointed queen and you'll never take that from me!"

Sparking energy flared from her eyes, knocking Nazarra back. The last thing she saw before it hit was Borismere's malicious smile as he lifted his mask. He wanted her to see, to know. This was a calculated move. Remove the sister from Akosha's ear to keep it for himself. But how to warn her sister when her loyalty was in question?

"Leave my sight," Akosha yelled. "I will find another to take up your duties." The queen turned away, unleashing a strand of black smoke that plucked the armband off Nazarra's arm. Borismere lowered the mask and joined her, his shoulders shaking with laughter.

Keep smiling, fool, she thought. *I'll hang you for this.*

8

"Dine with the dead and ignore your dread.
Those who understand the value of life will be the richest of all."

- Kui All, Salaz Demomancer

The morning storms passed, leaving behind clear blue skies and the promise of stifling heat. Salaz sprang to life in the aftermath, the residents all experts in maneuvering their lives around the brief and often violent storms. Lord Sem Orsava strolled along the streets of the Meskal, shaking hands with people outside of their homes and shops. In Salaz, the Orsava name was one of long standing. It carried weight enough for Sem to make his own decisions, but not enough to be instrumental in influential ones. A fine trade for Sem. It allowed him to be a man of the people and among them. Dressed in a smart white coat over top long cream robes, he stood out as a beacon of cleanliness in what Grint would describe as a city of dust, mud, and stink. But the Salazians ate it up.

Grint followed a few paces behind, content to watch without being seen. Anonymity was always preferable, but today, dressed in a bright yellow coat with puffed out sleeves and yellow pants, he imagined himself as anything but anonymous. The only contrasting color in the outfit came from the white belt tied snug around his waist. A sorry pair of yellow shoes made from velour flopped along the stone. Flimsy things designed for fashion, Grint felt water seeping through the fabric every time he stepped near a puddle. Perhaps worst of all was the yellow head wrap and white ascot Orsava insisted upon as the finishing touches.

"It's a piece of clothing to hide your face and hair," he'd said when Grint protested. "A disguise against any guards who might recognize you. I doubt your gods would get offended by that practical idea." Orsava didn't know how fickle those gods could be, or he wouldn't have scoffed at Grint's reluctance.

Stop thinking you're so important that the Gods pay you any mind, Hobbe said.

"Shut up, old man," Grint replied beneath the winding yellow fabric.

Orsava turned, having heard the mumbled reply to Hobbe. Grint waved him on. Wearing an armband with Lord Orsava's crest, people assumed Grint to be nothing more than a house guard. The outfit would neither help in a heist or getaway, but meant to portray him as someone who would engage in neither activity. An excellent thing. Along with the citizenry, city guards in tight clumps patrolled the streets in endless succession. Nervous men and women whose eyes darted within their masks and reached for weapons whenever anyone strayed too close.

Not a one gave Grint's loud yellow attire a second glance. In fact, most people they passed wore bright colors. Had this always been the case? Grint couldn't recall anyone's attire standing out in such a grandiose fashion before today. A bard's band of five danced through the street, playing hand-drums slung around their neck. The singer shook rattles, while another blew on wooden pipes. A procession formed behind the band, waving long colorful ribbons and singing along in thick accents and even stranger words.

With the crowd's attention pulled away, Grint walked beside Orsava. "I've been here a moon's turning and never once seen people get this excited about the rain stopping."

"They celebrate the coming of the Cognispyre," Orsava replied. The wind swayed a wooden figure dangling from the shop they passed. The thing was a jumble of twigs woven into form with carved accents and slopped over with a dozen paints. It brought to mind the night he'd returned from some minor larceny. Orsava stood over Angis, directing the manservant while he constructed a similar effigy.

"I liked yours better," Grint said, adjusting the head wrap to let him breathe.

"Each is unique to our grievances and sins against Ashgra. When we burn them, we are giving them to the god for her leniency," Orsava explained. The thought of burning sticks to beg for Hobbe's forgiveness made Grint laugh.

"Is that why everyone's dressed like mummer clowns?" Grint asked, reaching in vain for a spot on his back that itched like the wrath of Astapoor.

"Yes," Orsava admitted. "Just be glad it gives you a good disguise. Which, I might add, you need to stop fidgeting with or you will draw attention." Even as Orsava issued the warning, a group of guards turned the corner. They watched the pair, but kept moving.

"It feels like Angis stitched fire ants into the fabric," Grint said, squirming.

"He may have," Orsava replied with a flat look.

"What? He can do that?" The image of a thousand ants crawling over his skin made him fidget even more.

Orsava slapped him on the shoulder with a laugh, "He cannot. Relax. For someone who has traveled much of the world, you can sometimes be dense."

"In my defense, I rarely stay in one place this long. And what people have figured out how to do might amaze even you." Grint settled down, walking alongside the Lord, miming a protector's stance. "I only keep what I need in my head. Fill it with too much and the other stuff falls out."

"What a ridiculous notion," Orsava grumbled. "I hope that wasn't something your god taught you."

It was, in fact, something Hobbe told him. Wanting to change the subject, Grint whispered, "Why do all the guards look like someone insulted their mothers?"

"Yes," Orsava nodded. "The cobbler mentioned the Parthian ran amok this morning. Slaughtered several guards before attacking Queen Akosha."

"Inno janoi," Grint said a bit too loud.

"Indeed," Orsava agreed. "I don't know if it was of its own accord or through coercion from the Opposition, but that happened. Do you think it will affect what we're planning?"

"It shouldn't," Grint answered. "If this crew you've gathered is worth their salt, we should be well under the notice of the authorities."

"They'll do their job," Orsava replied.

Their destination was a place called the Overlook Cafe at the edge of the Meskal. A fine pastry and beverage cafe, named for its view of the Grand Runway and harbor. Passing under a garden trellis, they entered a secluded sitting area with shaded tables and cushions to sit on. The owner, a short fellow who looked to have a bit of goblin blood in his veins, greeted them warmly and led the pair to what he called, Orsava's usual accommodations - a wooden pergola carved with winding snakes and exotic flowers. Grape vines hung from the latticework, blocking out direct sunlight. The cafe was a regular destination for Orsava and his table sat along the edge, giving them a perfect view of Salaz.

Grint settled onto the cushions around the square table as Orsava removed his hat, handing it to the owner. In the shade, their coverings were no longer necessary. Thinking it best to keep his hair covered, Grint unwrapped the cloth around his face and leaned an arm on top of the wall, staring out while chewing on the end of his tabac pipe. Lightning forked across the sky, deep on the horizon, well beyond the harbor fort and prison island. Waves struck the breakwater, sending sprays of water a hundred feet high.

"Will be a sweltering day," the owner said, hands clasped behind his back.

"Yes, and thick," Orsava answered. "We'll be swimming in soup, as they say."

"May Ashgra be kind and burn the water away," the owner bowed. "May I get your usuals?"

"Please Marcel," Orsava smiled. "But bring extra, we are expecting guests."

"My pleasure," Marcel's eyes brightened at hearing he'd have more customers.

"And some of those lamb legs," Grint said. "Do you have those?" A delectable treat served in a scant few Salazian taverns, Grint did his best to order them whenever the opportunity arose.

"Whatever you desire, I will make," Marcel bowed and excused himself.

"What?" Grint said in response to a look from Orsava. "I like them."

"I don't think you ordered what you think you did," Sem laughed.

"The lamb leg things with the sweet jelly," Grint held his hands together, approximating the size of the food. Orsava laughed again and shrugged, leaving Grint to wonder what the owner would bring.

The rain washed away the worst of the city stink, leaving behind the fresh smell of wet stone. Sunbeams, free of the storm's shackles, began baking piles of wet garbage hidden in gutters or alleyways. Soon enough, the stink would overpower all the rest. Still, one couldn't help but wonder at the beauty of the city. Its stark architecture of sandstone intermixed with wood, the massive crimson statue of Ashgra matched only by the Seastone Tower, the placid water of the harbor, twinkling in the midday sun.

"It is one of the most beautiful things I ever beheld," Orsava looked around, breathing it in. "What about you?"

"Me?" Grint asked.

"What is the greatest thing you have seen in your journeys?" The owner returned with a tray of tall teas and flatbread. Orsava poured a bowl of olive oil for dipping, giving Grint a chance to mull it over.

A girl with short brown hair in wild tangles the color of baked cinnamon. She's sitting on the blanket we laid over a patch of golden grass, reading a book in her simple white dress, with hand-stitched blue flowers and birds in flight around the collar and cuffs. There are grass stains around the hem of the dress and she's tucked her bare feet beneath. As I stare, wondering how she could be in love with a scoundrel like me, the sun sets, silhouetting her in the most perfect light I have ever seen.

"Well?" Orsava said, sipping his tea.

"The pile of gold," Grint laughed. Jessua was his memory and he would keep it that way. But he'd be kry-damned if he wouldn't trade that mountain of gold to spend one more day with her.

"Your dedication and single-mindedness is why I love working with you," Orsava reached over and clapped his shoulder. "Ahh, and here we are! The first of our guests."

An old crone, bent as she walked, thumped the stone with her cane in an over-exaggerated way. Pale-skinned with thinning white hair, she wore no mask or veil over aged skin awash with wrinkles. Her clothes were in little better shape, sewn together in a hundred patches. A purple tongue, dried and cracking, flicked out every few steps, either tasting the air or clearing something unpleasant from her mouth. Grint could not believe this was who Orsava meant, but the crone settled on the cushions, regardless.

"Mrs. Millican, how wonderful to see you again," Orsava beamed, sliding a tea glass toward her.

"Old Millican, I am. Yes, yes, and yes," the crone said in a squeaking voice.

"Exceptional work," Orsava examined her face and hands before easing back. "Exceptional."

"A friend of yours?" Grint asked, losing hope that the crone was a friend and not a thief.

Perhaps the partnership needs rethinking, Hobbe said, agreeing with Grint for once.

"We're supposed to be friends?" A mountain of a man approached and sat beside the old hag. Recognition punched Grint in the gut. The tiger stripe tattoos, cat-face mask, and muscles that had muscles. Reacting as any sane man would in the situation, he drew his dagger. The tiger-man looked at it as something he might use to clean his teeth and held up his hands. "Please, don't scratch me."

"Ah, yes, you've met," Orsava said.

"You know about that?" Grint's jaw dropped open as he scowled, refusing to take his eyes off the tiger.

"Yes," he replied. "I needed to know you were safe. What I didn't tell him to do was throw you down three sets of stairs." It sounded like an argument the two recently had.

"No hard feelings," the tiger said, offering his hand.

"Sure," Grint shook it, returning the knife to his belt with the mental note to buy a much bigger one. "Just don't throw me down anymore stairs."

"I like friends," the old woman said in a wheezing laugh.

"Drop it, Billy. You know the magics give me the greens," the tiger said. After he spoke, the old woman shuddered and split into a hundred unraveling ribbons. The visage dissipated, replaced by a gangly adolescent with long black hair he kept slicked back with oils. His rich brown skin had a pleasant undertone of something cool. Billy, as they called him, also held out his hand.

"The Brothers Tagro," Orsava introduced the pair. "That is Billy you're shaking hands with and his brother Smit."

"Tagro," Grint said looking over at Smit. "Sounds close to tiger. Is that why you have all of that going on?"

"The stripes?" Smit asked in a deep, rumbling voice as he removed his mask. "No, it's because I bite like one." And he flashed sharpened teeth to punctuate the point.

"Lovely," Grint said. "And you, an illusionist?"

"Best in Salaz," Billy nodded.

"Dreaming," his brother countered.

The two bickered as Grint looked away. A flash of burgundy caught his eye. Just a taste of color mixed in the crowd. Was it a simple flight of fancy born from a paranoid mind? Grint couldn't shake the feeling that the woman in the floppy hat lingered nearby. A foolish notion. There was no reason for her to be coy. If she found him, then she would arrest him. But why? If it came down to it, he was an outsider to the city, and the queen put out new proclamations every day, damning those from elsewhere. He could close his eyes and point at one, and that would be enough to hang him.

A woman in pale green robes and a green tunic strolled down the Grand Runway. Did her gaze in their direction last too long? A man leaned casually against a brown mud-slopped building outside the square. He wasn't looking at them, but his demeanor and the way he shifted back and forth while loitering made Grint think of a time when Brotherhood Knights tried to surround his crew in Garth Morray. Grim business. Few of them survived the trap. A short man carrying a sack of herbs stopped beside copper pots, lifting the lids to release great puffs of gray and purple smoke. His eyes drifted up to the cafe three times as he dumped out handfuls from the bag.

"Are we boring you?" Orsava asked, drawing Grint's attention back to the table. Another colorful character joined while he'd been watching the Grand Runway. An outsider like Grint, who sat with his face in the sun. The warm light reflected off inconsistencies with the tone of his skin. Splotches of make-up covered darker markings beneath. Tattoos perhaps, or birthmarks if the man suffered from vanity. At the base of his fingers, in the space between digits, were tiny almost imperceptible webs. Together with a pinched nose that looked difficult to breathe through, Grint guessed he was half-Orrish. Orrish blood never mixed well with human, leaving the offspring spotted like cheetahs.

"Keranue," the man said. "The best cart man in the south of Terragard."

"That's an easy boast," Smit replied without any trace of amusement.

"I ran the Becklamaan Trail in two days," Keranue closed his hands into tight fists with an offended look.

"And I ran the Gaugrau Mountain Pass in one," Billy said, folding a piece of flat bread in half and waving a hand over it. In a matter of moments, it transformed into a tiny horse and cart that raced around the table.

Keranue stabbed a fork in the animated bread, and it fell apart. "Never heard of it."

"Exactly," Billy smiled.

"Enough," Orsava sighed, cooling himself with a blue folding fan. "We're waiting on two more. Let's try not to kill one another before they join."

Even as Orsava spoke, a new patron approached. A rotund man with sweat pouring off a bald head darker even than Smit's. His face widened in a smile each time he took a bite from a pastry wrapped in wax. The paper looked ornamental as frosting spilled over the sides, leaving puddles on the ground, each time he moved it towards his mouth. An oozing slop covered the man's left hand, so he held out his right to the cafe's owner. Marcel looked at his hand, then his pristine stone floor, and refused the gesture.

"Here Brott," Orsava called, waving him to the table.

"Yes, yes, my dear friends," Brott exclaimed as he settled himself on a cushion. "I am happy to be among so many smiling faces." No one at the table wore a smile except Orsava. Perhaps one was more than the usual number of people happy to see him.

Grint didn't need to wait for introductions to figure out Brott's role. Watching the deft wiggle of his fingers as he manipulated the pastry paired with the simultaneous pouring of tea and adding sugar cubes gave that away. This one was a lock pick. Keranue the driver. The Tagro brothers were mage and basher. And the creepy one in the long-beaked bird mask...

Flinching at the unexpected appearance of the final attendee, Grint dropped the tea glass onto his lap. The others hadn't noticed either, and Smit jumped to the side with a high-pitched yelp. Dressed in thick black robes, the dark-hooded figure remained still as everyone noticed their presence. Orsava held a hand over his heart and breathed, then smiled.

"The great Dusk Raven," he said. "You never disappoint."

The Dusk Raven didn't move as the thieves gathered themselves, giving away nothing. Not even their gender. What Grint gleaned from the scant few moments in their presence was what they brought to the team. A sneak thief, creeper, or Johnny Nightfoot in the old terms.

"Why the fan, Sem," Brott asked with a frown. "It is a beautiful day."

"The herbs they burn do not agree with my allergies," Orsava folded the fan, pointing the end at the braziers.

Twitching his nose, Grint noted a sour herb smell overpowering everything else. Now that he was paying attention, he spotted a handful of braziers around the square, all puffing smoke. "What are they for?"

"The swamp lands around the city, the filth in Harborside, the cemeteries beneath our feet," Billy said. "The lords

and ladies of the Upper Crust don't like reminders of us simple folk." Smit hit his little brother on the arm. Hard.

"What? Oh, sorry, Lord Orsava."

"No offense taken," Sem said.

"We're dining over a graveyard?" Grint rubbed the
gooseflesh popping up on his arms and tried not to imagine bodies climbing through Marcel's floor. Instinctively, he
dragged the toe of his boot beneath the table in the shape
of an old rune. Three circles and a square cutting the outer
two in half while framing the center. Protection against the
undead. The symbol wouldn't offer any real shielding unless
drawn in sheep's blood with a piece of dead wood, but the
action itself eased his nerves.

"Relax," Orsava said, leaning back on his cushion. "The
dead are dead."

"You've never met a necromancer," Grint mumbled.

"What?"

"Nothing. Do you still bury people here?" None of the
stones looked new. The mortar centuries old, with bits of
grime in the cracks despite Marcel's cleaning habits.

"No, it is an old practice. The elders created memorial
squares throughout Salaz to act as places of remembrance
without sacrificing the little land we had to build upon."
Orsava directed Grint's gaze to a statue by the arched gate
leading into the cafe. "Lord Hammon, a former engineer of
Salaz. In his visage, those who need to mourn their families
may do so."

"They burn those who die now, dump the ashes in the
Glades for the beasts," Dusk Raven said. The mask muffled
the voice, but couldn't hide that it belonged to a woman.
Grint's tension grew again, wondering if this was Floppy Hat
hiding beneath another disguise.

You'll go crazy if you keep on like this, Hobbe said. Grint had to agree. A healthy amount of paranoia kept one alive, but too much or too little led to death. The happy-place between was a fine line few could walk with any skill.

"We consign our bodies to filth by order of wealthy overlords who keep their boots on our throats," Dusk Raven went on. "And I mean offense," she finished, turning that black mask toward Orsava.

"Yes, well," Lord Orsava said as he cleared his throat. "I assure you, my ashes will end up in the same place as yours."

"Will they?" She asked.

"No," Grint answered for him. "None of your ashes will unless you want them to. In fact, if you stay, you'll be sitting at the top of the overlord pile. Staring down at the Upper Crust from palaces of gold."

The Tagro brothers laughed, a glitter in their eyes. Past them, the herb carrier paused beside the statue with his sack of herbs, tending braziers along the walk. Was he looking in? Faces were hard to read beneath the veils, forcing him to watch their body language. At a card table, Grint relied on minute changes in people's expressions to guess when they were bluffing. Body language was always Veselli's gift. That girl could tell you what someone ate a week ago by how they ran a hand through their hair. Thinking of the old crew, the one he grew up with, always brought with it a pang of sadness. They were all dead now, and the list of those Grint trusted died with them.

Doing his best with what little ability he had in Veselli's territory, Grint judged those passing by and relegated most to low danger status. It was the ones who stopped to mourn at the statue, merchants pushing carts back and forth, and

those sitting on their balconies enjoying an afternoon re-
past that garnered his attention.

The waiter brought out a tray of cups filled with black
coffee, setting them down. "Nothing stronger?" Grint sniffed
the bitter liquid they called coffee in Salaz. He'd be fine with
a dark, Taryn ale or one of their more potent mulled wines.
Orsava nodded when Marcel looked his way.

"Make that two," Smit agreed, pushing his cup aside.

A dozen children ran past, laughing as they flew long
streamers over their heads. True children at play, not the
cast-away urchins watching everything from the shadows. A
woman in pale green robes followed the children. Did her
look in their direction linger? The phantom woman in her
floppy hat haunted him, and he expected her appearance
around every corner. *Life isn't simple for a thief.* And that was
also true. Grint lived most of his by wits, luck, and a mid-
dling ability with a blade - which dug into his side. Adjusting
his belt offered minor comfort as the hilt of the long dagger pressed against him no matter the angle. Giving up, he
took it off, wrapped the leather belt around the sheath, then
placed the whole tangle atop the table.

"I told you there is no need for that," Orsava said, having
made his disdain of weapons known over the many weeks
Grint stayed with him. "These are friends."

"Showing our steel?" Smit asked, putting his scimitar
next to Grint's blade. Billy followed his brother's lead, rummaging through his pockets, he placed objects of varying
design around his plate. A domed piece of copper no larger
than his palm with a blue jewel on top, a stumpy candle that
burned at an angle, a worn piece of parchment, and a thim-
ble. Keranue brandished a stick the length of his forearm
with side grip. Brott had nothing but a loaf of bread in his

pockets, and shrugged as he dropped it, spreading crumbs across the fine tablecloth. The thieves looked over to Dusk Raven, who started producing blades, throwing knives and stars, slapjacks, pigstickers, and long needles.

"That is enough of that," Orsava hissed, raising his voice over the collective laughter of the crew. "Put all that away."

"No need to worry," Billy smiled. "I've got my slider." The young thief patted his hand atop the copper dome. "Anyone who looks our way will find a reason to look somewhere else. A little something I crafted."

"An illusionist," Brott nodded in appreciation.

"And what is the rest of it?" Grint asked, chewing on his pipe.

"This and that," Billy said. "Trade secrets I'm unable to reveal, but I guarantee our voices won't sound like much more than mumbles underwater. It's safe to talk."

"And since it is," Smit said, looking at the cafe's front door, waiting for their ales. "How about we talk about why we're all here."

"For that, I will hand this over to me associate, Grint," Orsava leaned back, working the fan as he closed his eyes.

"Sem called it Ashgra's Fortune," Grint said, striking a match to light the tabac in the pipe. "Maybe that's what it is. Maybe not. All I can say is that it's the biggest pile of gold I've ever seen. And I've robbed dragons."

All eyes remained on him. No one blinked. He'd worked alone for so long he'd forgotten what it felt like to run with a crew. The camaraderie, the mutual interest. *The betrayals*, Hobbe mused, as if happy about it. Grint couldn't fault him. Betrayals were an occupational hazard and even fun as long as no one got killed.

"Enough build up," Brott said, licking his lips. "Where is it and how do we get it?"

"First," Grint said. "I need to know this stays at the table."

Without hesitation, Dusk Raven plucked one of her knives off the table and stabbed the tip through her glove. Droplets of blood bubbled through the leather and she smeared it in the shape of a sun. "Where it concerns gold in significant quantities, my loyalty follows."

"Anyone can draw pretty pictures," Keranue said. "Blood magic without the magic is just a gesture." Dusk Raven pulled the tin of matches out of Grint's pocket with such speed that he wouldn't have believed they were his, had he not won the unique case in a game of cards. Lighting a match, she set the blood on fire.

"Oh dear," the owner said when he saw the fire burning his polished wood table. He set down the ale and doused the flames with a pitcher of water.

"I'll pay for any damages," Orsava said, placating the man with a few plicks. Availing himself of the ale pitcher, Smit filled his cup and then Grint's. His brother drained the water in his and held it out. Smit showed his pearly white fangs, having none of it.

"You're too young."

"I am not," Billy whined.

"Is my offering sufficient," Dusk Raven said, placing her hand gently on Grint's forearm. A soft touch, reassuring and familiar in a way that made Hobbe run for the deeper trenches of his subconscious. The woman hid something in the way she moved. Stunted. Tender. As if she'd been in a fight. The specks of blood spotting the long gray sleeves of her coat came from beneath. Bandaged wounds that had yet to scab. Somewhere Veselli's spirit was watching with great admiration.

"Yes, it works," Grint said. If Orsava trusted her, perhaps he should too. *At least until she betrays us. Or Keranue. Or Brott.* Grint drank, watching the table over the edge of the mug.

Not the Brothers Tagro?

You came back already? Grint thought to the phantom voice, but it didn't respond.

Pulling out the golden coin, he spun it on the surface of the table, letting it go until it fell onto its side and settled face up. Five hands reached toward it, but Dusk Raven got it first. She held it in the sun's light. Grint imagined her marveling at it beneath the mask. After an eternity in her possession, she handed it to Smit. And he to Billy. Then around the table, back to Grint.

"And there's more like this?" Keranue asked.

"Lots," Grint answered.

"You a skilled enough driver to handle lots?" Smit asked.

"Depends how many trips and how much time I have," Keranue answered. Maybe he heard the sarcasm, but it didn't faze him if he did. "And where I'm taking it. Hiding it from the guards will be a chore too."

"What's below us?" Grint asked. "Besides the ashes and bones."

"Dirt," Billy said.

"Beyond that," Brott said, before drinking from the pitcher of ale. Both Grint and Smit gave him a sour look that he ignored. "More below."

"The old catacombs?" Keranue asked. "Can't pay me to go down there. Not even for a mountain of gold."

"Why?" Grint asked.

"Full of Muddlers," Keranue replied, shaking his head. The term held no meaning for Grint, but the others shared a collective shudder at the name.

"Muddlers?" Grint asked, looking for a bit of clarity.

"Ogres," Orsava said.

"Bloody hammich," Grint breathed. "You've got ogres in your sewers?" Thinking back, it had been a long time since he'd last had a run in with an ogre. Tricky beasts. The scary ones were smart, but the dumb ones could be worse. Figuring out their intelligence before one twisted your melon off was a skill few mastered.

"That's a myth. A rumor," Orsava waved it away with the annoyance of a man who didn't put much stock in legends. Grint suspected that going to the lord without the coin would have led to a much different outcome. "What are you thinking, Grint?"

"Where does all the water go?" The reactions around the table ranged from who cares to this man is a moron, but Dusk Raven was the only one to voice it.

"It goes into the harbor," she said.

"Funny," Grint shook his head. "But that's not what I mean."

"Then what?" Smit asked.

"The Glades surround Salaz on three sides, and the entire place slopes down to the water. It's rained twice today, and the water is already gone. I've seen bigger cities turn into mud pits with half the rain." Grint watched a woman in light blue robes and silver mask as he spoke. She walked up the Grand Runway as the wind blew her silk robe. Was it the same woman in green he saw earlier? Long locks of flowing black hair fell around her opaque veil, as common a style in Salaz as the robes. Pausing beside a flower cart, she took her time inspecting the goods. Not unusual, but this was the third time that kry-damn cart passed through the square. Along with two bread makers and a cobbler's cart.

"We're dreaming of gold and he'd besotted with girls on the street," Dusk Raven said, still about the business of putting her many weapons away. "Perhaps you should rethink your decision, Lord Orsava, and leave the thieving to the professionals."

Grint couldn't help but smile. Dusk Raven was already trying to cut him out of the deal. This really would be a fun heist. Orsava didn't share the same sense of personal levity, frowning over the lip of his cup. Given the man's relaxed disposition, it was often easy to forget he was a lord and beholden to the same level of grandiosity as any of his class. Did he believe something distracted Grint? Or was he annoyed that his decision to put Grint in charge came into question?

"As far as I can tell," Grint leaned his elbows on the table, making eye contact with each member of the crew. "I'm the only one at this table who's paying attention."

"How do you figure that?" Smit asked, crossing his arms.

"I've been in Salaz for a moon's cycle. All of you much longer. And yet none of you ever asked where the water goes." Grint turned his gaze back to the Grand Runway, pointing at a pipe jutting from the stone. Water flowed from the open end, spilling into a grated hole to continue its journey to the harbor.

"Congratulations," Brott laughed. "You understand how drains work. If I knew the job required a knowledge of plumbing, I may have passed this opportunity by."

Grint laughed too, a bit too loudly and bereft of any humor. The sound, manic and angry, quieted Brott's laughter. "Anyone else wants to give me the high-hat? No? Good."

Perspiration coated the ale glass, wetting his hand as he picked it up to quench his thirst. When he set it down, he found them all watching him. Good, now they're ready to listen.

"My mentor taught me a lot of things about thieving. Some useful, others not as much outside unique situations, but the first lesson after 'Don't get caught' was to never steal when you can trick the owner into giving it to you."

"You think this lord will part with Ashgra's Fortune?" Keranue said, squinting his eyes in healthy skepticism.

"And what does any of that have to do with the drains?" Billy asked.

"We'll block the drains, break a levee, and flood the Upper Crust. Then smile as he hires us to move that mountain to a safer place." Grint leaned back, resting against the low stone wall overlooking the Runway.

"Flood the Upper Crust?" Dusk Raven said in a high squeak, unable to hide her shock at the idea. "You're a charffing madman."

"Aye," Grint replied with a satisfied puff of his pipe. "And soon, I'll be a filthy rich madman."

9

"When you find a snake in your home you don't burn it down. You buy a cat."

- Knight Monarch Augustum Belandrow

A drunkard leaned against a gas-lamp, belting out a tune he neither knew the lyrics or tune for. Each time he screeched toward a high-note or pre-mature crescendo, the post wobbled, adding a beat that made the cacophony a tad more bearable. As Grint and Orsava passed, he blinked his swollen red eyes and sang all the louder. Then slid down the post, passing out on the cobble street.

"The worst part of the Cognispyre," Orsava remarked. "A brilliant festival, but some don't know when to stop."

"True of festivals anywhere," Grint laughed, looking back at the drunk. He couldn't say he was in much better shape after going cup to cup with Smit and the endless pitcher of ale. "I'd say this one has been tame in comparison. Unless there's a parade in the next few days where everyone gets naked, dances in the streets, and well - you know."

"I would think not," Orsava shook his head, suppressing a shudder. "Can you imagine?"

Grint didn't have to imagine. He'd witnessed such a thing firsthand during a harvest celebration. Followers of Petra could be strange. *And free,* Hobbe chuckled. Before Grint followed his memory too far down the path, Orsava put an arm across his chest, stopping them short.

"What is it?" Grint asked. Orsava hesitated, staring at his manor, a beautiful gem highlighted by Effulg's cobalt light as the moon looked down with half a face. No guards walked the street, nothing appeared amiss. Angis even lit the lower rooms, adding to the brilliant sparkle.

"In your time with me, when have you known Angis to light the lower rooms?" Orsava asked.

Grint failed to see the significance of it. "Are you trying to save money on wax? You can buy all the candles you want soon. You can buy all the candles." The thought made the thief laugh.

"When the Countess Fatime came calling, we entertained her in the lower lounge," Orsava said, ignoring the remarks. "Otherwise, I remain in the upper rooms where the breeze is cool and the view palatable."

Grint nodded, picking up the thread. "Guests. We expecting any Countessessess - ians?"

"No," Orsava rolled his eyes. "I would say these guests are uninvited."

Grint rested his hand on the pommel of his blade. Smit may have laughed at it, but it would do what he needed it to if things got messy. "You need me to sneak in upstairs?" As he asked, he scanned the upper balconies and grimaced.

"Now it is my turn to ask. What is it?"

"The uninvited guests extend to the gardens," Grint said. "Don't look up. There are four of them, trying to stay hidden."

"How can you tell?" Orsava said, looking up despite the warning.

"Wearing black in blue moonlight." Hobbe hated the reliance on black. *How often are you in pitch-black conditions? Wear something brown or deep blue.*

"A trap to kill us?" Orsava's voice quavered, pitching at the end.

"If someone wanted to kill you, is there another room Angis would light?"

"We've never needed such signals or subterfuge," Orsava stammered.

They continued walking at a slow pace, Grint adopting the stumble of a drunk, leaning his weight on Sem. The lord understood and played along, but Grint could feel his fear in the soft shake of his chest. *Four on the roof, but none below.*

None you see, Hobbe countered. *Perhaps they wanted to reveal the ones up top so you stayed blind to the killers below?*

"Was there anyone who declined your invitation today?" Grint whispered, peering into the space between homes as they passed. Nothing moved but the rodents and mungles.

"No," Orsava answered. "Has one of them betrayed us?"

"All of them will try by the time we're done," Grint said, earning an irritated grunt.

"Shall we spring this trap then?" Orsava asked as they approached his door. Turning away now would draw whoever this was into the streets, but they had height advantage and could rain down whatever Hells of Astapoor they wanted.

Grint gave him a nod and straightened up, drawing the dagger and sliding it into his puffy sleeve. "I better not die in this ridiculous outfit, Sem."

"I hope we don't die at all," he replied.

Two steps from the door, it opened, silhouetting Angis in the warm candlelight within. The manservant looked well and in good spirits, wearing a gracious smile for his lord and guest. And that alone alarmed Grint. Angis tolerated him but that didn't extend to welcome home smiles.

"Keep your blades close," the manservant whispered to Grint.

The parlor, as Orsava referred to it, was a small sitting room to the left of the entrance. Two lounging couches faced one another over a mahogany table used for serving fruits and refreshments. A bowl of green grapes, half-eaten, sat in the center, surrounded by four silver goblets and a carafe of red wine. Three were in use, but only two people waited within.

"Mordechai," Orsava said with a nod to the first. A thin, but muscled man in a sleeveless shirt, the one named Mordechai looked like an over-worked dock-hand. Jaundiced eyes stared at them beneath bushy eyebrows showing the signs of age. The clothes he wore were simple, aged, and utterly anonymous. His only defining feature was the hint of a tattoo he revealed whenever he shifted positions.

Beside Mordechai, a man with smooth black skin and trimmed hair with highlights of blue bounced his knee with an impatient air. Gaudy blue, red and yellow striped robes made the Opposition armband of blue with white circles almost disappear. "Prince Mikil, a great honor. I was not aware you and the Harbormaster were friends," Orsava said, offering a bow, snapping his finger to alert Grint to do the same.

"Not a friend," Mordechai coughed.

"I am friends with every citizen of Salaz," the prince said, accepting the gracious bow from Lord Orsava. "And that is my associate, Tobor."

Tobor lingered in the corner, hidden in the dark recess behind the door. Hearing his name, he stepped toward the couch. Dressed in an equally garish set of robes, Tobor looked like a typical bodyguard, scowling with the hope he looked menacing, but scared of his own shadow.

"We didn't catch your associate's name, Lord Orsava," Mordechai said, sipping the wine. The rich color stained his lips and that of the Opposition men. They were all drinking. *So, who is the fourth cup for?*

"That is Grint," a woman said as she stepped through the servant's entrance. Earthy-skinned, she dyed her hair a myriad of shades ranging from red to green. No wine stained her lips. Smart enough to mistrust being served. Smarter than the others. She wore an armband Grint hadn't yet seen but heard tell of. Gray with the hint of a blue handprint. *Thieves Guild. Blue Hands.*

"The son of Blue Fingered Hobbe, God of Thieves," she continued, giving Grint a deep bow.

"You're a dennel?" Orsava asked, the color in his face draining.

"Son is an honorary," Grint said. "It's more of an adoption. Sometimes feels like an abduction." Needing another drink, Grint poured himself a cup of wine and drained it, then poured another. Meeting someone in Salaz who knew more about him than they should made him want to run far and fast. Not even Nazarra knew these details.

"I hope the manservant didn't poison that," the woman laughed.

Grint smirked and looked over his shoulder at Angis, who shook his head that it was not. "And it's the quality stuff. You're missing out."

"Racko, Master of the Thieves' Guild," Orsava said with no trace of humor. "To what do I owe the honor of so many important faction leaders visiting on an unimportant evening?"

"Enough of this proper halfling snot," Mordechai growled. "I told you he'd be coy about it."

"Mordechai," Mikil started, but reconsidered under the smoldering glare of the thin man.

"What my esteemed friend is trying to say," Racko continued, "is that we are aware you're putting a job together."

"A colossal job," Mordechai cut in.

"Yes," she said, displeased at the interruption. "My assumption is that it was a simple oversight. Otherwise, we would have had a seat at the table."

"Job?" Orsava asked as Angis produced a chair for him to sit on. "When I've had a job worthy of including you, I always have. What makes you think now is any different?"

"It seems not everyone in your little crew is as independent as you may believe," she said, stroking his cheek with the backs of her fingers.

As Orsava stood to object, Mordechai slammed a fist on the table, knocking over the goblets. Streams of red wine trickled over the edge, spilling onto the cream carpet. Orsava sighed at the loss of what was certainly another family heirloom. Racko whistled to calm the anger brewing and smiled a bit too large.

"We're here for friendly palaver, Lord Orsava," Racko sat on the arm of the couch, motioning for the wine pitcher. Prince Mikil leaned forward, handing it to her. "Thank you," she said, tipping the carafe onto the cushions and carpet. "If we can't be friendly, I'll get nasty."

"Enough," Sem shouted.

"Enough?" Racko smiled with the knowledge of someone who'd won.

"I will bring you in, but understand we don't know yet what we have," Orsava stared at the stains, water blooming in the corners of his eyes. "Your cut will be commensurate with what your respective guilds bring to the table."

Mordechai threw his head back and laughed. "The fool thinks we're here to negotiate."

"Then what do you want?"

"If you had come to us first, we could have negotiated," Racko set the carafe down, crossing her arms as she spoke. "That time has passed."

"Now you'll be lucky if we let you keep any of it," Prince Mikil threw his cup onto the rug. The gesture seemed like overkill to Grint. The rug was garbage at this point.

"Why would we steal something if you're just going to take it?" Grint asked. "Go get it yourself."

"You don't want us to hurt your friend, you'll do what we say," Mordechai pointed a bony finger at Orsava. Confused by the remark, he turned toward Angis, who looked none the worse for wear.

"Not him," Racko smirked. "Man-servants are replaceable. But dogs? They're family."

"Newman," Grint screamed, pushing past Angis to take the stairs two at a time. For the first time in the last two years, his heart pounded against his chest and throat closed tight to the point of choking. The staircase twisted in dizzying circles until he feared he'd fall up or down - who knew which was which.

Barging into Orsava's office, he screamed the dog's name, "Newman!" But the bulldog didn't come.

"The dog is fine," Racko said. "As long as you do what we say."

The knife slid out of his sleeve and into his hand. Grint spun, releasing it. It was something he practiced on the odd night, sitting alone in a rented room, on a rooftop watching a mark, or with a makeshift shiv in a prison cell. He'd become adept at it, wasting no movement or motion in his execution. Racko's smile faded as the blade flew toward the space between her eyes. There were many ways to avoid a knife in the face, and she must have practiced one as often as Grint did in throwing. She leaned easily to the side, swiping her hand in a half-moon gesture to knock the blade aside. As it bounced along the floor, Grint ran at her, fist cocked back.

Racko made a ball and chain of rough iron appear from the back of her coat and dropped the end onto the top of her foot, kicking it toward him. It was Grint's turn to dodge. His feet skid as he stopped his momentum to lean under the metal ball. Racko snapped it back quickly, using her foot to spin it round and wrap Grint's ankles. Off-balance, he got a foot out of the way before she yanked him onto his back.

Grint hit the floor and rolled as the metal ball struck where his gut would have been. The lost knife was within arm's reach and he rolled again as he heard her speak. "Why is Orsava's dog so important to you?"

Popping to his feet, the knife firmly in his grasp, Racko rolled her head back in frustration before whipping the chain round again. As she let it loose, Grint rushed, feeling the coils wrap around his waist, but that didn't matter. As he moved forward, he created slack in the chain she couldn't keep up with. A singular desire to drive the dagger into her chest, combined with a dizzying blood lust, overtaking rational thought. Grint's sole desire was to drown anyone who might hurt Newman in an ocean of their own blood.

At the last, Racko snapped three links tight between her hands, catching the tip of the blade in one and twisting it aside. "Stop, you fool," she breathed.

Grint rammed his head forward, catching her on the bottom of the chin. There was a wordless grunt as she fell toward the wall, but used her backward momentum to kick both feet into his chest. Grint churned his legs, but she won out, shoving him back to the floor.

"Enough," she coughed, wiping blood from her jaw.

"Give me back my kry-damned dog," Grint said as he picked himself up.

"Your dog?" She asked, sounding truly confused. "Orsava's dog, you mean?"

"My dog," Grint growled.

"Bloody, charffing, ip-swatted, drangoes," she shouted as she stalked back and forth. "I didn't know. I wouldn't have let them take him if I knew."

"Just go get him and we'll call it even," Grint felt a bruise rising on the back of his head from the fall. "Bruises for a bloody lip."

"It's not that simple," she said, bracing herself for another outburst.

"Make it simple."

"Mikil's Opposition has him," she said. "And he won't care who the owner is."

"Why do you?" Grint asked, unstopping a glass bottle of Pandinni Rum from the islands. He held it out to her, but Racko shook her head. Grint took a slug from the bottle and set it back on the shelf. The headache coming to life would need a little help to go away.

"My intention was never to cut you out," she said, dabbing her lip with a white kerchief. "You were always getting your cut, plus mine."

"Yours?" Grint asked. "Why?" But before she answered, he laughed and decided he needed another drink. "Hobbe. You want to meet Hobbe."

"Having the God of Thieves as a patron would bring an important level of legitimacy to my organization," she said.

Grint could tell her the truth, that Hobbe wouldn't care about her or her guild. The God would use and discard the lot of them to add one bauble to his depth-less vault of treasure. But that wouldn't bring Newman back, So he lied. "Sure, you make sure I get the bulldog back in one piece and I'll point you in the right direction."

Racko held her hand out, and they shook on it. "No fight for Lord Orsava's share? A cold draft of air is how I'd describe you."

"He's an adult," Grint replied. "I'm sure he can take care of himself."

"You're a scrapper," she laughed, examining her battle wounds. "Is that how you killed the God of Murder?"

"Killed? Inno janoi," Grint laughed as they walked downstairs. "Is that what they say? Trust me, no one has figured out how to kill one of them yet." And Grint prayed the God of Murder never heard that tale or he might come back to settle things.

"Are we done here?" Mordechai said, waiting by the front door. "The stink of entitlement this high in the city makes me sick. I want to leave."

"I have what I came for," Racko said. "And we all should have the same understanding of how to proceed. Let's not meet under these circumstances again."

"We'll be watching and waiting," Prince Mikil said, giving Orsava an impolite tap on the cheek and laughing about it with his cohort as they stepped outside.

"I will look after him," Racko added before closing the door.

The intruders gone, Angis flew into a weeping rage at the state of the parlor rug and couches. Sem did his best to calm the man, but the words had no effect. Grint didn't care about rugs. All he could think of was his dog in the hands of poisoners.

If Racko can't deliver on her promise, then I swear I will get Hobbe to curse this place so thoroughly that stealing a glance will get you a dance on the long rope.

"I'm sorry," Orsava said, placing his hand on Grint's shoulder.

"I'll get him back," Grint said.

"Yes, well, yes of that I have no doubts, but I am sorry I did not vet the crew in a more thorough fashion." Orsava sounded closer to tears than Grint felt.

"Don't worry about that," Grint said, watching Angis try to clean the rug.

"I am worried, and will find the culprit," Orsava said and noticed the cleaning. "Angis, leave it. It's not even the real rug. I stored that in the attic years ago. Filthy thieves everywhere. Present company excluded."

"I'm filthy too," Grint chuckled, ashamed to be laughing at a time like this. "And I already know who did it," Grint said.

"Who?" Both Sem and Angis gave him their full attention.

"Me," Grint said, feeling tired enough to sleep for a week. He took three steps toward the stairs when he heard the pewter cup slam on the floor.

"Now wait one moment," Orsava shouted. "Is this another of your poorly timed attempts at humor?"

"My humor is spot on," Grint shouted back. Sem's skin paled as he sat on the couch, slumping his head back with a lengthy sigh. The manservant pulled a fan from his coat and waved it, but Orsava would have none of it and knocked it away. The admission was not at all what he expected.

"I've tied myself to a madman," Sem said, holding a hand over his eyes.

"It's not madness," Grint replied, stepping back into the room.

"No?" Orsava sounded strangled as he spoke. "What I know is that you plan to flood the Upper Crust. A place where many friends live, might I point out. And the one thing you said you wanted to avoid when I put the crew together is the first thing you do. Bringing in the guilds? Utter madness."

"They would find out," Grint said. "Eventually, they would." He almost sat on the wine-soaked couch, but chose instead to lean against a table-looking thing by the hearth. Orsava would know what it was, but furniture never brought much value in a robbery, so Grint never learned the fancy names. Now wasn't the time to try. Exhausted by the day, and sore from the fight, all Grint wanted was a night's sleep.

"Would they?"

"Yes," Grint held up his hand before Sem said anything more. "I've done enough of these to know. This way I take away the surprise of the crew bringing them in. Now I control what they know and when they know it."

"You planned for them to take the dog?" Orsava dropped his hand, a look of horror in his eyes.

"No, that was unexpected and there will be blood if they harm him." Grint felt the tightness in his chest grow.

"No more surprises or secrets," Orsava said, leaning forward. "I think it's time you tell me the plan in all its ugly detail."

"I will," Grint said, rubbing the redness in his eyes. "In the morning. I need to sleep."

"Very well," Orsava said.

Grint excused himself, walking up the stairs with a weight on his shoulders. Orsava had given him a comfortable guest room on the third floor with a garden terrace and rotating fan on the ceiling that turned when the wind blew a contraption on the roof. The soft feathered mattress hugged him, and he kicked his boots off, too tired to remove the rest. In the moments before sleep came, a thought, unbidden, came to mind.

If I'm to tell Orsava a plan, I need to come up with one first.

Sleep would need to wait another night.

10

"Have you heard tell of the ship known as the Hermitage Roll? No? Finest black flag to sail the Krypholos Ocean and all three seas. Faster than an Islander Sloop. Stronger than an Orrish Destroyer, and hardier than an Imperial Man O'War. Though... I may be a bit biased.

- Captain Gaustauss

In the depth of night, while Effulg sank toward the western horizon and the shard-moon, Nacinth chased after her, a ship of ill-renown drifted into Salaz Harbor. The sentries atop Fort E'lo'Prakk's ramparts watched it pass. A beast with five masts, the unknown ship sat high in the water, its cargo light. Barnacles climbed the sides of its gray hull, and if you were close enough, you might notice that the space between planks ran wet with blood.

Mordechai stood on the rooftop balcony of his home, taking deep breaths of dank harbor air. He sipped a bitter spirit as he watched the ship. The hour late for libations, but the proceedings of the night left his stomach in a state of disarray. Bullying a lord provided a bit of sport to ease the mind, but the revelation that his thief was beholden to a god ruined it. Mordechai wore his mask during the day like a good Salazian, but didn't believe in Ashgra. That faith shattered long ago. But the outlander gods and the stories he'd heard of them? Those were too real. Maybe they weren't gods, but they'd walked Terragard for thousands of years and wielded enough power to be whatever they desired. Adopted or not, this Grint character was son to one.

Spitting off the roof, Mordechai regretted mixing the lord's wine and the sour spirit. The soft shuffle of feet and earthy smell of mud announced the fortunata's arrival. Some called her a salt witch, but that name fit her as ill as a noble's title. Crazed, unstable beings, salt witches wielded the deadliest magics. A fortunata looked the part, but their deep wisdom set them above the base creatures.

"It is late," he said.

"A dream of water flooding the city streets woke me. Ill omens atop of ill omens." Her voice crackled like burning parchment.

He'd come outside to calm himself in the sea air and perhaps even find reassurance that they hadn't rushed their earlier meeting. What he found was a black ship and prophecies of destruction. He'd never turned his back on the old ways of life in the Glades. A fortunate thing. So few in the city paid heed to portents of disaster.

"What would you have me do?" He asked.

"I do not know yet," the fortunata answered. "The dream is too fresh. I must return to the Glades and consult."

"Why tell me of a problem with no solution?"

"My visit is not about dreams," she said, stepping to the edge of the balcony. "You asked me to come. I am here."

"I did no such thing," Mordechai said.

The old woman grumbled and spit in her hand. She held it in the wind as the mucus slid down her palm. The trail would reveal truths Mordechai failed to comprehend.

"Odd," she said after a time of silence. "The echo of my meeting with you has changed. There has been a divergence."

Ill omens and a divergence. *Tonight is one best forgotten*, Mordechai reasoned. "Diverging visions aside, why did I invite you?"

"Yes, that," she said, reaching deep into the torn pocket on her tattered robe. Things clattered as she rooted around, and a night crawler slithered up her forearm, disappearing under her sleeve. What she found and presented was an unremarkable thing. No bigger than a slug, the black stone sat in her grimy palm. The longer Mordechai looked, the more it drew him to do so. Leaning close, he noticed the subtle vibrations of the thing. If he touched it...

"Fool," she spat on her hand, forcing Mordechai back. "You'll wake it."

"What is it?" He asked, both curious of its origin and why she would think he would need it.

"In full form, an Ochus." The fortunata wrapped it in a stained cloth, handing it over. "In this state, it is an Atchuous Seed."

"Why do I want it?"

"You don't," she said. "He does."

Mordechai knew better than to ask, but opened his mouth to do just that. "Sir?" A mangy youth named Karel whispered from the darkened doorway.

"Speak," Mordechai commanded.

"There is a man here to see you," Karel said.

"Man," he said with distaste. "I am a prince."

"Haven't I seen enough of you," Mordechai groaned as Prince Mikil sauntered onto the over-crowded balcony. He'd stepped out for a moment of peace and now found the quiet sanctuary to be quite the opposite.

"I would speak to you," Mikil said, hands clasped behind his back. Even two tolls from dawn, the man dressed as if he attended celebrations. "In private."

"Karel will leave us," Mordechai said. "The fortunata will remain."

The old woman nodded. Shuffling to the side, she plopped down beside a spider web and giggled like a child. Mikil's brow furrowed and mouth worked in masticating rhythm as he contemplated the choice of staying or leaving. Mordechai hoped he would leave.

"We need to discuss tonight's events," Mikil said, moving to a spot that blocked his view of the fortunata.

"That ship troubles me," Mordechai said of the boat dropping its anchor in the harbor. "What do you know of it?"

"You are the Harbormaster," Mikil said. "I leave the province of boats and fishing to you."

"You want something," Mordechai said, knowing he was to give the seed to the prince. The dark thing vibrated through the rag, clutched tight in his hand. In a single moment, Mordechai understood it to be a thing of overwhelming evil, and he was to hand it to this pompous fool?

"Yes," Mikil said. "To talk about tonight."

"What is there to discuss? The thief will steal something to make us rich." Mordechai couldn't help but feel cynical about the deal and what the aftermath of it might look like.

Mikil laughed, "Which thief? The one we can't trust, or the one we know we can't trust?"

"She is not your problem," the fortunata said, spitting in her hands before slapping them together. The soft, wet sound made the Harbormaster nauseous. "The other dances in a meadow of rain, supping on the breath of the endless sky."

"Cryptic," Mikil said, keeping his eyes away from her. A few hands moved about the deck of the ship, fleeting shadows who disappeared once they finished their jobs. "Wherever did you find her?"

"Mock not the fortunata," Mordechai said, rolling up his sleeve to show a long scar under his arm. "The penalties are harsh."

"Yes, well," Mikil said. "My humble apologies."

The fortunata went back to the spider, cackling as it climbed from one hand to the other. "Her warnings are wise to heed."

"Was that what it was? A warning?" Mikil asked.

"I'm tired," Mordechai cut in. "What is it you want from me?"

"Out," Mikil said. That surprised him. Of all the paths the conversation could have traveled down, that statement sat at the end of an overgrown trail. "I made a bargain intending to sit on the throne. The one I bargained with is not living up to their end, and I fear looking to remove me."

"If you want out, then leave," Mordechai grumbled. "Why tell me?"

"I," the prince paused, searching for his words as he leaned over to look at the fortunata. "I know you are from the Glades. And what that means."

"You want black magic," Mordechai said. "Doesn't your sun god frown on such things?"

"Our sun god," Mikil corrected, assigning the title of follower to the Harbormaster without care. "I would prefer not to perform the magic."

"I have what you desire," Mordechai said, feeling the vibrations grow once again.

"My portion of the thieves' loot. I don't care what it is or how much." Mikil slammed his fist on the balcony's rail, shaking the old shanty from foundation to roof. "They will not remove me from my coup. The throne will be mine."

"Hold out your hand," Mordechai said, showing him the dirty rag. Mikil smiled, lifting his left hand. As he placed the rag in his palm, a hand, old and gnarled, snatched his wrist. Neither heard the fortunata approach, but she locked him in a hold that looked both painful and impossible to break.

"What I give will bring the result you seek," she said, her voice powerful. "Add it to her drink. That is all you need to do."

"Yes, but," Mikil said as he unwrapped the rag.

"Fool," the fortunata hissed. "Touch it not. Keep it wrapped until use. That is all."

Mikil nodded and rubbed his wrist. The bruise she left would turn ugly by morning. A reminder for the prince of what power lay beyond these fragile walls.

"You may go," Mordechai said when Mikil lingered. The fool wanted to speak more, but now was not the time. Never was the time, but with him on the throne, that would be impossible.

"Our words are a binding agreement," the prince said, unable to remove his eyes from the rags. Karel waited in-

side the door to escort him out. A night bird cried from
its roost on the cliffs. The fishmonger contract to keep the
stone clear remained unsigned, and the birds were becom-
ing a nuisance to the fishermen. After the Cognispyre was
the only response he'd received from the palace.

*When their bellies go hungry, they will learn who rules this
city.*

"Ogg Willy said it's called the Hermitage Roll," the fortunata said, pointing a bony finger at the boat.

"Banshee's balls," Mordechai growled. Such frightful
news deserved a backhand or whipping, but delivering
such to the fortunata would prove fatal for his hopes of a
long life.

The Hermitage Roll was the nastiest of the black flags
since the Ballyhoot disappeared a good ten years past. A
death dealer. A dream breaker and widow maker. Word
was it scuttled the latest reinforcements from the Dhog
Empire. Then stole a year's worth of tabac on its way to
the Sandy Kingdoms. What was it doing here, berthing in
Salaz's eel infested waters?

Anchored beside the cliffs, it waited like a ghost ship.
No one came ashore. Not a soul moved on deck once the
sails dropped. The fortunata dreamed of floods as the
black flag arrived. And now he'd handed over a creature of
malignant power to an imbecile.

"Who is Ogg Willy?" Mordechai asked, but the fortunata had gone. By morning she would have traveled a hundred miles to sit upon a log in the most desolate stretches
of the Glades.

Parthian barbarians and a thief bringing sun-facer gods
to Salaz. Mordechai tossed his cup over the side, smiling at
the sound of it shattering. Destruction, when controlled,

was a thing of beauty. Mikil on the throne would not be the best thing for the fishmongers. Leaving the queen there was little better. The prince revealed a third option in his blathering. A partner willing to cut him out of the design. Mordechai very much wanted to meet this person.

11

*"When you don't know who to trust, make certain
you trust yourself."*

- Blue Fingered Hobbe

Gnawing on a crawberry, Grint walked beside Lord
Orsava, amused at how easily the two swapped moods in
a day. Just yesterday, Grint fidgeted with his yellow robes,
but today it was Orsava who writhed in the grip of nervousness. The sweetness of the tropical fruit danced through
his mouth with each bite. Scraps of tile fell from rooftops,
shattering on the stone street. A scrawny mungle hopped
from one roof to the next, eying the snack while streams
of drool dangled from its flat mouth. Orsava's nervousness
escalated as he shook bits of tile from his hat.

"I can't abide those things," Orsava said as he waved
the fan, the silk fluttering in quick snaps. The sound startled the mungle. It snarled as it darted off, the click of its
claws receded into the sounds of the city. Both knew it
would return in short order.

"I'd be angry if I had wings and couldn't fly." Grint spit a fat seed out of his mouth. They were the worst part of the fruit. Hard like stones and capable of shattering a tooth.

"Hurry and finish," Orsava rolled his eyes as Grint took a messy bite.

"I'm enjoying it," Grint mumbled through a mouthful of pulp, the yellow juices running through the stubble on his chin. Wiping the fluid with his sleeve, he'd only eaten half the fruit. A shame to waste. Crawberries weren't local to Salaz. Nothing sweet grew in the Glades, so the city relied on imported delicacies from the Sandy Kingdoms or further along the coast into Sangantide. Orsava mumbled something about Angis having to scrub the stains out of the shirt, a garment loaned to Grint, but such was the cost of business.

*****

The events of the prior night remained on the forefront of their minds as Grint stomped down the main staircase. He hadn't even yawned before Orsava pulled him into the study. As promised, while they dined on a bit of flat bread and honey, Grint relayed the plan. Most of it; The flooding, bringing in the guilds, walking away with the gold handed to them. It was the bits that Orsava didn't know that shook him. The lord coughed and pushed aside the grapefruit he'd been working on. Choosing instead to pour a glass of wine. Alcohol before the high-morning bells wasn't normal behavior for the lord. It said a lot to Grint, that he didn't fetch Angis to pour it for him.

"I wish now that I didn't know," the man said as he refilled his glass, holding it out to Grint as an afterthought.

"You needed to know at some point," Grint said, shaking his head at the wine. Early was never too early for a drink, but today promised to be a lengthy one and he needed to keep his head clear. "This isn't for the crew to know. I'll bring them in when I need to."

"Do I get special treatment because we're friends?"

"In my experience, a friend isn't a friend until they take an arrow for you," Grint leaned back, peeking through the blinds. One of Racko's Blue Hands sat in the shade of a chimney across the street. If she wanted Hobbe to take her seriously, she needed to do a better job of training her people to hide themselves.

Or perhaps that's the decoy, and the real tail is where you will never see, Hobbe whispered.

"If they take an arrow, don't they end up dead?" Orsava asked before Grint answered the phantom voice.

"Yes," Grint mumbled. A man walked along the street. Dressed in high-born robes, the wiry fellow with a sparkling red mask looked out of place - as if he were attending a ball and invited no one else. *Another spy? One of Floppy Hat's people? Or something to do with the kry-damned festival?* He felt somewhat relieved when the man bowed to a young lady whose flowing black hair bounced as she stepped out to meet him. Together the couple walked off, but Grint made careful note of the matching blue robes they wore.

"Must be lonely," Orsava said, sounding legitimately sad. "Living a life where all your friends end up dead."

"That's why I don't make friends," Grint tensed as he watched a woman in a large hat pass by. An older woman who didn't wear a mask. *Not her.*

"I had hoped you'd considered me among your friends by now," Orsava said, putting the wineglass down. "Now

I'm not sure I want to be."

"Probably wise on your part. Unless you enjoy arrows."
The woman in the hat walked with an aged limp. As if life
had gotten to her in a hurry. She stopped at the tree Grint
hid beneath two nights past, smiling at the manor. *Not a
woman. The bloody kid and his illusions...*

*****

After breakfast, they strolled through Salaz Plaza so
Orsava could visit a tailor and obtain festival robes. While
waiting outside, Grint availed himself of a crawberry from
a passing vendor. The offer of a robe stood, but Grint had
enough of that tomfoolery for one job. A loose white shirt,
brown leather pants, and the tricorn hat worked. A passing
local shook their head at the loitering sun-facer. *Maybe a
mask too*, he thought. *Something with a dragon.*

*Why don't you paint Ashgra's face on it and get their blood
boiling?* Hobbe and Grint laughed together, imagining the
salty reactions.

From the Plaza, they trekked across to Bushan, where
Orsava promised an even better view of the city. The people in this district didn't move out of the way or flock to Orsava's side the way those in the Meskal had. Here, narrow
streets overflowed with travelers from all over; merchants,
tradesmen, and sometimes mercenaries looking for work.
Few wore masks, and all the shops catered to sun-facers.
This amused Grint as Bushan was closest in proximity to
the foot of Ashgra's statue.

Grint struggled with walking around so openly. The
guards stopped looking his way, but someone had to have
his description. The net they'd tried catching him in in-

volved too many people, and those in authority didn't just give up. Orsava believed it had to do with the Parthian and the attempt on the queen's life. Whatever the reason, Grint turned every corner expecting to find Floppy Hat. An endless succession of scenarios involving her rolled through his brain. The guards may have moved on, but she was still out there - hunting him.

"What's the scariest thing you can think of?" Hobbe once asked.

"Standing on a needle above the clouds," Grint answered.

"Good," the god said. "Think of that and the other stuff won't be as scary."

Kry-damn bad advice, Grint thought as they passed a merchant selling brown face wraps. Grint stopped to buy one, breathing a little easier with a bit of anonymity. Until he met Floppy Hat again, he'd take the respite and get down to what needed doing. Stealing a mountain of gold and getting away with it.

This was a job even Hobbe would love - if he'd come up with it. Surely, he'd brow-beat Grint for daring to contrive such a plot. *It's too much. Take what you need to get you by. You'll get yourself killed!* Such needling and judgment from the god drove them apart years ago, and their relationship sat on rocky ground to this day.

No, he thought to himself. *It was what he let happen to Jessua.* Perhaps, but what if it was more? Grint wasn't one for deep introspection and let the thought drift away as he took his last bite of the crawberry. A quick toss of the core in the air sent the mungles into a frenzy. A fat mungle stepped on another's head to snatch the prize. The creature squealed seeing the pack descend on it, each looking to steal the fruit.

Walking beneath a simple archway spanning the space between two buildings, the cool shade offered a moment of relief. On a day like today, the sun beat down and wouldn't stop until dusk. Beyond the arch stretched a spacious park. An oddity considering the Bushan's crowded nature. Tucked behind two gray buildings, the overlook extended on an outcropping of stone. Paved with dusty yellow stones, the park had once been a spot of noble beauty, but fell into disrepair. Old roots and sprouting weeds stuck up from a multitude of cracks. A crumbling, dry fountain sat to the right, surrounded by rotting benches. Those who came to the overlook milled around, waiting their turn at the railing and the breath-taking view. Orsava described the overhang as a four-story drop. Seeing it for himself, Grint's stomach turned.

What's the scariest thing you can think of?

Shut. Up. Grint shouted at the voice.

Pulling his foot clear of a root, Grint noticed worn etchings in the stonework at their feet. The Overlook was another of Salaz's many graveyards, a realization that sent further chills up his spine. Every city had their own ways of disposing of bodies. Until today, Parameer's sunken crypts had been the oddest he'd encountered. But burying the dead beneath public squares and walking over them while on your afternoon stroll was something else.

Enough spirits lingering here to rival Zorn's army, Hobbe commented.

"Or make a Salt Witch dance," Grint replied.

"What's that?" Orsava asked. Grint gave a half-hearted shrug and shook his head. "Well then, here we are." They stepped to the edge of the railing. Orsava leaned on the wrought-iron with casual grace, but Grint lingered a step back. He'd fallen from worse heights and lived, but why tempt Lorelai?

"The only view more magnificent is from the queen's balcony in the Seastone Tower," Orsava said, looking at the glimmering blue jewel rising above the harbor.

"I'll take your word for it," Grint replied. His mouth had gone bone dry. Looking around the park for a drink, he saw the posted notice. Not a single merchant's cart or performer could enter the park. Chased away by another of the queen's edicts. "Unless you want me to steal her crown."

"Not today," Orsava laughed and looked around with a guilty smirk. "Come, you can see better at the edge."

"Why are we here? I'd much rather take in a view of some dancers or find the bottom of an ale keg." Sweat slicked his palms and he wiped them on the sides of his pants where Orsava wouldn't see.

"Perhaps for a moment of beauty," Orsava replied. "But also to have a frank discussion about our plan."

"Would be better at your manor," Grint wasn't only nervous about the heights. For the plan to work, everything had to go smoothly. Even now he counted six watchers in the crowd. The couple on the shaded bench pretending to have a lover's quarrel were Racko's Blue Hands. The three stalwart men in plain green masks and gray robes were Fishmongers. And the woman pretending to watch clouds was Prince Mikil's for sure. Over the course of their walk, he'd seen no less than twenty others in blue and white armbands who could just be supporters or spies for the Opposition.

"Perhaps," Sem said. "But there are ways to listen even there. I can make that argument about anyplace, I suppose, but few wear masks on the overlook. Easier to spot an eavesdropper."

"Frank, as in how do I feel about the crew you've assembled?" Grint said, raising his voice to match Orsava's.

"More about what you need to make this happen," Orsava said, fumbling with a pouch of tabac to fill his pipe. Grint helped steady him and then plucked his own pipe from a pocket.

"It's okay," Grint whispered. They removed their own veil and mask and lit the pipes.

Orsava recovered well, and the pair settled in, puffing wispy clouds of smoke. Grint leaned against the rail. His mind wandered to the job, forgetting for the moment his aversion to heights. "First thing will be city worker armbands. A warehouse by the harbor. Carts. Lots of carts."

"I have an old business license we can use once Angis forges unfamiliar names." The pipe dropped from Grint's mouth, and he caught it before it toppled over the edge. *Angis is a forger?* A newfound respect grew for the manservant.

"... I know a warehouse, one of Mordechai's," Orsava continued without seeing Grint's surprise. "The Fishmongers run protection on the businesses there, and they need to make themselves useful if they want their cut."

"Good," Grint said.

"I have to ask, are we planning to cheat the guilds at some point?" Orsava still looked less than thrilled with Grint's plan. "I know there's enough to go around, but I'd like to keep most of it."

"We will," Grint turned his face into the sun. Its warmth reminding him of the quiet days between jobs.

Admission of their planned treachery reached more than a few ears, which is what Grint wanted. All three of the guild leaders knew Grint would try to cut them out at some point. So why not reinforce the idea? Keep them focused on that detail and oblivious to others. What they don't know won't kill me.

I'll take that wager, Hobbe said.

"So how do we do it?" Orsava asked, his voice shaking.

Don't fall apart on me now, Sem. Grint wanted to say it aloud. Give the man some comfort, but the game would end if he did, and right now he had no other moves. They were playing a game of Krabbuk with a blindfold. Moving all the pieces across the checkered board by instinct. If he read his opponents right, he could move his Harrier across to steal their Heir and bring them back while the Infantry fought in the middle.

Since when do you play Krabbuk? Hobbe asked. The real Hobbe tried to teach him a long time ago. Grint understood the game, knew how to move every piece, but planning things ten moves ahead never sat well. Things changed too fast on a job. If you had the opportunity for three moves and they went off without a hitch, then Lorelai was smiling on you. As for the game - Grint usually just bashed his infantry into the opponents and caused as much chaos as he could.

"Once things get moving, they'll relax. When that happens, we slip away with the treasure and no one will be the wiser." Overhead, a pair of gulls stole the crawberry core from the fat mungle. The rest of them screamed in rage. The gray creatures flapped their useless leather wings and threw rocks. One struck, and the gull dropped the fruit into the gutters, where a massive rat helped itself to the treat. It disappeared into a pipe beneath the street before the gulls or mungles objected.

Thieves guild above, Mordechai and his thugs below. And I'm the rat, keeping them at each other's throat until they drop the gold right in my lap.

"Why is it the statue of Ashgra is red?" Grint asked, craning his neck to look up at it. "Why not yellow?"

"Ashgra?" Orsava asked his own question in response. The hints of annoyance and fear were plain in his voice. "Is that an important topic right now?"

"In Rhysin, there's a wrecked statue of Zorn being crowned." Grint held his arms up, miming the action. "A thousand feet of shining gold. Hobbe says it's fake gold."

Orsava whistled through his teeth, nodding. "The old Krypholos church in Rhysin. That is the God of Light doing the crowning. After Zorn's fall, it went to ruin. Did you know, in Sangantide, they named it the Golden Road because it led to the church and not because the road is gold?"

"I did," Grint said with a secret smile at the inane direction of the conversation. All the listeners were busy trying to decipher the code of this topic. Gold and statues, roads and churches. All of it was a bunch of nonsense, but let them figure that out. If they ever did.

Orsava continued speaking about historical oddities as Grint visualized the golden hoard in his mind. Some criticized him when he went away like this, saying it looked as if he wasn't listening, but it was just his way. *Concentration comes not from the moment, but from somewhere ten moves ahead. Examining each branch of possibility, weighing them, and wagering on the best outcome takes dedication.* Hobbe's words every time he beat Grint at Krabbuk. And every time, Grint sent his infantry forward to cause chaos.

A crawberry vendor pushed his cart through the district below. The vendor looked an awful lot like the man he'd gotten his discarded treat from. A coincidence that raised alarms, not because the vendor had reappeared, but getting a cart like that into the Baumer district took effort. There was only one stairway in or out. No roadways.

The robe is different. The mask too, he thought. That didn't mean much. Easy enough to change the mask and flip a robe inside out. Thankfully, the man didn't look up. His eyes remained on the army of urchins running around, drawing his attention so another could steal a taste when he turned his back. It's what Grint used to do on the streets of Dirty Gull. In the long-ago days of youth before Hobbe found him. This vendor was a foolish man, falling for the children's traps, swatting at one while another pulled fruit off the cart. Grint smiled, wanting to join them. The simple joy of their childish act called to him. *I bet I could take a full dozen.*

Exasperated, the vendor threw his arms in the air, shouting for guards. A shrill whistle followed, and the urchins scattered. They'd know the alleys, the nooks where bulky men couldn't fit, and... Grint watched a half dozen jump over a low wall and vanish below the street. A sight he'd seen before when falling down stairs by the Market - the urchins popped up from behind a wall and tried to get his bag, then disappeared again. *Where do you go?*

Two sea birds fought over smashed piles of fruit in the street as the merchant pointed the guard in all directions. The silence from Orsava was palpable. "Why did you stop talking?"

"You stopped listening," Orsava grumbled.

"Let's see, you talked about mermaids, sea monsters, ships from below the Sandy Kingdoms, and then listed the costs of acquiring the armbands and tools we'll need," Grint replied. "You also mentioned getting carts from a marine merchant who docks every fortnight. That will take too long. If we can't make or buy, we'll steal them."

"You have an odd way of listening," Orsava smiled. "But I thought we had the luxury of time?"

"We only ever have half the time we think we do," Grint answered.

"Another nugget from your god?"

"He's full of them," Grint laughed. "Among other things."

"Such piety," Orsava slapped the thief's shoulder. "He must be so proud to have you among his flock."

The sky darkened as clouds filled the sky with such ferocious speed as to elicit an undeniable feeling of terror. Thunder rumbled and the very world vibrated. A bright light illuminated the cloud's canopy before it punched through. A burning streak fell toward Salaz and all Grint could think was, *Is that heading toward us?*

The flaming meteorite tumbled end over end, trailing smoke. Orsava screamed along with a chorus of others, but Grint remained transfixed on the thing. Of all the ways he imagined dying, this had not been on the list until now. Heat emanated off its surface, itching his skin with the promise of burning. Another scream, this one in his mind, woke him up.

The illusion shattered, fizzling out just above their heads. So close, Grint imagined himself reaching up and touching it. That they survived made him laugh. He turned to share the moment with Sem, but the Lord showed no joy. Blood trickled from his nose and mouth as he clutched at the arrow shaft protruding from his chest. Orsava tried to mouth something, but no sound came out. Instead, he tumbled backwards over the railing.

Grint dove for him, grabbing his robes, but the weight and momentum pulled him over. Falling, he thought - *Now this is how I pictured dying.*

12

"Temper, temper, the God of Murder said as he slid a knife across the table. Keep on like this and you're bound to do something rash."

- The Corruption of King Baskis
First performed Annum 1174

"What happened to Lord Orsava?" The elder Tagro bared his sharpened teeth as they stomped down the cellar steps. Dust shook loose from the floorboards overhead, showering them in grains of filth.

"He's dead," Grint said, happy to be alive. He'd earned a dozen new scrapes and bruises from the fall, but the crawberry cart broke most of it, saving his fool neck. It was more than he could say for Lord Orsava.

"I know he's dead," Smit growled, having to hunch beneath the low ceiling. "I'm asking how it happened."

Gathered in a dank basement with dirt floors, the filthy remnants of Orsava's crew bubbled over like an alchemist's concoction, ready to engulf the world in flames. The dusty kegs and shelves of cobwebbed bottles belonged to the rancid tavern above their heads. A safe place Dusk Raven suggested, free from eyes or ears. Chain of Weebles. Whatever a weeble was. That the tavern had no patrons when they entered made it ideal for clandestine meetings. And the owner? As long as they paid him in silver, he didn't care what happened downstairs.

"I'm wondering that myself," Grint answered. He leaned against a support post, happy that a table separated him from Smit. It wouldn't stop the man if he got mad, but it would delay him long enough for Grint to pull a weapon.

"What does that mean? You were there," Keranue pulled the cork from a bottle and sniffed it before taking a drink. That was a situation that could turn into an actual problem if Grint didn't keep his eye on it. Standing beside Keranue, drawing in the dust on a shelf, was Brott. And to Grint's right, crouched atop a keg, was Dusk Raven, her long cloak draped over the edges. Angis joined them, mortified by the state of uncleanliness they met in. After city officials stormed Orsava's manor, the manservant had nowhere else to go. When a Salazian noble with no heirs died, they transfered their belongings to the crown. The poor manservant saved what he could and now looked around the basement with genuine disgust. Grint wondered whether his desire leaned more towards leaving or cleaning.

"I was there, but I still don't believe it." Grint shuddered. The heat coming off the meteor felt so real. "A big rock fell from the sky, heading straight toward us. Then it vanished in a puff of smoke." Grint snapped his finger and made an exploding sound. "When I looked at Sem, he had an arrow in his chest." Angis moaned and started crying. Something he'd been doing all evening.

Things turned worse after they fell. Destroying a vendor's cart being the least worrisome. Orsava landed a few feet to his left, face down. Ignoring his own pain, Grint scrambled away on hands and knees, rolling Sem onto his back. No pulse, no color in the skin, and the light gone from his eyes. Blood pumped from the chest wound. All that was Lord Orsava leaked into tiny cracks between the stones. Stolen by a coward with a crossbow.

The small Baumer square filled with guards. Six hulking men watched him, muscles twitching as they looked from him to the body. "Hey now," Grint said, trying to calm things down. Jamming the tricorn hat back on his head, he looked for the bandanna, but it must have fallen away when he hit the cart. The guards, seeing his red hair, muttered to one another about someone similar who'd gotten away. The chase was on again.

"Did someone stop it?" Brott asked. "The meteor, I mean."

"Or an illusion," Grint answered. "Where was Billy this morning?"

"And where is he now?" Dusk Raven asked right on top of Grint's question.

"You think my brother did this?" Smit shouted, clenching his fists. "There's eight other illusionists in Salaz that I'm aware of."

"But where is he?" Keranue repeated the question, holding the now empty bottle by its neck.

Stupid, I should have collected everybody's weapons before this started.

"Idiots," Smit shook his head. "He's making sure no one followed us here."

"Where was he this morning?" Grint lowered his voice, hoping to keep everyone calm. Betrayals were fine until the killing started. Then they became a nuisance.

"I was following you," Billy said as he walked down the cellar stairs. His sleeveless tan robes covered in mud, dust, roofing tar, and possibly blood. Red and yellow dust powdered his hair and gathered in the sweating creases on his face.

Keranue shattered the end of the bottle against a keg and held the jagged glass up, followed by Brott, who pulled out a pair of twelve-inch skewering forks. The one who concerned Grint most was Dusk Raven. Armed with a dozen swords and knives, she pulled out two curved daggers, planting herself in a spot where she could watch both Tagro brothers, but Smit didn't move or pull a weapon. He stared in disbelief at his younger brother. Billy waited for everyone to draw their weapons before holding up a fist. When he opened his fingers, Grint wished he hadn't. The kid held a firejack.

"Krypsie's sack, Billy," Grint said, horrified at the revelation. A firejack going off in the small basement was a death sentence for everyone.

"He's bluffing," Brott said. "Won't kill himself."

"From the look of it, you're planning to kill me anyway," Billy smiled. "Might as well take you with me."

"Easy Billy," Grint said. "No one here needs to die."

"Tell that to Lord Orsava," Billy stared right at him. *The kid looks like he might throw the firejack just for the fun of it.*

"You said you were following," Smit took a step towards his brother. It was unclear if the intention was to join at his side or wrench the firejack out of his grip. "Did you see the meteor?"

"Meteor? I never saw a meteor," Billy scowled, looking at each person.

"I didn't either," Dusk Raven nodded. "Something like that sounds noticeable."

She didn't either?

I know, Hobbe, I'm not deaf, Grint answered the voice. Dusk Raven had been at the overlook too. An interesting fact no one else caught.

"What happened then, boy?" Brott asked, lowering the forks a few degrees.

"I followed them like I said," Billy repeated. "And I wasn't the only one. A half-dozen thieves skulked around rooftops and alleys. Lost Grint and Lord Orsava when they turned into the park. By the time I climbed off the roof and snuck inside, Lord Orsava had an arrow in his chest. The two of them went toppling over the rail."

"No meteor?" Brott turned back to Grint, raising the forks.

"Put those down," Grint rolled his eyes. "You look like a kry-damn fool." A nervous laugh passed through the room.

"Could be the caster put the image just in their eyes," Billy suggested without lowering his own weapon of destruction. "Guild casters can do it."

"I'm out," Keranue said, tossing his broken bottle aside.

"That's not how this works," Grint replied.

"Excuse me? It works however I want it to work," Keranue raised his voice, eyes darting round for a fresh bottle to break.

"Grint," Dusk Raven said, and the way she said it made him itch with... *With what?* "If the Blue Hands are picking us off, perhaps it's best to melt back into the shadows."

"The thieves didn't do it," Grint shook his head, ready to draw his blade if Keranue went for the keg hammer, dangling from a hook to his right.

"How can you be sure?" Smit asked.

"Guilds came to see us at Orsava's last night," Grint replied. A wave of shock passed through the room.

"And that didn't seem important enough to tell us?"

"It was last night, Brott," Grint growled. "Listen, it doesn't change a kry-damn thing, except we can't back out. Not unless you want to re-locate from Salaz permanently."

"You said guilds?" Dusk Raven turned her creepy long-nosed mask toward him.

"Blue Hands, Opposition, and Fish Mongers," Grint answered to another moan of dismay among the group.

"This gets better and better," Smit slapped a bottle off a table. It shattered against the stone wall.

"How did the guilds find out?" Brott asked. "I know who I am, and the Tagros. Even you and Keranue. What about the woman? Why don't you take off the mask so we know you aren't Racko in disguise?" Brott even took a step toward the sneak thief.

Dusk Raven laughed within her mask, twirling her curved knives. "If you want to lose those puffy little digits you love licking? Please try to reach for my mask."

"Stop," Grint shouted. "This isn't helping. It could be one of us, all of us, or not a charffing one." Getting under the raven mask was on his mind as much as anyone else's, but a bloody fight in a dank basement wouldn't get anyone closer to the payout.

"What do you suggest we do?" Smit asked.

"We keep on with the plan," Grint said, relaxing a bit. "Billy, put the firejack away. No one will kill you today."

In the blink of an eye, the firejack turned into a crawberry. He tossed it in the air, caught it, and took a bite with an enormous smile.

"I knew it was fake," Keranue spat. There was actual laughter this time, and everyone relaxed. Those who still had weapons drawn put them away and gathered round.

"Without Orsava, where are we at?" Smit asked.

"We'll need a warehouse by the docks, those weird orange and white worker armbands, and a fake palace order for us to dig up a street in the Upper Crust," Grint ticked them off one by one.

"That will keep us from getting killed by the guilds," Keranue said. "What do we do about the assassin? If they're not working for a guild, they could be out there trying to kill the rest of us too."

"Someone who works for Borismere?" Dusk Raven asked. "They were rivals."

"Maybe," Grint said. "Could be him - if Sem was even the intended target. Might have been me they were after. I've had some crazy woman following me."

"Woman? Who?" Dusk Raven said in the loudest voice she'd used yet.

Grint smirked at her, "Jealous? If you want to have a drink with me, just take off the mask and we'll go upstairs."

The woman laughed, shaking her head. Grint shrugged, "You never know until you try."

"I'm not jealous, but I'd like to hear more about the woman," Keranue said.

"I know too little, to be honest," Grint answered. *Past time to bring them in.* Their local knowledge could dig out a kernel of information for him. "Big floppy hat and..."

"... burgundy coat?" Billy finished.

Nodding, he watched their faces pale. "What?"

"Charffing job get worse and worse," Keranue said after whistling.

"Guild is welcome to kill me," Brott said right on top of him. "I'll be at Pendarro's Bakery."

"Who is she?" Grint asked, and it was Dusk Raven who answered.

"Spymaster General and the Queen's sister. If she's on to you, that's bad, but I've not heard of her assassinating anyone."

"Someone that powerful never need admit to it," Smit said.

"One more thing to watch out for," Grint shook his head.

"I can give you something to make you look different," Billy suggested. "If she can't recognize you, she won't be able to follow."

"That'll work," Grint said. "Just don't turn me into the old woman."

"Fine," Billy rolled his eyes.

"Once we get what we need, we'll start the job. Two days good?" Everyone nodded. "Then in five we'll be sitting on a beach in the Sandy Kingdoms, haggling over which island to buy."

You'll be dead long before that, Hobbe laughed. Grint didn't have the words to argue with him.

The crew filed up the stairs one by one, but before Billy could leave, Grint took him by the arm and pulled him back. Careful not to hold him back too long and raise suspicion, he made his comment short and to the point. "Follow her if you can, yes?"

Billy nodded and walked away. He knew which 'she' he meant. *Too bad I don't.*

13

"I own all the little ones in this city. That makes me more a king than the fool on the throne. But I'm magnanimous, so I settle for being a gentleman."

- Hanging Ben, the Proprietor of Peach Street

The passing of Lord Sem Orsava saddened Nazarra. While not a major player in the noble landscape, his family maintained their loyalty to the Mahd's through eight successions. The revelation that he'd been the mysterious benefactor behind Grint surpassed the surprise of his death. A slew of unanswerable questions sprang forth. The most pressing being; *Why did a loyal Mahd supporter seek to undermine Lord Borismere, the queen's consort?*

That answer died with the Lord, unless he'd shared it with Grint. Nazarra would not have. To entrust someone you're paying to steal things with personal, sensitive information? A ludicrous practice. No, if she was Orsava, Grint would have been used to find something on his rival without disclosing why.

With her back against the sloped dome of a roof, she watched the stars twinkling in the night sky. Effulg floated through the ink in her brilliant blue way. As a child,

Nazarra often wondered if people lived there too. Did they look at Terragard and wonder the same? Ashgra might know, Or Blue Fingered Hobbe.

One by one the crew left the Chain of Weebles, even Orsava's manservant. Everyone except Grint. What took the man so long? It would be just like Grint to spend the night finding the bottom of a keg. The only other exit from the tavern was a side window outside her field of view. If it took much longer, she'd change clothing and go in as herself.

"And say what?" she asked the night. What pretense would she have to be there? What explanation for stumbling onto him once again? Finding him after the initial chase had been one thing, and even then, it raised his suspicions. The happenstance of walking into the Weeble would be too much, unless he was too drunk to ask questions - a limit she'd not seen him reach.

As she wondered if the illusionist hid his departure, Grint stepped out of the tavern. For someone under suspicion of killing a lord, he walked with casual grace, pausing only to wrap a yellow scarf over his hair and face. The rest of his garb comprised the dusty leathers, thick boots, and damnable bag he let no one touch.

The streets were quiet for it being so close to the Cognispyre. An attempt on the queen and assassination of a lord had everyone on edge. New edicts came out faster than before. Curfews, punishments, taxes. Nazarra couldn't believe her sister was behind them all. Akosha learned statecraft from their father and never displayed such tyrannical control. Or use of magic.

Grint said hello to a group of men walking past, all in blue Opposition armbands. None returned the greeting. Shaking his head, he turned down the stairway leading into the Termin district. Where the man went had always been a mystery, but even more so now. After Lord Orsava's death, the Royal Family reclaimed his manor as custom. City guards poured in, taking anything of value for the queen's coffers. The thief wouldn't return there, so where was he going?

Following from rooftops reminded her of chasing after the Parthian, without the dread or urgency. Being up high, away from people is where she felt the most at home. A tight rope stretched over the street, meant to look like a way to dry clothes, but this had the stink of the Blue Hands on it. When they first appeared in Salaz, Nazarra ordered their walking lines cut whenever they found one. For each they took down, five more appeared within the hour. Catching your prey took cunning and adaptation, so she eased up, letting the guild grow comfortable.

A misstep. Perhaps. The Blue Hands curried favors and traded illicit information to legitimize themselves. An agreement Nazarra stood against. The only thing worse than sanctioned thieves was the contract they signed. You can steal as long as it doesn't interfere in city business. And what did that include? No one knew for sure, so the guards let them do whatever they wanted if a few coins ended up in their pockets. Now that the guild had joined in on Grint's heist and partnered with the Opposition to do so, she might have cause to bring Racko down and kick the whole sorry lot out of Salaz.

Until then, she'd use their ropes against them. It let her watch Grint's progression through Termin without abandoning her advantage. He walked a good sixty feet below her now, but the yellow head wrap was hard to miss. Two taller homes blocked her view for a moment, but he reappeared on the other side, keeping a steady pace toward the Grand Runway. As a patrol approached him, her heart sank. The fool man didn't even bother to...

Three guards, armed with swords, walked past Grint without a second look in his direction. The cheeky bastard even danced a little jig behind them. *Billy*, she thought, freezing in place. The gifted illusionist must have cast something on Grint in the tavern, or was he also following - and watching Nazarra? She scanned the rooftops but saw no one. That didn't mean he wasn't there. Billy could be invisible himself, standing right behind her.

Nazarra suppressed the urge to swing her arms at the imagined phantoms lurking behind her. What a fool she would look. No, if Billy hid on the rooftops, there was nothing she could do until he made a mistake. If he made a mistake. *Control what you can.* A wise lesson from her old teacher. The trick to it was realizing there was very little you could control in any situation.

Grint ambled onto the Grand Runway, turning left toward Harborside. With no rooftops left, she climbed down, following at a safe distance. The mysterious sloop sat in the harbor. No one had come off it yet, and the Navy grew nervous. A half-dozen smaller vessels floated off its starboard side. Admiral Gaine was a coward and wouldn't force the situation unless ordered to. Even then, it depended on who the order came from. Was the sloop Grint's destination? Was even he so bold?

Alas, it appeared not. Nazarra watched the thief turn toward The Heap. The shanty homes piled on top of one another was just the place she would expect to find Grint. For all his attempts at clever humor and suave affectations, he was a mud-dweller at heart. An endearing quality, not because he tried to hide it, but because he admitted it to a select few.

The south road into Felsin was close to where Grint turned off, so she ran along the cobbled road and squeezed between two empty homes. Burn marks on the stone and around the empty windows signaled a fire, and a recent one as the smell of burnt wood remained strong. A parchment notice sat in the mud behind one house. An edict from the palace. Akosha had done this. Whatever else happened, she needed to find her way back into the Court and reassert her influence on the Queen.

Saving Borismere from embarrassment might be enough. Linking Prince Mikil to it would be. Exposing the heist would burn Grint, and he'd wind up on Allast Island, but family came first. Saving him from the hangman would be enough to assuage her guilt. Until he dies. Most who ended up on Allast died wishing for the rope. Grint could only blame himself. She didn't make him a thief.

Crouching beneath the low branches of a tree, she scanned The Heap for any sign of him. More people walked around than any other district, but she found the thief all the same. He sat on a broken stone wall, his bag upon his lap and scarf pulled down so he could smoke a pipe. Nazarra settled back, chewing on a piece of sugaroot as she watched, content to wait and see what happened next.

*****

It didn't take long after he sat to hear the first signs. A too-loud whisper. The shuffle of feet. Mischievous giggles. And that was when Grint saw them. Three tiny shadows ambling toward him. Dropping his head, he mimed falling asleep, keeping his ear attuned to the sounds the urchins made. They formed a line, leapfrogging past one another as they came closer. Someone taught them that. Or they'd taught themselves. The one in the back stumbled each time it was their turn to take the lead. Their slow march forward continued until a cat sleeping on top of an outhouse hissed. The urchins froze, waiting to see if it woke their target. It hissed again, followed by the thump of a rock striking wood. More giggles.

Grint waited until the footsteps were right on top of him, listening as the three fanned out. "Hello," he said, opening his eyes.

They froze, eyes wide in shock. A tall dark-haired boy, a smaller silver haired girl and a lyzan kidling. "Scatter!" The boy shouted, and the three sprinted in different directions.

Grint started after the boy. The other two had listened to him, so he might be their street-leader and one step closer in the hierarchy. Or it was a shell game, and they were getting him to chase the lowest one on the pole. Didn't matter, any of them would do. The kid was fast, slipping around and knocking over barrels to block Grint's path. Vaulting over them, Grint uttered disgruntled shouts about keeping up with the brat.

They wound through the bowels of The Heap, Grint slamming into walls as they made quick turns. He'd have fresh bruises after this but kept on. They crossed through a crowd of dockworkers and into a dark alley behind a warehouse. Grint lost sight of the kid, having to take more time climbing through junk and fallen timber. Grint put his hand on an old crossbeam crumbling with rot when a shovel clocked him in the face. The kid didn't have strength to put much force behind it, but it shocked Grint, knocking him into a wall.

As the boy wound up for another strike, Grint lunged forward and tackled him. The shovel fell away, splashing in a puddle of mud. Grint held the struggling boy by the wrist, dragging him out of the alley. A sharp sting clamped on the fleshy edge of his hand. Screaming in annoyance, Grint shook his hand, hoping the kid didn't break the skin or have rabies.

"What did you bite me for?" he asked as the kid bounced around on his feet looking for somewhere to go.

"Not going to let you send me to Allast Island or Madame Guigehr's." The kid balled up his fists. The dart of his eyes let Grint know he was planning to make a run for freedom. Inexperience in this line of work was a dangerous thing. *Better learn fast, kid. Life won't give you another chance.*

I gave you a few, Hobbe said.

"I'm not with the city guard," Grint answered, looking at his hand. "Kry-damn teeth marks. You charffing brat."

"If you're not arresting me, why did you chase? I didn't take nothing from you." The kid stopped moving, looking at Grint in confusion.

"I want to talk to the one in charge," Grint said, wrapping his hand in a soft leather strap.

"Happy Marv works out of a rug merchant's place in the Blau." Something sour and unsettling passed over the kid's face when he mentioned Marv. Grint knew Marv's type. He'd met him many times and even had a Marv of his own growing up.

"Not him," Grint said. "I want the urchin who runs the gangs. The kid in charge."

"How do you know about that?" The boy looked perplexed.

"Because I was him a long time ago."

"You're Matty?" The kid asked in astonishment.

"What? No," Grint shook his head. "When I was a kid, I was like you. I ran the gangs and kept the kids safe from Hanging Ben."

"Oh, that's less interesting."

"Fine. Just tell Matty that I want to talk," Grint said. Horns blared in the night. Warning sounds starting from the high streets and rippling down. Grint took a step to the alley's mouth and listened. Were they coming for him? After the boy? Not likely, not with the first alarm so far away. Grint turned to warn the boy, but he'd already gone. Nothing to do about it now except hope the message would get across. If not, he'd need to do this again.

"I can get a matching scar," he said, rubbing his hand.

Grint held his breath as a patrol ran past. Six masked soldiers with weapons drawn. Something had the hornets buzzing in a froth. *Billy, I hope you're still with me or I'm the one who'll get stung.*

*****

"Billy do this and Billy do that," he muttered as he followed Dusk Raven, who was following Grint. How the thief knew to mistrust her above the others was mystifying. Maybe it was luck, but Billy didn't think so. And it was wrong to get grumpy about having a job to do. This was the first time anyone had given him responsibility during a job. Smit usually made sure he was so far out of harm's way he was practically off the job, and that was if he brought him along at all. Grint trusted him, and that should at least earn him the respect of not complaining.

Dusk Raven was a renowned sneak thief and seeing her move across the rooftops made him understand why people spoke of her in awe. Even with a light bending charm on himself, she almost caught him saving Grint from a patrol. Since then, he'd stayed further away. He pressed himself against a wall when Grint went chasing after the kid, and her elbow brushed against his belt. Had she felt it?

Dusk Raven didn't stop moving, and Billy followed. Discovering her interest was what Grint sent him out to accomplish. If it turned out she was an assassin trying to bury an arrow in his chest - would Billy be able to stop her? Pulling out a long fir needle he'd gotten from an Orrish trader, Billy ran it through his fingers, re-shaping it as he whispered an incantation. Magic wasn't as simple as Smit thought. You didn't spout out a few nonsensical words or wave a hand like some street mummer making coins appear from a child's nose. It required preparation and the right tools. If Dusk Raven pulled out a crossbow, throwing blades, or anything else to harm the thief, Billy could toss the needle into the wind. The effect would muddle her a bit. Not enough to feel the magic, but more than sufficient to throw off her aim.

The woman slid to an abrupt stop as Grint continued through a dark alley. This time she didn't move, didn't look around, but the hair on Billy's arms stood up. Either she was sensing him, or they were both sensing someone else.

"Dusk Raven," the darkness said in a glib tone. Three shadows materialized on top of a cracked dome and slid down the convex structure.

"Racko," she replied in her flat whisper.

"You haven't been paying your dues," the guild mistress cocked her head with a smile that accentuated her round cheekbones.

Billy checked that his jaw hadn't fallen off. Not only was he seeing the infamous Racko for the first time, but he'd just learned that Dusk Raven was with the Blue Hands. Smit did the occasional guild job and at the end paid a royalty that let him use their fences. But paying dues meant you were a full armband wearing member. It was a simple step from that to believing Dusk Raven alerted the guilds to the heist.

"I haven't been working."

Racko laughed and shook her head. "That's not what I've heard. Is it boys?"

"No," Brim Cully, a thick-headed basher Billy recognized, said as he punched a fist into his hand. The other thief she brought was a basher too. A lyzan brute named Asher.

"You heard wrong," Dusk Raven answered.

"Did I?" The guild mistress walked to the edge of the roof and spat into the darkness below. "I don't think I did. Regardless, you're using the rooftops and that comes with a price."

"She's not even wearing her armband," Asher hissed.

"Right," Racko nodded. "That carries a stiff penalty. Do you remember Augus Bend? He liked to take the armband off. So, we took his head and fed it to the siren eels."

"Nothing helps you hide in the shadows like a bright blue handprint," Dusk Raven said. Billy almost choked on a laugh he didn't dare utter. Not quiet enough though, not with a lyzan on the roof. Licking the air with his forked tongue, Asher glanced around at the darkness. Billy fumbled through his pocket, pulling the fir needle out and tossing it up. Not what he intended it for, but it should keep his scent hidden by creating a wave of differing smells. Turned out to be enough, as the lyzan returned his focus to their quarry.

"I say we take her mask as payment," Asher laughed.

"No," Brim said. "I've heard the scars on her face are worse than the bottom of Scale Finny's feet."

"I think it's a smashing idea," Racko added. During all of it, Dusk Raven remained still. Crouched within her robes, the fabric never twitched. A fool's bet to think she hadn't armed herself, and Racko discerned that too, but it didn't diminish her confidence. At a three to one advantage, why would she think she'd lose?

Before anyone found out, a pillar of fire rose into the night sky. From this distance it was much further up the slope of the city. Somewhere as far as the Ashgra. Before the light faded, the alarm horns cascaded from one district to the next. A shrill sound, like a thousand angry crickets.

Distracted by the flames, Racko and her cohorts took their eyes off Dusk Raven, missing her escape, but not Billy. She had been in his line of sight, and he caught her cloak's movement as she dropped over the edge of the building. Chasing after her in a straight line led through the guild, so Billy circled round their flank, holding his breath and praying to Ashgra the lyzan didn't sense him again.

Beyond the cracked dome, he leapt to an adjoining building. The wet sound of guards running through mud came from all directions. Someone had been bad, and the city sought to make them pay. Why scour the Heap though? The fire originated elsewhere. Billy spared a moment to add Grint to his prayers. The thief was on his own. Dusk

Raven climbed a trellis, mantling a low wall. Her cloak slipped over the edge, snapping the air.

By the time Billy reached the trellis and pulled himself onto the low wall, his heart beat hard, and chest burned. Young as he was, he let magic do most of the work for him. Extended stretches of exertion were more of Smit's thing. As he caught his breath, a line of city guards filed past the gate. A rather inquisitive sergeant paused and lifted his torch.

"Who's there?" the man shouted. Billy froze, hoping it wasn't him they were talking to. If so, he'd need to re-think his decision to be a spy. Too many people tonight had been on the cusp of discovering him.

"I know you're there," the sergeant said as the soldiers stepped past him and into the small area. "Come out now and we won't hurt you."

A nasty wave of laughter spread through the ranks. None of them were looking in his direction. Had they spotted Dusk Raven? Even Billy hadn't... And then he saw her, sitting on the edge of a fountain, running her hand through the water. The mask sat on her lap and hood around her shoulders, but a deep shadow covered her face.

"Sergeant Wisk," she said. "I presume you have better things to do?"

"What's that?" the sergeant replied, sounding less than pleased.

"I asked if you had anything better to do?" she said again. The soldiers mumbled to one another as she stood, but they all shut their mouths as she stepped into the torchlight. Pulling a red armband with the royal sigil from her pocket was unnecessary. Everyone knew who she was.

"Spymaster General," the sergeant breathed. "My apologies. I didn't..."

"I know," she said as if speaking to a child. "Now run along and find whoever is creating havoc in my sister's city."

"Right away," the sergeant bowed, yelling at the guards to get moving when he straightened out.

This time Billy didn't check to see if his jaw had fallen off. He was sure it had. Dusk Raven was Nazarra Mahd, the Spymaster General and sister to Queen Akosha. The one who'd been following Grint. Dusk Raven. The exhaustion faded away beneath a deluge of anger. This was worse than a traitor bringing the guilds in on the heist. She was a mole for the crown and would hang them all.

Nazarra walked out of the courtyard and up the Grand Runway. He'd finished the job Grint sent him on. All he had to do was return to the tavern and wait, tell Grint the truth and figure out the next steps. Or... or he could keep following. Find out if she had a nest somewhere close by. He told himself if she made her way to the palace, he would let her go. If it was anywhere else, that would be useful. They could surprise her at their own time.

When she entered the Chantil he feared the worst. The cliff road into the Gutarr was in this district. But she stopped outside a bakery, looking around before walking in. Billy climbed onto a roof opposite the three-story building and watched the upper window light with candle fire. Nazarra moved around behind a thin curtain before pulling it away and opening the window. She leaned against the frame, looking toward the palace with a wistful, lost expression.

Here was a woman who ran the information network through Salaz. She'd played the Blue Hands for fools and a dozen other guilds besides. There was no point feeling sorry for her. Or maybe he should. Once Grint learned of it, the wrath of the thief would rival a Parthian volcano. As he mulled it over, a second person entered her room. The sad expression changed to one of relief and happiness. *Good,* Billy thought, *someone we can leverage against her.*

Except, as the man took her in his arms, kissing her deeply, Billy recognized him.

"Grint? What the charffing mungle is going on?"

14

"At dawn of the tenth day, the last horserider sat atop his mount, surrounded by the dead and a flood of blood-thirsty lyzan. 'Yield,' they cried in a voice ten thousand strong. The horserider laughed, 'No, for I am the flood.'"

- *Song of the Pale, composer unknown*

The sun beat down on Salaz, marking it as the hottest day in recent memory. Many took it as Ashgra's warning of displeasure over the meager Cognispyre offerings. The little people ran about, crying and gnashing their teeth. Over-paying for supplies in the market just to make their burnt offerings more appealing. Others paid significant sums to the temple so a priest would speak a few words over their efforts. And whst did it accomplish? Nothing. In a few days, the piles of ash left behind would sully the streets and discolor the buildings. And the sun would still beat down.

Lord Borismere took the heat as a personal affront to his person. The black velvet veil was admittedly an awful choice for the day, but it matched his tailored black coat and pants with golden dragons stitched along the seams. Ashgra should know better than to inconvenience him. *Conform to my will*, he commanded. *He who controls Ashgra's Fortune controls Ashgra.*

Borismere smiled as he fluttered the thick veil, cooling his face. A peasant's method, to be sure, but who would dare criticize him for it? Lord Borismere, consort to the queen - and soon to be king regent if things progressed properly. The idea pleased him. A man, not of Salazian blood, born in a refuse heap and left to die, now sat poised to wear the crown.

Walking to the edge of the gravel path outside his manor, hands clasped behind his back, Borismere surveyed the city. A panoramic view of Salaz spread before him. A blot of yellow haze hung over the harbor, created by this interminable heat, obscuring the naval fort and Allast Island. *All of this is mine.*

Lord Borismere admired the vivacity with which his wizard performed his duty. The pillars of fire caused quite a stir, over-extending an already exhausted corps of city guards. With him arrested and sentenced to Allast Island, they could free the Parthian from the inside. Time enough remained for the barbarian to complete the assassination before the poison took him. Poison. Such a foolish way to force someone to do your bidding. Prince Mikil had the imagination of a mungle.

Mikil had his uses but labored under the belief that Borismere planned to hand him the throne. Absurd notion. Their relationship would soon reach the point where the prince stopped being useful. Timing his removal required precision. Much like the skill he'd applied when claiming this manor from the aging Lord Senry. Lost in an ocean of senility, manipulating Senry had been far too simple. The fool never even knew what fortunes lay beneath his feet. Those who stood in the way met with untimely ends, courtesy of the wizard.

Borismere took notice of a street crew working along the lower edge of the district. Pickaxes cracked the stone retainer wall with their distasteful racket. A work crew in orange, white, and black armbands sweated under the sun. Indentured debtors on loan from Allast Island. Salaz law allowed them to work their debt off over time, but few did. Interest rates on the debt created more debt than the work paid. A vicious circle that tickled Borismere's fancy.

However, no one had made him aware that any such debtors were to work in the district. The vault lay well-hidden underground but having workers dig this close to it caused an unnatural wave of anxiety. The crunch of loose gravel announced the arrival of his expected guest. Borismere would not turn and greet the man. Not one of such low standing. No, they would make their presence known and offer the proper salutation.

"Lord Borismere," Captain Basto said mid-bow.

"You're late," he replied. Each strike of the debtor's pickaxe felt like the loss of a coin. An odd image.

"Apologies," the guard captain said as he stepped to Borismere's side.

"I trust everything is in place for the wizard?" Borismere asked. "I don't want him subjected to the usual tortures or counter-measures against magic."

"Yes," Basto said. Did he detect uncertainty in the man's voice?

"Were my instructions unclear?" Borismere glanced toward the captain. "I believe they were as simple as possible."

"No confusion, my lord," Basto said, this time sounding more confident.

"Good," Borismere dismissed the subject as he walked closer to the edge of the path. "Tell me what those debtors are doing here."

"Street crew," Basto said, trotting to keep up as Borismere walked toward the street. "Drainage repair. Allowed by the Interior Minister."

"I spoke with Minister Frea yesterday," Borismere shook his head. "He never mentioned it."

"Must have been an oversight," Basto offered, once more sounding unsure.

"One I shall remedy. All work and their approvals go through me from now on." Approaching the debtors, Borismere counted four. Nothing about them seemed wrong. Each displayed the proper deference, keeping their heads down as he inspected the armbands and their tools. Yet, he couldn't shake the premonition that this was wrong.

"Which of you is the foreman?" Borismere asked. A stocky man raised his hand to the question. "Come."

"My Lord," he said through the white head-wrap. There wasn't much he could tell about the man. Voice muffled, his exposed skin smeared with mud, and no sign of age.

"What is wrong with the drainage?"

"Wrong? Uh... sir," he added as Basto took a threatening step toward him. "Nothing is wrong, I think. Asked to clean out the drains."

"Asked by whom?" Borismere would find those who failed to inform him and see the proper punishment visited upon them. Much easier with the wizard, but he'd make do until they returned.

"Mapre," the man said. "Got our orders from Mapre."

Borismere looked to Basto, who nodded, "Work Officer in the Heap."

"Yes," Borismere said, staring at the hole in the ground. "Try to keep it down and be sure to finish by the end of the day. Basto, see that this Mapre finds a new home on Allast Island."

Having enough of the common people for one morning, Borismere turned on his heel and walked away. A refreshment was in order. Something to cool his throat and get him out of the sun. Perhaps a pitcher of the sweet sangria that he could take down to the vault. Staring at the gold calmed him, focused his mind.

For one who never believed in gods and even mocked those that did, he looked upon his discovery of the map as a gift from Krypholos. A retired Brotherhood Knight had it framed and hung in an old study. He'd looked at the map as a curiosity of the world and joked about finding the golden circle. Borismere, in his youth, had served as a page to the knight, and before long bedded the wife while siphoning off the man's meager fortune. When the couple died in a tragic fire that burned their home down, Borismere left with the map - and the tale the wife told of where the Knight came by the map. In Salaz.

"Begging your pardon, my lord, but why is the work crew such a concern?" Basto breathed with the effort of jogging up the hill.

"I suppose it's not," Borismere replied, mostly to himself. "The murder of Orsava, welcome as it may be, has many of us on edge. Have your men come to any conclusions?"

"My men?" Basto asked. "It wasn't you that did it?"

"Take off your mask," Borismere whispered in a growl as he spun on Basto. "Take it off now."

"In the sunlight? My lord, I must protest," he stammered.

Tearing his own veil over off, Borismere turned his face into the sun. "Ashgra holds no power here. Take it off."

Lacking the confidence that he'd proved his point, Boris-mere pulled a knife from his belt. "I won't ask again.

With trembling hands, Basto reached up and removed the scuffed, black mask, letting it hang at his side as he fought against burying his face in the closest shadow. What had Borismere expected? For a moment the answer had been an impostor, but here stood Captain Basto in a disheveled state with purple bruises on his right cheek and eye.

"Busy night?"

"Nothing outside the call of duty, my lord," he responded, lifting the mask halfway to his face before pausing. Borismere gave his permission with the flick of a hand.

"You can't be too careful is what I'm saying." The grim warning felt lost on Basto. "You would do well to remember that. I will secure the throne, but if you seek to be among those I raise up, you will need to use your brain. I won't set an imbecile as commander of the forces. And for Ashgra's sake, exercise. You're sweating like a stinking Glades-dweller." Resting his hands on Basto's shoulders, he meant it to be an encouraging moment, but doubt crept back. Had Basto gotten taller?

"Who is that?" The captain asked before Borismere could voice his concern. It was easy to determine who Basto meant.

"That dear Basto is one of my house guards." The man swung at the end of a rope; his face swollen purple face covered with foy flies that danced around his naked body. "We caught him stealing food and cavorting with the maids. It's good that you asked. This is a brilliant example of what happens when you fail."

"I'll bear that in mind, my lord," Basto said.

"Please do." The dog trotted up from some brush, an

old bone in her mouth. She fought him as he took it but let go with a whimper at the determined set of his eyes. The bone looked like something that came off a dead mungle. Filthy. The dog waited patiently until he threw it, then darted after it.

"You're useful Basto, but so is my dog," Borismere shouted, walking past the corpse. "Get the job done."

15

"Standing on a strand of beach in the lost depths of the ocean, the shipwrecked sailor knew survival would come down to one simple truth. Outsmarting the others who crashed with her."

- The Survival of Euchrydis - Benniof, p.Annum 9812

"This is a terrible idea," Smit said for the third time. "I'm telling you he knew something was wrong."

Grint didn't want to argue, not when he agreed, but as Hobbe always said, *The job decides for itself.*

Walking away was a luxury they couldn't afford. Borismere might be on to them, or not. They'd survived his inquiries in one piece, but had it been enough? Leaving meant the guilds would hunt and kill them, if they haven't already started. Brott and Dusk Raven had both mysteriously disappeared now. The kid followed the Raven until she lost him. At least that's what he claimed. True or not, she hadn't returned. Brott they'd seen last night, hale and hearty. As of this morning, he was a ghost. Everything screamed to run away.

Since when do you listen?

"We made the bangers. They'll be useless as of tonight. We use them today or the whole plan falls apart. Unless either of you has coin hidden away to buy extras?"

The few remaining thieves shook their heads. Smit and Billy, Keranue the driver, and Angis the butler. That was who survived to steal a mountain of gold and get away with it. Grint dragged a dusty table out of the basement's corner and they gathered round. Spitting on his finger, he drew a box on one side.

"This is Borismere's manor," he said, jabbing a finger into it. "Since Dusk Raven has stepped out and her backup in planting the bangers did too - The Tagro brothers and I will each take one.

"Set yours here and yours here," he told the brothers, drawing X's on the imaginary levee. "I'll set mine here and then we'll meet back on this roof overlooking the Ashgran."

"Right," Smit nodded, putting on a brave face, but the sweat popping up on his forehead proved he wasn't fool enough to disrespect the bangers.

"When it floods, Borismere will send a dispatch for the Arkhon Company. Keranue takes out the rider, then meets us with the wagons." Grint drew some wavy lines where he imagined all of it happening. "Borismere gives us the gold and we ride off into glory. Questions?"

"Just a few," Billy said. "Is that squiggle me?"

"This isn't a joke," Smit rolled his eyes, smacking the back of Billy's head.

"I do," Keranue said, studying the table as if it were a scaled map. "You keep saying a mountain of gold. Even with the five of us, it'll take a dozen trips. Once we get going, there won't be five anymore because one of us must stay up top to supervise and someone else will have to stay at the storage location to guard. So, three wagons and a lot more trips. Takes a while to get to the harbor and back. How long do you think we have?"

"And where in the harbor?" Billy asked. "Did Orsava set something up before... you know?"

Angis began crying again.

"We're not going to the harbor," Grint said.

"So where then?" Smit asked.

Grint drew a terrible rendition of a broken statue. "In the Ashgran, there's an old Kryphatic church, abandoned after the Temple of Ashgra reclaimed power."

"That place is haunted," Smit frowned.

"With the spirits of a million solid gold coins," Grint smiled. "Let's assume the guilds are watching or trying to. They don't know for sure it's today, but we'll pretend they do. When the carts turn into the Ashgran, Billy can conjure a phantom for them to follow down to the harbor."

"That'll take time to prepare," Billy said, earning a sour look from the others. "What? It will. I can do a lot, but that will be impossible without a few days to make..."

"Just do what you can," Grint interrupted him. "Send a dozen phantoms in every direction so they have to follow them all. I don't know."

"Okay," Billy puffed up his cheeks and let the air out slowly, mulling the idea over.

"Listen," Grint put both hands on the table, leaning in. "This isn't perfect. We may blow ourselves up or the flood might be a trickle. The guilds might catch on and string us up, or we ride straight into the queen and lose it all. The risk is worth it to me. Decide for yourselves what risks you're willing to take."

"Always was worth it," Smit said, crossing his arms.

"Yeah," Billy added right on top of his brother.

"I've got nothing better to do," Keranue laughed.

"Might I know what you need of me?" Angis asked.

"Stay with Keranue and when we get the gold into the temple, you'll be the one we leave to watch it. Sound good?"

"Yes," Angis smiled. "I was nervous you'd want me jumping around with a sword."

"Another time," Grint laughed. "And speaking of time..."

Walking past Smit, he clapped the big guy on the shoulder. Billy handed out the bangers. Slight things, no larger than a toy ball and half as heavy. Grint took care to place it in his bag. It may not have been the most lethal thing there, but it was the most volatile. He shuddered to think what the banger's blast would do when channeled through the refracting glass. Would that consume the entire city?

Grint did the unthinkable as he stepped out of the tavern. He prayed to Hobbe. *Old man, I've never come to you for a job, but if you're listening or watching... let this work. But keep your nose out of it. This is my job, and you can't have any of the gold.*

Ingrate.

Too many eyes followed them as they stepped onto the Grand Runway, heading north to the Upper Crust. Grint worried that everyone in the city had their own agenda and would stop at nothing to see them fail. When he caught sight of the desiccated corpses walking beside them, he understood the stares. Draped in leathers and chainmail, a rat poked its head out of an eyeless skull while wet sinew slid off the forearm, falling to the street.

"Are you kry-damned kidding me?" Grint spat, pulling the kid off the street.

Billy choked on his laughter until Smit slapped the back of his head. "Stop charffing about."

"Ow," the kid whined. "Leave off. I wanted to be sure I knew how to make them. In case we need to frighten the Blue Hands."

"Practice it where no one can see," Grint growled, pulling on his veil.

"Someone could call the guards," Smit kept at his brother as Grint scanned the street. People went about their business, forgetting the horrors they'd just witnessed.

"Don't threaten me, Smit. I'll trample you with a herd of cattle if you keep glaring at me."

"Enough," Grint said. "Get all the jokes out now. Once this starts its all business."

Both nodded. Grint walked along, no one saying a thing. The thieves' gut tingled like a million butterflies trying to burst free at once. Did the other two feel it and that's why they shut up? Keranue had it. The look he gave Grint before they left the tavern said as much. Keranue and Angis should have left by now, splitting off to complete their own end of it.

Each step of the plan rattled off in his mind. Had he measured Borismere right? The guilds? Given his druthers, he would have preferred setting up their own transport company and winning the contract outright. Time and circumstance didn't allow it. So many moving parts and any could turn into a dagger aimed at their hearts. *Where the bloody mungle are Brott and Dusk Raven?*

When they reached the cafe where the crew first met, the sun was well on its way to setting. They needed to pick up their pace. Grint wanted to time the first cart of gold with the tolling of the night bells. What illusion couldn't accomplish, the shroud of night would. *Another hope? You're starting to sound like Myrilee.*

Maybe I should pray to the Goddess of Hope, Grint snapped at the voice. An excellent sign. Arguing with Hobbe meant his mind was in the right place.

Pointing out the spot where they were to split up, Grint stumbled to a knee. Two steps behind, Billy juggled five bangers, making terrified noises whenever he let one drop. Instead of exploding, they burst into butterflies, floating off on the wind.

"It's fun," Billy said, dropping the illusion. "Only we could see it."

"Kry-dammit Billy, if we get killed, you'll deal with the disapproving glare of my spirit for all eternity," Grint brushed himself off. A part of him wanted to kill the kid for the jokes before he got them caught. *A small part,* he told himself.

"I'll keep him under control from now on," Smit leaned over as if to whisper, but said it loud enough to hear in the harbor.

"Plant the bangers and get out of there," Grint said when they reached the Upper Crust. "Once the rain starts, we need to be on that rooftop."

"Yeah, we got it," Billy said, still rubbing the back of his head. "Are you sure it will rain?"

The skies were as clear as could be aside from the flocks of gulls overhead. "If not, we do it the hard way," Grint said, pulling aside his coat to show the collapsed crossbow strung inside. "Just have to hit one and the water from the flooding will set off the others. But a seer assured me we'd have rain."

Both men nodded and started to their assigned spots. Grint waited a few moments, blending into the crowd before heading into the Upper Crust. His path would take him the closest to Borismere's. Mainly because he had the most familiarity with its layout and grounds, but also - well, he just didn't trust anyone other than himself.

The hanging guard's body, mutilated and bloated, still hung from the manor gate. Stray dogs had a turn at it, leaving the rest to the gulls and rats. The mungle weren't carrion eaters, but they kept close, throwing rocks at any gull who lingered. When they struck one, it was a mad scramble to claim it. No one appeared from the guardhouse to chase them off. In fact, there seemed to be no one around at all. If not for a candle lit in the front window, he would have thought it empty.

Shaking off the odd shudder the lack of guards brought on, Grint slipped around the back side of the property to the levee wall. The stalks of a hundred weeds recently trimmed tried to force their way through the cobbled ground. Nothing grew against the wall or came within a foot of its base. An enchantment? If so, it was old. As old as the city itself. And something he hadn't considered in the plan. Would the bangers work?

The levee was far from perfect in its construction. Enormous blocks of stone sat on top of one another, sealed with a dark, gritty substance. Grint found a nice groove to place the banger, saying a prayer to Lorelai for luck. Hobbe laughed at him as he jammed it in. The malleable form squished into the crack. He stepped back, happy to be alive, but lingered long enough to be sure it didn't fall out.

When they worked on the drains, the streets of the Upper Crust were as lively as any other. Merchants of the highest quality pushed their carts as the nobility strutted about. Today was different. The streets held onto an eerie calm as if the world had ended, leaving just the thieves behind. There were no lingering city guards, mustering troops, or even eyes watching from above. It was just quiet.

Quickening his pace, Grint made it back to the Upper Crust's edge and leapt across the two-foot chasm to land on the thick roof of an old temple. Its dome was ringed with raised edges deep enough for the thief to duck behind. The spot gave them a perfect vantage to watch both Borismere's response, the dispatch of the rider, and a view of Keranue arriving with the carts.

Not long after Grint settled in, Smit appeared, making the leap. Offering a nod that his job was complete, the two waited for Billy. Grint stared at the sky. At sunset, a deep orange replaced the blue sky with the blackness of night chasing behind. A handful of stars poked through the veil. Rotande, the Hunter Star. Gillum, the enchantress who led sailors to their death. Marvery and Wile, who some said were lovers while other cultures called them the bitterest of enemies. Hobbe liked the stars and the stories behind them, collecting them like the treasures he often stole.

Remember when we would lay on the Inn's roof and watch the stars? Hobbe asked. Grint smiled at the memory.

"What's so charffing funny?" Billy asked, dropping his veil of invisibility.

"Just your face," Grint put his hand over the kid's face and smashed it. Now it was Smit who laughed.

"Everything alright, little brother?"

"Yes," Billy said with a faraway look.

"What?" Grint said as it triggered his own unease.

"Went too well," the young illusionist replied. "Where is everyone?"

"Kry-damn charffers," Grint growled. The tingle of alarm scratching his brain grew. How could Borismere be on to them already? They just got here. But if they knew, then this was...

"A trap," Billy blurted out. "This feels like one I mean."

"I don't like it either," Smit poked his head up from their hiding spot to look around.

"Someone sold us out?" Grint said to himself. "What happened with Dusk Raven when you followed her?"

"I don't trust her," Smit added.

"You want to talk about that now?" The kid's face twisted into something dark and angry. Another illusion amplifying it?

"Yeah," Grint said. "It seems kry-damn relevant right now. If someone sold us out, it was her or..."

"Brott," Smit said in a flat voice.

"Sure, it's possible," Grint shrugged, unable to take his eyes off Billy and the darkening of light radiating off his skin.

Smit grabbed him by the lapel of his coat and yanked him round, pointing at the road along the Upper Crust. "Brott." And there the man stood, his portly frame and sweat-stained shirt as clear as the night sky. Beside him was the thief-master, Racko and three of her Blue Hands, each waving a banger over their head.

"Rot-gutted, dread-bolted, flappy gummed skainsmate." Grint punched the stone edging with each new expletive. "Why would Brott sell us out? He was Orsava's friend?"

"Hello?" Borismere shouted. Grint poked his head up again to see the Lord smiling at them from the road. City guards joined his house guards with more Blue Hands spreading out on the rooftops. "Yes, you three on the temple."

A chorus of laughter spread through the gathered troops. *This isn't ending well,* Hobbe whispered.

"We need a way off this roof," Grint said.

"No, we need a way off," Billy spat back. "You can go charff yourself."

"Billy," his brother growled, but the kid refused to back down.

"No, for once listen to me. You want to know what I found when I followed Dusk Raven? If it was her connection to the Thieves Guild that might have been enough, but that's just a cover. She's Spymaster General Mahd of the Royal Order." Smit's eyes widened with every word. Grint's did too, but he was too busy trying to tie why that was making the kid mad at him.

"Why didn't you tell us that?" Smit asked what Grint feared to.

"Because he's sleeping with her. The mole has been Grint all along," Billy pulled his knife and as his brother stepped beside him, he drew his.

"Guys," Grint said, holding up his hands. "I'm not sleeping with a spy. The woman I've been seeing..."

"I would enjoy your attention," Borismere shouted. The squat lock pick was now on his knees with Borismere standing behind him, holding a long sword to his throat. So much for Brott profiting off his betrayal. "I take it I have your full attention?"

"Do we answer him?" Billy asked.

"No," Smit said, pushing his brother further back.

"If you give yourselves up, I can promise you a stay on Allast Island," Borismere continued. "Otherwise, things are apt to get bloody."

"You don't have to do this," Brott shouted. "This wasn't part of the agreement!"

Borismere lowered the sword with an apologetic shrug. Brott's relief died as Racko yanked him to his feet and jammed a banger in his gut. Grint watched as two guards dragged a horse trough to the edge of the road, the water inside sloshing over the edges. When they backed away, Brott's cries filled the air. The thief-master shoved him. Stumbling, Brott fell headfirst into the water.

The explosion knocked Grint back, sucking the sound from his ears and replacing them with ringing bells. Red mist rained down, shocking him back to a state of clarity. Regaining his equilibrium, he watched those on the street picking themselves up, laughing as they did. Even Borismere grinned. As the sound came back, Grint shook the viscera from his hair and stood.

"Killing Brott doesn't fill me with confidence on my chances of surviving this," Grint yelled.

"What are you doing?" Smit coughed.

"He knows we're here. Why hide?" Grint whispered back.

"I tell you what, come down and I'll only kill two of you. The third can live," Borismere was having a laugh at them. He knew there were just three of them up here. How? Brott wouldn't have known Dusk Raven didn't show, or Keranue was somewhere else. How many leaks did the ship have?

"One can live? I have your word?" Smit and Billy glared at Grint, their concern growing. It sounded as if he were bargaining for his own life and not theirs. Did he care any longer? Chances are one of them was a traitor too.

"If I'm lying, I will remove my veil and face the sun," Borismere shouted. "I proclaim this for all to witness."

"Charffing liar," Smit said. "He doesn't fear Ashgra."

"I don't want to die," Billy breathed, paling at the idea. An inexperienced kid like him still thought he'd live forever and never get caught.

"We aren't the ones who will." Smit swung at Grint, who rolled on his back. In a vulnerable position, all Grint could do was position his feet under the larger man when he fell on him. Smit's eyes widened as Grint launched him, catapulting him onto the next level of the dome. Springing up, Grint kicked Billy before he could finish a conjuration, taking the air from his lungs. There had to be a way off the roof without jumping. On the front side of the dome was a window, something he could climb through and then down.

"Billy," Grint sighed before he took three steps. The rooftop twisted into unmanageable angles until he couldn't tell up from down. The magic broke, setting everything back so fast that it made him queasy. Smit tackled his brother, covering him with his own body. Before Grint figured out why, the first drop of rain fell on his forehead, rolling down to the bridge of his nose and into the corner of his right eye. Blinking it away, he saw the guards taking cover as the soft splat of a banger hit the dome.

"Charffing, hedge-born harpies," Grint cried as he jumped. A blast of air, more violent than the first, rocked the roof. What felt like a thousand tiny knives rained across his body as debris flew about. Disoriented, unable to see or hear, all he could go by was what he felt, and it felt as if the world tilted sideways. The roof collapsed, sending him into an uncontrolled tumble. Grint flailed through the open air. Somewhere before he struck the ground, something gripped his ankle and pulled hard. The muscles screamed and hip joint threatened to pull loose. *At least I'm not falling anymore.*

Thick plumes of dust made opening his eyes a challenge. Grint shook his head, trying to dislodge the tiny grunchels blurring his vision. Sound hadn't fully returned as he watched chunks of stone fall around him. Rain seeped through the gaping maw of the roof as the evening storm picked up. The wet flow of water streamed down his body. *Or is it blood?* Probably both seeing the discolored pool gathering beneath him.

Beneath, he thought. Grint came to understand his predicament. When the roof collapsed, he fell and caught a foot in the loop of a rope. Lady Lorelai was looking out for him. As he spun in a slow swinging circle, he reached up to free himself, but the rope tangled his ankle too tightly to just slip out. He fell back to hanging, breathing heavily from the exertion, and saw a tuft of hair beneath a pile of stone. Not a person or a stray. It was Borismere's dog. How had she gotten in here? Grint's heart broke. He liked Cur. Somewhere, he hoped Newman was faring better than he was.

The glint of light off a steel blade caught his attention. A knife sat on the ground, but it might as well be a mile away as he would never reach it in this state. As he stared longingly at the blade, shuffling steps he never heard brought someone into view. They reached out for the dagger, the tattoos on their arm covered in grime and congealing blood. It was Smit, of that there was no doubt. The burly tiger-man wavered on his feet as he looked at Grint. A moment later, Billy picked himself up from the rubble and leaned against his brother.

The elder Tagro took a step forward, knife held before him. Grint figured this was the end. Not that it was a bad run, but he'd hoped for it to end differently. As Smit took another step closer, he flipped the dagger over and held it, grip first. Shocked by the gesture, Grint almost dropped it, but Smit closed his hand tight to help him hold on.

Still unable to hear, he had to resort to reading lips. "Sorry," Smit said. "Like I said, we aren't the ones dying here."

The brothers left him there, stealing away into the stormy night. Armed now with a blade, Grint curled up, swinging his arm several times to catch the rope. On the eighth try - *Ninth*, Hobbe corrected - Grint caught hold and started cutting. It was slow going as everything hurt any time he moved. He almost gave up to wait for someone to find him, until he saw a chunk of stone with the last banger stuck to it. It must have collapsed inside before any water touched it. A situation on the verge of changing.

Water poured into the ruined temple from its non-existent roof, and a river ran toward the banger. Grint cut with furious speed, pausing only to take a breath and check on the water's progress. Without even trying to figure out how long he had, he acted as if it was no time at all. Cutting through the rope, he fell onto his back, rolled over, and scrambled on hands and knees toward the temple door. His feet slipped in the water, and he expected each breath to be his last as the world to turn to fire around him.

When he reached the street and the heavy downpour, he thought maybe the water passed the banger by. The next explosion threw him across the street and into an alleyway between shops. *Really Lorelai? Really?* Grint lay in a pile of muck, staring up at the rain. A mungle crawled onto his chest, curling up as one of its wrinkled hands pet Grint's face.

"I already have a pet," he coughed, struggling to sit. The mungle hissed and darted off, scratching his neck in anger. It wasn't deep, but he'd need something on it. Mungles spread disease faster than Orrish sailors.

Shouts came from several directions, but no one watched from their windows. Borismere must have cleared the Ashgran out the way he'd done the Upper Crust had to prepare for this sting. Grint knew that escape attempts would slip away quick if he didn't act, and stumbled into the street. With the rain and orders to stay away, no one came to light the lamps at dusk, giving him shadows to move through. *Where am I going?* The first place that came to mind was Orsava's manor. The guards had confiscated his belongings, but it should be empty by now. *At least to catch my breath.*

A young guard struggled to keep his torch lit in the rain. They never saw Grint as he lowered his shoulder, driving them both into a wall. Guard? This was a boy. Young enough that he struggled to grow a beard. The boy groaned and reached for his sword. Age didn't matter now. Grint swung hard, catching the guard's jaw. As he hit the ground, Grint collapsed on him, swinging a few more times to make sure he stayed down.

It hurt to pull the armband over his arm, but he managed. Then took a hood and mask from the kid's backpack and pulled them on too. *The disguise should hold with the help of darkness and rain,* he thought as he limped toward the Meskal. Grint kept moving, looking for somewhere he could climb down. Three guards ran toward him, and he tried waving them back.

"It's mayhem! Everything is falling apart," he shouted. They laughed and kept on, making jokes about Grint's manhood.

Just before the Gallery of the Sun sat a tall building with an open gate and tunnel. At the far end, in what looked like a stable, Grint heard voices and saw the bounce of torches. Laughter echoed off the stone, followed by cries of pain. With the stolen sword in one hand and dagger in the other, he walked toward it. Four guards passed the torch around as they took turns beating on Billy and Smit. The Tagro brothers hadn't gotten far.

Seeing the hood and mask of the city guard, the one with the torch smiled at Grint. "You want a lick? These are the ones Lord Borismere wants. Didn't say what condition he wanted them in."

"Yeah," Grint said, walking into the light.

Confusion overtook the guard. The mask and armband made sense, but Grint's tattered clothing and lighter skin didn't. "What outfit are you with?"

"Theirs," Grint said, cocking his head toward the Tagro's. Before the man could shout, Grint stuck the sword into his throat. Blood sprayed the stable walls. As he booted the man off the blade, he threw the dagger into the next man's neck. Two down before any of them had time to react.

The last two turned, ready to fight as their friends died in gurgling piles on the hay. Two-to-one odds weren't in his favor, not in the state he was in, but this was a better death than any he'd faced tonight. The closest guard tripped as Billy kicked a foot between his legs, leaving just the one to face Grint. They crossed swords and collapsed into close combat, dropping the blades as they struggled over a dagger in the guard's belt. Whoever won had the honor of re-sheathing the blade in the other man's chest. The guard elbowed him twice in the face. Grint spat out the tooth that came loose and drove his knee into the guard's groin. The fight fled from his opponent. Plunging the dagger deep through the guard's armor, Grint stood, holding up his fists, ready for the other. But the man never got up.

Smit climbed on him after Billy tripped the man, wringing his neck until the tongue swelled out of the mouth. Now, all three unarmed, beaten, bruised, and bloody, they stood staring, waiting for something to happen. Finally, Grint let out his breath and sat back against the stable walls. Blood from someone's wound pooled around the heel of his boot. The Tagros relaxed, easing down across from him.

Grint gave them a bloody smile and said, "Let's talk."

16

"Run, run, run. That's what I like to say to the thieves I hunt right before I kill them."

- Randorall Montfitzroy, Professional Thief-Catcher

Was it one day or two? Grint couldn't remember. He'd been on the run since Borismere's, never stopping for more than a moment to catch his breath. The sun set and rose and set again. Had it happened a third time? *Let's call it one day,* Hobbe said, his voice as tired as Grint's. During this blurred perception of time, he'd found his way in and out of a handful of fights. Underworld bashers, Blue Hands, Fishmongers, city guards, and a random fool with too much bravado. All with the bruises to prove it. Grint struggled against exhaustion, a constant drain threatening to take him down. How long since he'd slept? Or even eaten?

No time, he told himself. He needed to know what happened to Keranue. And what Mikil did with his bloody dog.

The subtle shift of wood and trickle of pebbles warned Grint of another fight. He looked up to see a falling shadow diving toward him. Rolling to the side, he dodged a dagger marked for his skull. The blade sparked where it struck stone. The tip ruined, the thief tossed it aside, pulling two new knives from his sleeves. Grint pulled himself up along the brass post of a gas lamp. With a deep sigh, he held his fists up, swaying in his stance as blood dripped from his chin. How many times had he fought this exact battle? Only now, there were no more knives up his sleeve. The last blade in his arsenal, and the one he liked best with its carved raven head on the hilt, broke in a fight with a hulking moron calling himself Jarry.

"Let's talk about this," the thief said, lowering his blade.

"You want to talk?"

"Racko does," the thief answered. "She says you're out of the gold business but she's willing to make a trade. Your life to meet with Blue Fingered Hobbe."

Grint found the offer so absurd that he fell back against the wall laughing. "She has to be joking."

"She's not," he said with growing uncertainty. "This is bad for business. Borismere is talking about hiring thief-catchers and we don't want that."

"I'll pass," Grint said, raising his fists.

"At least I can tell her I tried." The thief ran forward, slashing his blade in a crossing pattern. Grint turned his shoulder and charged. The blade cut through the fabric of his tunic, drawing blood, but he stole any time for a second strike. Grint tackled the Blue Hand into a wall. The knife dropped with an injured grunt. Grint pinned his throat with a forearm, hoping he'd just pass out. *Kry-damn!* The sneak thief raked his forearm with sharpened nails. Flesh tore away in ribbons in their frantic attempt to pry themselves loose.

"Enough," Grint spat as he took a handful of the thief's hair, stepped back, and with all the force he could muster punched the man in the throat. A wet choking sound accompanied the man's fall. Squirming on the ground, he clutched at his throat.

"I would have sent you back to Racko with a message, but I don't think you'll survive this." Grint picked up the dropped blade and tucked it in his belt.

"What's all this then?" A man asked as he wandered onto the thin street.

"A thief waylaid me from above," Grint said, watching the thief struggle to make sure they didn't get back up. Any hope that his stolen red armband would get him out of the next conflict faded fast. This was no ordinary man who approached. Neither was he a guard or thief. And he sure as Astapoor wasn't Salazian.

Wearing a neat brown vest with golden pinstripes, the six-foot eight man flexed the muscles on his tanned, tattooed arms. A mosaic of pirate ships, dragons in flight, and women wrapped in roses danced up and down his arms. Stringy white hair hung like cobwebs around his face as a single golden eye stared at Grint beneath a bushy brow. An eye-patch of pure black covered the other eye. *That's new.*

"Bloody Mavris Kane," Grint said, deflating. A thief-catcher of singular renown.

Two city guards approached from behind and blocked the other end. Mavris gripped his long club, Malfeasance, slapping it into his calloused palm. Tiny notches scarred the club's face, a cut for every victim it claimed. Trapped between Kane and the guards, Grint contemplated climbing. His fear of heights could kry-damn wait.

"Hello Grint," Mavris said. "I heard you were dead."

"Just took a long nap," Grint replied. "Simple mistake."

"Good for me. I found the prospect of not doing it myself to be a great disappointment. Now I can rectify that."

"Or you can look the other way," Grint smiled. "Nothing's been stolen."

"Yet," Mavris replied. "Not that it matters. There are bounties on your head from here to Papality City."

As they bantered, the Blue Hand turned purple, his arms waving in a last desperate struggle to live. As the spirit escaped him, he slumped over, kicking the base of a smoking brazier. The copper lid popped off, rolling and rattling as it came to rest. A small shovel protruding from the ashes teetered but settled back in place.

"And here I thought you had an aversion to killing," Mavris said, studying the corpse. "Something about the God of Murder?"

"Rent decided he had better things to do than chase me across Terragard," Grint shrugged.

"Good for you," Mavris laughed as he slid a set of brass knuckles onto his free hand. "Let's get started."

Grint didn't wait. Grabbing the end of the shovel, he flung hot ash at Mavris. The thief-catcher shrieked, lifting a hand to wipe his face. Grint used the moment to run, trying to squeeze past Mavris and away from the guards, but the thief-catcher was far from helpless. He swung Malfeasance to the side. The club glanced off the top of Grint's head. One step more and he would have been clear. Now he tumbled to the ground, rolling into a thick wooden door that rattled in its frame.

Recovered from the ash, Mavris lifted his face to the sky and screamed. A sound menacing enough to chill even the bravest of fools. "How about we go back to the banter?" Grint asked.

As if that will work, Hobbe said.

At least try to help.

How? I'm a voice in your head, Hobbe replied.

Mavris led with the club, thrusting it into Grint's gut as the thief punched him in the face. Keeping the cudgel out of the fight became the top priority. Grint got in close, pinning Kane's wrist, choosing to contend with the brass knuckles. The two traded blows, each left hook or jab from Kane felt like an assault from a phalanx of stoneskin warriors. The last blow missed Grint's cheek, splintering the wooden door. When he dropped the cudgel and tried to wrench himself free, Grint got a punch in that spun Mavris to the ground. Now was the time to run. Nothing left between him and an outlet into the Grand Runway. Mavris kicked at Grint from the ground, a weak, last-ditch attempt to win a battle he'd already lost. It almost made Grint feel bad to stomp the heel of his boot into the thief-catcher's face.

"Now where was I?" Grint twirled the knife in his hand and almost dropped it as he heard another blood-curdling scream. This time it wasn't Mavris, but one of the two city guards he'd forgotten were there. They'd been content to watch until now, but no longer. One guard backed away, shaking his head. The other dropped his mask, and when he looked at Grint, his eyes crackled red. *You've got to be bloody charffing me,* Grint thought. Orrish Drug Magic. Nacinti, to be exact. A rage inducer that numbed the pain centers in the brain while amplifying strength. There would be no stopping the guard, no fighting him. Anything Grint did would be like trying to tear a castle down with his bare hands.

"What is going on out here?" An old man shouted as he flung open the wooden door at Grint's back.

"City inspection," Grint clapped the man on the shoulder as he pushed past him, into the home. "Won't take a moment."

Grint looked for another way out as the guard shrieked and gave chase. Getting away wouldn't be as simple as outpacing him. Not when he'd become an unstoppable force able to smash through walls at the expense of flesh and bone, just to catch his quarry. Grint had to be smart and stay out of reach long enough for the Nacinti to run through his system. Of all the Orrish magics, this was the worst. The volatile powder gave many gifts, but when it faded - it faded hard. Many who took the drug didn't survive the crash. Until the guard dropped, Grint needed to slow the madman down or distract him.

The frame around the front door crumbled as the guard pushed through. Halfway out a back window, the rage monster caught sight of Grint and slapped the old man out of his way. Dropping into a central courtyard between buildings, Grint tried not to imagine the sound of every bone in the man's body shattering at once. He sprinted toward an alleyway that led back to the streets. Lines of laundry hung all around, but nothing to help him block the guard's path. The back window shattered as the guard leapt through, landing in a face first slide that would have torn the skin off anyone else's skull.

Grint vaulted over a series of low garden walls, stepping on plants and crushing vegetables on his way to the alley. The Guard kicked each wall into rubble like pieces of dried parchment. At this pace, Grint would tire long before the guard. He needed to climb, so he leapt from one wall to another, dancing over the clumsy swipes of the drugged guard, until he grabbed the edge of a low hanging roof. As he hung, a chunk of masonry smashed into the wall, shaking Grint loose. His leg caught the edge of a window as he fell and flipped him over to land on his head. Pain screamed in his ears, but the adrenaline of survival wouldn't let him stay down.

Legs shaking and body ready to give out, Grint bounced through the alley, using the walls to keep himself upright. His pace slowed, and the guard knew it, laughing as he followed through the tight confines between buildings. The guard would catch him, and when he did, there wouldn't be mercy. He wouldn't subdue or arrest Grint, instead choosing a more violent approach such as popping his head off like a wine cork. And that would be it. He stumbled into the street, bashing into a handful of soldiers. The leader, his face hidden beneath a shining copper mask, looked at Grint with wide-eyed anger. Tassels of silver along the length of his coat shook as he grabbed Grint, slamming him against a haberdashery sign.

"What's this then?" The captain's voice echoed within his mask.

Grint screamed in panic. A genuine emotion, but he layered on the melodrama as best he could. "He's coming! Bloody maniac has gone mad! He'll kill us all!"

"What is he talking about?" the captain asked, turning to the soldiers under his command.

"No clue, he's sun-addled," another answered, pointing at Grint's bare face.

A moment later the raging guard appeared, his red eyes filled with tears of blood that ran down his cheeks. The drug magic burned hot. In this most dangerous of states, his mind would collapse, confusing friend and foe as perception blurred. With a shake of his head, the guard slapped himself, acting as if a nest of hornets had taken residence in his skull. The clump of people in the street were to blame, and he screamed at them all. When the madman attacked, he punched a fist through the closest guard. The body stuck on his arm, and Grint gawked, watching as he tried to shake it loose.

As a unit, the other guards attacked. Encircling him with spears, they sought to drive him to a safe corner and keep him pinned until the magic wore off. Grint would have told them it was a fool's errand if he wasn't so happy about the distraction. The raging guard tore the body on his arm in half, and swung both parts in circles, knocking aside spears as the innards spilled out. Someone got a lucky jab in, driving their spearhead into his chest, but that only served to further enrage him. The madman screamed and stomped, punching and swatting, tearing apart anyone within reach. Three others died before the captain let Grint loose to join the battle. Striking with an impressive copper sword, he removed the raging guard's head in one swing. The magic fled the body as the headless corpse collapsed into convulsions.

"Get me a mage," the captain's scream faded as Grint rounded the corner.

A hundred people watched in horror, hiding in doorways and windows above. Grint lowered his head as he walked, trying to blend in. Impossible with his clothes torn apart. Horns blared from every direction. Blood oozed from the scratches on his arm and would need bandaged. Mavris wouldn't stay down long either. Grint needed to get off the street in a hurry. More guards flooded in from every direction, calling for backup with short horn blasts. When that backup reached the Blau, the dutiful citizens of Salaz would point them in Grint's bloody mess of a direction. He'd made a wrong turn for the Weeble. The fight turned him around, but if he kept along this road, it should lead him back.

In a small clearing stood wooden gallows. Citizens who had broken the law hung from frayed ropes. Judging by the state of the bodies, it was recent. They swayed in the soft breeze as mungles ran along the crossbeam, fighting with one another. A masked guard leaned against the scaffolding, head down. They looked asleep. Even the distant horns didn't draw them back from their slumber, but a handful of nosy buggers had been following Grint since the fight and now called out to wake the guard.

With a shouted expletive, Grint ducked into a rug vendor's shop. A small, dark room thick with the burning scent of incense. Black curtains pulled shut, blocked the daylight, making it difficult to see, and the candle on the counter had long since burned out. At first, Grint didn't think anyone was attending the shop. As he stepped deeper inside, the dread feeling that this might be a Salt Witch's lair paralyzed him. Fighting through it, he kept his back to the rug-covered wall. Outside, the people managed to rouse the guard, but had lost sight of where Grint ran off to.

"I am sorry for the incense," an old woman said. "I find it keeps the mungles out. Hard to sell rugs if they're covered in their urine."

Grint jumped at the suddenness and took a moment to catch his breath. An old woman stood from a chair with an enormous, padded back. She adjusted a white scarf wrapped around her eyes as she toddled toward him. *Blind*, Grint thought, realizing why she kept it so dark. "No problem, do you have a back way out?"

"That's an odd thing to ask," she said, pulling a cane off the counter.

"No need to help. I'm sure I can find it." Grint felt a tug of panic, trying not to think of salt witches.

"Always happy to help," she said. "But you've brought trouble to my door, and that I am unhappy about."

Grint backed away as she drew a dagger from the hilt of her cane. There had to be a door somewhere. Hidden behind one of the hanging rugs. *A salt witch for sure,* Hobbe whined. *She'll eat us, sprinkled with ashes.*

Not now, Grint thought back, slapping rugs, yanking them down when he could.

"I hear the guards gathering," the woman continued. "They skitter like roaches on the street. They'll infest my store because of you."

The woman lunged with her dagger. Grint side-stepped and slashed her wrist with his own dagger. High, strangled screams followed him as he ran to the rugs, peeling them away. Behind a blue rug with interlocking circles, he found a rickety wood door. *Locked.* The old woman advanced on the sound, shouting words in a thick accent that Grint knew no translation for. Old fingers, the skin like aged leather, wrapped around his throat. For an old woman, her grip held strong.

The guard, alerted by her scream, walked toward the open door. Grint just wanted to scare her back, threaten her, but when he twisted round, she pressed into him, driving the dagger into her own heart. The old woman's mouth hung open as she went slack in his arms.

"Rank, fool-born luck," he growled, setting her lifeless body atop a rug. Grint kicked the door open, finding a back room filled with piles of old junk. He slammed the door shut as the guard entered the store and pulled down junk to block it. A window, caked over with mud, hid behind a cabinet. Grint pulled it down and smashed out the glass. Careful not to cut his hands, he climbed out to a garden that had long since died.

Grint limped through an alley, watching the rooftops for any signs of roving Blue Hands. Ears ringing, he couldn't determine where the faint sound of running steps originated. When had the city up and gone crazy? The proverbial bell had tolled. *I should have gotten out. Found Newman and run.*

Grint pushed through a pile of rotting crates and stood across from the Chain of Weebles. He couldn't see them but would bet every coin in Borismere's basement there were at least eight thieves with nocked arrows crouched above. You live long enough as a thief; you learned the spaces to hide in and where others chose to. *Going into the tavern seems like the opposite of living long.*

Don't go coward on me now, Hobbe said. Or maybe that was his own voice this time.

"Just going to grab my bag and go," Grint called out as he crossed the street. "Time to move on."

No one rained arrows down on him. If they were even there. How stupid would he look if he'd shouted at no one? Grint chewed on his inner cheek as he stared at the tavern's tarnished knob. Dusk Raven knew about this place. Or the Spymaster General.

Stepping into a tavern he'd been in and out of a dozen times, the smell of rotting wine always surprised him. Gus at least lit candles today, which chased off the rodents, but that was probably because of the comely female sitting at the end of the bar, swirling her drink around in a dusty brown cup. *Nazarra.* Sitting on a stool with her feet kicked up, she didn't look at the door when he came in, but she'd heard him.

This one has eyes all over her bloody head, Hobbe cackled. Grint dragged his right leg as he approached the bar. He tore the tattered remnants of the red armband loose, tying it around his arm to stop the bleeding. Gus shook his head as if a few drops of blood would chase away his clientele and poured Grint a mug of something brown from the tap.

"Cheers," Grint smiled.

"You owe me for all them bottles you broke downstairs," Gus said as he walked away.

"Charming as always," Grint said, taking a drink that he found hard to swallow. Nazarra smiled, a mirthful thing.

"Glad this is amusing," he said as he took the ale and shoved her feet aside so he could sit. "You broke a few of those bottles yourself, Dusk Raven."

"You caught me," she laughed.

"Which Nazarra am I talking to today? The resistance fighter? Spymaster? Thief?" *Love?* That one he didn't ask, not wanting to know her answer. Another sip of the ale didn't improve its taste. Grint came close to spitting it out.

"I think he brews it in salt water," she whispered.

"With a chain full of weebles at the bottom." Grint guzzled the ale, deciding he didn't want to be sober right now. "Gus, what exactly is a weeble?"

The bartender mumbled something as he pretended to clean a mug.

"I never intended to betray you," she said, still swirling her drink.

"And yet you did," Grint shifted his seat, giving him half a chance to pull a dagger if she got antsy. "But don't worry about it, I had Dusk Raven pegged as a traitor from the moment I met her."

"You had Billy follow me the other night, didn't you?"

"Yes," Grint answered, rapping the mug on the bar for a refill.

"You want more?" Gus looked stricken at the concept.

"Keep them coming," Grint tried to smile, but everything hurt, so he coughed instead. When he finished, he wiped his chin and took a breath. "Brott wasn't as easy to spot. He was Orsava's friend. Now he is a spot. Brott the spot. Poetic."

"What about Billy and Smit?" she asked, setting her cup down. Grint tensed, unsure what her intentions would be. "Guards found them cut open and strangled with their own entrails. Was that you and your poetry?"

"Maybe," Grint said.

"And where did it get you?" Her eyes drooped, taking on a glassy glimmer around the edges. *Tears?*

"Same place it got you. A handful of rusty ales in a tavern full of weebles," Grint laughed this time.

"My duty is to my sister," Nazarra objected. "Everything I did served that."

"Everything?" Grint smiled.

"Why didn't you run? Or take Racko's offer? Why come back here?" she asked.

"Originally, I thought about killing you," Grint said. She didn't flinch. "But I like you too much. Then I thought to find Orsava's assassin. Honestly, this city is a mummer's fair in deep winter. You can all keep it. I just want my dog back."

"Someone stole your dog?" she asked. "I thought Angis was watching him,"

"Angis is probably dead too," Grint slapped the bar. "But you already knew that."

Except she didn't. For the first time the smile on her face faltered, replaced by genuine concern. It infuriated

Grint that she hid whose side she was on. *She's on all of them. Or none.*

"You should have stuck around for the botched heist. The things you could have learned," Grint said as he flipped the mug over.

"Why not tell me now?"

Grint slid off the stool, tipping an imaginary hat. "Get rid of the floppy hat. It hides your face. Nothing should ever do that." As he walked toward the door Gus ran down the stairs to the basement. "Well, that can't be good."

"Don't go out there," Nazarra said. "I negotiated to keep you alive."

Grint cracked the door and looked out. The street was full of guards in red armbands, Opposition in blue and white, Blue Hands, and even Mavris Kane. "Kry-damn luck," Grint chuckled. Nazarra walked up behind him. A sorry, pleading look in her eyes. She lifted her hand and blew dust in his face. Grint had a moment to choke on it before the world went dark.

17

Teelo Tane stood on the edge of the mountain, bearing its weight on his back. Those who thought to imprison the mighty warrior in a tomb of stone would soon learn the error of their ways."

- The Tale of Teelo Tane, Parthian Barbarian
p.Annum 9874

When the crow weeps. It is then you should expect your love to betray you. For Chell to have predicted Marra's betrayal, a murder of crows would need to weep an ocean, but the land choked with drought the day his love gifted him to Brasau, the Hangman. Tied to a post in the center of the village. Chell watched the Hanging Men rummage through the spoils of their conquest as others took amusement in torturing his warriors.

Hanging Men with their signature braids tied in nooses. Dozens of the trophy braids swung from each of Brasau's warriors. From their faces, their arms, backs, their legs, and chests. Each earned with a kill. Such chicanery. No one in all the valley believed Brasau or his warriors killed even half the number they claimed.

Their brazen attack on Chell's village should have failed. Brasau was no tactician, stumbling over his own feet when hunting boar. It succeeded because Marra dosed the victory feast, putting everyone to sleep. Brasau and his monsters walked through the gate unopposed. And where were Marra and Brasau now? Sullying his bed with their treacherous mating. Those of his tribe who survived looked at him with pitying eyes. Had he been a good warlord to them? He grew his territory and honored the old ways. What more could they ask of him?

To protect them from this, he told himself.

They could not execute him. Even Brasau would not dishonor Parthian heritage in such a way. Instead, when they finished destroying the village, a ceremony to strip Chell of title and honor would begin. A lone warrior expelled from Parthia to atone for the dishonor of losing in battle. Dishonor. Did the betrayal of a life-mate bring dishonor? It should be Brasau and Marra feeling the cold lick of the Gellanore River as they swam from home. Not him. But whining did not change his circumstance. The warriors he knew and loved were dead already. They gave the others a choice. Join the Hanging Men or die. Chell would not fault them for surviving.

Brasau finished his ill-deed and exited the chief's dome, tightening a belt around his briefs. Such malice twisted his features as he strutted about the village. The look Chell returned mirrored the conqueror's own. Brasau's stark white fur marked him as an oddity in the Parthian world. Hunting with bright fur alerted prey, so few wished to fight beside him. The bitterness of his ostracizing grew over the years, making his motives dark and his deeds worse.

Brasau slapped Chell's cheek as he stood before him. "Do you know why she betrayed you?"

"I hope because you bewitched her with your dreego witches," Chell said. All knew Brasau consorted with the dreego and even made them part of his tribe.

"You never gave her children." Brasau found a log and pulled it over. He snapped a finger and his Hanging Men shoved brave young Jesto toward the food. Jesto would have made a fine warrior in Chell's service, but under Brasau he'd become a food fetcher.

"I can," Brasau continued as he looked over the plate, picking out the most succulent bits of meat. As he chewed with an open mouth, the juices ran into the fur on his chin. A purposeful act, smelling Chell's hunger. "In fact, I did. Just now. And our child will grow to conquer all of Parthia. Let all know this."

"When I find atonement, and I will, I will come for you and Marra," Chell said. When he finished what he meant as a fierce proclamation, his stomach rumbled. Brasau laughed, mocking him with the help of his cowardly warriors.

"Even your stomach betrays you. What fear does a pitiful creature such as you pose?" The war-leader stood, leaving the half-eaten plate on the stump of wood for Chell to look at and smell. He closed his eyes and imagined Atonement. When he opened them, Marra stood before him with a torch in her hand. No words passed between them, just the silent condemnation of two loves torn asunder.

Marra swung the torch, striking Chell across the face. He writhed beneath the spreading fire as it consumed his fur and then his soul.

*****

Chell woke from his nightmare. Thick manacles meant for a dreego pinched his wrists, cutting off circulation to his hands. As he shook them, the chains leading to the wall rattled. The prison cell, his home for the last few days, was a cramped chamber of wet stone that crumbled against his back when he shifted positions. Sadly, he was not alone. The other occupants chattered without end. Even now, they argued like the angry tree monkeys littering the rooftops of Salaz. Each imprisoned for trespasses against queen or state.

Among the motley crew were two goblins, Trimbo and Puig, arrested for mischief in the queen's court that Chell did not quite understand. A dark-skinned magician called Tennebrue, who shot fire into the sky during a night of drunken revelry. A beaten man who was a thief of some sort. And a newcomer, his hair alight with the fire of a sunrise and gleeful roguery in his eyes. That one reminded Chell too much of Brasau.

"Look who's awake," the fire-head said.

"Ahh good," Trimbo lit up as he spoke. "Perhaps you'd like to join."

"Another is nice, but it's still unanimous against you," Puig added.

"Unanimous? Keranue, how could you?" The fire-head said in outrage. The injured man moaned something in response that they all accepted as a cogent answer.

"So how about it?" The fire-head asked, looking back at Chell.

"Does it hurt? The fire on your head," Chell answered. The man reached up, chains jingling, and then relaxed.

"You're talking about my hair color," he laughed. "No, it doesn't hurt."

"Odd," Chell said. "I have not met many dreego, but those few did not bear that color."

"It is unusual," the mage said. "Some say those with red hair are the spawning of demons or in service to them."

The fire-head's demeanor changed from mirth to outrage. "I'm not a charffing demon or in league with them. Hate those blasted kry-damn things." The injured man mumbled something, and they all nodded.

"What happened to that one," Chell said, pointing to him.

"Keranue made the mistake of getting caught in an act of larceny," fire-head said. "There's still a chance he might be why we got caught, but seeing him now, that doesn't appear likely."

"And that is why you're here?"

"Maybe," the fire-head said. "I caused some trouble for sure, but this seems extreme." The fire-head reached out, offering his hand. "I'm Grint."

"Chell," the Parthian answered but made no move to reciprocate. The distance between them was too great.

"Some trouble?" Puig laughed. "You tore apart half the city."

"I did no such thing," Grint protested. "That was the charffing guard on Orrish powder."

"You must have done something," Chell said, finding himself drawn into their banter whether or not he wanted it.

"True," Grint nodded. "But I didn't attack the queen."

"Yes, Parthian," Tennebrue said, his face hidden in a shadow, but Chell smelled... what was that coming off him? Enjoyment? "Tell us why you tried? What did you hope to accomplish?"

"Was it Atonement?" Grint asked, sitting back. The magician's demeanor changed, his amusement dying at the interruption. Anger in the quickening beat of his heart. Fire in the flare of his nostrils. Perhaps it should be this one he compared to Brasau and not Grint.

"What do you know of Parthian Atonement?" The last dreego he met knowledgeable in the ways of his people poisoned him.

"Enough to say that killing a queen is like shooting the moons with an arrow. Your atonement must be deep."

"This was not Atonement," Chell admitted. "They forced me into it."

"The poisoning trick?" Grint asked, his eyebrows rising.

"A coward's trick," Chell grumbled, ashamed to have fallen prey to it.

"I'd be afraid to meet someone who could force a barbarian to do anything," Trimbo shuddered, consoled by his goblin partner. Chell never cared for the dreego word barbarian. When they said it, they meant stupidity and mindless bloodshed. That was not the Parthian way, no matter what the dreego thought.

"How close did you get?" Tennebrue asked.

"I do not know," Chell turned away to signal his dismissal of the question.

"How can you not?" Trimbo asked.

"You were there. You must," Puig added.

"Unless you weren't there," Trimbo said.

"But then he wouldn't have gotten close. Think first," Puig slapped the other goblin on the arm.

"I thought, you maldungous fool," Trimbo replied, slapping him back. "The wizard asked how close. The Parthian never said he got close at all."

"Very true," Puig said, bowing his head. "Apologies."

"Would you try again if you could?" Tennebrue asked, leaning forward so his features caught the firelight in a most displeasing way. Twisted and elongated shadows ran at angles along his cheekbones, bringing back visions of Brasau's salt witches.

"I fear I must," Chell coughed. "They will not cure the poison unless I do. But I cannot remember if I stood on the precipice of success or not."

"You got close," Grint answered for him. "From the stories I heard."

"Perhaps. The queen is a sorceress. I did not fall until she blew the dust in my face," Chell said of the woman.

"Your harpy's sister put me here," Grint said. "Except I let her blow the dust in my face."

"Which brings us back to the start," Trimbo said.

"Yes, back to the wager," Puig continued.

"The thief says he will perform a magnificent escape before day's end," Tennebrue said to Chell. "The goblins and I disagree. And as goblins do, there is now a wager involved in the matter."

"Care to join?" The goblins asked in unison.

"No," Chell said. "I have no desire to engage in your foolishness. When my strength returns, I plan to leave myself."

"Do you now?" Trimbo said, his green eyes narrowing.

"How?" Puig mirrored the look of his compatriot.

"I will pull the chains from the stone." There was general laughter at the idea that Chell did not care for.

"Those chains can hold ogres," Trimbo smiled when his mirth faded.

"Not even a Parthian could break them," Puig said.

"Do I smell another wager?" Trimbo asked his counterpart.

"I do, indeed." Puig nodded.

"One bet at a time is enough," Grint scowled. "But I wouldn't pass up on this Chell. An inside source told me they stacked the odds against me. So, when I escape, you'll stand to make a lot of coin."

"Leave me be." Chell closed his eyes. This appeared to satisfy the lot of them, and they went back to speaking amongst themselves. Their inane chatter continued to no end.

The sickness ate at him. He could feel it gnawing at the walls of his gut, sprouting roots that wound around his chest, squeezing and scratching when he breathed. That was why he lost the fight against the queen. At least that was what he told himself. *If I were strong, I would have won.* Brasau laughed, a phantom of the mind that would not go away. How long did he have left before the poison stole his life? Two risings? Three? It was nothing but false bravado to think he'd regain strength enough to tear these chains loose. From this point on, he would only get weaker.

How did the fools who poisoned him expect him to accomplish the task if his body withered into decay before he finished? *They do not care,* Chell admitted to himself. There would also be no cure - if he wanted to keep telling himself the truth, but that was a hard path to travel and one that would render him without hope. Best to continue in the belief he would come out of this and continue his trek for Atonement - and then revenge.

Chell opened his eyes. The fire-headed thief stared out the only window in the cell and had been since Chell closed his eyes. What was he looking for? The answer appeared to come as the sun dipped below the portal.

"How about we sweeten the pot," Grint asked. The goblins shivered with joy.

"What did you have in mind?" Trimbo asked.

Puig followed with, "We demand something worthy of our time."

"The two of you have been wanting the Mantle of Hermadales. If I lose, I agree to steal it for you when we get out?"

"Bold," Trimbo said.

"And if you win?" Puig asked, more skeptical than his counterpart.

"I have a job the two of you would be perfect for." Grint waited for a response as the pair whispered among themselves.

"You know these two?" Chell asked, picking up on the thief's words of what the goblins wanted.

"I do," Grint replied. "Mainly by reputation, but we've crossed paths once or twice."

"This is all academic, to be sure," Tennebrue chimed in. "None of us are leaving this prison alive, so the thought of stealing things or doing jobs is ridiculous. If you get out of the cell, you would still have to get past the guards and out the front gate. And beyond them we're on an island. Do you have a boat?"

"I'm a strong swimmer," Grint smiled.

"Foolishness," Tennebrue laughed. "The harbor is full of siren eel. And I see by your unenthusiastic reaction that you're familiar with them."

"They make a horrible stew," Grint shrugged.

"They also have sharp, poison teeth that turn your limbs to stone. And if you survive that, they lay eggs with their bites. Tiny things under your skin that migrate into your gut. When they hatch, your body melts around you. It's a genuine horror to witness." Tennebrue smelled pleased at the downturn of Grint's mouth. "I think I would like to up my bet by one thousand plicks."

"Anyone else?" Grint looked around. "Keranue?" The injured man mumbled something to make the goblins giddy. "Okay, Chell you sure you don't want in?"

The Parthian waved his hand, unwilling to take part in their nonsense. "No. Besides, I have none of your money."

"That is of no concern," Puig said, drooling.

"Happy to make a loan," Trimbo nodded. "Just with a ten percent interest on the original amount."

"I'll give you it at nine percent," Grint laughed.

"Shocked I am at such low-ballery," Trimbo shouted.

"I'll give you eight," Puig said, rubbing his little green hands together.

"Eight?" Trimbo paled. "Now you're undercutting me too?"

"I'm undercutting Grint. We share our money."

"I beg your pardon?" Trimbo did not sound pleased with the revelation. "Since when have we done that?"

"Forever," Puig frowned. "Who do you think has been buying the drinks all these years?"

"You," Trimbo scoffed.

"Goblin arguments aside, Chell's 'no' stands. So that's everyone." Grint stuck two fingers in his mouth and whistled. The goblins watched in perplexed silence, furrowing their brows as the moments swept past. Before they could celebrate their victory, they heard tiny footsteps outside the cell.

The cell door was a latticework of black steel bars set into the wall with a single door in the center. Its hinges appeared stronger than the chains binding Chell. A locking mechanism kept the door shut, and Chell admired the design. The makers built it into a wall outside the cell to keep prisoners from exploiting it.

Chell jumped as a small face appeared between the lower set of bars. The quiet suddenness of it a shock. A dreego child with smudges of dirt across his face looked around, stopping only when his eyes fell on the fire-haired thief.

"Are you Grint?" the child asked.

"I am," the thief said as the manacles around his wrist fell away. With an exaggerated stretch, he stood. The child plucked his head back through the bars and disappeared. A moment later the lock rumbled and bars swung open.

"And just like that, I am victorious," Grint took a bow as if the room applauded the escape attempt. No one did.

"Cheating," Puig scowled, wagging a finger in the air. "This nullifies the wager."

"How so?" Grint looked and smelled offended.

"You already had a plan prior to the wager. Skulduggery at its basest form."

"Trimbo doesn't appear to agree with you," Grint added, staring down the silent goblin.

"I think it is a turn of genius and one we should have expected," Trimbo nodded. "We allowed him to bamboozle us. I say, well done."

The boy returned to the door, annoyed at having to wait. Grint got to work on the goblins' manacles, freeing the halflings. "You two owe me a job," he said as he worked on Keranue's wrists. When they fell away, he helped the injured thief stand.

"Mmmrphhdnna," Keranue said through bruised, cracked lips.

"I know," Grint answered. "We'll get you some ale when we're clear of this place."

"I think a mage might be worth the bother," Tennebrue added. "To whatever venture you have planned."

"I've had my fill of wizards on this adventure," Grint twisted his mouth.

"Even one that now owes you somewhere in the realm of ten thousand plicks?" Tennebrue held out his wrists with a hopeful smile. "Hard to pay you while I languish in this place."

"Right. Right. No need for you to rot here. Chell? How about you? Want another chance to kill the queen?"

"It would require a life-debt to you," Chell answered. "As you said, too many already on this adventure."

"Keep your debt," Grint said. "We'll call it square and you can go about your Atonement."

Chell thought about it, ignoring the eye rolls of the small dreego, then held out his wrists. "So be it."

Grint whispered with the goblins as the young dreego freed the wizard and then his own manacles. Rubbing his wrists, Chell followed them out of the cell. The posted guard slumped in his chair, drool falling from his mouth.

"Is he dead?" Tennebrue asked.

"No," the child answered. "Just sleeping with some help."

"I still don't see how we'll get off the island," the wizard continued as they walked with impunity through the corridors. Other cells, dark and full of prisoners, lined the hallway. Chell felt sickened by it. Most of those they saw were frail, underfed, and in the last days of life. The Queen of Salaz had imprisoned them all. Forced or not, there had to be some measure of Atonement for dispatching her. But that would not be up to him to decide. Only the Oracle could tell him if it paid the price.

Reaching a dead end in a hallway full of spider webs, the dreego child pulled a stone loose and reached inside. The opening was so small that no one else aside from the goblins could have fit their hand in. A moment later, a metal latch clicked, and the stones swung open, revealing a hidden room. A circular, windowless room with a single hole in the center of the floor. The kid pointed into it.

"This goes down?" Tennebrue asked, looking into the hole.

"That's the idea," Grint answered.

"Down to where?"

"The tunnels," the dreego child answered. "Just be careful of the ogres." There was a wicked smile on the child's face.

"That's just a joke, Trimbo," Grint said, shaking his head at the boy. "The kid knows how to move around the tunnels under the harbor. Now if you don't mind, I'd like to go before the guard wakes up."

"I hate ogres," Trimbo said, disappearing into the hole.

"Amazing," Tennebrue said. "I have always heard of the old tunnels, but never found the entrances. Amazing."

Chell stopped the thief before he went down. "Regardless of your denial, I owe you a debt."

"How about you make sure the ogres don't bite my head off?" Grint smiled as he started climbing into the hole.

"That was an attempt at mirth?"

"No," Grint answered. "Not at all."

Chell blew out an angry breath, shaking his head. "Dreego."

18

*"A darkened tunnel is only as long as the breath you allow it.
Your terror makes it no longer."*

- Kharlo Donne, The Philosophy of Nowhere

Grint often preferred the depths of a tunnel. Some turned to jelly underground, giving in to the nightmare of being buried alive. Not that Grint judged them for it. If you put him in a bell tower and told him to jump for his freedom, Grint would choose captivity and spend the next year planning an escape. This time, he didn't have to.

According to the texts in Orsava's library, tunnelers had created the old passages from the city to the island during the reign of an evil wizard. Lord Azzlebahn... *Angraball? Ashtigran?* The wizard had a penchant for icing things and froze the harbor to stop supplies reaching the people. The magic faded as it reached the island, so the rebellion directed their ships to land outside when dropping off supplies. Workers used the tunnels to carry them in. Orsava hounded Grint to read about it, as a lesson in understanding the Opposition.

Well, Angis read it aloud to me, Grint recalled.

A wandering hero from Bar Church killed the wizard, and the spell broke. The tunnels fell into disuse before being forgotten, but the architecture used in building them held for centuries, perhaps even millennia. The Ashgran Priests, never ones to admit they weren't in charge, struck most accounts of the wizard and hero from record, so none of the histories in Orsava's library were clear on when it took place, only that it was long ago. And among the dozens of tomes, only one mentioned the tunnels. Try as they might, such places never ceased to exist. Someone would always find them, use them - and that someone was the network of street urchins.

"The Opposition would love access to this tunnel," Tennebrue said. "The fighters we could free from Allast Island would turn the tide of our struggle."

"Our struggle?" Grint asked.

"You use the tunnel, you pay us," the kid snarled from the dark. The wizard acted as if he wanted to scoff at the idea, but Grint stopped him with a hand on the shoulder. Wisely, Tennebrue didn't push any further. Fighting against the queen was one thing. Going to war against the urchins was something the Opposition wouldn't be ready for.

"Yes," Tennebrue said in a softer voice to Grint. "Our struggle. I am a proud supporter of Prince Mikil and his Opposition against the unjust Queen Mahd."

"Sounds exciting," Grint said in his most sarcastic tone.

"We could use someone like you," the wizard replied, either not hearing or just plain ignoring the cheek.

"Like me?"

"Yes, someone who can get in and out of places you don't belong," Tennebrue said.

"I'm already spoken for," Grint answered. "And before you ask to buy me a drink, I'll pass on that too."

The low wheezing he heard after the comment turned out to be Tennebrue's laugh. The sound turned his stomach, reminding him of an evil lord sitting on a throne in their ruined keep. There were two types - the tyrant squeezing the populace of all their worldly goods, sitting on a trove of treasure, magic items, jewels, and coin. If timed just right, you could stroll in while some fool hero fought the lord and get the best of the loot. *Good times*, Grint smiled.

Then there was the other. The rotten ones into necromancy, blood magic, salt, spirits, and other vile corruptions. Instead of treasure, you'd find victims of torture, mutilation, and other experimentations. Horrible things to make even the heartiest knight fall to their knees. Tennebrue reminded him of that type, so he backed away from the wizard, letting the goblins take his place.

"Can we get some light?" Trimbo called out.

"Why? I have no interest in seeing what it is I'm stepping in," Puig replied.

Damp strings of algae hung from the arched tunnel ceiling, leaving behind green stains when they touched skin or clothes. The urchin lit a soft glow orb and handed it back through the line for the wizard to hold, allowing them to see in what otherwise would have been utter darkness. Rats scurried from the light, running in lines along half-sunken stones and congealed sludge. Everyone sloshed along, a somber hush settling in as the misery of their journey sank into their bones.

"Where are we?" Trimbo called back.

"Under the harbor," Grint said. "Keep moving."

"Are any of those eels in here with us?"

"Thank you, Puig. I hadn't thought of that," Grint growled, trying to see through the black water.

"I'll wager three silvers that we find one," Puig continued.

"Five," Trimbo countered. "That we don't."

Grint knew better than to get between goblins when they started betting. Focusing his mind instead on the next steps, such as getting out of the tunnel and back to the job of stealing the gold. Every voice he ever imagined in his head screamed for him to leave the job behind, find his dog, take the goblins and head out to Rhysin. After a few days to rest, they could steal a few jewels and cheat at a game of cards.

No, he replied. *Not with this much gold. No.*

Keranue walked on his own, reaching for the wall when his knees buckled. Without the room to walk beside him, Grint had him place a hand on his shoulder instead. Leading him through the tunnel, Grint whispered to the cart-driver.

"Angis?"

Keranue mumbled a response that Grint took as I don't know. From what Grint gathered before getting caught, Angis had disappeared - dead or alive? No one knew. Keranue kept his thick-mouthed mumbles coming, but it was hard to pick any word out of ten. *Separated. Guards. Thieves.* There was more to the story, but for now he'd have to fill it in on his own. They got separated by the guards waiting to ambush them. They tried to run, but the Blue Hands stopped them. *Close enough to kill a dragon*, Grint thought.

The cramped passage leveled out and then rose. Water trickled past them in an active flow, striking stones like a babbling brook. Trimbo demanded silver for the eel wager. Grint wished for a blade as the group entered a circular chamber with seven exits. The glow orb illuminated a raised stone platform in the center of the room. An altar for an evil wizard's sacrifice. The urchin's bare feet left behind wet foot-prints as he climbed onto the stone. Rummaging through his pockets, he pulled out a wad of grass and two stones that he struck together. The sparks danced over the dried grass until a small fire lit, at which time he stood, watching the dark doorways.

"What are we waiting for?" Trimbo asked, draining water from his boots. The boy held a finger to his mouth and hissed. The goblin shook his head and handed a necklace he'd been keeping in his pocket over to the other. Another lost wager, no doubt. What wouldn't they gamble on?

"Tell me about this job," Puig whispered to Grint.

"Later," Grint replied as he helped Keranue sit against the stone and approached the boy.

The Parthian had not come out of the tunnel unscathed either. Strands of algae tangled his fur, giving Chell a mon-strous appearance in the low flickering light of the fire. Every one of them looked tired and uncomfortable. Grint could relate. He was ready for warmth, a hot meal, and a change of clothes. And gold. Lots of gold.

"Are we waiting on Matty?" Grint asked and got the same shush the goblin did.

"They come," the kid grunted as large gray shapes emerged from the tunnels.

Muddlers, as Keranue called them. Ogres anywhere else. Foy strongmen with a taste for human flesh. They lum-bered in, their sagging gray flesh hanging across bone pro-trusions at every joint. Foy flies buzzed around their mouths and made nests in the ogres' giant ears. One ogre was too many to fight. There were five. Who knew how many more waited in the dark. Ogres were best known best for riddles and devouring intruders. That they didn't rush the group in an angry charge meant the urchins must have struck a deal with them. *Crafty buggers.* The wizard hadn't pieced that together. Grint saw the red spark of a spell forming on the tips of his fingers. *That won't go well.*

"Answer our riddle and you shall pass," the tallest of the ogres said in a voice as slow as cold honey.

"What is that?" Another ogre said, interrupting the first as they pointed a thick finger at Chell.

"A Parthian," Trimbo cried out.

"And a barbarian," Puig added. The goblins nodded at one another.

"So, we answered," Trimbo began.

"Now we pass," Puig finished.

"That was not the riddle." The lead ogre scratched his head, chewing on the flies who crawled into his mouth. The squint of his eyes was from a distaste for flies or displeasure at the turn of events.

Trimbo ad Puig talked back and forth. One, then the other.

"You demanded we answer a question."

"And we did."

"A correct answer."

"Not our fault that one asked a question different from what you intended."

"We won our passage square and fair."

"Fair and square."

"No one likes to be corrected, Trimbo."

"I apologize, Puig."

"Silence," the ogre roared, pulling a thick hunk of wood off its hairy belt.

"Bachha," the boy cried out in a guttural language Grint knew from one of Hobbe's many lessons.

Speaking the few words he recalled, Grint said, "Brahsh moya gelin." Then clicked and popped a few times with his mouth. The ogres took an interest in this, putting their heads together. After a whispered conversation, the ogres laughed, relaxing their weapons.

"I like you, man on fire," the lead ogre said.

"Thanks, now ask the riddle," Grint responded and brandished a fist at the goblins as they got ready to go off on another tangent.

"Forty-three and five. Ancestors wither and thrive. A map with no compass. Boat with no oar. A place where men fish no more. Where am I?"

"Well, that's just a rambled collection of words," Tennebrue scowled. The goblins didn't appear much more pleased about it.

"The harbor?" Keranue asked as much as answered with the first intelligible thing he'd said all day.

"That's not his answer," Grint held up his hand as two ogres walked toward Keranue, pleading without getting in their way. "We're just discussing. Harkest! Harkest, friend."

But Grint could not dissuade an ogre set upon its path. The two fell upon Keranue as the cart-driver screamed, tearing off his arms and passing them to the others as if they were collecting loaves of bread from a larder. Grint turned away. There was nothing he could do, not without bigger weapons and his bag. Tennebrue's conjured spark grew as the wizard chanted. Crimson light filled the room. That was at least one thing he could do.

"Stop it, you goat-snared maniac. You'll get us all killed," Grint shouted, making eye contact and trying to avoid the snap of the magic. The wizard looked confused, but nodded, extinguishing the magic. "Ogre skin is tough to penetrate with magic. You might hurt one, but the rest..."

"I understand," Tennebrue said. "That is good to know."

The lead ogre made a clicking sound as the other two finished dismantling the body. Keranue's eyes sat wide in his skull. Grint thought they might roll out as the ogre carried it away.

"What was that?" Chell coughed, his voice weak.

"You answer wrong and they tear us apart," Grint said.

"I thought that was a myth," Tennebrue whispered as he came close.

"No myth at all," Trimbo added.

"Lost my mother that way," Puig said.

"Your mother was..."

"Quiet," Grint snapped and shut Trimbo's retort down. "We don't have a lot of time."

"What are you thinking?" Tennebrue asked.

"Forty-three and five is a Bar Church reference. The city had forty-three rulers until the five-year siege that broke the wall."

"How do you know that?" Trimbo asked.

"I grew up around a lot of drunken bards and historians," Grint shrugged. "Hobbe keeps odd company."

"So that's the answer then?" Puig asked.

"I surmise only part of it. The rest is about water," Tennebrue shook his head. "The sea?"

By the sea, he meant the Sentent Sea, an inland salt water sea that nothing flowed in or out of. The stagnant waters were so thick with salt that nothing lived. No one fished it, no cities other than Bar Church sat on its shore, and using a compass near it made the needle go askew. Grint nodded to the wizard.

"The Sentent Sea," Grint answered, and the ogres smiled, pleased to have an answer at last. Each member joined in, saying the same.

"Choose your passage," the ogre said.

The urchin boy jumped down and waved them to follow. Without the boy, they could have wandered through these tunnels without knowing where they were until the life drained from their withering bodies. Making a last head count, Grint found they were missing the Parthian. He looked back to see him lying on the floor. Chell rocked in pain, clutching his arms tight as shivers racked his mighty frame. Grint whistled for everyone to stop as he knelt beside the fallen Parthian.

Chell's eyes squeezed tight. Grint feared laying a hand on him - imagining that mammoth paw and sharp nails swinging toward his face. *If he even has the strength.* Heat radiated off the Parthian like a blacksmith's furnace. The poison chose a poor time to strike him down.

Tennebrue nudged Grint aside and knelt over Chell, whispering words unknown as he delved. Blue light strobed from his palms and when he finished, he stood, shaking his head.

"What is it? Will we all catch it?" Puig asked as the goblins backed into the tunnel.

"This is your Opposition poison, isn't it?" Grint said with growing anger. "Fix it for him. He'll do what you're asking without it as part of his Atonement."

"I fixed it," Tennebrue answered. "The Parthian is free of the poison."

"Then why does he still look like a plague victim?" Trimbo asked.

"Something bit him in the tunnels," Tennebrue said, pulling a dead siren eel from the Parthian's fur. "The stone poison is working, but I have stalled its progress for a time."

"I want my money back," Puig shouted.

"Shut up, you two. Can't you heal this?" Grint asked, not wanting to lose the barbarian's strength and presence before they got out of the tunnels.

"I am not a healer, but I know those who can," Tennebrue stated. "We need to get him to my people."

"Your people?" Grint asked. "Your people put him here."

"Not the Opposition," he replied with a guarded look. Grint knew enough about avoiding a question to know that Tennebrue was hiding something.

"I'm not carrying him," Trimbo proclaimed as he and Puig passed coins to one another.

"None of us can," Grint said. "Can you at least wake him up? Once we get out of here, we can decide what to do next, yeah?"

"I can wake him," Tennebrue's demeanor stiffened before he spoke, but he turned and did as Grint asked. A few moments of magical nonsense, and the Parthian's fever calmed. His strength returned enough for him to open his eyes and stand, albeit on shaking legs.

"Move," the urchin boy called from the mouth of the tunnel, "before the ogres come back. And this time they won't ask riddles."

Tennebrue walked at the front with the boy, holding aloft the glow orb. The boy insisted he didn't need it for this leg of their journey. Their voices faded below the arguments of the goblins over wagers and rules. Grint took a final look back at the bloody mess strewn across the room. Keranue hadn't given him the answers he'd wanted, but

Grint was fairly certain he hadn't betrayed them. Not that it mattered now.

The Parthian's pace slowed, and he stopped to cough every few steps. A booming sound that echoed, shaking mortar loose. Grint walked behind him in case he faltered and found it hard to see with his massive frame blocking most of the light.

"What did you say to the ogres?" Chell asked.

"Brahsh moya gelin," Grint answered. "The taste of goblin will make you ill."

Chell laughed, a deeper sound than the cough, and it showered Grint with stones. Disgruntled shouts from those ahead quieted Chell, but Grint saw the broad shoulders moving with silent amusement.

"Who poisoned you?" Grint whispered softly enough for Chell to hear. "When you got here. Was it the wizard?"

Understanding the need for silence, Chell whispered back, "Two dreego found me in a tavern. One claimed to be a prince. The tavern owner poisoned me on his behalf. I was told they would issue a cure if I killed the queen."

From everything Orsava warned about the Opposition, the story matched. It was why Sem wanted him to stay clear of the taverns. The Opposition had a habit of poisoning sun-facers to do their bidding. But something else in the statement caught his ear. *A prince? Mikil?* Orsava mentioned the Opposition man at his manor was Prince Mikil. The question that remained wasn't so easily answered. Was Mikil pulling Borismere's strings or the other way around?

"If it's any consolation, the wizard says he cured you," Grint continued whispering.

"I am not sure he did," Chell answered. "The bite blinds with its pain, but I still feel the poison in my blood."

To Orsava's recollection, no one ever received a cure from the Opposition. Grint didn't believe they had one. Why would they? Once they cured the Parthian - healthy and strong, he'd rip through them. Better to let him die and tie up loose ends. That's what he would do, not that he'd admit it to Chell.

"I'll help if I can," Grint said.

"If you're trying to recruit me into this job of yours, I must decline," Chell said. "I have enough to handle as it is."

"There's a lot of gold involved," Grint replied. "I don't know anything more about Atonement than what I said, but I imagine you'd have enough to buy your way back with as much as we're talking about."

"A Parthian does not purchase Atonement. It must be earned through deed," Chell snapped.

"Your choice," Grint shrugged. *That's fine. He's a bit of an attraction and the purpose of my work is being unseen.*

"The wizard claimed you enter places you don't belong," Chell said.

"Out of them too," Grint laughed.

"If you were me, how would you get into the palace?"

"Through the front gate," Grint said without giving it any thought. The Parthian grunted and Grint realized that it must have sounded like a joke. "I mean it, I would go in the front gate."

"Just walk in?"

"As long as you act like you belong, people won't notice you. Go get yourself a robe and a veil. Walk hunched over. Don't fidget or look around. Blend in with a group if you can." The thought was simplistic, but the Parthian didn't sound like he had much time left to come up with something complex like a Harbor Drowning Man or Filley's Retort.

"And if that doesn't work?"

"You're Parthian, just kill whoever gets in your way," Grint laughed, this time meaning it as a joke, and got a face full of fur as he walked into the barbarian. The algae, still tangled in his fur, went into Grint's open mouth. Gagging on the sour taste, he yelped, "Don't stop short."

"Everyone has," Chell said, pressing against the wall to let Grint see past.

"What's wrong up there?"

"The boy ran off," Trimbo said.

"Why'd he do that?" Grint didn't like it. He had a deal with the urchins to meet Matty. Ditching him wasn't part of it.

"Heard a noise," Puig answered.

"It is fine, I see a light ahead," Tennebrue answered. Grint slid past Chell, confident the Parthian had enough strength to manage on his own.

"A light? Someone with a torch?" Grint asked, squinting.

"No, from above," Tennebrue extinguished the glow orb and let the darkness settle over them. Grint saw it then, a faint flickering light falling from above.

"Good, I am in great favor of leaving these tunnels," Trimbo said.

"No doubt foul spirits haunt them," Puig continued.

"We can find shelter with my friends," Tennebrue said as they reached a boarded up well with a ladder carved into the wall.

"Not yet," Grint replied as he tested the carved rungs. Given everything that had happened, falling into the Opposition's lap was not on today's menu.

One after another they climbed. The goblins, the wizard, Parthian, and finally Grint. He emerged in a covered courtyard with withered vines lacing through latticed wood.

Grint got the feeling he recognized this place. It wasn't a friendly feeling.

"My friends will take care of us," Tennebrue said, not letting it go.

"Enough," Grint snapped, turning his back on the group to look through the vines. Where in Salaz were they? If he could spot a landmark, he could figure out why this courtyard was familiar. And then Grint saw the crumbled warehouse he chased the urchin to just a few nights ago. *Fishmonger turf?*

And the Fishmongers are with Mikil, Hobbe warned.

And Mikil is Opposition. That makes this… charffing fish-guts. This is a trap.

"I must insist," Tennebrue laughed. The goblins howled as the Parthian slumped to the ground with a deep thud. Grint turned around, muttering things that made Hobbe's voice laugh. They were no longer alone. Throughout the courtyard were Opposition lackeys, all with their swords drawn.

19

"Only at the end do we become who we're meant to be."
                                    - Blue Fingered Hobbe

"I don't care who you are," Trimbo shrieked, adding to the already high timbre of his voice. From the muffle of the goblin's words, Grint assumed they were all in the same predicament. They had jammed a rough sack over his head, stinking of fish guts and seawater. Frayed patches of burlap provided the barest hint of movement outside the sack, but did nothing to dampen the rhythmic thump of wheels crossing cobbled streets.

"Shut up or I'll put a gag in your mouth," a gruff man answered. The goblin stopped after that, leaving them with nothing but the sound of the cart's squeaky axle. If they got out of this without the Opposition poisoning them, maybe he could tip off a city guard to where it was they took them. *Quick way to make some coin.* The driver did a poor job of hiding the route. First, they went up the hill, into a district - Wensley or Termin - around the streets, then back to the Grand Runway and down. The sack over his head may have stunk, but it didn't hide the smell of the harbor or sound of boats in the water.

Right back to where we started, Hobbe said.

The cart lurched to a halt, pulling Grint off his seat. A smaller lump lay beneath him - *a goblin?* - as they kicked and punched him. From the screams it sounded like Puig. Grint rolled himself off as the cart bed shook and someone pulled his hood off. A stocky, Salazian man wearing a pair of torn, re-stitched leather pants and no shirt stood over him, a tattoo of an anchor covered his chest.

"Good sir, did you know your anchor is upside down?" Trimbo asked.

"Or are we upside down?"

"No," Grint laughed. "His tattoo is upside down. How drunk were you..."

The thug back-handed Grint and scowled at the goblins when they opened their mouths. Taking his time, jailer tied a rope line, connecting their bindings together. "No talk," he scowled as he dragged them off the cart. Grint tried to help the goblins down, but the man yanked the line, dropping both to the ground. The Parthian wasn't with them, nor was Tennebrue, but the latter wasn't a surprise as he was Opposition.

The man Grint called Scowls, tied the end of their rope line to a thick beam and grunted, "No talk."

"Some talk," Grint said, and got another back-hand. The goblins remained silent for once.

They left them in the dark with no guards, but Grint heard the sounds of activity close by. *Sounds like an army.* Grint wondered where they might have taken Chell as he examined the rope tying his wrist. With his hood removed, working the knot loose wouldn't take long.

Why leave you here to escape? Hobbe asked.

I try not to think about those things, Grint answered. Either the Opposition were pure idiots or they had something else planned for the trio. The knot was fair, but he'd escaped better under worse circumstances. *Try unraveling a quadruple knot while tied to a boulder sinking in a lake.* Not something he wanted to revisit in Salaz, especially in a harbor filled with poisonous siren eels who laid eggs in your gut, melting your flesh when they hatched.

"I'm getting slow," Grint chided himself as the rope fell away from his wrist. The goblins smiled as he worked on theirs. They'd started on their bindings, using sharpened fingernails to claw at the hemp. "I'm shocked the two of you didn't bet on who would untie themselves first."

"An egregious lack of thought," Trimbo said.

"It shows the state of mental distress we are in," Puig nodded.

"To not place a bet," Trimbo said.

"Wasteful," Puig agreed.

"Where are we?" Trimbo asked, rubbing his wrists when he got free.

"Smells like a stable," Puig answered.

"I think it is," Grint said. "I smell hay."

With all three loose, Grint poked around until he found a glass lantern filled with amber oil. With nothing to light it, he left it hanging on the wall. Beside it, he felt a pitchfork and picked it up, hefting it in his hands. A poor weapon for anything except keeping someone at bay, but that might be enough to get them out. Trimbo pulled on his pant leg. When he didn't respond, the goblin did it again.

"What?"

"Grint," the goblin moaned.

Grint looked up at thirty Opposition fighters, men and women, all armed with crossbows. "Inno Janoi," Grint breathed, worried that an itchy finger would end his life.

"We can dispense with those," Borismere said as he entered the stable. "These three are now our guests."

At his command, the crossbows lowered. Borismere was the last person Grint wanted to see walk through the door. They learned he had a hand in Prince Mikil's agenda, but to see him in control of so many blue armbands was...

"They aren't real Opposition, are they?" Grint asked, looking at the soldiers.

Dressed in lordly robes, Borismere, clean shaven and unveiled, beamed. He clapped his hands and turned, having issued a silent command to follow. When they did not, the crossbows rose once more.

"We get it," Grint said as he started walking. The goblins trailed in his wake, complaining about pushy humans and mistreatment.

The stable connected to a larger building that he recognized as the derelict warehouse in Harborside. A hundred fighters milled around, preparing carts, stacking supplies, and sharpening swords. In their haste to step aside for Borismere, they dropped bits of armor and weapons few looked familiar with. Grint had seen enough battles to know they were preparing for one, but this lot looked no better equipped than a backwater militia. Aside from the dozen crossbowmen. That group looked mean enough to chew a stoneskin's head off. If Borismere hoped to win, he'd better find more competent fighters. The queen had a thousand swords at least.

Borismere led them through a cramped hall and further yet into a small windowless room with a round table, six chairs, and a box covered by an old white sheet. Dust marks on the table's surface led Grint to think something sat there recently, but moved in a hurry. *Strategic mapping of the revolution?* Borismere sat first and gestured for them to take other seats. A servant appeared with a plate of cheese and a pitcher of sweet crawberry wine. It reminded Grint of how Angis would enter a room with the exact thing Sem wanted. A bitter memory now.

The goblins dug in with abandon, spitting food as they critiqued the quality. Grint joined in, his stomach rumbling with a fond remembrance for what it felt like to be full. As he washed down his second mouthful, he remembered Orsava's warning of poison and sniffed the cup. Borismere laughed.

"You have nothing to worry about," the lord commented.

"Tell that to the Parthian," Grint retorted. He'd already drank, so if they poisoned it, he'd deal with it when he could. For now, he was hungry.

"True," Borismere nodded. "I've told Mikil to abandon that practice. It's foolish. How do they expect someone to succeed when they're dying?"

"Mikil? Not Prince Mikil?" Grint asked as he refilled the cup.

Borismere laughed again. "I like you, Grint. I do. Not these goblins. Miscreant finks who will find themselves back on Allast Island soon."

"Rude," Trimbo said after washing down some cheese.

"Uncalled for," Puig agreed.

Borismere ignored the duo, leaning forward on the table. The weight of his gaze focused squarely on Grint and made the thief frown. Such scrutiny rarely led to anything good.

"I'm glad to hear you like me so much," Grint forced a smile. "How about you set us loose and I'll just be on my way."

"Without us?" Trimbo asked, sounding offended at the idea.

"I wager three plicks he takes us," Puig managed through a mouthful of cheese.

"On your way to steal my gold? That is what you meant, yes?" Borismere leaned back, crossing his arms. "I assure you, it is no longer in the vault. Why not listen to what I have to say?"

"Are we bargaining?" Grint asked as the door opened once more. Tennebrue set a chair against the wall and sat. He didn't speak or acknowledge them. The wizard remained content to watch, running his hand over the top of the covered box.

"We know him," Puig smiled.

"Yes, the traitor who would have died ten times over if not for us," Trimbo said.

"We are bargaining," Borismere said. "If you desire. Tennebrue says it will be a waste of my time. I disagree."

Grint mirrored Borismere's posture, sitting back with his arms crossed. There was no way he would talk first, not when a deal was on the table. Time became a tangible thing as the two stared at one another and the sounds of the goblins eating magnified.

"My lord," Tennebrue whispered. Borismere held a finger up and sighed.

"I very much like you," he repeated, placing his hands on the table. A gesture meant to convey he had nothing to hide. "Forget the gold. Instead, let me offer you a chest. More than enough wealth for you to enjoy."

"And in return?"

"Yes," Borismere smiled. "You enter the tower while forces on the ground distract the guards. I've spent years laying the stones for this path and now Mikil is getting cold feet. I need to re-inspire him to..."

"Borey, let me stop you there," Grint said. Borismere squinted in confusion, mouthing the word Borey. "I don't care about your master plan. I've heard it - and seen it - before. Frankly, I don't care who sits on the throne. You want that? Have fun. I was in Tarynta when they assassinated King Gassore. It didn't end well for the usurper, but did for me. After a mob butchered the lot of them, I took an emerald the size of a fist off his corpse." Grint held up a fist, cocked his head and covered the hand with his other. "Two fists."

"Your point?" The lord asked, patience waning from his voice.

"Rhysin goes through monarchs with each new turning of Effulg. And the Crown of the Seven Kingdoms? Don't get me started on that incestuous lot of vipers. Politics bores me," Grint yawned.

"Bores me," Puig said with a mouthful of food.

"Borismere," Trimbo laughed, spraying wet chunks of bread across the table.

"You can fight over all the thrones you like. After you're dead, I'll be there to take whatever you leave behind," Grint smiled at the lord's discomfort.

"And look how well that has worked out for you," Borismere sneered. "Plickless and covered in muck, stinking like the bottom of a fishmonger's barrel. I am offering you real wealth for doing what you already do."

"Are you clueless?" Grint laughed. "You're offering me a slice of cake when I mean to steal the whole bakery."

Borismere slammed his fist on the table. The tremor knocked over everyone's cups, filling the room with the smell of crawberries. The darkness twisting Borismere's face faded as wine spilled onto the floor and the pleasant lord returned. "There's no need for nastiness."

"Nastiness? Like you killing Orsava?" Grint said.

"Me?" Borismere shook his head. "Nonsense. I enjoyed my rivalry with Sem. Respected him even."

"That's a charffing pile of lies," Grint said as he contemplated spitting in the man's face.

Borismere made a grunting sound and rolled his eyes. "I don't care what you think. Or your companions. Oh dear, do the goblins know what happened to your last companions?"

Trimbo and Puig stopped squabbling over the last scraps of food to look at the lord and then Grint.

"It seems not, so allow me to enlighten them. Captain Basto told me they found their dead bodies in a most unpleasant state." Wagging his finger and clucking, he continued, "Entrails here. Limbs there. Shame, you know murdering people draws Calabassus Rent."

"The God of Murder looks the other way with me," Grint snapped back. It wasn't untrue. Rent had his fill of Grint's antics for the time being.

"Grint may not be willing to make a deal," Trimbo said. "That does not exclude us."

"We'll do it, if you agree that after you're killed, we can help ourselves to your art collection? Some of it may fetch a pretty penny in Orr Moken," Puig said, draining whatever wine remained into his open mouth. A servant appeared as if they'd been watching and delivered a new carafe.

"We're talking galleons," Trimbo said. "Not the useless plicks you use here in Salaz."

"Art?" Borismere scratched his head, trying to discern what the two were on about.

"It's a fair deal," Grint shrugged. "I would take them up on it."

"I've brooked enough of this tomfoolery," Borismere slapped the table. A cue for Tennebrue, who lifted the old sheet off what appeared to be a cage. Inside, eyes heavy with exhaustion, lay Newman. Grint bolted up in his seat, but the wizard conjured leather straps to pull him back down. As Grint continued to struggle, Tennebrue formed a ball of static lightning in his palm and turned his hand to face the dog.

"There is no need to take it further. Do what I've asked and the animal will go free," Borismere spread out his hands.

"If you hurt a hair on his head," Grint said before a leather strap wound across his mouth.

"Tennebrue," Borismere sighed. "He can't talk if you've gagged him."

The leather strap relaxed and fell away. Grint flexed his jaw as he tested the bonds on his wrists. They weren't strong, but re-wound themselves any time he pulled one loose. "We're playing for lives then, are we? Fine. The gold and my dog. Give me those and I'll do what you want."

"The gold is off the table," Borismere gave him a sympathetic look.

"Gold is never off the table," Grint smiled.

"And us," Trimbo whispered.

"Don't forget us," Puig whispered over top.

"Gold, my dog, and the goblins," Grint stopped fighting against the bonds. "For that I'll break into the castle and kill your girlfriend." Borismere sat back, thinking. "That's what this is. You want her dead."

"You think I want my true love dead?" Borismere smirked.

"Yes," Grint answered.

"What would that accomplish? Mikil would just take the throne," Borismere said.

"Not if your fake Opposition army turns the people against him," Grint parried.

"That still doesn't put me on the throne." While they talked, Tennebrue made his crimson spark once again, holding it above Newman's cage.

"I smell a wedding," Trimbo shouted in giddy excitement.

"I love weddings. Such wonderful food," Puig nodded.

"And gifts to steal."

"Weddings take time," Borismere shook his head, feigning disappointment. "And the union approved first."

"Unless you have an Ashgran High Priest under your thumb," Grint smiled.

"How do you... Tennebrue, how does he?" Borismere stammered, perhaps concerned for the first time since he sat down.

A loud crash, followed by blood-curdling shouts, drew everyone's attention. Tennebrue extinguished the magic and cracked open the door. The telltale clank of steel against steel greeted them. Militia in heavy boots ran past. Then more. Borismere jumped up from the chair, threw the door wide and grabbed a passing soldier.

"What's happening," he asked, his voice muffled.

"City soldiers," the woman said. "Two squads."

"Basto? What in Astapoor is that moron doing?" Borismere cursed, shoving Tennebrue out the door, "Deal with this. I can finish with these fools later." Both men left the room, Borismere taking Newman's cage with him.

"Newman!" Grint shouted as the door closed. The steel turning of a lock clicked into place.

The goblins, unbound and free of the wizard's magic, jumped out of their chairs. Together, they pulled at the leather bindings, but couldn't budge them even an inch.

"Stand back," Grint said as he started rocking the chair. When his feet touched the ground, he launched himself back into the wall, shattering the wooden chair. Without the back support, the leather straps fell away with the splinters. Grint bit his lower lip, feeling the sting where a splinter - thick as a finger - protruded from his arm. Trimbo yanked it free while Puig tore a strip from the old sheet to tourniquet the wound.

"Now what?" Trimbo asked.

"Do you have any more urchins coming to save you?" Puig looked hopeful.

"Not this time," Grint answered. "As for what we do, that's obvious. We get out of this hornet's nest."

"A well-formed plan," Puig shook his head.

"No room for error with it," Trimbo looked disgusted.

"You have any better ideas?" Grint shouted at them. The noise drew a guard's notice. The door clicked and a slender man, his veil torn and hanging to the side, walked in. His short sword glistened with dripping gore as a Fishmonger bled out in the hallway.

"They told me to keep you quiet," he said. "Didn't tell me how far that allowed me to go. Don't make me find out."

Grint shifted his foot under one of the broken chair legs and kicked it up into his grasp, then kicked the edge of the table so it slid into the guard's midsection. With a grunt, he fell back into the door frame. It provided but a momentary distraction. When he righted himself, the guard gripped his sword in two leather wrapped hands, gnashing his teeth in anger. Grint used the table to leap, swinging his makeshift club at the guard's hands. Leather gloves gave moderate protection against sharp strikes, but not something blunt. The guard yelped and dropped the sword. As he bent to pick it back up, he tripped over the goblins who'd tangled themselves around the man's legs. When he fell back, his head cracked open on the floor.

Pinning the man down, Grint planned to bludgeon him unconscious, but the fall did the work for him. He tossed the splinter aside and picked up the sword. Two more fighters ran up the hall. They looked blankly at Grint and the goblins, unsure of their allegiance. When they noticed their compatriot on the floor, they charged.

"Find us a way out," Grint yelled at the goblins as he planted his feet. The two scurried beneath the first fighter and ran. Grint swatted a sword strike aside, starting to feel the fatigue of little sleep. The second guard came at Grint with the heel of his boot, attempting to bust his knee, but missing high. The pain in his thigh was sharp, but thankfully nothing broke.

Backing into the room, Grint shook off the leather tourniquet and cupped his hand under the wound. The closest guard raised his sword, while blood pooled in Grint's palm. When it felt like enough, he threw a handful in their eyes. The guard shrieked and scratched at his face as he fell away, leaving just the kicker. No longer unarmed, Kicker held two very sharp daggers, twirled them around as he stepped. Yet, before he got close enough to strike, two arrows whizzed through the door, one striking Kicker in the back of his head.

There was a moment of confusion as Kicker shuddered and dropped. The bloody faced fighter saw what happened and tried to crawl away. Grint followed him into the hallway. Two Blue Hands stalked toward the door, nocking fresh arrows.

"This charffing kry-damned day," he growled.

Chell appeared behind them and grabbed both by the neck, smashing them together. Their heads collapsed under the Parthian's strength. Grint looked at the bloody mess and decided that it ended better than he'd hoped. The goblins poked their heads around Chell's hairy legs and smiled. "We found a way out."

"What about that one, Fire-hair?"

The last guard crawled across the hall, shaking in fear as he put his back to the wall. Grint armed himself with the two daggers and knelt a few feet out of Bloody Face's reach. "You planning to follow us when we leave?"

The man shook his head.

"Good enough for me," Grint said.

"The stink of compassion amuses me," Chell said as Grint re-joined them.

"Aren't you dying?" He rolled his eyes. Chell threw his head back and laughed.

The four captives burst through the door leading into the warehouse where a viscous battle raged. Screams echoed from both sides as the bodies piled up. Red armband city guards. Blue Hands. Opposition. All fighting one another. Grint didn't understand what madness was at play. Trimbo yanked on his arm, pointing at a hole in the floor.

That was their exit? "I'm not going back in with those kry-damn eels," Grint shouted, unable to hear his own voice over the carnage.

Trimbo mouthed the word, *Sand*. The tide must have gone out.

A few steps from escape, Grint stopped. He couldn't leave yet. Not yet. The goblins pulled at him, questioning his hesitation. Grint shook them off and ran back into the fight. There was no way in the Seven Hells of Astapoor he'd leave without Newman. Scanning the warehouse, he found Tennebrue throwing fire at soldiers. And if he was there - Grint traced the path back to the hallway and beside a pile of crates, turned on its side, was the cage.

Newman looked less than pleased at being dumped in such a manner, and Grint would surely hear of it later. Dodging past two women fighting, Grint slid through a slick puddle to knock out a Blue Hand archer taking shots at city guards. One of Mordechai's lot appeared with a club, but he was slow in swinging it. Thus, he died with two daggers in his neck.

Tearing open the cage, he pulled Newman out. The dense lump didn't squirm for once and even wagged his nub of a tail. Back together, Grint sprinted with the dog toward escape.

A dozen steps from freedom, he saw the shocked eyes of the goblins. An amplified scream from the wizard pounded at his ears. Grint looked over his shoulder and slid to a stop. There was no escaping the fiery red blast coming his way.

"Sorry, boy," he said, giving Newman one last kiss.

20

"People speak of change as a benevolent thing. No. It is a nasty beast. A bloody, crying monster who does not abide other versions of circumstance. If you've come to fight for change, be warned, I fight for it too."

- The Succession of Queen Amorrey
Annum 360

Nazarra watched the mysterious boat from an old crow's nest. Warped from a decade of neglect, the wood creaked under her weight or when a gust of wind came through. Danger wasn't a concept she dwelled upon, at least not the danger of falling. Memories flooded her mind, repeating in a foul, timeless loop.

It was not bad enough for you to fail in your duty, but now you malign my consort? I don't recognize you, Nazarra. The woman before me - I expect her to wear the blue armband of Mikil's impotent Opposition. Should I execute you as a traitor? Hang you from the side of the Seastone Tower for all to see? No. For you are my sister and I will see you redeemed. As of tomorrow, you will depart for the Sandy Kingdoms. Exiled to the care of the Richii until you re-learn loyalty. Get her out of my sight.

Akosha had not been kind. Nor gentle. As she ranted, her sycophantic Court listening on, she beat Nazarra with the same jewel encrusted scepter their father once let her play with. That was a pleasant memory. This was not. After the beating, her sister tossed the scepter to the ground, flung aside like garbage until a servant cleaned and returned it. The guards dragged Nazarra from the throne room. Had her legs worked, she would have walked out, head raised high. But they did not, and the onlookers mocked her more for it.

Traitor. They spat at her.

The guards took her to a servant's room, tossing her onto the bare pallet that used as a bed. *Stay here and think about your future.* Calling this a future was a mummer's joke. Exiled to the care of the Richii was an ending, not a beginning. The fierce warriors would break her down. Shatter her spirit under a doctrine filled with more rules than Grint counted gods. It would be a hard life.

Grint. Thinking of the thief made her smile, but much like her other memories, theirs overflowed with bitter flavors.

She wished things ended on a better note - *Which Nazarra am I talking to?* - but duty to her sister outweighed all other considerations. Still, during that last meeting, the teasing way he mentioned what things she missed by betraying them - the knowing grin - haunted her. Grint could have lied. Or not. He often displayed a profound lack of subtlety. Then matched it with undeniable sneakiness. A contradiction, but when you knew him, it made sense. *I thought about killing you, but I like you too much.* Nazarra took the conversation to heart. There was more at play than a mere heist.

The mistake she'd made was looking at the puzzle as a straight line instead of a tapestry. Grint breaking into Borismere's manor. The Parthian's arrival and subsequent attack on Akosha. Lord Orsava's letter to Dusk Raven with the offer of a job.

Dusk Raven,

I hope this missive finds you well. I enjoyed our work togeth-er in repatriating the shipment of Taryn whiskey stolen from my trading ship. During our interaction, you displayed an equal amount of contempt for the perpetrator of the crime, and though they came away without tarnish, a fresh chance to remedy that has appeared as if a gift from Ashgra herself. We meet tomorrow where we met many moons ago. I hope to find you within our company, but bereft of any symbology.

L.S.O.

It sounded perfect. The man who organized the theft of Orsava's whiskey was none other than Borismere, though she could never prove that to the queen. The timing was un-doubtedly a gift from Ashgra, giving her the weapon she longed for. A way to enlighten the queen about the scum she'd let into her bed. That Grint's benefactor was Orsava came as a messy surprise, and she almost walked away. But she'd gone along with the caper, hoping to discover proof of Borismere's treachery. Until it all fell apart. Orsava died and Brott turned traitor. Having no choice but to distance herself from the thieves, she let Grint take the fall and even helped it happen.

What could she have learned by staying with them? No, not could have. Would. Nazarra would learn. It was not yet too late. The moment they took Grint away, she began. The first thread of the tapestry started with Borismere. Doing what a Spymaster General did; Nazarra hid in the darkest shadows, watching. The tools of her trade, safe houses, and minions were out of reach, but she had long ago learned how to do this job without such crutches.

If Grint's assessment on the size of the hoard were true, that would indeed be damning. As a citizen and supporter, the law obligated Borismere to disclose and pay taxes to the treasurer. As the queen's consort, Akosha even had rights to the gold herself. Keeping that hidden was a hanging offense. Greedy as he was, Borismere was no fool. After the failed heist, he moved the treasure using Racko's Blue Hands. A way to keep the gold while distancing himself from its ownership.

They used clever tricks to obfuscate the trail. Running several false carts on rotating routes. Vanishing behind false walls. Using the Cognispyre gatherings to blend in. Nazarra counted herself smarter, knowing it was only a matter of time before she found the new hiding spot. One more trip and their secret would fall apart. Except, she became distracted at a critical moment. While the Blue Hand carts departed, Nazarra froze, watching the approach of a palanquin carried by four muscled servants. She knew the conveyance well. Prince Mikil. In that moment, she made a choice. Whatever business the prince had with Borismere superseded the gold.

Nazarra needed to get closer, but there were so few spots unwatched by guards or thieves. A slow smile spread across her lips, realizing the answer sat in front of her. Three squads of thieves watched the Upper Crust. A dozen more came and went from the manor carrying squat brown crates. A cloak and armband from an oblivious Blue Hand, preferably one shirking their duties, would get her close enough to hear what...

Nazarra balked as the thief-catcher, Mavris Kane, pulled Prince Mikil from the palanquin at the end of a chain. The Harbor Master stepped out after them, free of bindings, but jumping at every sound. All three walked inside under guards dressed in golden breastplates. *Who are they?* Her head spinning, she stalked the rooftops looking for a suitable target to get her close. What precedent did Borismere have to detain a Prince? Even as consort to the queen, that should have been far beyond his reach.

By the time she stumbled on a Blue Hand, passed out with a bottle of rum in his lap, things in the manor had progressed too far. Prince Mikil's screams drew everyone's attention, rousing even the Blue Hand. Poised to scream in alarm, Nazarra shoved a hand over the thief's mouth, then slid a stiletto knife into the base of their skull. She nestled in a shadow beside the body, taking their hood and armband as she watched for any movement.

Mikil stumbled through the front door, clutching at his gut. They'd removed his chains, but he stumbled as if still bound by shackles. A dark substance seeped through his fingers. *Blood?* Mavris Kane walked out next, a leisurely stroll more akin to a day at the park. Mikil fell, waving a wet hand as he begged the thief-catcher to let him go. Unmoved, Kane twirled his cudgel, striking the prince to the cheers of the golden guards. Should she feel bad for Mikil? Or that his own guard didn't move to help?

Kane grabbed the prince by his hair and dragged him back into the manor. His screams of pain scared a pair of chattering mungles from their roost, and they climbed down the slope of Nazarra's roof to inspect the body she left.

Her own gruesome action nothing compared to this. Boris-mere and Mordechai appeared at last, sipping wine from fine goblets.

"Please," Mikil whined. The plea fell on deaf ears as Kane wrenched his neck.

If only you'd heard what we heard. Was this the mystery? Or would there be more? *Grint*, she should have begged. *Please tell me what you know.*

Mordechai spoke to the golden guards, their voices too soft to hear, but the Harbor Master pointed south. A full company of guards marched out of the manor, replacing their golden plate with black leather. They lined up in two rows as the commander inspected the garb, handing out Opposition armbands as he went. Not guards. Mercenaries.

In formation, the mercenaries jogged into Salaz Pla-za, turning toward the Grand Runway and harbor beyond. The Harbor Master was aligned with Borismere. Now there were foreign mercenaries in the streets, and a strange boat in the harbor. Nazarra feared the ship might be full of sol-diers waiting to come ashore. Who could she tell that would listen? *It doesn't matter*, she thought, knowing she needed proof first. Once she had it, they would listen.

And that led her to the crow's nest. How many times had she re-examined her steps? A dozen, maybe more. Waiting and watching could be a dull exercise with nothing to occu-py one except their thoughts. Even as she adjusted her legs and shook the feeling of needles out, the memory of Akosha tried to intrude once more.

"Not again," she said, slapping herself. Each step brought her here. Re-living them wouldn't change that. The boat hadn't moved since it arrived and remained just as quiet. Even now, in the grip of night, it sat in dark solitude.

The mercenaries spread out at the bottom of the Runway, content to sit and wait. But the Opposition was not. Rough men and women in blue armbands buzzed around a derelict warehouse like a hive. Did they know that Mikil was dead?

As if summoned by the question, the covered palanquin appeared. The mercenaries moved for the first time in hours, flanking it in a slow jog during the approach. Nazarra questioned the morbid nature of delivering the prince's dead body back to his people when the palanquin stopped and Borismere stepped out.

He had changed into a navy-colored robe and cloak, but the blue armband he wore was unmistakable. A declaration of intent or more subterfuge? Nazarra was no closer to understanding Borismere's actions than she had been a year ago. How long until she accepted the inevitable fact that her only option was confronting the man directly?

Another cart appeared, rumbling around the corner of the Grand Runway. Its bed covered by a thick burlap sheet, but not the driver. A stocky man, Nazarra knew him as a longtime supporter of Mikil. Someone her own spies kept watch over. Rumors swirled of Mikil using the bald-headed man to make others disappear. The cart shook as its crooked, chipped wheels struggled over the uneven street, eventually turning into a stable beside the warehouse.

Two Opposition supporters closed the stable doors behind it. It must have been a signal of some manner as the buzzing activity ceased. Everyone stopped what they were doing, retreating inside. The suddenness of it chilled her, leaving the Harborside quiet, lit only by Effulg. A cool breeze shifted in off the water, and the heavy smell of salt reminded her of her impending future.

Nazarra turned toward the mighty statue of Ashgra to pray. A twinkle of blue moonlight glinted off the edges of the sun the goddess held aloft. It hadn't dawned on her until now what tonight was. Firelight Eve. A time for quiet contemplation about sins and the last chance to add them to the effigies before tomorrow's burning. Everyone would be in their homes with families. Everyone except the Opposition, it seemed. Borismere's grip must have been tight to cajole them out of the yearly ritual.

Through all of this, the three-masted ship sat dead in the harbor. Its mysterious appearance and connection to Borismere's plans remained unanswered. Gossip escalated into tall-tales of undead pirates waiting to storm the city during the Cognispyre. Nazarra wished for pirates, and not the waiting swords of an invading army.

A cry of pain broke open the night's silent vigil. Two dozen Blue Hands crawled across the rooftop network, converging on the warehouse. Another stood, clutching an arrow in their chest, then fell over the edge, their scream trailing after them.

"What madness is this?" Nazarra whispered as she scanned the street. A squad of city guards in loose black silks and leather plates converged on the warehouse. A trio of point men carrying coffin shields protected the archers as they shot at any Blue Hand foolish enough to peek over the edge of their roof. Captain Basto barked an order at the rest of the troops. The man wore a black steel cap with chain veil even at night.

"The fool," Nazarra breathed. "What is he doing?"

The Blue Hands lit the end of their arrows and returned fire. Flames marred the beauty of Effulg's light and burst outward when they struck the shields. A blinding flash to distract the guards as the rest swarmed to fortified positions on the warehouse roof. Darkness failed to hide their movements from Nazarra, and she watched them prepare blades with poison.

Captain Basto and six men ran beneath another volley of arrows, leaving the rest of the guards to hold the street. An impossible task for the remaining ten as the Fishmongers appeared from the other end of the street. A motley bunch armed with nets, tridents and spears. They crawled from shadows and shattered walls like roaches until they numbered a hundred or more.

Only then did horns scream throughout Salaz.

Nazarra watched as Blue Hands and Fishmongers fought together to protect the warehouse. Together with the Opposition, their army would triple the guard. *Borismere doesn't need a mercenary army*, she thought, horror-stricken.

A lone Fishmonger stepped out of the line, throwing his trident high. It struck a Blue Hand in the throat, and they fell screaming. *What?* To misjudge such a throw seemed impossible. Had it been on purpose? The attacker disappeared back into the throng as a Blue Hand retaliated, killing a Fishmonger. Chaos erupted as those who fought at first to protect the warehouse, turned on one another. More attacks came from the shadows beside the warehouse. Arrows and bricks rained down. The Blue Hands stopped fighting the guards and turned on the Fishmongers, who turned back on them. Each fought the other, attacking anyone other than themselves.

Armed with nets and tridents, the Fishmongers overran the Opposition, storming through the stable doors. Nazarra lost track of who was for who, except for her own people. A handful of guards hid behind their make-shift barricade, but that would change when gathering Opposition reinforcements flanked from behind. Unable to watch them slaughtered, Nazarra wrapped her scarf around a rope line, slid down the side of the perch, and hit the ground running. One fool stood to cheer and choked on a sword as it punctured his throat. Nazarra drew two eleven-inch assassin daggers and flipped them to an underhand grip. Leaping over the dead guard, she flew at the Opposition killer, driving both blades into the soft trapezius tissue on either side of his neck. Amid the fountain of blood, she stood ready, joined by others who nodded with wicked smiles. Either they hadn't heard or did not care about her upcoming exile.

As the first wave of Opposition fighters approached, a flaming arrow struck the street. The eruption blinded them all, spewing fire in every direction. Nazarra fell back, clawing at the spots clouding her vision. Something solid struck the side of her head.

When she again gasped for breath, the scene had changed. A dozen injured city guards lay on pallets around her. The healer, busy bandaging a woman's arm, jumped to his feet as he saw Nazarra stand. The spots faded, but sounds ran together as if she were underwater.

"Spymaster General," the healer said as he placed a hand on her arm.

"That is no longer my title," Nazarra said, tearing the bandage off her head.

"Please don't do that," he asked, but she smacked his hand as he tried to stop her. "I must insist you lie back down."

"Am I dead?" A simple question, but the man couldn't form the words to respond. "If I am not a corpse, I see no need to sleep." Nazarra yanked her arm from his grip and walked toward the warehouse.

The guards she passed exchanged whispers. Some flattering. Others decidedly not. Trying to explain her relationship with Akosha would eat up time, so she ignored the latter, looking for the one in charge. Swords swung and clashed. Archers climbed on crates to get a better vantage for their shots. Flaming spools of cloth flew, creating smoking piles to hide troop movements. The Fishmongers dragged broken carts, doors, and barrels into the street, setting up their own barriers.

Lieutenant Argus held the city line with two squads. Runners came and went as he surveyed the scene and issued orders. "Where's Basto?" she shouted over a Blue Hand arrow explosion, ducking behind a sack of grain to keep out of sight.

"Spymaster General," Argus smiled at her. A kind man, the lieutenant had once been a general under her father. Akosha demoted him to make way for one of Borismere's cronies. The argument being that Argus was an outlander. Light-skinned like Grint, the veteran soldier with his frosty white hair and bushy mustache hailed from the service of the Geldens. Nazarra hated the decision to demote him. It was unfair and she hadn't been afraid to air the opinion.

"I saw Basto, where is he?" she asked again.

"Captain Basto, did you say?" An aide whispered in his ear, and he nodded. "It seems the madman ran into that mess."

'That mess,' was the warehouse each faction now fought to control. "I'm not Spymaster General any longer," she said, knowing he could sympathize. "But I would ask a favor."

"The sun has not risen, and your exile has not begun. The title stands and I am yours to order." Translation, *Serving you needs no favors. Ask and we will follow.*

"I need inside," Nazarra replied. "Borismere is within."

The lieutenant paled, "They have the Queen Consort?"

"No," Nazarra said, pinning him with her stare. "He is inside. Wearing a blue armband."

Argus went from pale to red in an instant, his hands shaking in silent rage. "Then I guess we'll be hunting that traitor together."

Two scouts broke through the rear lines, falling to their knees as they reached Argus. He offered them a moment to breathe before his patience vanished. "Out with it, or do you expect me to wait until next Cognispyre to receive your news?"

"Opposition in Meskal, Market and Graht," one said.

"Blue Hands in Chantil and Blau. Fish Mongers in Bushan," the other said after.

"Blood and the last shade of Krypholos," Argus said. "This is Firelight Eve. What happened to civility? Barker, get a signal out to the fort and tell Brayan we need the garrison. Firelight Eve. Bloody mess."

"I'm still going in," Nazarra said. "Keep the streets. I have this."

"I know a hundred women in the guard who would take your place on that boat," Argus said, placing a hand on her cheek. "A hundred more who would stand with you after it sailed."

"Traitorous bastard," she smiled, holding his hand.

"Stay alive," was the last thing he said before turning to issue orders.

Nazarra dashed through the last open space as arrows whizzed by and slid the last two feet into the shadows. The door Basto had gone through hung limp from a single hinge, but a dozen cracks in the rotting wood gave her easy access. Climbing over a pile of crates, she searched for the captain, finding instead a Blue Hand archer within reach. Nazarra snuck up behind them, holding a knife to their throat.

"Don't kill me," he moaned as he dropped the bow.

"Why are you here?" She asked.

"Supposed to guard, but they started attacking us. Racko says enough. Now she wants the thief," the man said.

"The thief? What thief?" Nothing in his response made sense. Before learning anything more, a Fishmonger's spear plunged into the archer's chest. The force ripped him from her grasp, and he gurgled, spraying blood as his body fell back. The Fishmonger waved a net over his head as he ran. Countering attacks was a lesson learned before wielding weapons. With nets, the best course was to take them down before they got close. Nazarra picked up the Blue Hand's bow and drew it back, her arms shaking under the weight of the string. She screamed as she let it loose, aiming for the man's head. Blood drenched the crate, and she slipped to the side. The shot flew wide. Stopping to laugh, the Fishmonger flexed and taunted her - until a city guard tackled him, and the two rolled off in hand-to-hand combat.

Nazarra jumped to the side of the crates, intent on finding Basto first and Borismere second. Two steps into the battlefield, ribbons of fire began spraying in terrifying arcs. A bit of demomancy Nazarra recognized well. *Tennebrue?* But that was impossible. The insane wizard was jailed on Allast Island.

"Tennebrue, contain yourself," someone yelled. "You're torching our people too!"

Tennebrue. It was him. A sadistic, un-sympathetic killer they'd finally locked in the deepest, darkest cell on the island. The crimes he'd committed in the name of the Opposition were considered egregious by everyone, including his own people. The queen wanted him executed, but changed her stance after a word from Borismere.

Nazarra rooted through a dead Fishmonger's gear, finding a bolo with barbs on each end. If she could get close enough, perhaps she could shut the wizard down once and for all. But then she heard Basto's voice, booming out orders. Crawling to the side, she peeked past the edge of cover and saw the captain leading a younger soldier across the battleground. Why was the private familiar? Not his appearance, hidden beneath armor - but the way he moved.

The chaos grew more dire when the Parthian appeared, cutting down anyone he could. Carrying two swords, the fighter made no judgments on who that might be. Everyone was his enemy. Tennebrue and now the Parthian. Both should be on Allast Island. When the two goblins appeared with a third man behind them...

"Of course," she said. "The thief." Nazarra smiled despite herself.

The four ran toward Basto until the thief slid to a stop and turned back. "Run, you fool," she whispered. Grint fought through the battle just to pick up a cage. "The dog."

Clouds of smoke swirled through the warehouse as the Parthian and goblins disappeared down a hole. Grint was a dozen paces from freedom when Tennebrue volleyed his fire, dousing the thief in temperatures so hot they melted him in an instant. Even Tennebrue looked surprised by the violence he'd unleashed, jumping back as the explosion rebounded. Nazarra submerged herself in a horse trough, watching the fire wash over the battle. When she came back up, the fire had dissipated and all factions retreated. The wizard ran off with the Opposition, but there had been no sign of Borismere in the fighting.

Nazarra looked for Basto. With his help, perhaps she could find the lord, but there were no traces of either the captain or the private tagging along. Both vanished in the smoke... *when the others scurried down that hole*, she finished the thought. Basto must have gone after the escapees and would need her help. She circumvented the last few fights as the city guards cleaned up the insurrection, and jumped into the hole.

A dozen sets of footprints left behind a messy trail in the wet sand. Nazarra followed, changing direction each time they did. The trail disappeared at the mouth of an old drainage pipe, where a metal grate lay in the sand, torn and tossed aside by the escapees. By the Parthian in particular, if she had to guess. Stories floated around of the urchin children using small and often collapsed tunnels, but no one ever verified the rumors. She may not find out about urchins, but she would see where the tunnels led. If the Parthian could fit, she could too.

The stone aqueduct streamed with water that stank of decay and defecation. Enough to make her gag. An almost imperceptible trail led the way. Scuff marks on the right, a discarded glove on the left, and wet boot prints at the edge of the stream. The darkness deepened the further she ventured, but the sides of the tunnel never shrank. At the first junction, she found a bloody handprint on the wall. *Fresh, from someone injured in the battle? Then why haven't I seen blood before?*

A child's voice whispered in the dark. Tiny footsteps echoed in the tunnel behind her. Off another branch someone laughed. More running to her right. Nazarra closed her eyes and followed the sound. Each passage she crossed screamed at her with hidden voices. Her heart beat, pounding against her ribcage. They knew she was here, but were they chasing her or running?

"Captain Basto," she called out in a loud whisper. Her voice echoed back at her and then again as the hidden children chanted it. Whenever she got close to one, the chanting stopped. Three times she retraced her steps when she'd followed the voices into a dead-end.

Finally, the voices led her into a much larger tunnel where the stagnant water glowed iridescent green. What created the light? A riddle she couldn't answer. Hanging from an old hook embedded in the stone was a red armband. Basto or his private? But no signs of a fight. They were in danger or already captured.

Nazarra hugged the wall, keeping clear of the water as she followed distant sounds. The urchin voices disappeared when she found the tunnel, and the escapees had dropped their guard. Did they think no one would follow? Sloppy, and something she would use to her advantage. Deep underground, there weren't landmarks to guide her, but she must have traveled the length of Salaz by now. That these tunnels existed without the queen or her knowing was a serious problem. What if a marauding army found them? Forgotten passages from the old city - it was something out of a fairy tale - or nightmare.

The green light beneath the water vanished, dousing her in sudden darkness. Nazarra never lost a step. The way forward was flat, and she trusted her memory, allowing the sound of voices to navigate for her. In a crouch, she approached a chamber at the end of the tunnel. Silhouettes danced across the open doorway, while shadows spilled over walls. How many were in there?

Nazarra heard a strange sucking sound to her left and in the dim light found an urchin sitting on a rotted barrel. The girl smiled, pulling a candied treat out of her mouth. Nazarra held a finger to her lips, hoping the child would remain quiet. The girl cocked her head and waved with a sticky hand. Two more urchins appeared, each carrying jagged blades. Nazarra stepped back, never hearing the splash of feet in the water. Before she could escape, a dozen more urchins filled the tunnel, penning her in. With the element of surprise gone, she drew her assassin's dagger and waited to see what they would do. And promptly dropped it.

Grint walked out of the chamber with the dog at his heels. Seeing Nazarra, he smiled and held out his arms. "Great, we're all here!"

Before she could reply, the urchin girl hopped off her barrel and blew a handful of dust in her face. *So that's what it feels like*, Nazarra thought as the world went black.

21

"The enemy of your enemy is not your friend. Whoever sold you that lie is a kry-damn idiot. Find yourself someone who's never wanted to kill you, but neither of you care if the other dies. Now that's someone to storm a castle with."

- *Robber-Baron Gillicus*

Nazarra climbed back from the deep sleep forced on her by the powder. Confused thoughts swirled around her mind, making it difficult to separate fact from fantasy. A child blew powder in her face - but was that real or the fragment of a dream she inserted? The thief lived, even after watching Tennebrue disintegrate him. Is this what her powder did to people? As clarity settled in, she felt the bindings on her wrists and ankles. They had her in a chair. Moving her tongue and jaw, she suppressed a smile, discovering they hadn't used a gag. Nor could she feel a blindfold.

Nazarra kept her eyes closed, listening to voices behind the dark void. Maintaining her breath, she wanted to make them think sleep still had her while learning all she could. The air carried a stale odor of something damp, rotted, and moldy. Water trickled across stone and fell in shallow puddles, echoing in what must have been a narrow chamber. Farther away someone was breaking stones with metal picks. Three voices argued in harsh whispers., but it was the two voices to her right she found herself most interested in.

"We want to help," a girl said.

"You'll get paid for what you've done," Grint replied. It was Grint, she knew his voice well enough, but how did he cheat death?

"Want to do more," the girl said. Other voices chattered. It was a wordless noise, but came from every part of the room.

"Maybe," Grint replied. "When I meet Matty."

"You already have," the girl laughed.

"Clever," the thief joined her in laughing, finding humor in the deception. Nazarra didn't know what was so clever about the child or Matty. Or why the thief was dealing with children. "So, why is it you want to help?"

"You killed Happy Marv," she said. The laughing stopped. "We owe you."

"What makes you think I killed Marv?" Grint answered, his voice guarded. More chattering.

"Guards found her body with a dagger standing tall in her chest," Matty answered. "Dirty Paul said you went into her shop but no come back out."

"Inno janoi. Watching me this whole time," Grint grumbled. "Wait, her? That mean, blind woman was Happy Marv? Thought she was a kry-damn salt witch." Nazarra hadn't heard of a rug merchant dying, but why would Grint have killed her?

"The woman is awake," a callow boy said in a sing-song voice. Startled by the nearness of it, she opened her eyes to see a scruffy child in torn clothes perched atop another chair.

"Welcome," Grint said. "Though I hadn't planned on seeing you again." The children, numbering at least thirty, started their chattering laugh which was much more frightening to see than hear. The girl with the treat, the remnants of which were still on her face, clapped her hands and the urchins stopped. When she jerked her head, they left in a mass wave. So, this was Matty, the true head of the urchin snake.

The cracked barrels sitting around the room reminded her of the Weebles basement, but the stone here had a worn quality that spoke of age. Thirty paces long in one direction and ten in the other, she struggled to comprehend what the original intention for it might be.

"A smuggler's den?" She asked.

"Why don't we start with you? Who are you are this time," Grint asked. The urchin girl covered her ears as he dragged a chair to sit in front of her.

"You're alive. Billy is good at what he does," Nazarra replied. "Watching you die looked very real."

"You're avoiding the question," Grint said.

"You know who I am," she said, pretending not to see Matty tapping a knife against her knee.

"Without an armband, it's hard to tell," Grint countered. Newman trotted into the room and laid at his feet. The dog licked the air as Grint scratched his back, both happily reunited. Behind the dog came a stocky man in black steel cap and chain veil. His red armband was missing, but she knew him well. Was it the one hanging in the tunnel? Basto walked with purpose toward a barrel of water that he dunked his waterskin into. The captain wasn't a prisoner, but working with them. "Why are you following me?"

"I wasn't following you," she smiled. "Didn't you hear? I thought you were dead."

"Did you shed a tear at least?"

"Rivers," Nazarra said, trying to find the weak thread in her bindings. When she got loose, the first to die would be Basto. Matty next. Could she kill Grint?

"That's heartwarming," Grint nodded. "So again, why are you here?"

"I'm here for him," Nazarra said, using her chin to point at the captain. "I assumed he went after the Parthian and thought he'd need help."

Grint furrowed his brow, confused by the admission. When he looked over his shoulder, he blew out a breath, shaking his head. "Take that kry-damn mask off. It's creepy when you wear it." Grint shuddered as he looked back at Nazarra. She understood. Or thought she did.

"Just being cautious with this one here," the false-captain replied.

"He makes an excellent point," Grint smiled. "I don't think we should we trust you."

"It's not a mystery anymore," she said. "That's Billy."

"Wrong," the young illusionist said as he walked in. "I can change my appearance, but haven't figured out how to master it with others."

Basto took off the helmet and dropped it to the floor. The face beneath was his, but blurred. Almost as if the lines of his face had lines of their own.

"Some answers have consequences," Grint said. The warning in his voice unmistakable. Nazarra nodded. "Do it."

"This is a terrible idea," Basto-not-Basto grumbled. Tearing at a seam of flesh on his neck, he peeled the skin from his face and dropped it on the floor. Nazarra screamed in horror, expecting a bloody skull. Instead, Smit flexed his jaw, taking a towel from his brother to clean the residue off his face.

"You killed them," Nazarra said. "I heard the reports. Tore out their guts."

"A little over the top," Grint said, frowning at Billy.

"Basto made the report," Billy grinned. "Our Basto. Smitsto? Smasto?"

"I like Smasto," Smit laughed.

"There you have it," Grint smiled. "Mimicrum used to copy a face. It's not elegant, but when you can hide the imperfections beneath a veil it evens out. Now, we find ourselves at an impasse. You made it clear where your loyalty lies. We can try to keep you tied up or I can have the urchins toss you in the harbor. I hear the fish are friendly."

"There's no need for that," an unfamiliar voice answered. Nazarra thought her shock had reached its peak, but that was just not true. "I am sure if we put our heads together, we can find a solution without further bloodshed."

"Sem," Grint's smile broadened as he stood. The two threw their arms wide and embraced.

"When did you return?" Lord Orsava asked, grabbing Grint by the shoulders and nodding.

"Just now," Grint said. "They told me you were sleeping, and I didn't want to wake you."

"You're dead," Nazarra mumbled.

"A bit of showmanship," Orsava said in a solemn voice. "I thought I acquitted myself."

"Angis," Grint shouted as the manservant entered the room. The thief grabbed him in a bear-hug that was not immediately returned, but then Angis softened and returned the gesture. "I worried they had killed you."

"It seems I am adept at hiding," Angis said with a shy smile and shrug.

"A hidden skill to be sure," Orsava said, laughing at his own pun. Knowing Grint's distaste for such humor, it surprised her he didn't comment.

"Should I assume Brott and Keranue are alive as well?" Nazarra asked, looking around for the remaining two members of the crew.

"I knew Brott for many years," Orsava said. "It pained me to learn of his treachery, but no, he is dead."

"Keranue?" Smit asked.

Grint shook his head, "Almost. Ogres got him in the tunnel beneath the harbor."

"I told you there were muddlers down there," Billy whispered. Nazarra couldn't believe it. They had been told those tunnels collapsed a century ago.

"Yet, I see we have three recruits to replace them," Orsava looked out the doorway as he spoke.

"Two," Grint said with a shrug. "The goblins are in, but the Parthian has his own agenda."

Nazarra railed against the bindings, trying to will them into breaking. "The barbarian is here?"

"Can I have the room?" Grint said, closing his eyes.

"I know you've been against killing her," Billy started, but stopped as Orsava put his arm around him and led him from the room with Angis trailing behind. "What? It's true and I have a point to make."

"We've been at this for two days," Smit said. "It's not going fast enough. We could use the Parthian."

"The goblins are more than enough," Grint said.

"The goblins?" Smit laughed. "They're in the next room betting on which rat eats the other first."

"We need demomancers, and those two are the most destructive devils in all of Terragard," Grint took on a far-away look as he spoke, as if imagining some past destruction he may have witnessed.

"Fine," Smit said. "I'll try to get them to work."

"Smit?" Grint called out before the elder Tagro left. "Bet on whichever rat Trimbo backs. He wins more often than Puig."

Almost alone with Grint, the urchin girl had something to say. The cold steel of a blade pressed against Nazarra's wrist as Matty spoke in a dead, emotionless voice, "If you attempt escape, a flood of urchins will devour you before thirty paces." The blade eased off, cutting away the bindings one by one.

"So, you don't want to kill me," Nazarra smiled as Matty left the room. "How sweet."

"That can change," Grint said as he crouched down to rub the dog's belly. Nazarra stretched out her stiff muscles as she walked around the back of the chair. An urchin left a long cudgel leaning against an old barrel. At least the length of her arm. The weapon looked sturdy enough to use on ten, fifteen opponents before it broke.

"I'd die for my duty," she shrugged, giving up on the thought of escape. Street urchins had been a problem in Salaz as far back as she could remember, even if no one paid them much mind. There were few enough to begin with, and those who survived to adulthood could join a guild and gave back. No one imagined the true number of them or how they'd organized. How many had she counted in this room? How many more had she heard in the tunnels?

"Why are you down here, Grint? Borismere hired Racko to move the gold. Even I don't know where that is."

He'd given her cause to doubt everything she'd seen. And now this too. "Right?"

Grint walked to the moldy door and swung it open. Outside, she could see a much larger chamber with arched ceilings and a watery canal. A dozen or more torches lit the area as urchins carried buckets of dirt into the tunnels. Further back, they'd built a wooden scaffold - *to do what?* Nazarra took a long look at the brothers and urchins. All of them covered in stone, dirt, and muck. Where in the city were they?

"You're digging," Nazarra breathed. "But how do you know where?"

"Racko moved the gold where we wanted her to," he answered. "I kept dropping bread crumbs. Had to lead her to it."

"That was your plan?"

"No," Grint said as he closed the door once more. "It was further down the list. Think of it as Plan J."

"It's not going fast enough, so you brought in demomancers," she reasoned. The idea was almost laughable. "You'll bring half the city down."

"I'd die for my duty," he answered. "But that's Plan S. We're still somewhere around M or N."

"I can't let you destroy Salaz," she said, looking back at the cudgel.

"It won't come to that," Grint said. He watched her eyeing the cudgel, but there wasn't an ounce of tension in the man. "I've seen those two maniacs do incredible things."

"What are you doing?" Nazarra asked as he crossed the room to take her hand in his. A gentle hold that almost melted her resolve when paired with the determined stare of his steel-gray eyes.

"Last time I ask," he said in a soft voice. "You can still be a part of this. Forget the city, the queen, all of it. Come with us."

Nazarra yanked her hand away. "And forget my duty? My very destiny?"

"Destiny," he screamed as much as laughed. "Darrow doesn't care about destiny or what you do with it."

"Darrow?" The reference was odd. "Is that the God of Destiny in your strange one hundred?"

"Destiny is just an excuse people make when they're too stupid to see the ax swinging toward their neck," Grint stomped around until he found something to kick. The noise woke the snoring bulldog, who barked, yawned, and went back to sleep.

"I'm stupid?" she asked, crossing her arms.

"If you can't see your own death in the cards? Maybe you are," he retorted with just as much ferocity.

"The queen is my sister," Nazarra argued back. "Borismere already killed Prince Mikil and took control of the Opposition. He now means to kill Akosha so he can sit on the throne. A fact you knew but neglected to tell me."

"I didn't see it as pertinent information to share with Dusk Raven," Grint shook his head. "And I wasn't in the giving mood when you blew that charffing dust in my face. Which is horrible stuff by the by. The kry-damn nightmares I've been having."

It was Nazarra's turn to cross the room, taking his hand in hers. "You claim you don't have a heart, but I know it's not true. This excuse of some young love destined for tragedy is just that, an excuse to push people away. Stay with me. Fight by my side. We can stop Borismere and you can live like a king. No more risking your neck for a bauble you'll drink away in a single turning."

"Sounds cozy," he smiled. "And too safe. What's fun about that?"

"Insufferable," she growled, shoving him away. Nazarra spun on her heels and threw the door open. Two dozen urchins blocked her was as she stalked toward the tunnel door.

"Move child, or I will move you," she said.

"Blood for blood," Matty said, and the urchins chattered.

"No," Grint called out. "No one is killing her."

"Are you going to let me go? Or does this get messy?" Nazarra said over her shoulder.

"I vote for messy."

"Shut up, Billy," Grint yelled. "Nazarra, come with me."

"I told you no," she answered.

"Not on the job," he said with a frustrated huff. "Literally, come with me."

"No."

"Stop being a mungle-haired weeble and just bloody listen," he yelled. Nazarra turned, seeing a handful more doors beyond the first room she'd been in. There was also a skiff in the canal with thirty more piled behind it. *They're floating the gold out,* she thought. *To where? The mystery ship? Clever.*

Grint opened the second door as she approached, and what was inside horrified her. Nazarra dropped to her knees, consoling the prisoner. Basto lay bloody and chained in a room no larger than two paces. As he saw and then recognized her, the captain's face lit with hope, and he mouthed the word, *Please.*

"Let him loose at once," she commanded.

"No," Grint replied. "We might need another mimicrum of his face."

"You're a monster," she snapped, standing up.

"He works for Borismere," Grint shrugged.

"Lies," the captain hissed in a voice strained from disuse.

"Why show me this? Are you implying this is my fate?" Nazarra wished she'd taken the cudgel.

"What? No," Grint answered. "I just opened the wrong door is all."

Grint walked away without waiting for her to follow. Against her better judgement, she followed, leaving Basto and his whimpered pleas behind. Did she take the thief at his word that Basto was a traitor? Grint was many things, but not a liar. The captain delighted in beating the prisoners he took, bloodying his knuckles on their faces. All in the service of the queen's edicts. Which originated with Borismere. It might explain how Grint came by so much knowledge of Borismere's plots.

"How long have you been planning this?" she asked as he paused at the next door.

"I think this is it," he said, more to himself.

Inside was a room much like the one she'd woken up in. Crumbling stone walls, dirt floors, and two pallets pushed together to accommodate the Parthian's gigantic frame. Lord Orsava and his servant sat beside the pallet, administering herbs and liquids to the barbarian. When last they met, he'd looked so strong, menacing. Now, a withering frailty hung over him, sapping the life from every limb.

"I believe this will stave off the poison for a time," Orsava said. "It has not cured it, but your strength will return in small bursts. Once we can leave this place, I am confident I can find an antidote."

"I must leave now," the Parthian said.

"That is not advisable, Chell," Orsava replied, patting the giant on his shoulder.

"You're healing him?" Nazarra snarled. Hearing her voice, the Parthian sat up, his head swaying with dizziness. Chell showed his teeth, and she was sure he would have lunged had the energy existed for such an action.

"Chell, you mean to finish what you started, yes?" Grint asked. The Parthian nodded.

"We should try to dissuade him," Orsava said, glaring at Grint.

"You'd as soon dissuade the sun from rising," Grint replied. "What if I told you the queen wasn't your enemy? That it was the man in the warehouse."

"Borismere," Chell grunted.

"He's taken over the Opposition and means to kill the queen," Grint added.

"His villainy knows no bounds," Orsava said in a sad voice vibrating with anger.

"What are you doing?" Nazarra asked, still feeling a raging inferno of anger burning in her belly.

"I'm offering you a solution," Grint said, turning his own anger on to her. "You need to stop Borismere and he needs Atonement. Saving a queen from betrayal and bringing peace back to a city should do it, shouldn't it Chell?"

"It would fare better than killing someone because they forced me to," The Parthian agreed.

"You know the layout of the palace and he has the desire," Grint said. "I've known heists that have gone off without either of those."

"You're suggesting I work with the barbarian?"

"This is your way out," Grint answered. "Unless you want to slaughter a bunch of children."

"And what do you get?"

The look he gave her in return made her feel stupid for asking. "The gold," he said. "Go save your sister. All we ask is you keep everyone looking the other way as we sail into the sunset."

"That's all this was for you," she breathed. "Another heist."

"Yes," he said, leaning against the wall and rubbing his eyes. "I'm a thief."

"You could have ten times the gold," she said. "If you stay."

"I don't want that," Grint yelled. "I've never wanted that."

"No," she yelled back. "You just want to waste all your gold, spreading it across the land like dead seeds that never grow. And then what?"

"And then I steal more," he said. "Or I take it all back from the places I spent it."

Nazarra wanted to scream at him, to cry, rage, and wail. She wanted to keep arguing the matter until he opened his fool eyes and saw a sliver of reason. But the soft voice in her head told her something different. People didn't change their view because you made an articulate point. Change came from within, when you stopped believing in the thing you held to so tight. Things had changed in Nazarra. She no longer believed there was a reasonable way to remove Borismere other than death. And she believed as Grint did, that the barbarian could help her. That Argus was correct and others in the palace would stand by her. Finally, she believed that the love she and her sister shared was stronger that the hate Borismere had poisoned her with.

"Barbarian," she said. "If you can find Atonement in destroying Borismere, I would aid you."

"Call me Chell," the Parthian responded. "And I find the arrangement agreeable."

Without another word, Nazarra stormed out of the room. The urchins tried blocking the way until Grint shouted at them to move. There were several groans as he explained why he was letting them go, but the urchins parted. The barbarian strode up beside her, two swords of questionable quality in his hands. The tunnel door opened and together they stepped through.

"Chell," Grint said. "There's a way up. The third tunnel on the left."

"Thank you, Firehair," the barbarian smiled.

"Nazarra," the thief said and then went silent. The sound of water dripping into the sludge at their feet trumpeted like celestial screams. When the time came, he said one simple word. "Goodbye."

Turning her head, she refused to look at him from anything more than the corner of an eye. "If I ever see you again," she said. "I'll kill you."

22

"I'll wager ten coppers you used too much."

*- Puig Dustfeeder to Trimbo Albottom on the day
they brought down the Sentinel of Stone.*

"That could have gone better," Sem said with a sympathetic pat on Grint's shoulder.

"No," he answered. "It could have gone much worse."

Grint paced back and forth as the pair disappeared into the tunnel. With nothing left to see, he turned back to the job at hand, trying his best to re-focus. If he was being honest, she almost had him. An old friend once got out of the life and for a time seemed happy about it. Why couldn't Grint do the same? He pictured himself lounging on cushions, drinking fine wine, getting fat and gray with age. Never again looking over his shoulder for a dagger. But it felt hollow, like the life some other man should live. Not him.

That's my boy, Hobbe said.

"What are you two doing?" Grint shouted at the goblins. "I didn't hire you to bet on rats."

"Didn't hire us at all," Trimbo said.

"Tricked us," Puig added.

"You befuddled us with your red-haired demon magic," Trimbo continued.

"Befuddled is correct."

"I like them," Billy laughed as he shoveled dirt off the top of the scaffold. Smit and a handful of urchins worked on filling buckets with the piles while others took the buckets into the tunnels to create dams that would control the flow of water. Something they needed to do or risk losing it all in miles of twisting darkness.

"That kry-damn Parthian's help would've made this part easier," Smit said as he dragged a pile of stones away from the scaffold.

"He's dying and has other business to attend to," Grint said, turning to the tunnel mouth as an urchin scampered in chattering.

"Dying? How do you mean?" Smit stopped to watch the tunnel too.

"Opposition poisoned him. Tried to kill the queen." Another visitor approached. Was it who he hoped it was? Or something worse? *Like Mavris?* The urchins would only speak to Matty, and she might not tell them anything at all. If it was bad, and they scattered - that would serve as warning enough.

"Charffing Opposition," Smit spat as he dropped an enormous stone in the canal. "We expecting someone else?"

"Yes," Grint said, and relaxed when Matty waved him over with a dirty hand.

"Who?" Smit's tone told Grint that he hated splitting up the gold as much as the rest.

"Our way out," he said as a dozen rough dressed sailors sauntered through the door. A wretched man with an elaborate hat and pet mungle on his shoulder followed them. Newman caught sight of the winged monkey and barked. This upset the mungle, who screamed back. Coward that Newman was, he ran across the chamber to hide in Orsava's room.

"Gaustauss," Grint shouted.

"Captain Gaustauss," the man replied as he calmed his pet. "I hope your animal will not upset Nigel any further."

"Don't blame Newman for having enough sense to not trust a mungle," Grint responded.

"How I've missed this," Gaustauss said as he looked around the chamber. "You called, and I came. What is it you need?"

"Grint, who is this?" Smit whispered.

"This is Captain Gaustauss of the Hermitage Roll. The last of the dreaded black flags to sail the Three Seas, and the answer to how we're getting the gold out of Salaz," Grint proclaimed. The urchins chattered, and a few clapped. Orsava, Smit and Billy looked a little more skeptical.

"You're trusting a pirate with the gold?" Smit asked.

"Not just a pirate," Gaustauss smiled. "The pirate."

"And he's demon possessed," Grint added with a rise of his eyebrows.

"You say that like it's an offensive thing," Captain Gaustauss sneered.

"It is," Grint gave him a winning smile. "But it also means I know eight hundred ways to ensure he doesn't cross us."

"I expect when this job's done, that nasty piece of parchment you've been holding over my head will go up in smoke?" Gaustauss asked. "Or I'll start testing the boundaries of what it will and will not allow."

"A deal is a deal," Grint said. He didn't like demons and cared for the possessed even less. Who knew what type of person Gaustauss was before, but demons didn't take over unless you had a black heart and invited them to. "And there's a full share for you and your crew. That should suffice, yes?"

"We have an accord," the pirate captain held out his hand. With the deal done, Gaustauss ordered his men to help however Grint needed.

Smit pulled Grint aside as Billy hopped off the scaffold to join them. Each with growing concern on their faces. "What's this about?" Smit said.

"You didn't mention pirates," Billy added.

"Listen, it's good. We're down Keranue, Nazarra, and Brott. The two goblins and a share for the pirates evens it out."

"Don't forget the urchins," Billy said. "Matty gives me the creeps."

"Okay," Grint shrugged. "We're down a share, but it would have been worse if the guilds still had their hands in the pot.

"And you're certain we can trust them?" Billy asked.

"No," Grint said, clapping him on the shoulder. "But a boat is the only way we're getting the gold out. How far do you think we'll get with a caravan of gold wagons on the Krau Plains?"

"I never thought of what we'd do with the gold once we had it," Smit said.

"It's not like we can keep it under our beds," Billy laughed, earning a back-handed swipe from his brother that the kid ducked.

"That's what you have me for," Grint said, walking back toward the goblins. "The pirates will take us to the island of Lira Cellas. I know a banker there who will exchange it for Gelden Notes."

"Yes," Puig said, rubbing his hands.

"Those are good from here to the Papality," Trimbo said, nodding in time with Puig's hands.

"But not the Papality," Puig scoffed.

"Well, no," Trimbo scoffed in return. "Who wants to go there?"

"Do you two have everything you need to make a river of gold?" Grint asked before their banter swallowed them all in its brutal banality.

"I gave the boy our list of requirements," Trimbo said.

"Once he brings the proper items back, we will be rich," Puig smiled.

"Beyond our wildest dreams," Trimbo continued.

"Unless it's a nightmare," Puig cautioned. "What if only five coins fall from the sky?"

"Do you recall that explorer, Puig?"

"Why Trimbo, do you mean Brasan Farthermew the Eighth of his Name?"

"None other," Trimbo nodded.

"Who is that?" Billy asked, causing Grint to groan.

"Don't you know," Trimbo frowned.

"No one knows," Puig shook his head.

"Yes, true, we should enlighten the boy," Trimbo said.

"Farthermew discovered the Tomb of Polius."

"Cracked it open."

"Did he find gold?" Smit asked, drawn in by the story.

"No," Trimbo said, holding his tiny three-fingered hand over his heart.

"He found sickness," Puig bowed his head in solemn prayer, tapping his temple and heart.

"Died?" Billy asked.

"Gruesome-like," Puig laughed, making a choking sound as he rolled his eyes back.

"Everything else is ready," Smit said. "I don't see why the goblins can't get the supplies though. It's an awful risk for Billy."

"Look at our faces," Puig said.

"How can you not want to arrest us on sight?" Trimbo nodded. "Not that we're not stunning in our good looks."

"They told me what we need to do to break the levee," Billy said. "I can do it. The rest I'll bring back for them."

"Good, but I'm coming with you," Grint said. And for the first time in ages, he thought they had a chance in Asta-poor of pulling this off. "Should be a piece of cake."

*****

"You had to jinx it," Billy said as they watched the Blue Hands loading the last of the gold into the old Krypholos church. Except it wasn't just the thieves. A mercenary company had joined them, a nasty one out of the Thousand Rivers region. The Golden Few they called themselves and Grint had run from them on at least seven occasions.

And bought them off another three, Hobbe said.

"There has to be fifty of them down there. How do we get the gold without them hearing?" Billy rolled onto his back, punching the sky in frustration.

Grint didn't have an answer. Yet. "I'll figure it out," he said. "Come on, we still have a job to do."

"Who hired the mercenaries?" Billy asked as they slid off the roof, landing in the bed of their wagon.

"Borismere." Grint tried to assign logic to the lord's actions. Hiring the Golden Few was a decent backup in case wresting control of the Opposition away from Mikil failed. Now, with the prince dead, they could monitor the thieves - make sure the gold didn't mysteriously vanish.

An all-out battle raged across Salaz, courtesy of their crew. New skirmishes between guilds sprouted every time they extinguished another. Billy had laughed when he told Grint how they'd done it. Making illusions of one faction attacking another. It had been meant as a diversion to get in and rescue Grint after the urchins reported he'd been taken. No one thought it would spread across the city.

Maybe it will help you too, Nazarra.

Borismere had his eyes set firmly on the throne, betting both ways. If the queen died tonight, he would ascend as the Opposition leader. If she lived, he could use the gold as a dowry to marry her, become king and then make something untoward happen on their wedding night. Not a bad jump to go from money lender to Lord and then all the way to King. And the thieves? If Racko and her Blue Hands behaved, they'd make a great clandestine force.

The cart rolled along; the horse whinnying at the sounds of steel clashing. People unwilling to fight hid in their homes, shutters closed tight. *So much for the Cognispyre. They'll disappoint Ashgra with this behavior. Or maybe she'll dance in the empty streets.* Ashgra seemed a strange god - even for one made up.

Their first stop after leaving the tunnel had been the curio shop in Meskal. Her selection of illicit goods included everything the goblins wanted and more. Just in case,

Grint bought the bangers she'd once offered and stored them in a side compartment on the wagon. Something to scatter a few troops who might get nosy.

Getting out of the Meskal was harder than in. Roving bands of Fishmongers, Opposition, and city guards slowed their progress to a crawl - causing them to hide every thirty feet. Sweat broke out on Billy's brow from the effort of concealing them so often.

The Upper Crust didn't see as much battle. Manor guards stood sentry outside each home, chasing off anyone who came close. Whoever won the guild battle would dictate what happened next, but for now, it was business as usual. Grint and Billy took their time in the district, following a circuitous route to identify any followers. So far, no one looked to be trailing them above or below.

"Do you think they're waiting for us to do something?" Billy asked as they approached the first stop.

"No," Grint said. "The best thing we have going for us is they think we're all dead."

Billy nodded and pulled out the first two demomancer concoctions prescribed by the goblins. His hand trembled as he passed the glass bottle filled with bubbling amber liquid to Grint. Stupidly, both failed to ask how volatile these were. If dropped, would it send them to the spirit realm? Grint decided he'd avoid finding out. They unstopped the bottles and carefully poured half across the levee stones. The liquid hissed as it seeped into the cracks, but not enough to cause panic. When they finished, they noticed the color draining from the rock, and that effect spread into areas they hadn't doused.

"One down, three more stops to go," Billy smiled, wiping his brow with the back of his hand and almost spilling the liquid onto himself. Grint hissed, stepping back. The kid mouthed the word sorry.

"Did Trimbo tell you how long it takes?" Grint asked, worrying about the time they had. The effect was spreading faster than they could pour.

"No, but I'm hoping they added in the time it would take for us to get back and enter the church." The young thief shrugged as he climbed into the cart. Knowing the goblins like he did, Grint wasn't sure they had.

Do you remember that bush lord's tower? Hobbe asked. Grint actively tried to forget that job, afraid that thinking about it would summon the old fool's ghost to haunt him.

Their next stop went smoothly, as did the third. They finished pouring the liquid and stooped over to wash their hands in a trough when the horse shook its head. They both froze, watching the horse's nervousness grow. It whinnied and stomped its feet, trying to pull the cart. It acted as if a swarm of foy flies assaulted it, but the air was still. The horse screamed and bolted, dragging the cart behind it.

"Krypsie's sake, why is it always the last one when something goes wrong," Grint groaned as they gave chase. The horse slowed and stopped a block away, but continued shaking its head until it laid down. Convulsions followed as skin tore away and bones cracked. The horse transformed from a beast of burden to something horrifying, standing on two legs and heaving deep breaths.

"Please tell me that's you doing this," Grint said to Billy. The boy shook his head.

A robed man strolled along the street, humming a jaunty tune. The horse-beast bowed its head for him to pat. Pulling back the hood with a smug, self-satisfied look, the wizard laughed.

"Tennebrue."

"I had my suspicions you were alive," the wizard said. "Never seen my magic vaporize someone so completely. I applaud your illusionary skills, child," he said looking at Billy.

"How about we just go our ways," Grint smiled. "I broke you out of prison. You owe me one."

"If you think I was a prisoner there any more than you, I mistook the depths of your intelligence," Tennebrue said.

"Then what do you want?" Grint asked, pulling Billy close, ready to run.

"What are you up to?" Tennebrue looked into the cart as he ran a finger along the wood. "The two of you in a farmer's cart on a night like this? You're up to something."

"Just trying to enjoy the Cognispyre," Grint smiled.

"That's how it is then," Tennebrue sighed. The horse-beast roared before it charged. Grint and Billy held their hands in front of their face, crying. The monster charged through them, the illusion shattering into piles of hay. Tennebrue and the monster screamed in unison while the thieves watched from a nearby roof.

The boy's skills are strong, Hobbe agreed.

"I guess we're no longer dead," Billy said.

23

*"Be not afraid," the wolf said. "Man is the one who kills for
nothing but the wool on your back. I have no interest in wool
and will protect you. If you but serve me."*

- The Treachery of the Wolf, Farahl's Foy Tales

Chell waited for the double vision to subside. It wors-
ened with every hour but passed quickly, allowing him moments of clarity and strength. That too would dwindle - of
this he held no disillusionment. The salve provided by the
one called Orsava helped, but even he admitted it would
not be enough.

"Please," a small dreego male moaned, holding his
head as he crawled across the floor.

"What is the purpose of this?" Chell asked.

"The purpose?" The angry Salazian woman replied.
"We need the gear and clothing that Nasdo is more than
willing to provide. Unless you'd like to assault the castle
with rusty swords?"

Chell could not fault the need, even if the method felt
brutal. The Salazian woman - Nazarra - scared him, an exciting admission to make of a dreego. Not since the ferocity
of his first love had he experienced such a warrior. Chell

forgot where he was as he followed her. Was this a dreego city or the jungles of home in disguise? A foolish notion, amplified by the sickness in his blood.

The pair moved through the city with care, avoiding unwanted conflicts. Dreego fought one another to the death, painting the winding streets in their own blood. As they passed an armorer's shop in the Gutarr, Nazarra's mood changed. According to her curt growls, this shop displayed a symbol of the Opposition. Like a tornado come alive, she rushed in to take what they needed.

"Be glad I am leaving you with your life," Nazarra said to the dreego as she pointed out a two-handed sword behind the counter.

"You have no right," the owner said, pushing himself against a wall.

"Nor did you and your lot in poisoning me," Chell said as he strapped the sword and scabbard across his back. In the empty loop of his belt, he slung a curved dagger and wrapped a long cord around his shoulder. Such a thing was useful for climbing or strangling. A pair of thick leather vambraces struggled to close around his forearms, and none of the boots came close to fitting. He settled for a wide pair of moccasins like the children of the village wore in summer.

"I had nothing to do with that," the dreego said.

"Quiet," Nazarra said, pressing the heel of a boot against his throat as she tied it.

A thick robe caught Chell's eye. Such garments would normally lie beneath his notice. A proud Parthian showed their fur. It let others know them by sight and smell. To hide it beneath extraneous fabrics was akin to cowardice, but the thief's words stuck with him. To get through the gate, he would need to exercise a level of subterfuge he had not before.

"I'll call the guards," the dreego choked as she set her foot down.

"I am the guard," Nazarra laughed.

"You're a traitor."

"Another word and I will not leave you alive," Chell said as he slipped the robe over his head. It stretched tight across the chest and hung only to his thighs. Far too short to be an effective disguise. Flexing his muscles, the flimsy thing tore at the seams, falling into a pile on the floor.

"Sneaking through the gate is not the plan," Nazarra said, using a small club to knock the merchant unconscious.

"What is the plan?" Chell asked as they walked through the door.

The streets of the Gutarr remained quiet. Far removed from the screams of battle and raging fires below. Yet, the dreego here were not cowards, quaking in their homes. Archers stood in stone windows, their arrows ready to rain down upon intruders. Killing holes on street-level walls glinted with the promise of spears, as they pushed steaming barrels of tar into position above. The dreego were smarter than he imagined. They'd creating the perfect killing field and hidden it beneath a facade of civility.

"Why do they not attack?"

Nazarra glance to either side before she answered. "As long as you're with me, they will hold. Just don't make any sudden moves."

Chell grunted a muted laugh. As they continued, he recognized this street as the one he'd first failed to strike down the queen. "I believe this is where we first met."

"Sorry," she said with no trace of sincerity. "Protecting my sister is my duty."

"I admire your goal but find fault in how you dreego accomplish it," Chell replied. Poisons and spells were the work of wickedness.

"Sorry to prick your barbarian sensibilities," she sneered.

"Parthians are not barbarians," he hissed. "We are strong warriors."

"And dreego aren't salt witches," she answered. "Sometimes magic is useful."

Now that was an interesting notion and one he'd never considered. "I shall speak to the Oracle when I return home. Though I doubt she will give that thought any credence. A warrior must battle without crutch or aid."

Nazarra drew her knives, and in the darkness he heard the soft pull of bowstrings. "If you want to duel, I am happy to put you down. Like magic, you're useful, but not needed." Feet shuffled in the kill-hole to his left, and he positioned himself to catch a spear if one came through.

Chell wanted to laugh, but such a sound would frighten the dreego soldiers into attacking. "I doubt that very much. If so, you would not have agreed to join me."

"You're joining me," she said, continuing on. "Not the other way round."

"As you say," Chell answered. "You knew deep love for Fire-head."

"Love?" She laughed. "There was no love."

"One thing I have learned is that you dreego - humans - feel your emotions with great ferocity," Chell said. "You're unable to hide them."

Nazarra shook her head, keeping her expression hidden.

"I do not say this as a hurtful thing," Chell continued. "I loved quite the same and endured the bitter sting of betrayal. It is how I came here."

"You talk a lot," she said.

"Yes," Chell said in a softer voice. "It helps to distract me from the smell of anger, the sound of weapons gripped tight, the wave of fear that makes dreego panic."

Nazarra looked around this time, perhaps seeing for the first the imminent danger they were in. The knowledge did not slow her pace or change her direction. A commendable level of bravery for any Parthian, let alone a dreego. The stuff of songs.

"What was life like for you," she asked. "In Parthia?"

"I was a great chief. A war-leader much like your sister," he answered, proud of what he'd accomplished even if it they stole it away.

"Akosha is not a war-leader," Nazarra laughed. "She knows nothing of holding a blade and less about battle formations."

"By how she handled the magic against me, I would beg to differ."

"That's not her," Nazarra said with a profound wave of sadness pouring off her skin. "Borismere corrupted her as he did you, just with different poisons."

The palace walls rose above the buildings, growing taller with every step. Massive stones of glimmering blue stacked on top of one another and lined with soldiers. The gates stood open, giving him a view within. A green courtyard, lit by torches and moonlight, edged with trees. Six men in steel armor and red armbands blocked the way forward.

"Let me talk," Nazarra said. "But if this goes another way, promise me you will not strike Akosha. Only him."

"You have my vow," Chell replied.

"Spymaster General," the lead dreego called out. "I am pleased to see you, but must question your company."

"Is that the Parthian who attacked the queen?" The soldier beside him asked, scratching his chin. At their backs, the hidden forces stepped onto the street. The stink of anger, their mumbled words, flex of muscle all led him to believe a battle was imminent.

"Jaspar," Nazarra called back. "Argus told me I'd find friends at the palace."

"Always," the one called Jaspar answered. The two parties approached one another, leaving Chell alone with the growing mass of soldiers.

"Borismere is here?"

"Yes," Jaspar answered. "He arrived after the fighting started. As did many of the noble families."

"Let me past so I may introduce him to my friend," Nazarra said in a voice of icy steel.

"You know I can't," Jaspar replied. Chell could smell the care this dreego held for her, and his deep sadness at denying the request.

"Borismere is a traitor and means to kill Akosha - the queen," she said, turning to the soldiers, addressing them all.

"What proof? Don't roll your eyes at me," Jaspar replied as he started pointing out various guards who'd gathered around. "None of us are supporters. Lord Borismere bankrupted Corro's father, indentured Slago's sister, and sold the contract to the Fishmongers. Had Regneir sent to a post in the Glades for looking at him."

"I'm done with proof and excuses," Nazarra interrupted the soldier. "Borismere killed Mikil tonight. Killed him and took control of the Opposition. Borismere's forces are who your friends are fighting in the city. All of it to distract from him killing my sister and taking her throne."

"That can't be true," Jaspar said, eyes widening in shock.

"It is," she answered. "I'm done asking. Let me pass..."

"Or I will let her pass," Chell answered in a deep, rumbling voice as he drew the two-handed sword.

"I'm not fighting a Parthian to protect Borismere," Corro said, stepping back. The others joined him, each clearing a path until only Jaspar remained in the road.

"I can get you through the gates," Jaspar said. "I can't get you into the tower."

"They're all loyal to him?" she asked, the dread realization of how much danger her sister was in now dawning on her.

Chell studied the wall and grounds beyond. Two grand structures lay between them and their goal. The one to the left did not interest him, but the one on the right...

"The High Priest of Ashgra's residence," she said when he pointed at it.

"Does it connect with the palace?"

"No," Jaspar said.

"What are you thinking?" Nazarra asked.

"This wall," Chell said. "From the city, I saw it run across the cliff. Does it come close to the palace?"

"No," Jaspar said again. "There's a ten-foot gap between the wall and palace."

Chell laughed. "That is but a stride. And will be our entry. Can you get us onto this wall?"

"I don't see why," Nazarra said. "Chell, there is no way into the tower from the top of the palace wings."

"Not there, little one." Chell pointed a thick finger at the balconies around the upper tower. "There."

"Madness," Jaspar groaned.

"I appreciate your fervor," Nazarra said. "I've seen ten men try it for sport. All ten died."

"Were any of them Parthian?" Chell asked.

"No, but neither am I," Nazarra said.

"Then you shall hold to my back," he proclaimed, the matter settled.

Whether she was on board with the plan, Nazarra joined him as they climbed the innards of the palace wall, reaching the wall-walk as a column of Opposition troops flooded the Gutarr. A cloud passed across Effulg, highlighting flaming arrows fired from both sides. Nazarra gripped the edge of the parapet, her knuckles turning white. Which would give out first, the woman or the stone? Chell would not dare to weigh his opinion.

"Let's go," Nazarra said. "If I stay, I will fight."

Chell understood. Would he do any less for his home? *Yes,* Marra mocked. *You slept while Brasau stole your kingdom. And knelt at the post in defeat. You crawled away with your fur in tangles. Coward.* The truth and the lie of her accusation stung in equal parts.

Side by side they ran along the wall-walk. Soldiers called to arms by the blaring horns ignored the pair as they rushed to hold the gates. A harsh pain consumed Chell, taking his legs out from under him. With flailing arms, he toppled, grabbing the closest merlon to keep from collapsing. Nazarra was at his side in an instant, helping him drink from the canteen Lord Orsava prepared. Giving him a moment to rest, they looked down on Salaz between the crenelations. From this height, the city glistened like a faceted jewel, but the twinkling lights were not reflections of beauty. Each fire represented a scar of violence as the city tore itself apart.

Along the rising crest of wall-walk, opposite the High Priest's home, Chell smelled the oiled veneer of worked leather. On the next breath, the gritty texture of dust mixed with sweat. Then trepidation and relief. Nazarra hissed when she spotted the hidden dreego and drew her blades. Chell had not found him with his eyes until the warrior-woman attacked. Crouched in gray leathers, the dreego watched Salaz with a farsight to his eye. The garb did not match that of the city guards. Nazarra's blade was an arm's length from his back when he lowered the glass and back-flipped over her. The gray-dreego drew his own blade, focused on Nazarra. Ignoring Chell would be the dreego's undoing. Chell struck from behind and palmed his entire head. The stranger struggled, swinging his blade as Chell dragged him to the parapet. The tiny blade he wielded found nothing but open air in his frantic strikes. Chell outmatched him in size and strength. At the edge, with a nod from Nazarra, he tossed the man over. A terrified scream cut off when he struck an outcropping of stone and began again as he fell further to his death. The dreego did not know how to die with honor.

A candle flickered to life in a window of the Priest's home. Nazarra pulled him to move. Chell followed, amused by her superstitions of deities and priests who communed with them. The only god one needed was the spirit of battle and ecstasy of victory.

"Who was that man?" He asked as they approached the tower.

"A Blue Hand."

"Blue? I saw nothing blue. The man wore gray, even on his hands," Chell said, wondering if he missed some symbolism in the meaning.

"It means he was a thief," Nazarra said as they slowed their pace, crouching low to avoid unfriendly sentries.

"Like our friend Grint?"

"Your friend," Nazarra snapped, easing the tension in her shoulders a moment later. "But no, Grint is not with them. He's worse."

"How so?" Chell asked from a place of curiosity. Learning about the dreego, the depth of their emotions and what drove them sparked a desire to learn more. Was this what Brasau felt when he met the dreego? Could that be why he brought the witches into Parthia? A question he would ask before he removed Brasau's head.

"The Blue Hands picked a side," Nazarra said, oblivious of the Parthian's musings.

"So did Grint," Chell answered. "It just was not a side you appreciated."

Nazarra's rage boiled over. Chell sensed it in the tightening of muscles, the chalky, burnt smell of anger, the raising of hairs on the back of her neck. He believed she would have attacked him, or tried to, had a guard not appeared. Venting her wrath, she flung a blade, end over end, running behind it as the tip plunged into their eye. The man struggled to scream in the moment of life she allowed, but fell silent under her knee.

"Peace," Chell said as he approached. "I sought only to understand. Not to judge."

"Understand this," Nazarra stood, a map of blood staining her leather while droplets fell from the blade's edge. "We are not friends. We are not allies. Each has a goal to accomplish and if we can help the other do it, we will. When that's over, you will leave Salaz. If you die, I will not shed a tear."

The woman lied, but Chell did not speak it. Dreego were terrible at masking emotions. "So be it," he said. "This is where we cross."

Nazarra stepped back and ran, leaping over the edge of the wall and rolling on to the roof of the palace wing. An impressive effort that Chell hoped would not diminish beside his standing jump. Yet, the woman didn't watch or experience jealousy at his prowess. Nazarra struck him as one who did not seek or even need validation from anyone. A truth that deepened his admiration for her.

Chell uncoiled the rope around his shoulder, wrapping it around his body in a criss-cross. He wove two loops for footholds and a larger one for her waist.

"No," she said. "I won't need that."

"Are you certain?"

"If you get weak again and fall, I'll have a fighting chance to finish on my own." A grim smile and satisfied smell wafted off her. Chell laughed, unable to contain his booming cough.

"Fool," she said, shaking her head as she climbed onto his back. "Do you want to alert the entire city?"

"I believe they have enough to deal with," he replied, digging mortar loose to create the first hold.

The side of the tower was not smooth, as he'd expected from the glimmering sheen. Uneven facets, some required digging, provided hand and footholds. The conical shape of the tower was enough to provide an easy slope, but when free-climbing, any slope was better than none.

"It is no wonder Zorn conquered this land," Chell said as they ascended.

"Zorn had his troubles with Salaz," she replied. "Not enough, but some."

"A great dreego," Chell said.

"You knew him?"

"Not personally," Chell laughed. Already his muscles ached from the effort. "I am not a thousand years old, but our histories sing of him and his battles. To hear a song-weaver sing the Zorn Ternary is something to behold."

"It's too bad you killed him," Nazarra laughed, gripping his shoulders. The moisture on her palms alerted him to a growing nervousness.

"Kill him?" Chell said, his own nervousness growing in time with hers. "We did not kill him."

"All of our histories say he died in Parthia," Nazarra said. "If that's not true, what happened?"

"To tell that tale takes preparation, and now is not the time for such things. Besides, I am an abominable singer."

She nodded into his back as they continued up. Neither spoke again, letting the howl of the wind and carried screams of battle lull them into the rhythm of the climb.

Their ascent brought back a memory never forgotten, but rarely visited. A childhood remembrance of scaling the Cliffs of Moore with his father. A rite of passage taken by the hardiest among Parthians. Only one in a hundred survived. But Chell's father beamed with pride when his son attempted it. *Better to die trying than live with the shame of avoiding challenge.* Bracha joined his son, himself a powerful warrior and hunter who made the climb once before. His father wanted to witness the entire journey as his son ascended.

A third of the way up, his father faltered as a flock of grawks flew into him, losing his grip. Chell watched him fall in silence. *The winds scream, so a Parthian need not.* What he remembered most from that day - even in the moment of death, his father looked upon him with great admiration.

Without the strength of his father to bolster him, Chell needed to continue alone. It was an arduous journey as the winds battered him and grief worked to beguile. *You will fail as he did*, the winds whispered. *How can you succeed?* Chell focused his mind, blocking out the noise. The spirits tested him and he would prove their superior.

When he reached the top, tribal elders waited. Each celebrated Chell for not only conquering the cliff, but do-ing so in the face of loss. It was the first step in his journey toward ruling. And eventual downfall.

Climbing the tower tested him with equal ferocity. His arms shook as the winds whispered their mocking lies. *Your arms shake - as did his before he fell. The woman weighs you down, shake her loose. This time you will fail and fall. But for you, there are no cubs to look upon. You are alone and without a tribe.*

Chell smiled. The challenge strengthened him. The mocking enraged him. It would push him past the weak-ness brought on by poison or doubt. The voices would lose and he would accomplish his task. Atonement may not come from it, but he would not let that deter him.

"We are here," Chell said as they reached a balcony's ledge and grasped its side. Nazarra went over first, breath-ing from the effort, and reached back to help Chell. With her aid, he pulled himself over, and then collapsed, his breath wheezing and stomach threatening to empty. The cool stone refreshed against his face. A soft kiss to spur him on. Chell pushed himself to his knees and listened with Nazarra, their ears pressed against a curtained glass door. Music played within and dreegos chattered... and laughed.

"Laughter? While the city fights and dies?" Nazarra spat in disgust.

The time for subtlety was at an end. Chell drew the mighty sword from his back and kicked the doors open. Within was a room of merriment draped with red velvets. A table of dreego sat feasting and looked only mildly surprised as the doors flew open. Then they beheld the Parthian in the threshold. A woman in cream silks fainted while a dreego man dove beneath the table. Two others fell back in their chairs, curling into balls as they wept. Was there no one brave enough among these dreego? No one willing to face him?

Chell threw the table aside, laughing as the terrified dreego scurried away like a rat. Nazarra gestured for him to follow. Their path continued through a larger room filled with many more tables and silken dreego. A band sat upon a stage playing music while they ate. Guards in ornamental armor looked uncertainly at one another as the crowd panicked. One guard brandished a long spear, the end tied with pastel ribbons. Nazarra smiled and stepped aside when he charged her. Chell waited behind, and his great sword cut through the spear's wooden shaft in a single stroke. The ineffectual guard dropped his stick and ran, tripping over fallen chairs.

Others attacked and broke like waves against stone. The Parthian grabbed the nearest by the back plate of his armor and threw him. His limp body flew over three tables before crashing into the fourth. The last living guard tried to hide, but Nazarra found him, and dragged her thirsty blade across the dreego's throat.

"Where do I find the queen?" Chell asked a silken dreego who stunk of terror.

"In the throne room," he choked out.

"And where is that? Tell me now," he roared, catching urine's pungent stench as the dreego wet himself.

"Chell," Nazarra called. "Finish him and let's go. I know where it is."

"As you wish," he replied. The man screamed as Chell crushed his skull.

More dreego gathered in the hallway. All waiting for the guards to finish the intruders so they could return to their revelry. A woman screamed upon seeing the bloody visage of Nazarra and fainted when Chell stepped through. The herd of dreego ran where they could, trampling the weak in their rush to be anywhere but here. Chell paid them no mind, for there was no honor in killing what amounted to pampered children. Keeping his attention focused on Nazarra, he followed her through twisting corridors lined with golden carpets. No further guards appeared. *Odd. The one called Jaspar mentioned stiffer resistance.*

The carpet ended at a set of doors so grand they made Chell feel insignificant, but he found a reason to smile - they'd found the fight they sought. Thirty armored guards formed two lines, shields in front, spears in back. A defensive maneuver meant to block the door. *This will be a song-worthy battle.* And if he perished, it would be in the arms of his mistress, Battle. *A good death,* as his father would say.

Nazarra stepped forward. The smell of anticipation flooded his nostrils. Yet, the guards shifted. Each line to a different side, creating a clear avenue to the double red doors.

"What trickery is this?" Chell whispered.

"I do not know," she answered.

"The queen awaits," a man with a large feather in his helmet said.

"She wishes to face us?" Chell had not expected this.

"She awaits," the dreego repeated awkwardly.

"Remember your vow," Nazarra said, eyes focused forward.

"Borismere," Chell nodded.

He kept a tight grip on the sword in case the guards tried something, but they did not. The doors opened for them, revealing a throne room full of soldiers and silken dreego. The queen rose from her seat, spreading her arms wide as the prey they sought, Borismere, lounged with legs up, eating from a bowl of fruit.

"Dear sister," Queen Akosha said. "I have been waiting for you."

24

"I am the richest man alive."

- King Benizoa Gelden, The First Jewel,
Crown of the Seven Kingdoms

"What happened?" Smit pushed past the pirates, shouting as Grint and Billy limped through the tunnel door. The noise did nothing to help the headache blossoming at the base of Grint's skull.

"Charffing wizard," Grint said, helping Billy sit before checking himself. During their escape, he'd torn the leather coat, shredded it to be more accurate, but at least he could mend that. Blessedly, the beast never broke the skin. Krypsie knew what poisons or disease such a manifestation carried with it. Tennebrue and his beast found them twice after Billy's illusion. And the last time nearly became the last time.

"Wizard? That wasn't some hedge wizard or salt witch. It was Tennebrue," Billy groaned. Smit whistled, making a two-fingered sign over his eyes.

"You two know him?"

"Yeah," Smit nodded, checking his brother for injuries. "Worst of the worst. He was the one Borismere wanted to break out with the Parthian. Except I was Basto when Boris-mere ordered it. Not sure how he got out."

"With me," Grint said.

"You?" The Tagro brothers said in unison.

"Goblins, Parthians, sadistic wizards," Billy ranted, shaking off his brother's administrations. "Who else did you bring out of there? Astapoor?"

"Astapoor is place," Grint said, tossing the ruined coat aside. With the gold, he could buy a new one. A hundred new ones.

"Maybe you should have left him there," Smit suggested.

"If I knew who he was, I would have," Grint snapped. "You'd think he'd show some gratitude."

"Not everyone is as cordial as you," Orsava laughed as he dragged a crate over. Angis followed, handing the Lord a silver cup with glimmering blue gem embedded in the side. Where they found such a thing was beyond his under-standing.

"Were you followed?" Smit asked.

"I don't think so," Billy grunted as Smit yanked him back onto the crate to clean the bleeding scrapes across his fore-head. "I kept us shadowed."

"Where are the goblins?" Grint looked around the chamber. Four pirates helped the urchins remove the main door to give the canal freedom to flow. Other urchins milled about, some dragging skiffs into place, the rest chattered and played games. But there was no sign of the goblins.

"They're up in the hole," Smit cocked a thumb back at the scaffolding. "Getting the last part set."

"Billy, bring them the supplies," Grint said. "I don't want to be sitting here with empty pockets when the water flows."

"Yes," he said. "But what about the mercenaries?"

"Go," Grint said, waving the kid away. Billy kicked a stone into the water, making the urchins laugh. Moments later, the lot of them searched for things to throw. Grint ignored the noise, walking over to the water barrel, soaking a rag and pressing it against his neck. It sent a much-needed chill through him.

"Mercenaries?" Orsava asked.

"The Golden Few," Grint said. "Borismere hired them."

"Ashgra," he breathed. "He would have to have executed the contract months ago. Will they be a problem?"

"They're mercenaries," Grint shrugged. "Who knows?"

"I don't know if doing nothing is a reasonable plan," Orsava argued.

A rattling jumble of bones fell through the hole, bouncing off the scaffold and finally the ground. A cracked skull rolled like a ball when it landed, stopping at the edge of the canal. The urchin children laughed as they whacked it with sticks.

"Did Smedley break?" Puig called down.

"Are you done yet?" Grint shouted back.

"Grint," Orsava drew his attention back. "We need to alter this plan. The mercenaries..."

"Changing the plan isn't an option," Grint said, to which Orsava grunted. "It's been a long night, Sem. We'll deal with the Golden Few when we need to."

"I don't think that's wise," Orsava continued arguing, but their words fell into silence.

Billy dropped out of the hole first, eyes wide in terror. He waved his arms as he dove off the scaffolding into the canal, vanishing beneath the surface. The goblins slid down the rope, expressions of manic joy as they danced around in anticipation. A moment later the air sucked out of the room as if a giant breathed in. Grint's ears popped as needles stabbed his skin. Angis and Orsava stumbled, but Grint kept his feet, holding to the edge of the water barrel. And then it was over.

Everyone but the goblins looked scared, staring at the hole. Billy re-surfaced, wiping the water from his eyes. A ringing sound followed the first rumble, like bells over breaking glass. Grint put his hand on Orsava's shoulder and started shaking him, a gesture the demure lord returned. A sense of nervous excitement filled Grint, a fluttering in the belly unlike anything he'd felt since... well, since he fell in love as a boy. But this was much more powerful. A pull, a yearning like none other. They were moments away from claiming a hoard of gold to make the King of Dragons envious.

The room shook as golden coins rained down. A torrent of wealth spilled throughout the chamber. And more fell every moment. More than any of them could ever have dreamed of seeing. Jewels and ornate weapons. Armor and candlesticks. They backed away with half-panicked screams of joy as more flooded the room.

Grint heard music as he watched, a sound more beautiful than a siren's lure. A thousand trumpeting horns joined by the deep bass of pounding drums. He conducted the symphony as he danced around like a fool, laughing along with the rest. Smit fell backwards under the deluge, holding his hands out as a golden sword slid over the coins, narrowly missing his face. A moment later he was on his feet, wielding the golden blade in a battle against phantoms trying to steal the hoard. Even Lord Orsava dropped his noble demeanor, falling to his knees and cupping great handfuls of coins he threw into the air.

The only moment of dissension came when an urchin boy pocketed a handful of coin and pushed his way through the tunnel opening. Matty's head spun round, and she grunted a command. Ten urchins chattered, picking up blunt weapons as they gave chase. When the urchins returned with bloody weapons, they dropped the coins into a skiff. Of the thieving urchin, there was no sign.

"Each will get their lot when I allow it," Matty said in her flat tone.

"That one would make a great pirate," one of Gaustauss's crew remarked.

"I feel bad for the boy," Trimbo said, watching the tunnel.

"Let's bow our heads. Dear gracious, sun-filled Krypsie," Puig prayed.

"For the love of Myralee, will you two stop?" Grint shook his head. "How much time do we have until the levee breaks?"

"A tolling of the grand bell," Puig answered. "Then the flood begins."

"Okay then, all hands ready," Grint jumped around in excitement. Smit clapped him on the shoulder, handing over a golden crown encrusted with jewels.

"Don't know who else deserves this more than you," the elder Tagro said, placing the crown on Grint's head. Billy whistled from the water while Orsava and Angis applauded. The goblins mocked from their perch atop the scaffold.

"Off with his head!"

"Down with the monarchy!"

"No monarchy is a good monarchy!"

"What are you going to call your kingdom?" Orsava asked. "Something with an interesting backstory I imagine."

For a moment, with the weight of the crown on his head, he imagined a sprawling castle of gray stone sitting atop a hill. People milled throughout the streets, celebrating and drinking. In the throne room, he pictured himself lounging with his legs up on the arm of the chair. Beside him sat a queen in white. In a world where he'd saved her, who else besides Jessua would he have as queen? The memory of her burned through the daydream until the taste of ash filled his mouth. Grint pulled the crown off his head and tossed it back to Smit.

"I'm no king," he said. The room quieted as he climbed the piles of gold to get up the scaffold.

"Grint?" Billy asked as he climbed out of the water, accepting a towel from Angis to dry himself.

"Load the boats," Grint answered, fighting away the tears. Through the hole he could see faint highlights from torches coloring the edges of stone. They'd dug it in a sloping corkscrew pattern, and even with a brief inspection he could see golden coins and jewels that had not fallen all the way.

"Is there more at the top?" Puig asked. For once, the goblins didn't launch into a spiel.

"Lots," Grint smiled, letting the past go. "Grab the shovels. Time is running out."

As he climbed, he heard Orsava shouting orders. The urchins chattered as they scooped golden piles into buckets. The gold would then go into the skiffs, through the tunnel to the harbor, and onto the pirate ship. If this all went right - *because it's all been perfect so far* - they'd set sail by dawn with a ship full of gold.

If greed hadn't embellished his recollection of what was in the vault, what fell would only account for a fraction of the gold. And it was all his. *Not all, boy,* Hobbe warned, but the gold fever burned bright and he didn't hear the whispered warnings of his conscience. All that mattered was getting what remained.

Grint reached the top. His first attempt at a handhold slipped in coins that fell in a sliding heap past him.

"Hey!" Trimbo shrieked through a face full of gold as he appeared beneath.

Clearing the way, Grint stepped into the ruined interior of the temple's basement. The remaining gold was at least two to three times larger than what was below. And there was enough accumulated wealth below for all of them all to live like kings.

"Krypsie in the north," Trimbo said with a glassy-eyed, slack-jaw grin.

"You must break us out of prison more often," Puig said a moment later.

"With this," Grint laughed. "None of us will ever have to see the inside of a prison again."

Billy joined them with shovels, followed by two pirates carrying buckets. Each of them froze as they beheld the treasure. It wasn't until Grint threw handfuls of gold at each, that they broke out of the trance and set about working. "Best work I've ever done," a pirate said, grinning from ear to ear. The goblins shoveled heaps into the hole as the rest started at the outer edge, pushing it all inward. As engrossed with the task as they were, none of them saw the Blue Hands until it was too late.

"What do you think you're doing?"

Grint froze, seeing a crossbow rise to the level of his face. Three thieves stood on the stairwell, each with a bolt aimed at someone. Grint's crew outnumbered this lot two to one, but they had Billy and him well covered and the pirates were too far back to be any use. The third crossbow alternated between Trimbo and Puig, who were about as useful in a fight as Newman.

"Racko sent us to make sure the next stage of the gold relocation got started," Grint said, standing straight.

"Did she now," the center thief said. None of them had identifying features other than their armbands, but he talked like someone in charge. "We all know that's not true, Grint."

"You have me at a loss," Grint replied. They knew him, so trickery was off the table.

"You killed my brother the other day. Crushed his head with a brazier."

Great, he thought. "No offense, he tried to kill me first."

"I would love to repay the favor, but Racko wants you alive. The rest of your miserable crew weren't on the request," the head-thief spat.

Heavy boots rumbled across the floor above. The Blue Hands looked up, following the path from the temple door to the basement. Five mercenaries of the Golden Few joined the party. The leader, a young man with blond hair and a nasty scar across the chiseled line of his jaw, looked first at the hole and then the thieves.

"We told you to remain outside," the Blue Hand said.

"We go where we want," the golden captain answered. "Is this what we are guarding?"

"We have this under control."

"The Golden Few," Grint said. "I've heard of your company and their great deeds."

"Shut up or I shoot a goblin," the Blue Hand warned, turning his crossbow onto Puig.

"As great as you are, Borismere must have paid you a hefty sum," Grint continued. The crossbow swung back to him.

"I'll kill you then," the Blue Hand said. "And tell Racko it was an accident."

"It seems our pay is not enough," the captain said, the gold fever burning behind his blue eyes.

"As the new owner of the gold, I am happy to rectify that," Grint said, praying no one's trigger finger slipped.

When it happened, it happened fast. Blades flew from their scabbards, dropping the three thieves of the Blue Hand in a matter of breaths. The Blue Hand leader squeezed the trigger of their crossbow, but the bolt flew well wide of Grint's head. With their bodies twitching, the captain removed his gloves and crouched, picking up a single coin.

"Take what you can carry," Grint offered, signaling the others to keep working.

"Morin," the captain said. "Tell the others to remove the remaining Blue Hands from the field. Dump any non-essential gear and come down."

One by one the Golden Few filed down, filling their bags with as much as they could carry. Grint hated to see so much go, and even thought of trying to stop them after the sixth bag, but kept his mouth shut for once. Eighteen mercenaries helped themselves, including the captain who took two bag's worth.

"Captain," Grint said with the man halfway up the stairs. "You'll want to leave Salaz."

"I don't need you to tell me that," The captain sneered.

"No," Grint replied. "You'll want to leave straight away."

"Noted," he said, in a much more cordial way.

After he left, Grint picked up his shovel and found the others staring at him. "What?"

"Did you know?" Billy stammered. "That they would turn on the thieves?"

"I've escaped from the Golden Few on a handful of occasions. They're renowned for their moral flexibility with a higher bid." No one moved even after he finished speaking. "The gold won't move itself."

"Trimbo would have killed you if you let that man shoot me," Puig muttered as he shoved gold through the opening.

"Well," Trimbo said with a shrug.

"What?"

"It's a lot of gold," Trimbo answered. "I would expect no less of you."

Grint laughed, listening to their arguments as he continued to work. Time was against them, but they were all in agreement on getting every last coin into the skiffs. They were doing well enough to make the tolling bell. *As long as there aren't any further interruptions, it should work.* Hobbe laughed at the thought.

"Someone down there is shouting," Trimbo said, pointing into the hole.

Grint wanted to ignore it, keep shoveling and pretend whatever was happening down there wasn't. The shouting grew louder, and he grumbled, handing the shovel off to Trimbo as he shoved his head in the hole. The echo made it tough to understand what they were saying, but he caught his own name a few times. "Keep working," he ordered as he slid into the passage.

Orsava jumped back as Grint dropped in a shower of coins. The pile atop the structure was growing, so Grint kicked it over the side in heaping sweeps. The lord hadn't spoken, but Grint could see why he called for him. Across the chamber, Gaustauss railed, whipping a pirate into bloody strips as his crew watched,

"Inno janoi," Grint said as he climbed down.

What was that about further interruptions?

Shut up, he told Hobbe.

"He's gone mad," Orsava shouted.

"Not madness at all," Gaustauss said to Grint, offering a turn at whipping the pirate.

"We have enough to do," Grint said, shoving the whip away. "Is there some pressing need for this?"

"Beyond the fact that I enjoy any opportunity to punish these humans?" Gaustauss laughed, his demon eyes glowing red. "I sent this one to guard one of the tunnel exits. Decided he was thirsty though, went up into the city for a drink. Now we have those blue armbands sniffing around."

"Are they in the tunnels?" Grint asked, leaning over the canal to see through the wall.

"Not yet, but they will be soon," Gaustauss replied.

"Put extra men along the tunnels," Grint suggested.

"Already have, but if they come down in force, I don't have enough men to hold," Gaustauss took a jug from one of his pirates and drank until it was empty. "If that happens, whatever we've gotten out will be it. Can you live with that?"

"No," Grint admitted. "I want the whole bloody pile."

"Now you sound like your father," the demon laughed.

"Hobbe isn't my father."

"Close enough," Gaustauss shrugged. "Just come up with one of your squirrelly plans or we won't have a choice." The captain walked away, ordering his crew to get rid of the body.

"He's a genuine delight," Smit said.

"A necessary evil," Grint replied.

The sound of chattering urchins echoed through the tunnel, growing louder every moment. Angis yanked on Grint's sleeve, dancing in an exercise of nervous terror.

"Master Grint! Master Grint," he shouted.

"What now?" Grint said, unable to decide which direction's issue was more important.

"Lord Orsava has gone up to the temple," Angis said, nearly in tears.

"Bloody fool will break his neck," Smit said, staring at the constant rain of gold falling through the hole.

"Calm down, Angis," Grint said. "He's safe."

Matty tugged on the back of Grint's coat. Once. Twice. And a third time with great intensity. "Everyone stop bloody pulling on me!"

"They're here," the girl said.

"How close is here?" Grint couldn't see anything moving in the tunnel except the slow float of skiffs.

"In the black tunnels where we tricked the woman," Matty smiled.

Gaustauss and three of his pirates appeared with torches and swords. The demon nodded at Grint with the look of someone who wanted to say, *we've gotten what we can. Let's go.*

"How long until the bell?" Grint asked, grabbing the manservant who'd devolved into full tears. "Angis, how long?"

"Imminent," he sobbed.

"How much is up there?" Smit looked ready to run for the hole.

Too much, he thought. "Almost done."

For all of a moment, Grint thought about abandoning the ones in the temple. Collapse the scaffold and ceiling to cover what they'd been doing and run with what they had. Gaustauss wouldn't cry over his pirates, and no one but

Grint would miss the goblins. Orsava though? And Billy? Newman sat at his feet, whining for a treat. That broke the spell. Grint blinked, feeling the gold fever subside. Was he willing to lose any of them?

"I'm getting Billy," Smit said, as if reading every thought in Grint's mind.

"No," he said. "I'm going."

Gaustauss shouted from the tunnel entrance, "We leave with what we have. Won't be long before those fools find the canal."

"Keep them busy until the levee comes down," Grint shouted back. "We'll still get it all when the water pushes us. I'll draw them out of the tunnels."

"I'm coming with you," Smit said.

"Not this time," Grint smiled and clapped him on the shoulder. "Get Newman on a skiff. Make sure the pirates don't leave without us."

"What are you going to do?"

"The dumbest thing I can think of," Grint replied.

Plan Z, I think you'd call it, Hobbe cackled.

25

"Let my battle be your guide and my death your warning."

- *The Tale of Teelo Tane, Parthian Barbarian*
p.Annum 9874

"I am not here to fight you," Chell said as he stood before the queen and her court.

Akosha clapped her hands three times, summoning warriors bedecked in armor meant to instill dread. Each warrior's garb painted red to simulate blood and wrapped with chains. They lumbered with slow steps, each a head smaller than the Parthian they would fight. Chell surmised they would be his equal in this diminished state. Nazarra remained by his side, squeezing the hilt of her sword in nervous repetition.

"My sister proves herself a traitor," the queen announced. "I am grateful for my betrothed in bringing it to my attention." The one called Borismere laughed as he placed bets with those at his side. A sweaty, white-haired man stinking of greed and malice stood behind the lord. *Now that is an adversary worth facing.*

"If you marry that swine, I'll kill you both," Nazarra said, blood dripping from a gash on her cheek. The queen closed her eyes as bright sparks of light flew from her up-turned palms. The intensity blinded Chell for a moment, and when his vision cleared, he saw snaking tendrils of cloth wrapping around Nazarra's face, sealing her mouth.

"If you best my warriors, perhaps I will allow you to face me," Akosha said, sipping a goblet of wine. The Court applauded.

"My love," Borismere looked concerned. "It would be prudent to not..."

"Silence!" Akosha commanded Borismere, but the force of her voice quieted the entire room. "Begin."

Chell took a deep breath, determining what strength remained. Was it enough to fight the four warriors? Perhaps if he finished them quickly. If. An ugly word. A hiding place for those too afraid to try. For those who would use circumstance as an excuse to remain sedentary. Not Chell. There was no if. He would succeed and face the queen. No, not her, Borismere. The architect of his misery would produce the promised cure or fall under Chell's blade. The Oracle would grant Atonement for saving the queen from insurrection. He'd return and reclaim his home from its own festering parasites. There were no ifs.

"This I know," he growled as he side-stepped the warriors' attempt to flank him and twirled his blade.

On the left, the first carried a morning star and wooden buckler. The next wielded twin swords. The third pulled their wrapped chains loose, swinging them in flowery patterns around their body. On the far right, the last carried spear and net. Heavy steel sacrificed speed and movement for protection. A foolish trade when armor offered so many exploits. In particular, Morningstar's armor had vast gaps around the shoulder to allow him movement to swing the weapon. Chell grinned as he sheathed his sword. The four warriors exchanged glances before they charged. Chell yanked a Salazian noble from the crowd and tossed him at Morningstar's feet. Too clumsy to move, he became entangled in the nobleman's robes and tripped. As he collapsed, his spiked cudgel swung wildly into the faceplate of Two Swords, taking him down in a screaming heap. The silken dreego noble bent in half under their weight, convulsing to the great joy of his peers. And they called the Parthian a barbarian.

The one he called Chains lashed out with his barbed steel links. Chell held up his arm, letting them wrap around. The barbs dug in, but the resurgence of the poison dulled the pain flowing. From the corner of his eye, he saw Nazarra flung into the air by the queen's magic. Chell pulled the chain taut and yanked the warrior into the air. The crowd gasped as Chell swung him around, throwing him at the queen. Nazarra fell as Akosha re-focused her magic onto Chains. The links contracted, crumpling the dreego's armor until he burst in a crimson mist. More cheers.

Nazarra wiped her bloody face and nodded to Chell. Outnumbered two to one, the man with the net kept his distance. As Nazarra reached for a length of discarded chain, he thrust the spear toward her and swung his net to tangle Chell's feet. Two Swords climbed to his feet, so Spear took to the defensive, falling back to protect him. A tactic the queen disapproved of, given the snarling twist to her face and summoning of black magics.

Chell and Nazarra saw what the champions did not and dropped to the floor as the queen swung a flaming scythe.

The magic cut through their armor and flesh with ease, bisecting both Spear and Two Swords before continuing into the crowd of nobles. Fountain of blood blossomed into the air as screams of terror filled the chamber. Nobles ran toward locked doors, trampling ill-prepared guards trying to keep them back.

In the mayhem, Borismere stepped toward the queen. "My love," he said. Her right hand extended toward him, palm out. A wave of invisible energy knocked him onto his back.

Morningstar was the last of the warriors. As he found his footing, he advanced. Chell drew the two-handed sword as the warrior spun the namesake weapon. Focused on Chell, he paid no heed to Nazarra, the spear she picked up, or the shouts of warning from the crowd. Nazarra threw the spear, skewering the unprotected part of his neck beneath the lip of his helm.

"Treasonous witch," Akosha shouted. "I showed you mercy with exile and you spit it in my face."

"I am not here for you," Nazarra replied. "He has poisoned you. Corrupted you with evil. And he now seeks to take your throne."

"Lies," Akosha answered, walking down the marble steps to the throne room floor.

"Lies? Look outside at the rebellion Borismere fomented tonight." Nazarra wanted to find the good in her sister. To connect with her and bring her back, but such redemption was rarely possible. Chell's own life, love, and fall were testimony to that truth. The queen needed struck down before she visited a deadly fate upon Nazarra. Yet, he had given his vow to abstain from such an action.

Borismere, the architect of all this misery, sat up, gleeful malice in his eyes. Chell would end this, drive the blade
through his black heart and perhaps free the young woman from his poison as he wished to be. The white-haired
devil intervened, throwing a brazier full of ash at Chell.
"I learned that move just days ago," he laughed, grabbing
Lord Borismere, and ushering him toward the door.

Nazarra screamed, locked in battle with the re-animat-
ed corpse of Morningstar. Akosha laughed at the cries of
heresy, rewarding each with death. Chell abandoned Borismere to help Nazarra. The corpse suffered none of the
setbacks the living warrior had and moved with graceful
speed. It took three strides to flank the Parthian and slam
the spiked head of its weapon into his back.

A dreego would have had their back shattered by such
a blow, but Chell was no mere dreego. It drove him to his
knees as his great sword clattered against the polished
marble. The undead dreego spun the morningstar over his
head, waving another hand for the crowd to cheer. And
they did, nervously at first, but the sound grew into roars
of appreciation. Chell retrieved his blade and stretched his
shoulders. The crowd fell silent.

Chell looked at the wight, and smiled. "Let us find the
succor of Mother Battle together."

The undead dreego screamed and slapped the buckler on his left arm. Chell leapt, spinning through the air
in a dizzying twist. Whatever magic's were used to bring
the creature back, gave him strength enough to absorb
the blow against his buckler, but forced him to discard the
weapon. Unarmed, it braced for another strike, hissing un-
intelligible words. Chell hacked in relentless assault until
the buckler's leather veneer split and wood cracked.

"I grant you the warrior's death you missed in your first life," Chell whispered as he beheaded the creature. It gurgled and slumped to the side, black blood pouring from the open wound. An audible gasp spread through the onlookers, followed by the queen's scream.

The diminutive ruler held Nazarra in a grip of ice, stamping her feet as she shouted at the guards. "Kill the barbarian!" None moved. Who among them wanted to share the fate of soldiers more capable than themselves?

"Die," Queen Akosha screamed. "All of you. Die!"

Black sludge flooded from her hands and open mouth. Akosha spewed it toward the court, consuming anyone it touched. Guards, nobles, servants. Rank and status mattered little to the magic. Borismere recognized the madness and unlocked the throne room doors to release those who survived and save his own skin. Great marble columns toppled as the sludge ate through both animate and inanimate objects.

Chell smashed the ice holding Nazarra and tried carrying her away, but the queen redirected the sludge toward them. Standing over her, he blocked its path, the fur on his back sizzled away in smoking tendrils. The pain he experienced in those few moments was excruciating. Fragments of memory re-surfaced. Flashes of life, love, and more recently loss. Nazarra looked upon him with deep sadness. Did she understand the cost of what he did? The sludge wrapped around his arms like jungle snakes, squeezing tight, but he refused to give in. Chell shifted to keep the sludge off of her.

"This magic," Nazarra wept. "It's an Ochus. Borismere poisoned her with an Ochus!"

"I care not what it is," he groaned. "Run, you fool!"

"We go together," Nazarra replied.

"Don't waste this time," he said as his mouth filled with spit that fell in long strands to the floor. "I saw Borismere leave. Find him. I'll be right behind."

Nazarra cocked her head. She knew it as a lie, as did he when he uttered the foolishness, but said nothing. The woman stood and brushed his cheek. The feel of a hairless, dreego hand was odd, but he accepted the gesture with a nod.

"I release you from your vow," she whispered. "My sister is no longer here." Spinning on her heels, she darted off, dodging the sludge as she leapt through the last open doorway.

Chell stood upright at a considerable cost and turned. The queen looked upon him, a maniacal sickness in her eyes, and parted the black magic. His hand trembled to hold the sword, the little strength left slipped away with each breath. The poison, the eel attack, the dark sludge. All of it took its toll and came back to collect the rest.

Not yet. Atonement first. Death second.

"What are you waiting for? You wanted to face me," she laughed. "Here I am."

26

"The last opponent one must face is always the first who bested them."

- Unknown

Nazarra's mind reeled with the horror of what her sister's magic wrought. The black sludge of the Ochus, a frightening tale from their childhood. Aside from a handful of reports involving salt witches, Nazarra didn't believe such raw power possible. What had Borismere done to her? Exposed her to dark magic and allowed an Ochus to take root? It must have been him. The nightmare throwing tantrums was not the girl she grew up with. Sweet young Akosha; the caring queen, always so gracious to those serving under her. These were memories now. The depths of Borismere's poisoning struck deep. Too deep to redeem Akosha now. Nothing could once the Ochus took hold. And so Nazarra let the Parthian loose upon her.

The sludge magic spilled through the door behind her, shattering pillars in the outer hall. Nazarra avoided being crushed as she rolled forward. A guard in burnished plate did not, screaming as a chunk of marble flattened him. A

lord and lady she recognized from her father's inner circle failed to escape. Both screamed as the sludge devoured
them. Crawling on her belly, Nazarra spotted the malignant master of this farce, Borismere. And he saw her. Their
eyes locked until he recognized she was free to pursue him,
and then he ran as his pet thief-catcher cleared a path. The
Ochus magic swirled about, dissolving anyone it touched.
Kane threw a young couple holding one another into a
surging wave to get Borismere through the door.

"No," Nazarra cried in a voice cracked from pain. Uncaring of any fate beside the one that let her destroy Borismere,
she walked toward the door. That the magic did not strike
her down was either a stroke of fortune or a spark of hope
that her sister remained buried in that dark shell.

She pushed away thoughts of what she could have done
to end this sooner. Such dalliances into guilt were dangerous things. *Time sets the past in stone stronger than a mountain,*
as her father used to say. The past existed to study your mistakes. To dwell upon them too long led to questions, and
that led to something far more dangerous. Fear. Many a general fell to the fear of indecision.

Nazarra felt no fear as she stepped past the sludge. Smiling, it came to her that fear drew the magic, fed on it. Chell
stood strong because he was not afraid. It was her own fear
that cost the Parthian.

"Borismere," she screamed, looking down the curva-
ture of the tower's winding stairs. Borismere stumbled when
he looked up, horror-stricken that she'd survived. Kane
pulled at him and they vanished from sight. A sea of people
swarmed from the tower, and Nazarra let them carry her in
their wake. It all led to the same place. Borismere had nowhere to run. No escape.

At the base of the tower, city guards fought a battle between those fleeing the tower and the Opposition forces attempting entry. One idealistic fool, a blue and white flag tied to the base of his blade, attacked Nazarra. The strike she dodged cut a young nobleman's belly open. Nazarra grabbed the attacker's wrist and kicked him in the groin. As he fell to his knees, screaming to the sky in pain, she took the sword and jammed it in his open mouth, sheathing it in his throat.

A woman with long locks of black hair screamed in Nazarra's face. She opened the woman's throat with her dagger, bathing in the warm spray of blood that followed. Had she been Opposition? Or a noble, terrified for her life? Nazarra could no longer tell.

"General, what is happening?" A man shouted. Three red band guards pushed through the crowd, clearing a path for her. Nazarra looked at him, struggling to put a name to the face. Seeking to find any thought in her mind beyond the death of Borismere.

"Nazarra," he said, and she blinked.

"Jaspar?" Nazarra woke from a dream. The man nodded as life returned to her eyes.

"What is happening in there?" He asked as a squad of guards set a perimeter around the base of the tower.

"My sister has gone mad, captain," Nazarra said. "Do not send your men in or they will die like the rest."

"Ashgra save us," he breathed.

Nazarra looked upon the faint smudge of the promised morning sun rising in the east. The Cognispyre, when Ashgra blessed those penitent and punished the wicked. Today, we're all wicked. The thought made her laugh, a deep throaty sound that terrified everyone around her. "Jaspar, I don't think Ashgra has any intention of that."

"Are you well? Where is the Parthian?" Jaspar did his best to hold her attention, but there was only one thing on her mind.

"Where is Borismere," she interrupted his line of inquiry. Opposition forces pushed against the guard lines. They bowed for a moment, but held.

"I don't..." Jaspar stammered and then grabbed the arm of a passing guard. "Felz, have you seen Lord Borismere?"

Jaspar's utterance of the title sent nettles down her flesh. The man was no lord. He was not even a dog. Felz stood on his toes and looked around, then pointed toward the Guest Apartments. The place where the nobles lavished themselves when visiting Court. Nazarra slipped away from Jaspar, disappearing into the crowd. The captain had much to deal with.

Two mercenaries in golden armor blocked the pathway. The greedy demons demanding a toll to pass. Nobles, terrified by the reminder of their own mortality, threw money at them in great showers. Few offered enough to buy their way through. Most did not. The great Borismere had no trouble securing his way, taking the thief-catcher with him. *Soon*, she thought, pushing her to the front. Two noble brats confronted her. They died in agonizing pain, chewing on their own entrails.

As the crowd ran, Borismere looked back. The color drained from his face. All the strength and power he claimed to possess. The endless supply of smugness. It all evaporated in an instant as he came to understand the consequence for his actions. *When you reach too high, the sun burns you*, Nazarra thought. *Didn't you listen to the High Priest before he died screaming?*

"Where do you think you're going?" The golden mercenary asked.

"There," she said, pointing at Borismere.

The two looked at her, and then at the dead nobles she left behind. Without pause, they stepped aside, giving her the path. "Our contract doesn't include dying."

"Then leave Salaz," she growled. "Now."

The Seastone Tower shook as the black sludge pushed through the upper floors. Massive chunks rained down, falling at random, killing the noble and peasant alike.

"Kill her," Borismere shouted as he shoved Kane in her direction. The thief-catcher walked toward her, gripping his famed cudgel in both hands. Nazarra yanked a sword from the chest of a dead guard, spinning it as she ran. Ten feet from contact, a chunk of marble the size of a head bounced across the field, striking Kane on the temple. The thief-catcher fell over, twitching as his cudgel rolled from his grasp.

Nazarra tossed aside the rusty sword, availing herself of the cudgel. Borismere pushed through the panicked throng and sprinted toward the closest apartment door. When it didn't open, he ran around the side, trampling a bed of golden peonies shaped like the royal crest.

"That's a hanging offense," Nazarra sang as she walked around the corner.

Borismere threw a stone at her. It missed. Picking up a second stone, he aimed it at a window. The pane shattered and a woman within screamed. Borismere crawled through as Nazarra followed at a walk. There was no rush in catching him. He had nowhere left to go. Shards of glass slick with his blood made her smile. She took her time knocking the rest out before climbing in. Spots of blood marred an ancient rug stitched a century before Zorn. An easy trail to follow.

"What are you doing?" The woman shrieked as Nazarra walked through her sitting room.

"Quiet," Nazarra replied. Lady Rhodellum wore a platinum wig and frilly silk dress. A loud woman who loved to make garish statements, the lady was at a loss for words. Unless you counted her strangled gasp as a word. Glimpsing herself in a mirror, Nazarra understood the reaction. Blood painted her face, matted her hair, and ran in tiny rivers down her torn leather jerkin. But now was not the time to admire such horrors. There was hunting to do.

Nazarra stepped on Borismere's trail of blood as she walked, imagining it caused him pain. A silly thought, but deliciously pleasant. The trail continued out of the apartment and led up the center stairs. One floor. Two floors. All the way to the fifth and down a hallway. *How the portly bastard must be perspiring.* The door at the end dangled off a single hinge, the wood along the frame splintered from a powerful kick. *I didn't know he had it in him.* Nazarra paused beside the broken wood, listening for labored breaths or movement. Nothing yet. She stepped through the opening to look around.

A pristine apartment with ante-chamber, sitting room and bedroom suite. Nothing appeared disturbed. White marble floors sparkled from their most recent cleaning. Hand-woven rugs from the northern fields of Hallity displayed patterns of swirling color among lush mountain trees. A basket of fruits waited beside a decanter of wine, a gift for the next guest to claim.

"Where oh where oh where is Borismere," she sang as she jingled a loose chain hanging around her neck. Hoping to scare him loose, she jumped around corners, ready to strike with Kane's cudgel. There was no sign of the man. So focused had she been on taunting him, she failed to see what was missing. *No blood*, she thought as she inspected the floor. Nazarra returned to the front door, running her hand over the bloody hand print left on the wood. As she did, the door across the hall opened and Borismere charged out. Twice her size, he lowered his shoulder, knocking her flat onto the marble floor. Instead of finishing her, Lord Borismere backtracked into the hallway.

Nazarra got up, berating herself as a twinge of pain shot along her right leg. A sloppy mistake and one she would not make again. Whatever effort he'd made in stanching his wound failed as the blood trail doubled in size. It amused and befuddled her to find that the lord hadn't gone down - but up. *Why is he going to the roof?* Nazarra could not answer the thought, but she'd soon find out. *Does the fool mean to jump?*

A wooden ladder led through a hatch onto the flat stone roof. Gravel crunched under her boots as she looked for him. Borismere stood at the edge a hundred feet away, measuring the distance to the next manor. Even the Parthian at top physical condition would have trouble making that jump. Borismere had no chance. But the odds didn't concern him.

Thinking of Chell, she glanced at the Seastone Tower, hoping he still lived. Hoping Akosha may yet live. The sludge oozed through the upper windows and balconies. Great pillars of smoke rose from where it touched. If left unchecked, it would consume the tower, the palace, and perhaps even the city.

Borismere backed up a few steps, preparing to jump. He licked his lips as he saw her approaching and backed up another step, as if that would help him accomplish the impossible. Nazarra did not run, Borismere had a sizable lead, and she'd never catch him before he went, but she quickened her pace. Rational thought must have taken over, for at the last moment he stopped - or tried to. Skidding and waving his arms, Borismere tried to arrest his momentum. Nothing would stop him from falling now.

Nothing aside from Nazarra.

With the tips of his feet hanging over the edge, Borismere struggled to keep balanced. It was a battle he was losing. As he tilted over the edge, Nazarra swung the chain, wrapping the end around his neck. She pulled it taut without yanking him back. The man's sheer weight threatened to pull her over, but she dug her heels into the stone and stalled their momentum.

Nazarra heard him choking as he swatted at the chain. The fool didn't know he was dead. Even if she let go, the fall would kill him. But Nazarra had no intention of letting go. Careful not to pull him away from the edge, she wrapped the chain around her elbow one step at a time. Stopping beside a stone gargoyle, Nazarra looped the chain around its neck and tied it off. Borismere shook as she walked to the edge.

"That would be quite the fall," she said, slapping the cudgel in her free hand.

"This doesn't have to end this way," he choked out the words between gasping breaths.

"This is the only way it ends," she growled. "Tell me how to help my sister. Why did you give her an Ochus?"

"I didn't," he cried. "Mikil. It was Mikil."

"But you stood by and let it happen," she said, tapping the backs of his knees with the weapon.

Borismere got his fingers around the chain at his throat. "I can help her. The Parthian too."

Nazarra laughed, "Now I know you're lying."

"Please," Borismere choked. "I have gold. Lots and lots of gold."

"Not anymore," she whispered. "Grint sends his regards."

The man spasmed as fury and anguish turned his face blue. They'd bested him - not just Nazarra, but the thieves. "Lies," he squawked.

"You have nothing left," she said. "Your gold is floating away on the mysterious ship in the harbor. Your hopes to rule Salaz, done, as is your life."

Nazarra batted his knees out from under him. Borismere's feet flew and his head cracked the stone edge before his body went over. Nazarra stared at the bloody remnant left behind as he gurgled his last breaths. Jerking until the end, his motions stilled and body went limp.

"I told you you'd hang, traitor," Nazarra said, leaving his body as a warning for others who might try such foolishness.

Weary from the events of the past day, her hands shook and legs gave out. Nazarra sat hard in the gravel, trying in vain to will herself enough strength to stand. Instead, she lay back, feeling the warm kiss of the rising sun. Nazarra felt no need to cover herself. No fear from a deity who'd done nothing to help them.

"If you want to punish me, here I am," she laughed.

Her mirth ended as the Seastone Tower shuddered, shaking the very world as it cracked with the noise of thousand lightning strikes.

27

"In my experience, a friend isn't a friend until they take an arrow for you."

- Grint

Halfway through the hole, the gold stopped falling on Grint's head. Climbing into the temple, he found them celebrating by slapping shovels together and dancing around a dented gold vase. They piled the dead thieves in a far corner, their crossbows now the property of the pirates. Of Ashgra's Fortune, only a single mound remained by the stairwell. Billy sat on it, slapping his knee in time with the tune. When they stopped, he dragged a rag across his sweaty brow. Orsava beamed with pleasure as he inspected the temple for any bits they missed.

The pirates approached the mound, but Billy waved them away. "This is Ashgra's cut," he said.

"Ashgra can jump off the Roosting Cliffs," the pirate said.

"What was all the racket down there?" Puig asked, handing Grint a skin of something tasting like fire mixed with ogre piss. He coughed as he swallowed and shoved the skin back at the goblin.

"Never give me that again," Grint coughed a second time feeling the liquid burning his throat.

"You're not taking it," Billy said, standing firm. The boy's fingers twitched as he got ready to cast.

"The racket?" Puig asked again.

"Calm down," Grint raised his voice. He stepped between the rising confrontation, hoping things didn't boil over now. Not when they'd done it. *Congratulations boy, you did it*, Hobbe said, sounding pleased, if not also surprised.

"Thank you," Billy said as he lowered his hands.

"Don't," Grint replied. "They're right. Ashgra can jump off the Roosting Cliffs." It was something he'd done once and would welcome anyone else to try.

The pirate laughed, "I like him."

"That's not a good idea," Orsava intervened.

"It's the only idea," Grint answered. "But it's not going down the hole. We saw a few carts when we scouted this place. We'll load it in one of those."

"Why would we do that?" Trimbo asked. "We have a fleet of perfectly good boats below."

"Plan is we go through the hole and cover it with the mimicrum. Then we ride the wave to the harbor," Puig said.

"That was the plan," Grint said. "Still is for them. For us, we're loading what's left onto a cart."

"Why? What were they yelling about?" Puig asked a third time.

"Opposition is poking around the tunnels. We need to give them a reason to leave," Grint said, and they all nodded. All except the pirates.

"A Jealous Kregger?" Billy asked with a widening grin.

"What?" Grint scratched his head. The terms they used in Salaz made no sense.

"Who in the long depths of Asper is Kregger?" The first pirate asked.

"Why's he jealous?" Puig continued.

"I don't know," Grint shook his head. "I'm talking about a Tooney Run. Load the cart, let them see us, and get them to chase."

"Yeah," Billy grunted. "That's a Jealous Kregger."

"We call it a Sea-Serpent Surfaces," the one-eyed pirate added.

"I don't care what we call it," Grint said, exasperated by the running commentary.

"That's well and good, but if it's all the same, I'll pass on the cart and take a boat instead," Trimbo said, walking towards the hole.

"There's no time," Grint shouted. "The levee is coming down. You want to drown halfway through the tunnel?"

"Tooney Run could work, but only if the right people see us," Puig mulled it over, scratching his chin. Trimbo remained silent, standing at the edge of the hole and staring down. The dart to his eyes, back and forth, spoke of weighing his options. What were the odds of making it? What outcome was most likely?

"No good wager ends with you dying," Orsava said, smiling at the diminutive goblin.

"Aye," Trimbo replied. "I suppose you're right."

"Let's get this topside," Grint said.

Billy stood his ground until Orsava pulled him away with an arm across his shoulders. "Grint is right. Ashgra won't mind if we wait a bit to give her the proper cut. And we'll have plenty of time to decide what that is when we count it up."

"It's coming out of your end," Puig laughed as he followed the pair.

"Trimbo," Grint said. "Come on." With a last glance down the hole, the goblin followed. Grint was thankful he did. For a moment he imagined having to climb after him and carry him back up. Kicking. Screaming. Biting.

Throughout Salaz, the battles raged. Fires ran rampant through the many districts as swords struck in heavy cadence. A dozen or more Blue Hands lay dead on the ground. Slaughtered by the Golden Few for a share of gold. Thick smoke drifted through the air, filling the streets with a choking fog. Macabre shadows floated through the clouds, each looking like monsters from legend, instead of people running for their lives.

Two carts sat beside the burned-out stable, but only one had a horse attached. The brown mare stomped a hoof as they approached, but settled down when the goblins fed her carrots. Grint inspected the cart, littered with hay and old burlap sacks. When he nodded, they set about loading the last of the gold. The pirates climbed in with the treasure, setting their stolen crossbows along the side as they loaded them. Billy and Orsava got in back too, the former pulling bits of parchment from his pocket and whispering incantations while the Lord dug himself a place to sit.

"Don't hide us, Billy," Grint said as he and the goblins climbed up front. "We want them to find us."

"I know what a Jealous Kregger is," the kid replied, straining to see through the smoke.

"Fine," Grint said, looking around. The battles were close, but none close enough to draw attention. *You know this is a bad idea, yes?* Hobbe asked.

Yes, Grint replied. The last time he'd run a Jealous Kregger, half the crew died, and the rest landed in prison. *Great, now I'm calling it a Kregger.*

With a gentle flick of the reins, the horse lurched forward, keeping at a slow trod. Far beneath them, an armada of skiffs floated toward the harbor. How much would they lose if the plan didn't work?

"Light a pillar of fire above us," Grint said, looking for the Arch of the Sun.

"What?" Billy gawked. "That'll bring Tennebrue."

"I know."

"Tennebrue?" Puig asked, brightening. "The fine fellow from the prison? I liked him a lot."

"Very personable," Trimbo said.

"He never tried to disintegrate you," Grint replied.

"Or transform a horse into a monster with an appetite for your brains," Billy added.

"Hmm, I like him less now," Puig said.

"I like this plan less," Trimbo grumbled. "Is there still time to go back to the hole?"

"Light it up, Billy," Grint said as he urged the horse into a trot. The tolling of the bell would happen soon, and they needed the Opposition out of the tunnels before it did. A brilliant shaft of fire roared into the sky, painting golden hues throughout the clouds. Blue Hands appeared along the rooftops as they reached the Arch of the Sun. A dozen or more onlookers came to their windows, drawn in by the spectacle of Billy's fire. Grint watched without making it obvious and kept the horse moving.

"What if we make it to the gate?" Trimbo asked. "Do we go through?"

"We won't," Grint kept his eyes forward, catching glimpses of shadows moving in the alleys.

"I'll bet you one hundred gold we do," Trimbo continued.

"Two hundred," Puig added.

"Five hundred," Grint said to great hoots from the goblins.

"Is now the best time for gambling?" Orsava asked, popping his head up.

"I'll take that bet," the one-eyed pirate laughed.

"For shame, Lord Orsava. There's always time for a gamble or two." The goblins were entertaining one another without realizing how much Grint agreed with them. They were all gambling with their lives. *Can't spend gold when you're dead,* Hobbe said.

"Pirate, what's your name?" Grint asked, trying not to think about the odds.

"Guillard the Pyklops," he said. "And he's Kiln Ben."

"Kiln Ben can't speak for himself?" Puig asked.

"In fact, he can't," Guillard answered. "Gaustauss took his tongue when he disagreed with an order." The goblins whistled.

Grint always appreciated pirate nicknames. Colorful as they were, they often described the person perfectly. "Well Guillard, get ready to be five hundred gold richer." He pulled the horse to a stop beside a statue of a mounted general.

"Yes, the statue of General Keastenair. A fine soldier. Did you know he beat back a horde of goblin marauders using trained alligators?" Orsava spoke, always so proud of Salaz and its history. "No offense meant to my new goblin compatriots."

"This is cheating," Trimbo scowled, paying as much attention to the history lesson as Puig.

"Unfair," Puig said.

"Maybe you'll want to tell them," Grint pointed the reins at figures emerging from the smoke. Eight men on foot, two on horseback, and one in the seat of a rickety cart pulled by a grotesque horse-monster. Tennebrue stood in the driver's seat, his off-putting smile melted in the hazy atmosphere. The wizard waved a hand at the rooftops on either side of the street like the grandmaster of a traveling circus. Grint stole a glance and lost count at twenty Blue Hands.

"Foolish to think we didn't prepare for this," Tennebrue called. "Although I applaud your tenacity. I don't know how you emptied the church, but you will return every sliver."

"Did he say silver?" Guillard asked.

"We didn't take any silver," Trimbo laughed.

"Can't give back what we didn't take," Puig continued, laughing louder.

"What will you do if we refuse?" Grint yelled.

"Refuse? How foolish of you. I will exact the toll in blood." Tennebrue's Opposition flunkies laughed as he looked at them for reassurance of his humor. Mordechai sat beside him, hidden from view at first but revealed as Tennebrue moved about. The perpetual glower on his face clarified that nothing was ever funny in his eyes.

"Well, sadly you missed it," Grint said, joining the laughter. A fake sound that rose in volume. It quieted the Opposition and stole the grin from Tennebrue's mug. "The gold already got past you."

"Liar," Tennebrue spat. "Your illusionist is talented, but not to that level. Where is it?"

"Is this part of the plan?" Orsava asked.

"Yes," Grint smiled. "And so is that. Hold on."

Ashgra's Temple tolled its bell for the hour. A deep sound that drowned out all the others. As the copper gong faded, the levee broke. One section at a time, each cracking like a glacier in the Ice Fields to the far north. Tennebrue dropped in his seat, covering his head, confused by the noise. Grint winked at him as he looked up and snapped the reins. The horse lurched into motion, making a hard turn.

Arrows rained from the sky, striking the shield of air Billy prepared. The Blue Hands kept firing until the cart distanced itself from their range, rolling down the hill toward the Grand Runway. The rush of flooding water grew louder as it chewed through the city. They couldn't outpace it, but hopefully they'd make it far enough that it wouldn't bite them in the backsides.

"Tennebrue," Billy shouted over the rumble of hooves. Grint looked back to see the wizard and his horsemen in pursuit. "They're catching up!"

Tennebrue's creature was faster than their horse. Grint yanked the reins hard to the right, banking the cart on two wheels into the Market district. He counted on the tight streets to keep Tennebrue's monster from catching them. A fool's wager. Grint had to swerve around stalls and between effigies meant for the celebration, but the beast smashed through them with ease.

Rounding a sharp turn, Grint shouted, "Keep them busy!"

"What do you think we're doing?" Orsava yelled as Billy cast illusions. Gusts of fog meant to confuse, flocks of gulls and rabid mungles to terrify them, but Tennebrue destroyed each the moment Billy cast them. The pirates fired crossbows at the beast, handing the spent weapon to Orsava to reload. The bolts deflected off its thick hide and slid past the wizard as if he wasn't there.

"Where are you going?" Orsava called out as two Blue Hands jumped onto Tennebrue's cart. They drew back bows and fired. The arrows struck the cart with a high-pitched twang, vibrating as the cart rumbled over stones meant for walking.

"There," Grint shouted as an arrow flew past his face, the wind close enough to feel like a kiss from a springtime maiden.

"Where?" The goblins cried in unison, looking at the end of the road ahead.

The cart went over the top of a staircase leading down to the Graht district. In an airborne drift, Grint turned back to Billy while laughing, "Your brother threw me down this staircase last week."

They landed with a thump that jostled them all. Gold jumped into the air, a fair amount falling outside the cart. Orsava held on for dear life as Kiln Ben struggled to hang on after falling out.

"I'm thinking of throwing you down it myself," Billy snarled, his teeth chattering with each bump.

The water reached the top of the steps as they hit the bottom. Grint pulled them left and whipped the reins for speed. It wasn't enough. The beast reached the bottom and struck the back of the cart. Everyone held tight as the impact spun them in circles through a battle between city guards and Fishmongers. Everyone an enemy, the cart did not discriminate as it bashed fighters aside. When they came to a stop, a guard climbed in, raising his sword. Orsava kicked him in the gut, and the man fell backwards into a Fishmonger. The horse stomped and blew out its nostril before it found its footing. She reared back and darted forward. The battle gave them a brief moment of separation from Tennebrue as they raced toward the Grand Runway.

Tennebrue's beast regained its stride as it tore through the few remaining fighters, pulling alongside and slashing at the horse and goblins as they skidded onto the Runway. Without needing to hold on to reins, Tennebrue conjured fireballs and threw them in unyielding succession. Billy dispelled as many as he could before they left the wizard's hand, but more and more got past, striking the side of the cart or whizzing over the heads of the crew. Splashes of fire lit the night, and the wood smoldered wherever the fire struck.

Kiln Ben fired a crossbow, taking one of the Blue Hands in their eye. They fell away with a grunt, bouncing on the cobbled street as flood waters raced to meet them. Four horses appeared from the upper Termin road. Grint recognized them from the warehouse. Opposition fighters loyal to Borismere. They leapt from their horses, grabbing onto the cart. The pirates struck at them with scimitars, trying to keep them from climbing in. Grint kept looking back, wanting to help, but was stuck on the reins, huddled between shields the goblins held to block arrows.

An Opposition fighter screamed as a scimitar cleaved into his skull, taking the weapon with him as he fell. Kiln Ben looked at his empty hands for a moment before an arrow hit him in the chest. Blood blossomed around the wound and he dropped, knocking another fighter loose as they tumbled.

"Ben," Guillard shouted. "Kry-damn bastards!"

"Take the reins," Grint shoved them into Puig's hands. The goblin dropped his shield and whipped the leather as Grint rolled ungracefully into the back. His feet slipped on gold coins - a lucky circumstance as an arrow darted past his head. Orsava grabbed Grint's coat and kept him from falling unceremoniously off the back. Expecting a thank you, it shocked the lord that Grint shoved him aside. Grint dropped a blade from his sleeve and stabbed the Opposition fighter who'd climbed aboard. A fireball whizzed past his shoulder, the heat singing his ear. Billy was losing the battle.

One thing at a time, he thought as he struggled to help the pirate with the final rider. A fireball struck Guillard on the side of the head, deflected by Billy, who could no longer dispel the attacks. Both the pirate and Opposition fighter had been grappling. Both went up in flames, falling over the side. Another arrow flew past. Mordechai, now armed with the dead Blue Hand's bow, had started shooting. Grint chucked a handful of gold into the Harbor Master's face and then a dagger. Before it hit the crusty old man, the last Blue Hand fell in the way. The thief cried out and fell backwards from the cart.

The flood waters licked the back of the cart as they rumbled toward the docks. Tennebrue's beast punched the side of their cart, knocking the back gate open. Gold spilled out, disappearing into the frothing water. Grint dove for the gate, screaming as he pulled it back up. He would not lose another coin. Not one more coin.

"Grint!" Orsava screamed behind him. And then he heard a grunt, followed by the thud of a body falling in the gold.

The lord lay on his back, an arrow in his chest. *An arrow meant for me,* Grint thought. All because he'd focused on saving a few coins. Sem looked on him with a weak smile. His hands trembling as he struggled to breathe. Billy gave it his all, casting illusions to hamper Tennebrue. Grint cradled Orsava in his arms. Until the end, he'd stay with him.

"Sem, why?" They were almost to the harbor. Almost out.

"We're friends," the Lord replied. "Friends take arrows..."

"Sem." Hot tears burned in Grint's eyes.

"Grint! The firejacks you bought. They're in that cart," Billy yelled, pointing at the rattling side panels on Tennebrue's cart. Not Tennebrue's cart, not really. It had been theirs until the wizard transformed the horse.

"Firejacks? The ones we made for the fortune teller? You'll kill us all," Trimbo yelled.

You're all dead if you don't, Hobbe counseled.

That's the truest thing you've ever said, Grint replied.

Orsava spit up blood as he helped Grint pull the arrow out. With his last breath, Lord Orsava nodded and threw the arrow high. Mordechai ducked behind the cart's panel, nocking a fresh arrow of his own. Billy saw the bloody arrow fly, and cast a spell to ignite it, then forced it to fly at the cart.

"Time to die," Tennebrue shouted in glee as he threw a wave of blue energy at Billy.

"Puig," Trimbo yelled. "Hold on to something."

Tennebrue's beast tore the throat out of their horse and she faltered. Grint watched the flaming arrow hit the firejacks. Saw Billy go stiff as Tennebrue's blue energy engulfed him. Felt Sem's blood flowing over his hands and heard the raging flood waters beneath them. *Enjoy the gold, Smit,* he thought as Tennebrue's cart erupted in a glorious blaze of fire, consuming the wizard, his beast, and the Harbor Master. The concussion from the blast toppled Grint's cart, dropping them into the flood. He tumbled through the current as gold and fire rained from the sky.

28

"The Parthian Reaver is the most dangerous fighter of all. They are not driven by Atonement or a need for home. They have no home to return to. They live for blood and more blood. Weep for the wretched that stand in their way."

- Wizen Alanna, Magicai of the Third Order

"Hello, my love," Marra said, walking behind the mad queen, Akosha.

"Impossible," Chell answered, rubbing his eyes to clear away the phantoms haunting him. "You are not here. Cannot be here."

"With you this close to the veil," she said, holding out her hand. "I can find you anywhere."

"Not yet," he turned his face away from the apparition. "Not without Atonement."

"Atonement?" she cried. "You will never find Atonement. Chell, thus named Chell the Heartbreaker. The Butcher. The Reaver. Atonement is not a gift you will receive."

Chell roared at the queen, "What trickery do you burn in my head, witch?" The mirth Akosha reveled in faded, replaced by confusion. Chell's lips peeled back, drooling blood onto the marble floors. Chunks of ceiling cracked and fell around them as the sludge multiplied, tearing down everything and leaving nothing.

Lashing out with black tendrils, Akosha ensnared him, wrapping him tight in an anaconda's grasp. Chell gripped the magic, squeezing it tight. Akosha wailed in shock as it first cracked, then shattered. With everything he had left, Chell broke the magic and fell, cracking a bone in his left leg as he hit. Discarded weapons littered the ground, but it was the two-handed great sword he wanted. If this was his end, he'd die with that in his hands.

"Don't die. Not like this," Marra whispered. "Your death should be so much more unpleasant."

For a moment, he saw a golden field with crooked trees providing the perfect amount of shade. The Gellanore flowed beside it, the fierce river rumbling with great rapids. In a small shoal where the water sat stagnant, Chell washed his hands. The blood upon them thick and refusing to come clean. He scrubbed with a porous stone, but even that did not help. It formed like a memory, but couldn't be. He remembered his crossing of the Gellanore. Riding atop Fleck, he... He rode across a bridge? What bridge other than the dreego structure in Last Zorn existed? And they did not allow Parthians to pass.

"The memories you concocted are falling apart," she whispered in his ear.

Was this a hallucination of the poison? Magic? Or worse - real? A hard slap spun him, slicing open his cheek. Blood poured through his fur as he gripped the great sword, limping toward the queen. Akosha conjured six arms, each carrying a sword twice the size of Chell's, but the queen was not a swordsman or a true fighter. She lashed out with simple attacks, choreographed motions, easy to spot. Chell rolled beneath, intending to stand before her, driving the great blade into her heart.

The sickness within had other ideas and he struggled to remain upright. Collapsing, another image invaded his mind. The night Brasau took the village, leaving Chell tied to a post. It felt real, looked real - even the smell of burning thatch mixed with morning dew sat heavy on the air. The rope Brasau tied him with frayed and as Chell pulled at them they came loose. As he stood, the rage boiling deep in his gut bubbled up. Marra lingered a few steps away, disbelieving that he'd broken free. Chell felt his hands around her throat, heard her pleas even as he fought against the vision.

This is not what happened. It cannot be!

A pummeling barrage of arms broke the trance. Chell came to with the queen straddling his chest, beating him. With a war cry, he swatted her aside. She spun through the air, but the many arms broke her fall, setting her right in an instant. Screams of rage flew like bats from her mouth as she set back on a path to attack. This time, Chell prepared himself. Leaning to the right, his upward stroke was as perfect as his waning strength would allow. Enough still to shatter her left arms into tiny shards that floated through the air, swirling in a great vortex overhead. The queen screamed for her lost arms as if they were cubs torn from the womb.

Not wishing to waste the chance, Chell pressed the attack. Lurching to his feet, he held the sword steady with all intentions toward removing the remaining arms. Marra stepped in his way, lifting her chin to reveal the deep bruises around her throat. Horrified, he dropped the sword to cover his eyes.

"Look at what you've done, Reaver. Look long at it and tell me you deserve Atonement."

"Begone foul revenant," Chell shrieked.

A thick paw slapped the side of his head, knocking him over. Brasau joined Marra in the undead mockery. Blood flowed freely from a hole in his chest, his black heart beating within. The grotesque wound looked like someone reached in and tore the ribs out.

"Not someone. You," Brasau said. In a horrifying display, the war-chief pulled at one of his exposed ribs until it came loose with a sickening crack. He held the end and ran his hand along the length, straightening it into a sword. Dropping into a fighting stance, Brasau held the bone sword at the ready.

The queen remained in mourning, staring skyward at the swirling maelstrom. Chell retrieved his sword, ignoring Brasau as he strode toward the only target he knew to be real. Ghosts were not his enemies and as incorporeal things, they could do him no harm. Or so he thought.

Brasau struck at the back of his cracked knee with the flat of the bone sword. The pain he experienced as he dropped was very real. Lightning bolts of searing agony rose through his torso and into his upper extremities. How was such a thing possible?

"You will face me," Brasau said.

"I will not," Chell said, gathering his strength. His left leg was useless now, so he favored the right. *A warrior needs not his body*, the Builder commanded. *The spirit of battle drives us.*

"Then you will die." Brasau touched his blade against the side of Chell's neck. The wind whistled across its many imperfections as he drew it back.

"Of that, I have no doubt," Chell whispered, listening to the blade reach the summit of its back swing. As it began forward, he rolled into a somersault, then leapt with only his right leg. The blade held firm in his grip, each knuckle ached with cries for release. Brasau's ghostly scream chilled him, stinging his ears, but there would be no stopping him this time.

Chell brought the blade down, aiming for the queen's head. She rocked in misery, falling to the side as he struck - her remaining arms. No, he thought, hearing the fragile glass appendages shatter. Feeling the pieces cut through his skin to join the rest. What more had he to give? *As much as I need. I will not fail.*

"You have already failed," Brasau screamed as he swung his blade.

Chell raised his sword, deflecting the blow, but strength was no longer his ally. The force behind Brasau's anger grew mountainous, and Chell reeled under the blows. The Parthians fought while the maelstrom expanded. Chell knocked aside attack after attack, struggling to hold his sword. What chance would he have for victory if he didn't turn the battle and issue his own blows?

The sludge was an ever-present threat. Shooting sharpened lances across his path, the black goo cut deeper than steel. The flesh tore away from his arms as Brasau stood back, laughing at the misery befalling his rival. Marra joined him, watching the dark magic tear through Chell.

See what you are, Marra's voice spoke in his head. A hundred corpses littered the floor. Parthian warriors of the Hanging Men - and the defeated of his own tribe. A single blade brought them all low with equal prejudice. Chell's blade. His captains, loyal to the end, cheered at what they thought was rescue and screamed like cubs as he slew each in front of the other. Even the children did not escape. Young Jesto, whose corpse sat up, pointed a finger at Chell, *I met a fate no Parthian cub should.*

Reaver, the corpses chattered in an unending discordant chant.

"This cannot be," Chell cried out. "I would not do this."

"You did," Marra spoke, now at his side. Her touch was soft, the sound of her voice pitying. "You closed your eyes against the post, and when you opened them, you knelt at a pool by the river washing blood from your hands. What did you imagine happened?"

"I fought a were-bear, or rexian stalker," Chell lost hope as he said the words. The voices of the dead were too strong. They cracked his armor with the single repeated word. *Reaver. Reaver.*

"Reaver," Marra said, stepping away.

"Allow me to remind you why they call me the Hangman," Brasau said at his back. The war-chief grabbed the sludge and pulled it, stretching it around Chell's neck. When he let go, the strand contracted, choking the Parthian. He did not fight it, dropping his sword one last time.

The queen lay on her back; the sludge oozing from her eyes and nose. One body among a thousand dead Parthians. Yet, her life had not expired. Weakened, she moved to gather the sludge back into her body. Was she weakened enough for Nazarra to save her? Saving lives? Did he deserve such an honor?

"No, you do not," Brasau said.

Fool, his father whispered. *Have you forgotten the Builder's most profound lesson?*

"I am not worthy of the Builder's love," Chell answered before the magic constricted his throat.

Every Parthian is worthy.

To know truth, first know yourself. The lesson was an old one and taught to young warriors on the day of their first battle. They were to give themselves over to the bloodlust. Drink it deep and revel in the ecstasy of destruction. Only then could they know their own depths. Those who went too far, or could not return, died by the enemy - or their own tribe.

Chell knew well the state of bloodlust, for he abided by the laws of the Great Builder. Why would he, on this singular occasion, betray what he'd spent a lifetime honing? Closing his eyes, Chell shut away the corpses and their endless mockery. He let Brasau fade into the sound of a gentle breeze across a meadow. The strand was killing him, but far too slowly.

And Marra... "You cannot escape us," she said, holding his hands against her throat. The re-creation of the deed brought to life its dishonesty.

The black magic was all around. Bits fell from the ceiling or divided from the strand around his neck, slithering across his skin. It burrowed into his open wounds like maggots on rotting flesh. He could feel it inside, moving to a central spot just beside his heart. A shard of Brasau's bone sword remained in his shoulder. Chell took his hands from Marra and pulled it free. She reeled back, expecting an attack, but the blade was not for her.

Chell drove it into his chest, cutting a deep gash that he reached into. The pain was something he'd never experienced. A searing flame, both agonizing and freeing. A transcendence of the physical. The black magic squirmed in his grasp, and Chell tore aside more flesh, pulling it out in his fist. It formed white fangs and snapped at him until he tossed it. The thing shattered on the marble floor like much of the queen's magic.

With the creature dead, the noose released him, and he gasped for air. The false corpses melted into sludge, sliding back to the true host. Brasau and Marra lost pigmentation first, laughing at him as they too melted. How he remained on his feet while his blood flowed from the many wounds was a miracle of the Builder. Perhaps there was one last task to complete before he rested.

"You tried to trick me," Chell wheezed in a hollow approximation of his once powerful voice. "Tried to make me think I was a Reaver. I see now you are nothing but evil and I will send you to the wicked place you so wish to find. I believe the thief called it Astapoor."

The queen stood, armless and bloody, and shook. A small shudder at first, but it grew in violence until her skin cracked and she fell apart in a heap of glass shards. Was that it? Was she dead? Chell shuffled forward, stepping on the glass, testing it with the bloody end of his foot.

A slow clap brought his eyes up. The queen - the true Queen Akosha - sat on her throne. The Ochus rose from her back, her arms, and her head. A deep void lived behind her eyes and the way she moved, tried to clap, made it difficult to tell if she possessed control or the Ochus did.

Lifting her on strings of blackness, the queen floated off the dais like a marionette. No longer was this the woman Nazarra grew up with. That any of her kin would have remembered. This was now but a shell, filled with devilment. It opened its mouth as it approached.

"Chell," she said. "I can give you a new life." Then she conjured Marra from the mass of writhing darkness. "Or even old life."

"I seek nothing you give," Chell said. He looked at his hands to be sure they were making fists, for his hands no longer had sensation.

"Fool," Akosha said in quiet ferocity. A wave of blue energy struck him, flinging him back. Chell slid across the marble, through glass shards that tore his back apart, until he came to rest on the center crest. His sword lay a foot away. When it fell, it dropped hilt first into a crack, but stopped point up before falling through. With great cries of pain, he rolled onto his stomach and crawled toward it. Yet, he could not budge it from the crack. Was he not strong enough? The steel cut his palms as he tugged. The sword did not move.

Tendrils of dark magic wrapped around his shoulders, standing him upright and turning him round. The queen's feet dragged as she moved, her head lolling back and forth like a cub fighting sleep. A breath away, she stopped. The Ochus lifted a hand to touch his face.

"You seek death? I shall grant it to you," Akosha said. "I will leave this place and devour the city outside. The land, the sea, the stars in the inky sky. Nothing shall stop me."

Chell blinked, trying to discern what it was he saw as she spoke. Within her mouth, behind dark, stained teeth, was something white. White like the teeth of the thing in his chest. Except this thing blinked. A single eye. Akosha no longer existed, but what remained would eat the world. Chell knew what he must do.

"I seek death," he smiled. "Let us journey there together."

Chell pulled her into his arms and fell back. The blade slid through his heart and out the other end where the queen waited to kiss it. The dark thing squealed as the blade tore apart its brain. Chell went to his rest, knowing he'd accomplished the one thing he'd set out to do.

Atonement.

29

"Swim in the river, go down down down.
Into the sea, don't drown, drown, drown.
If they catch you in town, town, town.
The last you'll wear is the hangman's gown, gown, gown."

- *Mummer's Rhyme, Author Unknown*

The watery mess eased off and the flood waters ebbed. Grint emerged, taking a gasping breath before he threw up. After being thrown from the cart, the current dragged him in sweeping circles. It would have carried him into the harbor if he hadn't gotten lodged in a doorway with a pile of broken chairs and half a sawhorse. Even the slightest movement brought jarring pain. He'd cracked at least two ribs and dinged his skull eight. At least he was alive. Were the others?

The initial rush of water had passed, but swamp water continued to flood through the streets. Grint waded knee deep through the current as he looked for any sign of the goblins, the kid, or Sem. The lord had stepped in front of an arrow for him. *Why in the charffing name of Maguire would he do that?* Grint asked, but Hobbe had no answer this time.

Broken sticks of furniture floated past, along with the wreckage of carts, baskets of fruit, and effigies meant for the Cognispyre. Grint dodged a door carried on the current. Rats covered the surface, fighting to stay out of the water. In its wake, three drowned mungles drifted down to the harbor. *Thank Krypsie*, he thought, seeing the bodies of dead guards who looked to have died fighting each other. None of them were his friends. *Not yet.*

People shouted from far-away places as the sun dawned on the eastern sky. Most asked if someone else was okay. Smoke clouded the streets, making it impossible to see past a few feet. No one came outside, but many opened their windows and watched Grint as he passed. Obscure silhouettes hiding in unreachable towers.

Where the Grand Runway met the harbor proper, he found the goblins. He'd almost missed them and would have kept going if he hadn't heard them squabbling. The pair had climbed onto a gas-lamp to keep above the water, but turned at his sloshing strides.

"Grint, good to see you," Trimbo waved.

"You owe me a gold coin," Puig kicked his friend.

"And I'll pay it when I'm not fighting for my life."

"What was the bet?" Grint asked as he reached them.

"Trimbo said you were dead for sure," Puig answered.

"Pig-gutted goblins," Grint muttered.

"Rude," Puig scowled.

"My father was the pig-gutted one," Trimbo nodded. "I am the very essence of fitness."

"I told you we needed a flow of water," Grint slapped the surface, splashing them with water. "Never meant we should drown the charffing city."

"Perhaps we were a little exuberant," Trimbo admitted, watching a wardrobe full of clothes drift by.

"Rushed," Puig corrected. "Time was of the essence. We did our best to guess."

"Have you seen Billy?" Grint asked, looking for any sign of the kid. The best he hoped for was he got clear and wasn't at the bottom of the harbor with the eels. *Or he died fast.*

"No," Trimbo said. "We never saw each other until we climbed onto the post."

"Perhaps you can help us down?" Puig asked.

"Just jump," Grint replied. Neither did, choosing instead to scowl at him. He realized then that water up to his knees would reach their chests. One powerful surge and both would become memories.

"Let us onto your back," Puig smiled.

"I'm not a horse," Grint coughed up more water and grabbed his side as the pain renewed. "Besides, I think I cracked a rib."

"We can't stay up here," Trimbo said.

"Wait," Grint replied. The rat door came to a stop across the street, caught between two fishing shacks. Most of the rats had escaped onto the remnants of a thatch roof. Grint waded over and pulled the door loose, dumping the few remaining vermin into the drink.

"Did they crap on it?" Puig asked, wrinkling his nose.

"Probably," Grint said, flipping the door over to the other side. "Better?"

The goblins climbed down, settling on to the old door. Grint stood behind, pushing it through the water, holding onto a coat hook to keep it from getting away. The smoke turned white, but was just as thick. *Means the flooding put the fires out and maybe cooled tempers too.*

Keep telling yourself that, Hobbe said.

Go away.

They needed to find the dock closest to the palace cliffs. There they could signal Gaustauss to pick them up or even paddle the door out on their own. Keeping their direction straight in the smoke was a challenge, but as long as they kept moving with the flow of water coming from the left, Grint felt confident they'd find the dock. All three stole glances toward the harbor, trying to find any sign of the ship. A light, a flag, any sound at all. Any sound but the labored grunts of a fight.

Smoke hid distant fighters, but the way sound bounced off buildings made it tough to know if they were walking toward it or away. A muffled scream came from the right and a bellowed shout echoed behind and then again ahead. The goblins strained their necks, looking one way and then the other.

"It's in the Wensley," Trimbo said, sounding only half-confident.

"The Heap," Puig said.

Before they could place a wager on the differing opinion, Grint shouted, "Ahead, see that?"

"What?" The goblins asked.

A flash of red light burning bright and then fading fast as it moved. Blue light further back. A flicker of white followed by an angry screech and another grunt. Sideways lightning and a crack of thunder that made them duck. And through a sky thick with smoke, they witnessed a falling meteor, seeing it as clear as can be.

"How are we seeing it through the smoke?" Trimbo asked.

"Billy," Grint shouted, letting go of the door. The goblins shouted for him to come back, but he wasn't stopping. Every person reaches the point where they're unwilling to lose anyone else, even at the cost of themselves. This was Grint's. *Not the kid. Not the kry-damn kid.*

The pressure dropped and air pulled inward. A clap, akin to a dragon's tail slapping him, spun him round. There was time for a moment of confusion as the world rotated faster and faster. Then he fell face down in the water. A small hand fished for him, pulling his face out of the water. The goblins looked roughed up, but kept their footing and helped him stand.

"What was that?" Trimbo asked.

"Magic," Puig shrugged.

"Two terrible spells countering one another," Grint shook his head, trying to coax the hornets out of his skull.

With the door gone, Grint ignored the pain in his side to keep them above the water. They leaned on him as he waded toward the epicenter of the strike. The flood had decimated a dozen shanty huts along the docks, leaving behind trace remnants of a frame or crumbling brick and mortar. The stronger structures opposite fared better, but not much. Stone walls stood close to falling under the weight of collapsing roofs. Somewhere in the center of all that chaos, Trimbo spotted Billy lying on top of a pile.

The goblins swam to him, leaving Grint behind. The kry-damnned clap added to the number of cracked ribs and he moved like it. "Is he alive?"

"Yes," Trimbo said, and then after a long pause. "Yes, he's alive."

"Going to need you to sound a little more confident," Grint groaned.

There was little warning of what was to come. Nothing more than a trickle of water. A ripple on the surface. Puig shrieked and pointed as Tennebrue grabbed Grint from behind. With a scarred hand, its flesh sliding off the bone, the wizard conjured fire, holding it in front of Grint's face. The two struggled as Grint grabbed for the wizard's wrist. Surges of fire burned through his shirt and he screamed. Without a weapon, he could only hope the goblins...

A rock glanced off the side of Grint's leg as a rotten tomato hit him in the chest. The goblins shrugged and started looking for more things to throw. "Stop helping," Grint yelled.

"I will burn you," Tennebrue yelled, and for a moment he caught sight of the wizard, his hair scorched clean and face a ruin. One eye sagged, and the eyeball threatened to pop out. "I'll burn them next and find every member of your mis-begotten crew and turn them all to ash. And when that's all done? I'll burn your dog."

"Krypsie's balls," Grint yelled, slamming his head back into Tennebrue's nose. It didn't shake the wizard loose, but Grint broke free long enough to snatch a swimming rat. The rodent screamed as he shoved it in Tennebrue's face. Or it was the other way around? Free from his grasp, Grint grabbed his burned shoulder while Mister Rat gnawed on the wizard's nose. Tennebrue yanked it loose and threw it aside, conjuring a fireball to roast the fleeing rodent. Grint charged and swung a right hook. The fireball flew high, landing somewhere in the rubble. The wizard's singed robes existed as only a few tattered strands that broke apart when Grint pulled at them, but the thief kept at it, gathering enough fabric to hang on and beat the wizard. One punch led into another, and another. He kept hitting Tennebrue until his teeth caved inward and legs buckled.

They fell together into the water. Neither had much fight left. Grint straddled him, pulling a small sticker-knife from his boot. He wanted to say something clever, name the people Tennebrue had killed, say it was for them. But he was too kry-

damn tired, and it would have been a lie. This was for himself. Shoving the wizard beneath the water, he held him there
until the air escaped his lungs, letting him feel the terror of
drowning. At the last, he jammed the knife in his chest, keeping it there until the wizard stopped moving.

"Grint?" Trimbo said.

"I'm here," he answered, getting up. "I'm okay."

Sloshing through the water, he looked out to where the
harbor should be. He needed a healer. He needed rest. *I need
a drink.* He needed to swim through the piles of gold in the
Hermitage Roll's belly.

"Gaustauss," he yelled as loud as he could. "Gaustauss!"

The goblins took up the shouts, turning to bang rocks
against walls, or metal pots floating by. There was nothing but
the distant cries of Salaz and the lap of water against the cliffs.
"Kry-damn pirate. If you've left without us, I'll escort you to
Astapoor myself."

"Astapoor is a place," Billy said in a small voice.

Grint smiled, throwing his head back in laughter as he
swam to the kid. "Thought we lost you. How are you feeling?"

"Everything hurts," Billy said.

"I know the feeling," Grint clutched his side. "I can't find
the boat."

"Trinavad," he said, waving his hand in a circle. A small
breeze tickled Grint's cheek and picked up, swirling the
smoke and carrying it through the harbor. In the breaks between clouds, they caught sight of a lantern, a faint waving
back and forth.

"Can someone bring Tennebrue back to life?" Grint
laughed. "We need fire."

"Let me see what I can do," Billy coughed.

"An undead wizard is not what I want to end the day with," Trimbo shook his head.

"Begin the day, you mean," Puig said.

"I meant what I said."

"But it's a new day."

Puig is right, Grint noticed. The sun had risen in the east. It was time to go. Daylight was a thief's worst enemy as Hobbe might say. *Hobbe?* But his conscience had nothing to add.

"You think they got it all?" Billy asked, struggling to move.

"Lay back down," Grint said. "We've got it." The fear that they'd lost it or the demon had run off with it was eating at him. Hearing the kid mention the same did nothing to ease the anxiety.

"What is that?" Trimbo asked.

"Looks like a Kelavite ooze beast," Puig responded.

"A Kelavite? Here?" Grint needed to see that. He'd heard tales of ooze beasts, but never encountered one. Grint scanned the water and ruins for it until Puig pointed his gaze up to the Seastone Tower. The shining stone tower was a marvel in the morning sun and it stung, bringing back a memory of Orsava just days ago. But the goblins were right, the tower was not pristine. Black ooze ran from the upper windows, marring the face of the stone.

"Maybe the Parthian is doing it?" Trimbo shrugged.

"Inno janoi," Grint paled, looking back to the harbor. "It's a kry-damn Ochus." The lantern's light grew stronger in the haze. The pirates were coming to them.

"Gaustauss," Grint shouted, delighted to hear his name called back to him.

"That sounds like Smit," Billy laughed.

"They made it," Trimbo and Puig danced around in the water.

"At least one thing went right," Grint said.

Their joy ended abruptly. A crack, softer than the magic clap, but louder than the levee breaking interrupted them. They all ducked, terrified that the wizard had returned without their help. Tennebrue's body floated, bumping into a pylon on the dock. "Another levee?" Grint asked.

"Can't be," Puig said.

"Too close," Trimbo nodded. Another crack made them jump.

"No," Billy coughed, pointing at the tower.

They watched as the Seastone Tower cracked; the ooze pulling inside, taking the stone with it. The great tower listed over the cliff. In that moment, they all saw it. All realized what would happen. Though they were impotent to change the course of events, they waved their arms in panic, jumping along the dock.

"See me, you idiot! Get that ship moving! Go!" Grint shouted, willing the pirate ship to safety.

Smit shouted for them to light a fire, unaware of the disaster above. The goblins screeched in unison until Smit looked up. Gaustauss must have too. Activity sprang to life on the deck as sails unfurled, catching Billy's wind, and the ship slowly began turning. The Hermitage Roll inched toward the mouth of the harbor.

"Go, go, go," Grint cried. "Billy, more wind." They could meet them after, down the coast. Anywhere but here. "Go, go, go. Billy?"

The kid wasn't conjuring. Wasn't even watching. With his eyes closed, he cried. Grint understood the anguish. Billy was about to lose his brother and all the magic in the world would not change it. *I'll watch for you.*

The first chunk of the cliff side broke free and fell in the water, narrowly missing the ship's stern. A massive wave rocked the boat and for a moment he thought it might capsize. Then another crack. Grint could do nothing now but watch as chunks of sea stone broke away, pulling the cliff down with it.

In a massive fall of debris, the pirate ship disappeared. Grint screamed and braced himself as impact wave rose and struck the docks. The goblins held on to Billy, pulling him beneath a fisherman's stall. The wave hit Grint, throwing him against a stone wall. He choked on the brackish saltwater as his foot tangled in a fishing net. When the water subsided, he stared at the morning sky, a dying eel flopping on the ground beside him.

"Yearghhh," he shrieked as he rolled away from its lethal bite. Stars swam across his vision, but he climbed to his feet, holding to the side of a chunk of wood that hadn't been there before. Smaller waves struck the docks. The few bits of wood left of them. Asper could be mean when humans disturbed her.

Grint's heart sank as he realized what it was he was leaning against. The shattered bow of the Hermitage Roll, or what remained of her. Its tall mast rose above the brine, teetered and cracked, then sank.

"No," he whispered. Then got louder. "No. No. No. No. No." He ended in a scream and tried to dive in after it. Trimbo grabbed on to his tunic, yanking him back.

"Let go!" Grint screamed.

"Fool," Trimbo croaked. "You'll die."

"I have to get the gold!"

"The eels will devour you before you clutch a single coin," Puig yelled, helping Trimbo. But Grint hadn't come all this way to leave empty-handed. Not after everything they'd done.

"Not when we were that close," he shouted, trying to shake the goblins off.

Billy swung a piece of driftwood, hitting Grint on the side of the head. The rotting wood snapped, falling apart in the kid's hand. All it did to Grint was stop him from screaming. He reached up to where it hit and looked back at Billy with questioning eyes.

"I wasn't trying to hurt you," Billy said, swaying on his feet.

"I know," Grint slumped. Too tired to fight, he fell into a group hug with the goblins. Billy joined them, his face streaked with tears. Together, they looked at the empty harbor. All the gold lay below its lethal waves. Every coin, bauble and jewel. His friends and his dog. Grint wept, watching the harbor waves slow to a calm rumble.

And then he heard Newman's bark, a single joyous sound. Grint turned to see the urchin, Matty, poling a skiff out of the tunnels. Newman stood with his front paws on the edge, the little nub of his tail wagging. Matty docked, and the bulldog jumped out, running to Grint, covering him with kisses.

"How?"

"Smit said to wait for you," Matty said in her flat voice. She looked at the water, no trace of emotion on her face. "The boat sank."

"You did your part," Grint said, just happy to not have lost everything.

"And you did yours," the urchin girl said. When he cocked his head, she smiled for the first time. "You killed Marv."

"Right. That. There's always another Marv," Grint said. "But you're smart. Next time make sure it's you. When you're too old for the tunnels."

"Yes," she nodded. "Happy Matty."

"Sure," Grint stood, feeling every injury. He had more wisdom to impart. A lifetime's worth. But the girl had gone, vanishing back into the tunnels with her chattering masses.

Horns blew from every corner of the city. Frantic calls. The streets would be swarming with city guards by the next bell. And militias with pitchforks if the belltower still stood.

"I think it's time to go," Grint said. "All of us."

"I agree," Trimbo said.

"As do I," Puig answered.

"If I agree, you don't need to. It's implied."

"Nothing is implied."

"Billy? You want to come?" Grint said. The kid stared at the harbor, the blank look of someone with nothing left to go home to. He wiped a tear and nodded.

"They'll kill me as dead as the rest of you," he said. "And I've never seen the Crown of Seven Kingdoms."

"Crown of the Seven Kingdoms," Puig said.

"Nobody likes to be corrected," Trimbo grumbled.

Four thieves limped away from the harbor, looking for a way out of Salaz. Grint imagined what a sight they must appear. Newman waddled beside him, looking up every few steps. Looking for a treat to give the dog, he found something else. In his pocket was a single gold coin. The first coin. The last coin.

After - 1

"Celebrate the Cognispyre, not for the sins Ashgra burns clean, but for the gift she gives and the promise she made. Salaz will stand forever."

- High-Priest Palas, Annum 359

The morning sun rose high above the horizon, sending out rays of comfort for the people on this Cognispyre. Blue skies promised a morning without rain, which for once was not what the people wanted. Columns of white smoke rose beside black in every district. Smoldering fires unleashed sparks that ignited new blazes. The people formed lines, scooping flood water to douse the flames, but they struggled to stay ahead of it. A torrent of rain would change that.

Nazarra stood on the palace wall, staring down on the ruined city of Salaz. Her hand shook as she touched the merlon with her fingertips. This spot was where she and the barbarian... the proud warrior fought the Blue Hand.

Above it all, the statue of Ashgra stood. The Arch of the Sun and Temple too. A few meager pieces of history for the people to look upon as they sifted through the destruction. Flood waters poured through the broken levee, turning the winding streets into rivers. Homes fell, shops collapsed, parks and cafes washed out to sea. It would take years to re-build some of it. Generations for the rest. An unfortunate few would never return.

Was it worth it, Grint?

A dozen paces to her left, the palace wall ended where the Seastone Tower fell, pulling enormous sections down with it. Glimmering blue stones twinkled below the surface of the harbor. Perhaps the engineers could reclaim and re-fashion some of it, but the tower would never be what it was. That at least, she could not lay at the thief's feet. The per-petrator of that travesty dangled still from the side of the apartments. As for her sister and the barbarian... *Parthian. Stop calling him barbarian, you fool.* She assumed both per-ished with the tower.

I hope you found your Atonement, Chell. Bitter tears burned her eyes. In her anger, she'd told Chell that she would not shed a tear for his passing. Did he know it was a lie when she spoke it? *I hope you did. I cry for you and your sacrifice and promise we will sing a great song.*

"My lady," Jaspar said, "It would be best to cover your face."

The captain stood sentinel behind her, unwilling to move from her side since she climbed off the apartment roof. In his words, "I don't trust anyone beside myself." Nazarra didn't need the protection, but understood how some need-ed to feel useful in the face of overwhelming disaster.

The Battle of the Guilds, as some of the guards now referred to it, had all but ended. A few pockets of fighting existed below, but the grounds of the palace were secure. Borismere had hired mercenaries to fill out the Opposition forces, handing out blue armbands to blend in. The Golden Few they were called. Punishments for their part in this fell to the Council to decide. A parade of prisoners sat in lines on the grass, priests and servants brought them water as healers dealt with the wounded on both sides.

"My lady," Jaspar said again in gentle reminder.

"If Ashgra has something to say about my face, she can come down and say it," Nazarra replied.

Two of Jaspar's soldiers escorted a runner along the wall. The young girl, out of breath, removed her veil to speak. "I have reports," she said.

"Go on," Nazarra replied, watching an old man in Wensley sift through floating debris.

"They found Prince Mikil dead at the manor of Lord Borismere," she stopped and flinched as Nazarra slammed a fist into the battlements. Hearing that traitor referred to as a lord still sat poorly in her gut.

"Continue."

"The Krypholos Temple collapsed into a sinkhole. It will take time to discover if there is any gold inside or a chamber beneath. There were several bodies found, but the sergeant couldn't tell if they died there or floated." The girl paused, waiting for questions Nazarra didn't ask. "They also found the catacomb entrance you used, but the tunnels remain flooded and impassable."

"There is a girl in charge of the urchins. Her name is Matty. Issue her description to the squads. Four feet tall, dark skin, hazel eyes and straight black hair," Nazarra said.

"Yes, general," the girl answered.

"You've just described the entire urchin population," Argus said as he limped along the wall.

"I'm glad you survived," Nazarra said, struggling to smile.

"As am I," he took a stance beside her, removing the dented chest armor and dropping it. A servant handed him a crisp red coat, with golden epaulets and a chest full of medals. Argus buttoned the first clasp, but stopped, letting it hang open in the breeze. His effort to stay strong impressed her.

"A little hot for dress reds," she said, hoping that the act of making a joke would allow her to experience an emotion beside rage.

"Salaz is too hot for any clothes," the old battle commander replied. "That you don't run around naked all day has always been a surprise to me."

Following Argus was Admiral Brayan from the Fort and the surviving members of the Salazian War Council. Those that remained. The mercenaries had killed most when the command building fell.

"If you don't mind," Brayan asked. "What are you looking for?"

Since dawn, Nazarra had been sending runners into the ruins to dig up information and deliver reports. The methods of the Spymaster General applied perfectly during this crisis. "Borismere had a trove of gold he used to manipulate events," Nazarra said. "A group of thieves was working to steal it from him," she continued. "They were using the old tunnels to move it into the harbor with the help of the urchins."

"Our sentries saw skiffs loading onto the ship before dawn," Brayan reported.

Nazarra's anger boiled over. The thief-catcher's cudgel hung at her waist, and for a moment she thought of brandishing it at the admiral. Instead, she chose words. "Why did you not board the vessel sooner? For a time, I believed it full of Borismere's mercenaries."

"We inspected it," Brayan said, his tone one of deep offense. "My captains made the report. A charter ship out of

Rhysin. We thought it a harmless export vessel, so I am un-happy to report we ignored them."

He was right. Nazarra didn't know the navy had inspect-ed the ship. How could she after being banished from her sister's presence? "I am sorry, Admiral. Protecting the city was the right choice," Nazarra replied.

"Thieves. I cautioned your sister against legitimizing the Blue Hands," Argus said.

"This wasn't the Blue Hands," Nazarra shook her head. "They were an independent crew."

"They were successful in loading the gold, but they won't ever spend it," Brayan leaned over the wall. "The tower de-stroyed the ship. Whatever it was carrying is at the bottom of the harbor with the eels, or washing out to the Sandy Sea on the current."

"All hands with it," Argus added.

"No," Nazarra whispered. "He's alive."

"He, your Grace?"

Using the title shocked her. "Grace?" she said, looking at the gathered party for the first time. The leaders of the queen's court assembled before her. "I'm not the queen."

"Begging your pardon, my Grace," Argus bowed. "You, in fact, are."

As one, the rest bowed with him. The Admiral, the Counselors, the soldiers on the wall. There was no crown to place on her head or High Priest to confer the rites, but those were details they'd put in place later. Salaz needed a leader, someone strong to pull them from the brink of destruction. As the sole remaining Mahd, that duty fell to her. *Duty.*

"I am not queen yet," she said, uncomfortable with the bowing. "I want it done right. Find me the new leader of the Opposition. I want to sit with them and hammer out a treaty. Then we bring our cases to the Council, as has always been the tradition in Succession."

"That would be me," Lord Torran Boggs said as he stepped forward. An older man who walked with a limp and lost his right hand to an alligator as a child, the lord was second cousin to Mikil and now the senior member of the Opposition. "I am much too old for the rigors of rule. I cede my claim to you."

"And we accept," the Councilors replied.

"We may have lost Akosha, but your efforts saved our city," Lord Boggs said.

"Saved? I did no such thing." Nazarra stared over the wall, lamenting the destruction.

"We can replace stones," Argus said.

"That simple?"

"You were three when the last hurricane hit. Flooded the levees and gate. Destroyed a lot, not as extensive as this, but a lot," Argus said. "Your father, he went down to the streets with the people and started rebuilding. Council thought he'd become Ashgra-addled, down there in the muck, carrying stones. But he looked me in the eyes and said just that. We can replace stones. It's a person's spirit, once torn away, that can't be. We need a leader. We need you."

"Get the engineers working on levee repairs. Stopping the flood is our top priority." Nazarra walked along the wall, the gathered leaders following in her wake. The time to stare with pity had passed. "General Argus, dispatch the squads to quell the fires. And have someone tear down the edicts, they hurt the city more than help. That includes the Blue Hands. As of now, the thieves are outlawed."

"Very good, your Grace," Argus said.

Waves of people were filing through the city gate, setting up refugee camps on the outskirts of the Glades. "Open the Palace Apartments to the people. They will need housing while we rebuild. And start sending aid to those camping outside the city. Guards to protect from bandits and hunters from the wildlife."

"Your father would be proud," Argus said.

A guard escorting an outlander in chains caught her eye. "You, yes you. Bring that man here."

Shocked at being singled out, the guard shoved the prisoner inside the wall. They stepped through the stairway door and into the sun. The outlander, with shaggy white hair and a beard, had his forehead wrapped in thick bandages. His chains rattled as he stepped, tripping him often in his attempts to keep pace. As a thief-catcher hired by Borismere to kill Grint, he'd failed in that task - and in protecting Borismere from her wrath. He kept his eyes down as the guard shoved him forward, but it wasn't an act of deference. After such failure, the man fidgeted like someone with a bruised ego. It couldn't help that she also had possession of his weapon.

"Unbind him," she said.

"General?" The guard asked. "He's scheduled for execution. Taking him to the cutter."

"That is the queen you are speaking to," Jaspar said, drawing his sword and resting it tip down with his hands on the pommel.

"Apologies, your Grace," the guard stammered, unlocking the chains.

"Congratulations on the crown," Mavris Kane mumbled.

"You'll look upon the queen when she speaks to you," the guard said, slapping the back of Kane's head.

"I came by it because of my sister's death," Nazarra said. "It is not a moment for celebrations."

"My apologies," he replied. "When last we met... I meant no offense, your Grace."

"You know him," she said with only half a question in her tone.

"Borismere? No, I did not. He paid me for a job. I was not a follower of his," Kane said, the stammer was that of a man hoping to keep his head.

"No, you know *him*."

Understanding dawned, and a malignant glare appeared beneath his bushy eyebrows. "I have been to a hundred kingdoms and a thousand towns. The one thing they all have in common? Wanted posters with his image."

"And yet, you've never caught him," she said, failing to be anything but impressed by Grint's exploits, though she loathed to be.

"No one has paid me enough to do it," Mavris said.

"Until Borismere," she added.

"Until," Kane nodded. "Would have done it too if that guard didn't start snorting Orrish powders."

"Name your price," she said, disinterested in explanations of failure.

"One thousand gold pieces," Kane said. The leadership laughed, expecting Nazarra to join in. "Up front. For that I'll drag him across Terragard and drop him at your feet."

"Two thousand," she countered. The laughter stopped. "And all I want is his head."

"Consider it done," Mavris bowed. "Your Grace."

"I have no great confidence you'll succeed, so I will give you one hundred now and the rest upon completion. Let him loose," she finished, pointing at the guard. "He has a job to do."

This time she pulled the cudgel loose from the loop on her belt, feeling its weight. "A fine weapon. You'll be needing it." Kane took it back, offering his first moment of joy since they'd brought him to her.

"Nazarra," Argus whispered in her ear, pulling her aside. "Forgive my impertinence, but what is this? Who is he looking for? Borismere is already dead."

"Borismere and Mikil may have started the fighting," she leaned against the wall once more. "But he did the rest. Broke the levee, turned the guilds against one another." *Broke my heart.*

"He? Who is he?"

"The thief," Nazarra said, smiling too, for the first time in days. "Grint."

After - 2

"On a long and dusty road.
The thief rides again.
Doesn't know where he's going.
Doesn't care where he's been."

- The Ballad of Grint, Annum 1587

The cart's axles squeaked with every grinding rotation and the back left wheel thumped each time it rolled over the chip missing from its face. Somewhere north of a Glades town called Sumerik, the goblins turned the racket into a song. The lyrics changed with every verse, which numbered around fifty by now. Or maybe it felt like fifty.

"Do we have any more rum?" Grint asked, pulling back the hood he'd been wearing. The sun fell well past its apex, but without shade, the rays cooked the thick fabric and his head beneath. Humid, stagnant air made Grint want to tear off the robe and clothes beneath, but they needed to remain cautious if any travelers happened past.

"A bit," Trimbo said, climbing over the driver's seat with the flask. As Grint drank, the goblin took a seat beside him, staring out at the swamps. Long-winged white birds took flight over the water as alligators floated in amiable currents. A beast cried deep in the trees, a high-pitched keening that cut off. The hunter claimed the hunted. *A poor portent,* Hobbe said.

"And it's time to drink," Puig sang.

"Bump," Trimbo added in time with the wheel.

"And it's time to sink."

"Bump."

"And it's time..."

"To shut up," Grit snapped.

"Bump," Trimbo said after an awkward silence. Grint laughed with the goblins and took another drink.

Escaping Salaz had not been the harrowing journey each of them feared. Soldiers waded through flooded streets, but they had eyes only for Opposition fighters, Fishmongers, or Blue Hands. The citizens only became a concern when someone needed help. Grint, Billy, and the goblins faded into the mass exodus of people escaping the flood and fires. No one stopped them at the city gate, on Tiber's Bridge or anywhere beyond.

Past the bridge, where the ground flattened, people set down belongings hastily gathered. Some pitched tents while others strung sheets across the trees to provide a bit of shade. The growing camp would remain until the city set itself right, or would develop into a new city. Few wore face coverings, even on a day meant for celebrating their deity. No one looked twice at the fair-skinned man, the beaten up Salazian, or the goblins traveling with them.

The four walked until the sun sat at its apex. They'd found the first border town, Grase by then. It was little more than an inn with stable and two supply shops. The innkeeper wasn't willing to sell the donkey and cart until Grint slapped the gold coin on his counter. They received a single silver and twelve copper bits in change, which they spent the greater portion of on food and the flask of rum.

All of it would run out before they traveled beyond the Glades, but this wasn't the first time Grint had been on the road with nothing to his name except the clothes he wore. He may even have been better off since he had a donkey and cart, friends, and a dog. *No bag of tricks,* Hobbe said.

Another adventure. Another lost bag, Grint replied with a half-cocked smile.

Newman snored in the shade of a blanket, curled up beside Billy, who slept off his injuries. Grint didn't think he'd have to worry about the kid. Losing his brother would sting for a long time, but he'd proven himself resilient. Wherever they landed, Grint would find a job. Maybe they could all put their minds on something beyond who and what they'd lost.

So much gold. A mountain of it sitting in the harbor's mud. A century from now it would be another layer and lost forever. With twenty wizards, a handful of years, and the help of the city guards, maybe they could retrieve a fraction of Ashgra's fortune. They had none of those things, and considering how they'd left Salaz, they weren't likely to have a hero's welcome if they returned.

Move on, put the town to your back and find the next, Hobbe would say.

True, his own version of Hobbe commented. *But I would also have gotten the gold.*

"The far gull cries," Puig sang, starting the song again.

"Bump," Trimbo muttered out of habit.

"Where the sea dies."

"Bump," Grint and Trimbo said in unison.

"I found my share of gold."

"Bump," Billy said, sitting up and rubbing his head.

"But lost it again and again," Puig finished.

"Ruff," Newman barked with the wheel.

All four burst into hysterical fits of laughter. Something rich and true. The kind of laugh you experienced when you let go of everything else and just lived in the moment. A cool drink of water against a parched throat. As they settled, Grint passed the rum back to the kid,

"You earned it," he said. Billy took a swig and coughed. Then coughed some more.

"First drink?" Puig asked. The kid nodded and took another. This time he only coughed once.

"Second drink too," Billy smiled, handing the flask to the goblin.

Grint sensed the silence before he noticed it. The cries of the swamp, the bugs, the frogs, the birdsongs, they were all gone. All that remained was the creak of the wheel. *Bump.* And an unnatural stillness. Oppressive. *Bump.* How did the others not sense it? *Bump.*

"Get in back," Grint whispered in a low voice. Trimbo gave him a questioning look, his smile faltering.

"Hide," Grint said. "All of you. Now."

Trimbo hopped over the seat, joining Billy and Puig under the blanket. When they all settled in, Grint pulled the cart to a stop, scanning the Glades. Many things could have caused the silence. It didn't mean a trap or pursuit. But he'd weigh the options first. Figure out if they needed to make a run. Grint pulled up the hood and flicked the reins. The donkey brayed, offended at starting again so soon, but plodded ahead.

Between a pair of willow trees, a rider stepped their horse onto the road. Grint halted just a pace away from the shade and kicked himself for it. Of everyone he expected to come after them, this individual had not been high on the list.

Racko maneuvered her horse and walked it toward the cart. The Glades came back to life as two lyzan swam onto shore, long spears held ready. Three more Blue Hands appeared behind them. Thick muscled louts with large clubs and sweat-drenched faces.

"Hello Grint," Racko said when she was close enough.

"Who's Grint," he replied in a crusty old voice. "Name is Simple Scatt. Alligator poaching is my trade."

"Cute," she said, pulling back her own hood. Someone had gotten to her, cutting up her arms and bruising her face. That she was still alive meant she'd gotten the better of them instead. "We've been following you since Grase. The goblins are in back with Billy."

"Should we come out?" Trimbo asked as the goblins poked their faces beneath the sheet.

"We don't have any of the gold," Grint said as he pulled back his hood. "If you're looking to rob us, we have five coppers between us."

"Maybe I'm here to bring you back," Racko said. Her face remained still, making it hard to read, but Grint knew a lie when he smelled it.

"Sure," he replied. "But if that was true, you'd have brought more goons."

Racko laughed, despite the displeasure Grint's remark sent through her people. With a sharp whistle, she called two of the goons forward, a heavy chest held between them. They dropped it on the road as Racko dismounted. She used her foot to open the latch and kick the lid open. The inside over-flowed with coin and jewels.

"Congratulations," Grint said, swallowing the taste of ash in his mouth.

"It's for you, charffing mungle," she smiled.

"Why?"

"Our original bargain stands. A chest of gold for Hobbe's location," she said. *Don't you dare, boy!* "The Blue Hands' time in Salaz has come to an end. I'm an outlaw again."

"Sorry," he shrugged.

"Don't be," she replied. "You want the gold or not?"

"I'd tell you not to waste your time," Grint said. "But you'll go looking for him anyway, and yeah, I want the gold. Go north, past the Sentent Sea to a place called Grimble. Follow the road east out of town. They'll tell you there's nothing out that way, and for most people there isn't. But if you're looking for it, and he wants you to, you'll find it."

"It?" She asked.

"The Red Goat Inn," Grint answered. "It's where he lives."

Racko nodded and closed the lid. Whistling again, the lyzan and her goons joined her by the horse. With a tip of her cap, they turned.

"Racko," Grint called out. She didn't stop walking, but looked back. "Don't expect too much. And if you do find it, tell Alanna I said hello."

The goblins jumped out of the cart and threw open the lid of the chest, their eyes alight with joy with what they beheld. Grint and Billy were slower getting down and even slower in loading the chest in the old cart. The way the bed settled when they shoved it in made Grint wonder how long the axles would hold before cracking. *A trouble for when it's time.*

"It feels nice to be rich again," Trimbo smiled, petting the chest like a dear companion. Newman cocked his head.

"You're rich?" Grint asked as he got the cart moving. Billy climbed into the seat beside him. "When did that happen?"

"Don't you pull any nonsense now," Trimbo scowled.

"Equal shares," Puig said with a stiff nod.

"Our equal shares are at the bottom of the harbor," Grint said, trying not to laugh. "This was a deal between Racko and I. Don't see how you're entitled to any of it."

"Of all the dirty, rotten..." Trimbo stammered.

"Villainy," Puig said. "Base villainy."

"May the foulest of stenches emanate from your bowels."

"I hope you wake as a toad in the morning."

"Cursed to croak, forever in loneliness," Trimbo said.

"Bump," Grint said, but this time, he was the only one laughing at it.

"Are you going to keep it all?" Billy asked, a hurt sadness in his eyes. Grint ruffled the kid's hair.

"No," he said. "I just like hearing them squabble."

"Rude," Puig said.

"The very essence of rudity," Trimbo agreed.

"You both still owe me a considerable amount for the jail-break," Grint added with a snap.

"Our exemplary work excused that," Puig said.

"It did not," Grint spat. "I sweetened the pot. That doesn't erase what's already owed."

"True," Trimbo agreed. "Let the naysayers not say nay, and we don't pay what we owe."

"You could just say we pay what we owe," Puig muttered. "Instead of the jumble of words that fell from your mouth."

The bickering continued as they rode along the path. *Bump.* The sun would set soon, but Grint would keep them moving. He wanted to clear the Glades before they camped. *Bump.* Nobody wanted to end up a midnight snack for the ga-tors. *Bump.*

"What does everyone want to do next?" Grint asked.

"Could go after the Red Rider's crop and saddle," Puig said.

"The Cup of Petra," Trimbo said. "I hear it gives endless wine."

"The Mantle of Hermadales," Puig shouted.

"Billy?" Grint nudged the kid, who'd taken on a faraway look.

"There are eighteen mercenaries out there with sacks full of gold. Our gold," Billy said. "I say we go steal it back."

"I like how he thinks," Trimbo said.

"Mercenaries it is," Grint said, cracking the reins. The donkey looked back at him, but went no faster.

"On a long and dusty road," the goblins sang together, with Grint and Billy adding the bumps.

"The thief rides again. Bump."

"Doesn't know where he's going. Bump."

"Doesn't care where he's been."

Bump.

GRINT WILL RETURN
IN
HARD TIMES

BUT NEXT...
DHOG SOLDIERS

Will you remember your past or become what you're accused of?

The Empire of the Dhogs have arrived. Disgraced Imperial Lieutenant and Thornslinger, Kyra Larr was imprisoned for the crime of decimating her former command with the very magical weapon she wields. Released back into service, she's been sent to the western front of Trindian Island in preparation for an invasion of Terragard.

The plan is simple. Sneak a company of dhog soldiers behind enemy lines and open a portal. But when the landing goes wrong, Kyra must lead a ragtag company through hostile territory. In the heat of battle, where the stakes are deadly, a conspiracy of lies surfaces and threatens everything she believes in.

Are the lies real? Or is the magic she possesses making her go mad?

Lieutenant Kyra Larr. Guilty or innocent? Hero or villain? Dhog soldier or traitor?

Connect with

D.S. TIERNEY'S
WORLD OF TERRAGARD™

www.DSTIERNEY.com

[Instagram] World.of.Terragard

[Facebook] /worldofterragard

[Twitter] @dstierney1

[YouTube] World of Terragard

[TikTok] @d.s.tierney

[Patreon] /terragard

[g] D.S. Tierney

YOUR ADVENTURES IN TERRAGARD DON'T END HERE!

Terragard Tales tells new stories full of exciting action, intrigue, and magic! Each story features new characters, monsters, locations and journeys spanning the world of Terragard and its history.

The Terragard Tales Audiodrama Podcast is available everywhere podcasts are found.

iTunes - Google Play - Stitcher - Spotify - Amazon
www.dstierney.com/podcast

Season 1: The Lunar Sundering - Available Now!

Season 2: Gods & Monsters - Available Now!

Season 3: The Longest Tale - Coming Soon!

ABOUT THE AUTHOR:
D.S. TIERNEY
BY
GRINT

So how does this work? I just tell you? Okay.

D.S. Tierney is the scribe who first wrote about me in 2012 when I robbed the *Seventh Tower* along The Papality's pilgrimage trail. There was a demon involved. And a Rope. Bad business. You can read about it on the *Aphelion* webzine. I have no charffing clue what a webzine is, but there you go.

I think he was a bard before that, writing mummer shows and performing in them. Yeah, kind of like a jester without the monarchy nonsense involved.

There's also the podcast about Terragard. It's called *Terragard Tales.* Stories from around the world. None about me yet. I guess I'll have to steal more stuff to get a story on there!

He lives in Boston, MA but also has a web address: www.dstierney.com

Web address? Webzine? Is he a spider? Gross. Okay, that's good? Great, time for an ale. No. No, I didn't pickpocket you. I will not empty my pockets. Let's not be hasty. No need to call a Brotherhood Knight into the room...